MW00960720

Wizard Storm:
Scirocco

CHANDLER YORK SHELTON

DEDICATION

I want to dedicate this book to my parents, Jim and Yoshi Shelton who loved and shaped me but never got to see this novel in this world.

CONTENTS

BOOK 1

Chapter 1	10
Chapter 2	22
Chapter 3	31
Chapter 4	40
Chapter 5	49
Chapter 6	54
Chapter 7	60
Chapter 8	66
Chapter 9	71
Chapter 10	83
Chapter 11	91
Chapter 12	96
Chapter 13	104

BOOK 2

Chapter 14	115
Chapter 15	125
Chapter 16	133
Chapter 17	139
Chapter 18	146
Chapter 19	154
Chapter 20	164
Chapter 21	172
Chapter 22	177
Chapter 23	190
Chapter 24	196
Chapter 25	200
Chapter 26	210
Chapter 27	224

BOOK 3

Chapter 28	236
Chapter 29	244
Chapter 30	247
Chapter 31	258
Chapter 32	264
Chapter 33	273
Chapter 34	277
Chapter 35	281
Chapter 36	287
Chapter 37	295
Chapter 38	302

ACKNOWLEDGMENTS

Any acknowledgment in anything I do has to start with my wife, Jennifer. Without her I would not, could not be who I am. Her love is the mana of my existence. Next I have to thank my two sons. If my wife is the fuel for my life, my sons give me direction and the desire to be even more than I thought possible. Next I have to thank some good friends, Trish, Steve, and Craig who helped me make this book better than I thought possible. Lastly, I want to thank the high school English teacher, Dr. Leonard, whose belief in me was so powerful it stayed with me over 30 years until this book was finally finished.

Book 1:

SAND

Chapter 1

The sound of the grazing goats changed. Mellik glanced up from the weathered, leather-bound book he was reading. Several of the goats near the ridge of the hill were looking down where the Northern Road crossed below them. The goats only glanced down for a moment before returning to the flowering shrubs and weeds. Mellik figured he should check, just in case. Goats were smart about some dangers, not so much with others.

Mellik placed the leather strip he was using as a bookmark back in his book and carefully stowed the book in his canvas satchel. There were only four books in their small village, and they all belonged to his mother. He wouldn't risk her wrath if something should happen to it..

He levered himself up with his hooked shepherd's staff and strode over to the ridge. In the distance he could see two horsemen moving along the rutted track on the far side of the river, followed by a small wagon. Another half-dozen horsemen trailed after. He could just make out the plumed helms of the two lead horsemen, and all carried spears and other arms that glinted in the afternoon sun. Several of the soldiers glanced up at him, but none seemed to pay him any mind and simply continued on.

Mellik called to their dog, and she began gathering up the goats to follow him down. The goats were a bit uncooperative at being hauled away from their hilltop meal so long before sunset, but the dog was an experienced herder and brooked no nonsense. The soldiers would have to go a ways to reach the ford where the wagon could cross, and his father would want to know before they arrived. He wondered why they were come to Hillsford village in the spring. He could only remember them coming at tax time in the fall before.

*　　　*　　　*

Mellik peeked out through a crack in the front shutters. His father and two of the other men from the village were standing in the commons and had turned to face the North Road, so the soldiers must be close.

"Mellik, come away from there and shut the shutters," ordered his mother.

"But Ma," protested Mellik, "They can't see in here where it's dark anyway, and I want to see."

His mother was silent, studying him for a moment. Mellik could feel her weighing her options and whatever risks she thought might be involved. She finally nodded, but slowly, holding Mellik's eyes with her own.

"Alright, but not a sound."

Mellik put his eye back to the crack -- just in time too, as two of the horsemen rode into the commons. They looked far more striking than the guardsmen who accompanied the tax collector each year. One man wore a breastplate and helm that shone in the late afternoon sun. His red cloak and sash seemed exotic and rich. Mellik guessed the man must be a lord by the bright trappings of his horse. The second man wore a more familiar leather jerkin studded with blackened metal and a simple kettle helmet blackened in the same style. He held a long spear braced in his stirrup, and weapons bristled from his saddle, back, and waist. The lord rode toward the three villagers, his eyes never wavering. The second glanced left and right constantly; not nervously, but with a casual awareness, as if curious. That man looked right at Mellik's shuttered window the window. He seemed to pause, studying it, and in the next instant he moved on with his inspection of the village: dismissing whatever he'd seen or sensed. The warrior kept a horse-length behind the lord.

The two men stopped their horses a few paces away from the villagers. The three villagers bowed low with palms up and outspread in greeting.

"Welcome to Hillsford Milords," said Mellik's father as the three men straightened up. "How can we and our village be of service to you?"

The lord slid from his saddle and handed the reins to his companion.

"Are you Mellor Ackins?" he asked.

"I am," replied Mellik's father.

"And you were a sergeant in the imperial army?"

"I was."

"Good to meet you," said the man taking a stride forward and extending his palm to Mellor with a smile. "I am Lieutenant Guardsman Aaron."

Mellor took the proffered hand.

"And this is my compatriot, Warden Hake."

Mellik shivered in excitement at the mention of the title Warden. They were the stuff of legend: said to be warriors almost superhuman in their abilities. This was the most thrilling thing that had ever happened in Hillsford.

Mellor bowed again to the mounted man, "It is an honor, Warden."

The Warden nodded in acknowledgement.

"You can tell your villagers to relax," continued the Lieutenant. "We're not here to collect extra taxes, and we're not conscripting your boys. We're here testing for talents. Do you know what that is?"

"I grew up in the Lakes Province, so yes," replied Mellor.

"Good, than you can explain it to the other families. If you made sergeant, then you can read?" Mellor nodded that he could.

"I have my paperwork here if you'd like," and the man reached for a sealed wooden tube hanging from his belt.

Mellor held up a hand to forestall him, "Your word is good enough. I'll talk to the other families."

"Ah, good. You have no idea how hard it can be in these frontier towns the first time we come testing. I almost think the Conscripters have it easier in some ways. Make sure to mention that the Emperor is paying one gold crown for any youth that tests out for a talent, and the family will be excused from taxes for the next three years as well. I have the gold and the imperial writ of exclusion with me."

The eyebrows of the two men with Mellor shot up at that. It was a handsome payment for whatever these men were asking from the villagers.

"Many of our youngsters are out in the countryside right now," said Mellor. "When and where would you like me to gather them?"

"We will come back here an hour after first light tomorrow. I have my men camped just on the other side of the ford."

Mellik nodded, "I understand and will explain it to the other villagers."

The three villagers bowed again, and the Lieutenant swung himself back into the saddle. The two horsemen turned in unison and trotted out of the village square.

*   *   *

"Should we hide him?" asked Mellik's mother with a slight tremble in her voice.

They stood in their house now that the soldiers had left. The windows stayed shuttered, and the small cottage was stuffy with the warmth of the spring day. Mellik looked down at his pallet by the hearth, his satchel laying where he'd left it when he'd come back with the news.

"No," answered Mellor. "They have the tax rolls from the fall, and with your ancestry it would only cause suspicion."

Mellik's mother made an "O" with her mouth and touched her face with a glance at Mellik. She was darker than the other villagers, with jet black hair and dark brown skin, but what made her stand out were the lighter stripes of tan skin that trailed down like tears from her hairline: some ending on her face, some continuing on down to the neckline of her blouse. One went all the way to the tip of her pinkie on her hand, and during summer you'd see the few that trailed down to her ankles or ended on her arms. Mellik had the same black hair, but his skin was a shade lighter, almost as light as his father's sandy brown, and his stripes were a pale almond color.

"He's a half-blood," continued Mellor. "We have the documents from his birth. Father Hiram is still alive if they want testament from someone. The prophecy and the laws are very specific. Only a full-blooded Kamori would be in danger.

"Mellik, you remember the prophecy and what you need to say if asked?"

"Of course," replied Mellik, reciting the passage from memory though he had not had to defend himself from scrutiny in years. ""Full blood of the earth blood shall he rise, though raised by the old blood." I am only half Kamori, and we are not the old royalty of the kingdom."

"I'm sorry," said his mother with a deep breath. "I'm just a mother – I worry."

"It's alright," said Mellor, coming over to give her a hug and rubbing her back as he turned back to look at Mellik. "He'll be fine."

*   *   *

The next morning Mellik stood in a cluster with the other children of the village. Everyone between the ages of eight and sixteen. The youngsters hung behind the older children, and at twelve, Mellik stood towards the front of the twenty three kids. His hooded cloak was pulled up over his head to ward off the early morning chill. They stood in the middle of the village green, a few garlands of early flowers already dotted it well ahead of the spring festival. The village cottages circled the green like men around a campfire on a chilly night.

Mellik's father had explained what the soldiers were looking for. Mellik was excited.

"Talents are just that," his father had explained. "Some people are born with or grow into abilities far beyond what ordinary people possess. Two of the most well-known are wizardry and the fighting abilities that the Warden's possess, but I've also heard of men who could seemingly talk someone into anything, and a woman who could speak seventeen different languages."

"So one of us could be like a warden?" asked Mellik hopefully. All the children had heard tales of the Wardens daring deeds.

"Don't worry," said Mellor, misinterpreting the reason for the question. "I've been watching all the youngsters, and I've not seen any abilities out of the ordinary. Even if someone does show some talent, they'll be well taken care of. The Emperor values talents very highly."

Mellik stood wrapped in a hooded cloak against the morning's chill peering around at his friends from the shadow of his hood, trying to catch a glimpse of what the testing might entail. But where were the soldiers? Mellik had no way of telling the time, but it seemed as if the entire village had been standing there waiting forever. Finally, from between the low hills, the Lieutenant and the Warden appeared. A wagon followed with two of the other soldiers Mellik had seen from his hilltop the previous day riding behind the driver.

The wagon rolled into the village commons and stopped. Without a word, the two soldiers who hadn't come into town the day before dismounted and pulled a table and two chairs from the wagon. They set the table with the two chairs on one side next to the wagon. The wagon driver dismounted and began to rummage in the wagon for things. He was oddly dressed to Mellor. He wore long, loose pants with a similar shirt. Although they were worn and dusty, they were made of a grey cloth Mellor had never seen before that seemed to shimmer slightly in the morning sunlight.

"This half," Mellik was broken from his study of the wagon driver by the Warden, who had come to stand in front of the bunched children and was now pointing down their middle with his left hand and gesturing with his right. "Take a step to your left."

Mellor was on that side of the group and took a step with the other children.

"Good, now follow me," and the Warden strode off back down the road the soldiers had come by.

One of the soldiers followed them and glancing back, Mellor saw that he had a bundle of smooth wooden sticks in his arms.

The Warden strode up the lane, forcing many of the children to trot to keep up. He went just past the last house and fence and turned onto a small, bare field.

"Form a line on the fence," he said, pointing at the low stone wall that ran on the village side of the field.

The children lined up.

"You'll be first," the Warden said, pointing at an older boy, and then glanced at Mellik. His hand came down and drew his sword as he seemed to glide toward Mellik. Before Mellik could flinch the blade came up, flicked off his hood and came back to rest on his breast just below his neck. Mellik was entranced by the speed and precision of the Warden's movement. He had watched his father practice with his old sword and thought him quite the swordsmen. Now that seemed like watching one of the little ones whack at trees with a stick.

"What have we here?" the Warden whispered to himself, but loud enough that Mellik could hear.

"Warden Hake!" Mellik heard his father yell and could hear his boots pounding up the road.

"Stay!" the Warden commanded, pointing down the lane with his free hand. "And be quiet. Sergeant Mellor is your father?"

Mellik didn't sense any malice or any other emotion in the Warden's tone or face.

"Yes," answered Mellik. Somewhere in the back of his mind he wondered at his lack of fear for the blade at his throat. He felt strangely calm, almost detached from himself.

"And what is your heritage?"

"I am half Kamori."

"On which side?"

"My mother's."

"And has she told you the prophecy?"

"Yes."

The sword flashed down and slid into its scabbard with a hiss.

"Good. I'll take you first," the Warden turned towards the road, and Mellik saw that his father had stopped several paces back. The soldier who had carried the staves was standing in the lane with his sword drawn. "Go back to the village. Your son is safe with me."

Mellor nodded and turned to head back. The soldier sheathed his sword and stooped to pick up the pile of sticks he had dropped. Striding forward, he dumped the pile at Mellik's feet.

"Choose something that feels comfortable," instructed the Warden.

Looking down, Mellik saw that the sticks were not just rough pieces of wood, but had been carved smooth and rounded off at the ends. They were of various lengths, a few were curved, and some had rough crosspieces, imitating swords. Mellik had played with such toys when he was younger and was tempted to take one, but his father had taught him the use of the spear and staff, so he chose one of the longer sticks that was roughly as tall as himself.

The Warden drew his blade and waved Mellik toward him, "Attack me. Don't worry about the sword. I'm not trying to hurt you, so I won't."

Gripping the staff near one end and the middle like a spear, Mellik advanced forward in a slow shuffle. The warden stood unmoving as Mellik advanced, his sword held motionless at his side.

"Now attack me," he commanded when Mellik's fake spear point was less than an arm's length away.

Mellik gave a tentative lunge. The Warden didn't even bother to raise his sword, but just grabbed the spear below where its point would have been and pulled it to one side and past him, pulling Mellik along with it. The Warden grabbed him before he stumbled past and held him close.

"I'm here to test your fighting ability," the warden whispered in a growl. "I can't do that unless you attack me with everything you've got. You're not going to hurt me, and I don't want to hurt you, but if that's what it takes to make you fight me, I will."

The warden gave the shaft a shove that sent him reeling to land hard on his backside in the dirt.

"Get up and try again," ordered the Warden.

Mellik got to his feet and gripped the pole like a staff. The spear was good for holding off wolves, or keeping something at bay, but if his purpose was to attack this man, he felt more confident attacking with two ends, not one.

He approached slowly again, but this time he advanced in the slight fighter's crouch his father had taught him. He also circled to his right. Mellor had told him that whenever fighting it was best not to come straight at one's foe, and against a man, their left was usually their more vulnerable side. This time the Warden raised his sword in defense when Mellik got close, but he remained standing rigidly upright, only turning slightly to stay facing Mellik.

Mellik jabbed and was parried. Several more jabs resulted in the same. Mellik tried the few combinations he knew, but the Warden barely needed to move when defending himself. The Warden seemed to be not worrying about any kind of counterattack, so Mellik launched into a full-out assault. Left, right, up and down; he swung the staff in a flurry, abandoning any chance of defense, but he could not break through the single dense blade that rang from the blows and seemed to be everywhere. Without even seeing what the Warden did, Mellik felt himself spun about and pinned against the Warden's solid body. Mellik's staff was gripped in the Warden's free hand and the Warden's sword was held carefully to one side.

"Enough," the Warden stated, releasing him. "Your father has been drilling you, yes?"

Mellik nodded, breathing too heavily to speak.

"You did well," he said. Mellik felt a huge grin spread on his face. "If you ever have the desire for it you should consider the army when you're of age."

The grin evaporated from Mellik's face, and he nodded.

The Warden sensed his disappointment and put a hand on his shoulder.

"Son, everyone is born with different abilities. The talent at arms to be a Warden is just one of them. None of our generals are from the ranks of Wardens, yet they command Wardens, so who is the more powerful? Now, go over to Sergeant Cade, who has some more tests for you."

The Sergeant had Mellik sit and watch as the Warden put the younger half of the group through the same paces. When five more of the village children were with him, the Sergeant began to test them in physical activities. They ran a short race, jumped over things, and climbed the sheer side of a sinkhole. They attempted to juggle, tumble and perform all sorts of feats of strength, dexterity and flexibility.

Mellik was the eldest and the only boy in the Sergeant's group, and he was feeling good about himself again by the end of the tests. The Sergeant, giving no indication of their performance, dismissed them and told them to go back to the village commons for further testing. Mellik had noticed other children from the village were trickling up the lane to be tested as he had been doing the activities. He didn't get to ask them about the testing in the village however, as they joined the Warden's group.

Entering the village, Mellik could see that the remaining children were sitting in a line on the grass with one of the soldiers standing by them. The Lieutenant was sitting on the wagon speaking to one of the girls. The horses had been unhitched and were grazing in a pasture. The man with the strange clothing was sitting at the table. Sitting next to him was one of the eldest boys, who held something shiny and square in his hands. The soldier gestured Mellik and his group over and had them sit in line with the last few children.

Mellik made sure he sat next to the last girl waiting in line.

"What's going on Tara?" he asked.

"I don't know. They call the next one up to sit with that man," and she gestured at the table. "Then they look at that mirror for a while, talk, and then he sends them over to the soldier on the cart. They seem to just talk. What about out there?"

"All kinds of races and stuff, and the Warden tests you with weapons, of course."

"Even the girls?"

"I guess even girls can be Wardens," replied Mellik with a shrug. He'd never thought of a girl being any kind of soldier before, but the Warden had been testing them, so he assumed it was possible.

They lapsed into silence and watched as the children took their turns, first with the man at the table, and then with the Lieutenant. Mellik wondered at the silver square that each child held and looked into. The man and children were facing them, so he couldn't see what was on the front of the piece of metal, but he could see that the edges had been sculpted into some kind of swirling pattern. Neither man took long with each child, and in what seemed no time at all, Mellik was next.

He concentrated very hard at what Tara did with the piece of metal, but she did nothing all the youths before her hadn't done, and strain as he might he could not hear a word that was said between her and the man. Soon she was moving on to the Lieutenant, and it was Mellik's turn. He felt strangely anxious and afraid. He began to tug at the cuff of his sleeve while he waited to be called forward.

"It's your turn," said the soldier, coming to stand before Mellik and gesturing towards the table.

Mellik rose and approached the table. The man was rubbing his eyes, and Mellik could smell alcohol on him even from across the table.

"Sit, sit," said the man impatiently, waving at the chair next to him.

Mellik obediently crossed to the chair and sat down. Looking down, he was surprised to see that the square object really was an old silver mirror. He had thought it must be something far more arcane than that. It must have been very fine once, as Mellik could see that the swirls were a pattern of vines and flowers around its border, but now it was pitted and warped with half-repaired dents.

"Please pick up the mirror and look at your reflection in it," the man instructed.

This seemed a very odd test, and Mellik wondered if the mirror was some amazing magical object that would see inside his mind as he gazed at his distorted reflection. He wanted to stick his tongue out at himself and see if he could make it look extra long in one of the creases, but he restrained the urge.

"Now try and empty your mind of thoughts and just gaze into your own eyes. Think of their color and pattern and nothing else."

This was relatively easy for Mellik. His mother had often done similar mental exercises with him when he was younger. He had been terribly afraid of the dark as a child, and she had taught him this concentration trick to help him relax and go to sleep. He automatically relaxed his muscles, rapidly going from his toes and fingers, right up his spine and out from his nose. He released all thought except to gaze at his own eyes, and even then he did not think consciously of any color or pattern but just let his eyes focus down on the points of his pupils, becoming lost in their depth.

"Now think of the face of someone that you love. Fix it in your mind."

The voice came to Mellik, and thoughts of his mother floated back up to the surface. He saw her face, bending over him at night giving him similar instructions. Then he realized that the image was not just in his mind, but was actually reflected in the mirror. He smiled as he saw her beautiful face and then lost his concentration as he realized that this beaten old mirror was indeed a magical device, and his excitement broke his thoughts.

He turned toward the man, ready to apologize. He stopped when the red eyed man smiled for the first time Mellik had seen. It was a crooked smile that didn't move passed his lips.

"Congratulations," said the man. "You are now an Apprentice in the Exalted Emperor's service."

Chapter 2

"But it will be dangerous," Mellik's mother protested.

"Jozella, you heard Mage Arbret. He is in **more** danger if he does not receive training," replied Mellor patiently for the fourth time that Mellik could remember.

Mellik was still in something of a daze – he was a wizard! The mage had introduced himself and then sent him on to the Lieutenant. The soldier had questioned him about the other people of the village, mostly about the children, but he wanted to know about anyone unusual or anything odd happening. Mellik didn't remember answering. He just remembered sitting, wondering about what it all meant, what his future might be.

"But what if he's lying? They lie all the time," she argued.

"A wizard is far too valuable to waste. He will be coddled and receive the best care and food next to the lords themselves. He will also become wealthy and powerful beyond anything he could hope to achieve here. This is a good thing for our son, Jozella, a great thing." Mellor came to stand behind his wife, hugging her around her shoulders and nuzzling an ear.

"But it's so far away," she protested, leaning back into Mellor.

"Mom, I want to go," Mellik said, looking up from where he had been scratching at a knot in the table.

"What, love?"

"I want to go. If I have this gift, I need to learn to use it. I want to learn to use it. And this isn't just good for me, you and dad will be able to live better and save some with me gone and no taxes. Mage Arbret said I can come back and visit after the apprenticeship."

"We've raised a strong, wise son," said Mellor softly. "It's now time to let him go. And besides, you know we have no choice."

"I know, just give me some time to adjust to it."

"The Lieutenant was kind enough to give us until tomorrow morning," said Mellor. "I know that won't be enough, but it's what we have. It's really not up to us . . . or even Mellik."

Mellik's mother only sighed in reply.

*   *   *

That night held little time for Mellik's family to say goodbye. All evening long the people of the village came by to say farewell. Some even brought gifts.

"They wish to be remembered well," explained his father. "They know that when you return, you will be one of the most powerful men in the empire."

Some also brought sick livestock or kin.

This completely baffled Mellik, until his mother saw his expression and came over to whisper in his ear.

"They don't understand what you might be able to do. Just touch the afflicted one on the shoulder and say you wish the best for them. It will be enough."

To Mellik's surprise, it was. Mellik found it unfathomable that villagers who had cursed him for being a clumsy goat the day before, now were asking him to cure their child's twisted foot.

Children, the old, people's sheep and goats were even brought to him. Mellik's blessing became nothing more than a mantra he repeated over and over, not even noticing who or what he was blessing. He did notice, however, that the village girls would give him shy, furtive looks from the doorway: even girls several years older than him.

Some of the mothers would notice these looks and quickly usher their daughters out. Mrs. Corly smiled crookedly and pushed her daughter forward. Mellik had no idea what on Assa Corly he was supposed to bless or cure. She was almost three years older than he, and considered the prettiest girl in leagues. Rumor had it that men from neighboring villages had already come courting.

"Um, hello," said Mellik.

Assa merely blushed in reply.

"You know my Assa has yet to accept any man's hand," said

Mrs. Corly, pushing Assa forward and forcing Mellik to take a step backward.

Jozella came forward to save him.

"I'm sorry, but I think Mellik is done for the evening. Mellik must pack and prepare for a long journey in the morning," she continued when Mrs. Corly opened her mouth to protest. "Our own family has yet to say its goodbyes, and I'm sure you understand how important that is to us."

All the while, she had been backing Assa and her mother out the door. Jozella followed the two out and shut the door behind her. Mellik could then hear her making the same apology to those still waiting there. There were a few muted grumbles and protests, but his mother had always had a way of cowing the people of the village when she wished to.

She came back in a moment later, latching the door behind her.

"Come Mellik," she said, sitting down at their table. "You have a long day ahead of you, but we must talk tonight as a family. Mellor, will you bring me my knitting basket please?"

Mellor picked up the basket by their bed and placed it on the table.

Jozella took Mellik's hands from across the table and held his eyes with her own.

"Mellik, I have something for you," she said, lifting the fire opal necklace from around her neck. "This is yours."

"But Dad gave that to you," protested Mellik.

"No, this ring has been in our family for many years. It came to me from my grandmother, and was always meant to go to you when you were old enough. That time is now."

"What do you mean, ring?" asked Mellik, looking at the teardrop shaped pendant.

"Wait," she instructed. Then, she cupped the pendant in both hands and closed them about it. She brought her hands up to her mouth and breathed slowly into her hands.

A brief flash of light, amber and crimson, shot from between her fingers. Startled, Mellik almost tipped his chair over backwards. His mother only raised an eyebrow at him and her eyes sparkled with contained laughter as she continued to breathe out into her hands. The glow slowly subsided and then went out. She smiled as she opened her hands to reveal a rough gold ring.

"You can do magic!" exclaimed Mellik.

"Shush," ordered Jozella. "There is a reason we have kept this a secret. You are young, but you need to know that it is your life and ours too if the Emperor were to find out."

"Why?" asked Mellik in bafflement.

"Your great grandfather was a king of our people. When the Emperor came to take his kingdom, your grandfather waged war on the empire. He resisted for many years, but in the end, the sheer weight of the empire wore him and our people down. As punishment for his resistance, the Emperor ordered that he and all his kin should be put to death.

"Your grandmother was the only one to escape that I know of. Before she died, she passed that ring on to me. Now it is yours."

"But if it could mean our death, why don't we just throw it away or melt it down and sell it?" asked Mellik.

"Because then the Emperor wins. Then the death of your grandfather and all our family were for nothing," Jozella was becoming teary eyed and she reached across to clasp his right hand tight in her own. Mellik could feel the ring digging painfully into the back of his hand but could not speak nor look away.

"This ring is important. You are important. Someday I hope to tell you about that war and our people and your family's role in both. You also need to learn about the empire and the Emperor himself. But now is not the time, so you must trust us now and keep this ring and your heritage a secret," she turned to look at Mellor and Mellik followed his gaze. His father looked at Mellik and slowly nodded his affirmation.

Mellik's father almost always took the lead, with his mother backing him up. This reversal, and the intensity with which she held his gaze, made Mellik confused and afraid.

The silence held for several seconds as his parents waited for him to absorb all this.

"So are we all wizards?" he finally asked.

"No, Mel. We didn't know until today that you had the potential in you," she let go of his hand and took the ring off the chain. "As for what I just did, I have barely any ability in that area, certainly not enough to be considered a wizard. No, the ring itself has an affinity for magic, which makes these things easier for me. That could be important for this next part."

She looked over at Mellor, "I will need a bucket of water and my burn salve."

Mellor nodded and gave Mellik's shoulder a squeeze on his way by.

Jozella rummaged in the bottom of her knitting basket and came up with a small jar stoppered with a wooden plug. Opening it, she scooped out a small piece of shiny green clay.

"Do you remember this?" she asked as Mellor returned to set a small pail of water and an open jar of ointment next to her.

"It's slime rock," answered Mellik.

"That's right," replied his mother. "As you know, it's a clay used mostly to entertain young children, because it never seems to dry out. Please try the ring on."

Mellik took the proffered ring and slipped it onto his right index finger. He was a little surprised at the perfect fit, as it had looked much too large for him, but he supposed it was due to the odd swirls and crests of its design that ran even to the ring's inner side. It was very odd looking: rough and seeming almost unshaped, as if someone had only taken the time to smooth out its inner surface.

"Good," Jozella commented, holding out her hand again. Mellik returned the ring to her. She began to take pieces of the slime rock and mould them onto the outside of the ring.

"A secret that our people found many generations ago is that when heated to temperatures well beyond what the best blacksmith's furnace can produce, slime rock becomes something else," she looked carefully at the clay covered ring, turning it back and forth in her fingers before giving a satisfied nod. "You need to hide the ring's true shape from the Emperor's mages. Many of them would recognize it, and a pendant would look suspicious on a boy.

"Mellik," she said after a deep breath, "I'm going to need your help. As I said, I don't have much skill in this, but with your magic potential, I think I can borrow enough energy to work this spell. I'll need to be touching you, I think, so why don't you come around behind me and give me a hug.

"There, good," she said when Mellik had complied. "Now put your cheek against mine. Mellor, this is probably going to hurt quite a bit, so please keep me from crying out."

Mellik's father moved to Jozella's other side and crouched down next to her.

"Mellik, I've never done this before, but you might feel week, light-headed, even cold, but no matter what, don't break contact with me until I drop the ring." Mellik nodded against her cheek in reply.

"Okay, here we go."

For one instant, Mellik felt nothing. Then the weakness came on quickly. It was like the weakness from the winter sickness, but he could feel the strength draining from him, his arms wanting to drop to his sides, his knees wanting to buckle. The cold came quickly after, but not the cold that stole in from fingers and toes, but something coming from within: like his chest grew shards of ice that began to spread out and up his spine. He heard a muffled whine and knew that Mellor was keeping his mother from crying out. The ice was becoming painful and it was taking a concerted effort for Mellik stay upright.

His mother jerked up out of his grasp and Mellik was sent sprawling onto the floor in a ragged heap. He heard her whimper of pain and the hiss of something hot hitting the water and something else heavy and solid striking the table.

Looking up, he could see his mother standing at the table, her hands sunk in the bucket of water and a trace of steam rising around her. Another trail wafted up from somewhere on the table. His father was down on his hands and knees next to Mellik.

"Mellik, Mellor, are you alright?" she asked, seeing them both on the floor for the first time. She pulled her hands from the water to crouch beside them, then hissed and pulled away in pain when her hand grasped Mellik's shoulder.

Mellik looked at her hands, gnarled into claws by the pain, and he could see the heat: not as smoke, or waves of heat like sometimes came up off the rocks in summer, but as pulsing waves of light that were wrong and foreign to the light that he knew as his mother. The feeling of coldness had dimmed from its sharp pain to a dull emptiness that engulfed Mellik.

An urge gripped him: an instinct so strong he felt like an observer to his own actions. He reached out and grabbed her hands, holding on with a strength that surprised him as she pulled back in pain. He could physically feel the heat there now, almost painful to his touch. He could still feel the coldness within him too, like a blackness that could devour the bright red of her heat. So he pulled the red into himself: pulling only the pulsing redness that was not her, leaving the soft, glowing pinkness that he knew as his mother.

Mellik felt the prickly heat all about his skin, and then a black far from cold took him and he saw no more.

* * *

"Mellik! Mellik can you hear me?" shouted his mother.

"Please don't yell," mumbled Mellik, his head was throbbing and for some reason his clothes were soaking wet. Maybe the bucket of water had tipped over. The bucket, the ring, his mother's hands: suddenly it all came rushing back to him.

"Mom, your hands," Mellik tried to blink the fuzz from his eyes and sit up, but he was so weak his mother held him down with only her fingertips.

"They're fine," and she held her two bandaged palms up for him. "Thanks to whatever you did, but whatever that was, don't you dare ever do that again until you're trained. What did you do?"

"Wait, where's Dad? Is he okay?"

"I'm fine," Mellor said, stepping out where Mellik could see him. "Answer your mother's question, it might be important."

"I don't really know exactly," answered Mellik. "I remember seeing the heat in your hands and I felt so cold, I just thought the two could cancel each other out."

Mellik's mother bit her lower lip, but said nothing.

"Jozella?" asked Mellor softly.

"Demons, I just don't know," she swore. "I was so young when my mother explained these things, but that sounds wrong. The coldness was a loss of energy, I remember that, but I don't think you can replace it by force. What Mellik took in was pure heat so he could shape that and redirect it, but I think it's dangerous to just hold it in like that. I just don't remember," she continued with a deep sigh. "I guess that settles the matter of you needing to go for training."

"No harm done looks like," commented Mellor as he reached down to feel Mellik's forehead. "The fever is already going down. I'll get some more water. He needs to replace as much of that as he can. At least that I know."

"What happened?" asked Mellik.

"I just told you I don't know," bristled Jozella but quickly softened. "I'm sorry, Mellik, but I've been frightened out of my wits for the better part of an hour."

"I've been out for an hour?"

"Yes. My best guess is that you drew the heat from my hands and then let it spread into your own body. You could have killed yourself. Lucky for you this was a fever your own body wasn't producing, so it came down quickly. You'll not try something like that again without instruction?" she asked again.

"No ma'am."

Jozella helped him to slowly sit up.

"Good," commented Mellor, returning with a tall mug of water. "Now drink this."

Mellik needed no urging and quickly drained the mug.

"What of the ring?" asked Mellik, remembering the cause of all this.

"Sitting on the table where your mother dropped it," replied Mellor.

"Oh my, I'd forgotten," Jozella echoed his earlier thought.

"Stand slowly," she instructed Mellik. "Any dizziness?"

Mellik shook his head in reply as he slowly climbed to his feet. Standing at the table, he gazed down at the small ring lying near its center. The deep gold was still visible on its inside, but now the outside face of the ring was a lustrous dark red stone.

"Bloodstone," said Mellor.

"Can I pick it up?" asked Mellik.

"It likely cooled off quicker than you," replied Mellor. "Should be fine."

"It's yours now Mellik. Take it," urged his mother.

Mellik reached out and lightly touched the ring with his index finger. It seemed slightly warmer than it had before, but not hot. It rested in a small ring of charred oak. Mellik took the ring between his thumb and forefinger and held it up to the light of their lantern. He had thought it a shadow or a reflection of the charred table, but where one side of the ring was the bright red of fresh blood, it had darkened to almost black on the other side. Mellik rubbed a finger against the stone experimentally, but it was the stone's coloring and not soot.

"It must be from where it touched the wood," commented Jozella, looking over his shoulder. "I've never seen that pattern of coloring before."

"If I'd known you could do that, I could have gotten rid of the goats," commented Mellor.

"Trust me," said Jozella, holding up her hands, "I won't be doing that again. Go ahead and put it on, Mellik. It's yours now."

Mellik slipped the ring onto his right ring finger. It felt warm and heavy, but not uncomfortable. The moment felt oddly important, like horns should have played, like in a book. Of course, Mellik had no idea what a horn sounded like. Then a huge yawn broke from him.

"Come," said his mother. "You obviously need some sleep, but I will try to shove as much of our history into you as I can before you pass out. Mellor, can you help me pack his things and fill in as many holes in my history lesson as you can?"

Mellik's mother guided him toward his bed and began to teach him the history of a land and a people.

Chapter 3

The next morning was something of a blur. Mellik could remember being awoken and dressing quickly, followed by a breakfast with bacon he wasn't allowed to savor. The tearful farewell was very clear, however. Even his father had cried for the first time he could remember.

Now Mellik found himself trudging along beside the mage's cart in a world only a few miles away from the one he had grown up in. It could have been the hills around his own village, but then it would have been his father's cart and his day would have been filled with his father's pleasant voice and the occasional burst of laughter or song. Instead, he trudged along in almost complete silence. Mage Arbret had hardly said a word to him except to tell him where to go and what to do with his things. He had only grudgingly allowed that Mellik could ride in the cart if he needed to. Mellik preferred walking. At least then he could pretend to brighter company.

Being a shepherd's son meant being used to one's own company. What made today difficult was that he could hear the soldiers ahead and behind talking amiably. He wasn't sure he would be welcomed into the conversation in any case, but Mage Arbret had made it clear that he was expected to stay next to the cart if not actually riding in it.

He comforted himself with the thought that they were headed to Benton's Hollow, the only other village within a day's walk. The two hamlets had many familial ties and Mellik knew the boys and girls of his age from Benton's Hollow from shared festival days and visits. Wouldn't they be impressed that he was a wizard!

*   *   *

That night was not as fun as he had hoped. Arbret informed Mellik that he was to be his assistant and to stand one step back and to one side, keep his mouth shut, and do as he was instructed. The Mage proceeded to then declare his meager selection of clothes inadequate. Arbret found a tattered cloak that was not too voluminous and told Mellik to keep the hood up and his hands inside whenever possible. Luckily, Mellik was tall for his age, and had broad shoulders. It didn't look too ridiculous.

After considering the costume for a moment, Mellik decided that it furthered his goal of impressing his neighbors with his status as an apprentice.

"Mellik!" screamed the Mage.

"Coming, Mage Arbret," Mellik called. The wizard seemed grumpy and smelled of cheap wine again, so Mellik would be on his best behaviour.

Arbret was leaning heavily against the wagon as he watched Mellik scurry up the road with the voluminous cloak held up to keep from tripping over it.

"Can you drive a cart?" asked the wizard.

"Yes, Mage Arbret."

"Good, you will drive into town then. Here," and the Mage held out a small bone needle, "pin the cloak in front of you so it looks more like a robe."

The Lieutenant had ridden ahead that morning, so the village was already prepared for their arrival. As they rode into the center of the village of thatched wooden homes, Mellik spotted the children huddled in a mass and wanted to pull down his hood, but knew it would get him in trouble.

The Lieutenant was standing in the middle of the road waiting for them, so Mellik stopped the wagon a few strides from him. The Warden had walked alongside the wagon this time, and now he strode forward to the children. One of the two soldiers trailing behind grabbed the bundle of staves and practice swords from the wagon and jogged to catch up. The other soldier pulled the small table from the back of the wagon.

Mellik had been told that the silence of their setting up was important for making the children slightly off-balance and more likely to answer truthfully about someone with a talent. Mellik turned and hopped off his side of the wagon. He had forgotten about the oversized cloak that was now pinned around in front of him, however.

The cloak caught under his foot, and Mellik was sent tumbling from the cart to land heavily on one shoulder. Mellik heard a girl's giggle, quickly contained. Then Arbret was there, grabbing Mellik's arm and pulling him roughly to his feet. The Mage put his face right up to Mellik's ear and his grip was painfully strong.

"You idiot," whispered the Mage. "Break the mirror and I'll make you wish you were dead by the time we reach the college."

Arbret shoved Mellik away. A steady hand caught him, and Mellik looked up to see the Lieutenant. Without a word, the Lieutenant placed a thin leather strap in Mellik's hand.

"Tie that ridiculous thing up out of your way," whispered the Lieutenant. He gave Mellik a wink before sauntering off.

Mellik hiked up the cloak and tied the strap tight about his waist to keep it up before scurrying to help bring the rest of the supplies to the Mage.

When everything was ready, Mellik stood just behind and to the right of the Mage, as he'd been instructed. He'd been told to keep the hood up, but he slid it back slightly, hoping that one of the village youths might recognize him.

The first few candidates were nervous and barely glanced at Mellik while Arbret took them through the mirror test. At first, Mellik was intrigued by how Arbret would take more time with some of the children than others, sometimes coaching and cajoling a few of them before moving on to the next. Mellik could see no rhyme or reason to it however, and became bored. He began to fidget and look around.

He had been too nervous to notice how most of the people in his own village had taken the testing as a holiday from chores and had stood around watching the uneventful proceedings. He remembered it now, seeing the people of this village do the same. He recognized several of the youngsters in the group waiting to be tested, but the names of only a couple of the boys his age came to mind: Jory and Willit.

Then he noticed that many of the youths in the group were looking back at him.

"Mellik?" Jory called to him.

Mellik raised a hand to wave and then stopped as Mage Arbret turned to glare at him. He realized in that instant that the hood of his cloak had fallen completely from his head.

Arbret set the mirror down and stood. Mellik opened his mouth to apologize, but Arbret's slap across his face stopped the words in his throat.

"Can't even stand still properly," commented the Mage. Mellik saw an expression cross Arbret's face that might have been regret, but it was quickly erased. "You're an apprentice Mage now. Pull the hood up and try to act the part. We'll start with standing still and being quiet. See if you can accomplish that."

Mellik felt the blood rushing to his face and quickly pulled up his hood. His father had only struck him once: when Mellik had argued with his mother and called her a name he'd heard from one of the older boys. His mother had never struck him.

He spent the rest of the day looking down at the ground, not wanting to see the faces of the youths he knew. Occasionally Arbret would ask him to fetch or hold something, and he would comply with a meek, "Yes, Mage Arbret," and then return to his silent post.

That evening, when they returned to the soldier's camp, Arbret informed him that he would be sleeping in the cart to guard it and then Arbret disappeared into his tent.

That became the pattern of his days. They would travel a day or two to the next village, test the young and then move on. Each day was the same for Mellik; he would walk next to the cart in silence, do as Mage Arbret instructed, usually only the most menial, simple tasks, and then sleep with the wagon. He tried to talk to the soldiers, but Arbret came and made it clear he was not to be welcomed at their fire.

Arbret was his only companion, and the wizard would speak to him only when he wished him to do something, or when he wished to berate him for doing something wrong. He learned to be extra cautious when he smelled wine on Arbret's breath.

After a week of this, Mellik was bored, resentful, and fit to burst.

That night, he couldn't sleep. There was a full moon and he found himself looking at the grain of the bench where Arbret sat each day to drive the cart. The wood was smooth and almost polished from use. Arbret had the lazy habit of sliding across the seat to the middle. He was lucky this cart was well used or he would have gotten a sliver long since: he was sliding right into the grain.

Mellik pulled out his belt knife and idly began to pick at one long grain of the wood: if it were to come up just a fraction...there! The sliver of wood stuck up just enough to pierce a plump buttocks when it slid over the bench -- a perfect gift for Mage Arbret in the morning.

He crawled back under the cart and drifted off with a smile on his face.

*   *   *

Mellik awoke to the full light of a new day, and his smile vanished. The thought of hurting a wizard who seemed largely indifferent to his continued existence now seemed a dubious idea at best. He looked around and saw that Arbret had for once awoken before him and was already breaking his fast by the wagon.

He stalled and fussed at the wagon loading, but Arbret spent the entire morning sitting or standing right next to the seat. By the time they were loading up to leave, Mellik was almost shaking with nerves. He was so frightened he couldn't seem to move or say anything. He just stood and watched the Mage climb up into the wagon. Arbret lowered himself onto the bench, slid over... The wizard vaulted up out of the seat with a howl. Everyone, even the wagon's horse turned to look at the Mage. Cursing non-stop, Arbret reached around and pulled out the huge sliver from his left cheek.

Suddenly it was funny again. Mellik bit down hard on his lip to keep from laughing, but it wasn't enough. The wagon was parked on some rough gravel, and Mellik dropped down and drove one knee forward into the rocks. The pain shot up from the knee and drove the laughter from his lips. He gasped in pain and clutched his knee as he rolled onto his back. It hurt like crazy, but it had stopped him from laughing.

"What's wrong with you?" asked Arbret, looking down at Mellik while still massaging his rear.

He looked up at the Mage, one hand still holding the sliver, the other on his wounded buttocks, and knew it was a good thing his knee still hurt, the wizard's pose was so comical.

"I heard your exclamation and stumbled," replied Mellik.

"Let me see that leg," said the guard Lieutenant as he rode up and dismounted. He glanced up at the Wizard with a grin, "Unless you want me to inspect your wound first, of course."

Arbret flicked the sliver away with a great show of dignity.

"I'm fine. Thank you," he said, but Mellik noticed that he was still surreptitiously rubbing at his left cheek.

The Lieutenant pulled up the pant leg and rinsed the blood away with some water from his water skin.

"You'll likely live," he pronounced, then took out a clean handkerchief and wrapped it around the knee. "Ride on the wagon at least through the morning. Rinse that cloth out whenever we stop and tie it back on there. Even after it stops bleeding make sure to keep the scab covered for a couple of days.

"Let's go," he shouted suddenly as he turned and quickly mounted his horse.

Mellik was forced to sit next to the taciturn Mage all morning, but the way Arbret shifted around on the bench and cursed under his breath at each unexpected bounce kept Mellik in a good mood.

*   *   *

That evening, after the horses had been taken care of, the Lieutenant came back to the wagon again.

"Mage Arbret," he called out. "May I borrow your apprentice?"

"He is not **my** apprentice," grumbled Arbret. "He's an initiate of the Imperial Academy Magica."

"Then you have no objection."

"He is supposed to be guarding the wagon."

"My men guard your wagon," and he motioned to two men stationed on a nearby hill. "This one's only purpose is to deter rodents. I think we're safe enough until nightfall."

"It matters not to me," and the wizard turned away as he waved them off.

"Grab your staff," instructed the Lieutenant as he strode off into the dry, sparse grass.

Mellik noticed then that Lieutenant Aaron was carrying a quarterstaff. The soldier was inspecting a gravelly, barren patch of ground and kicking the larger rocks away. He ignored Mellik for a moment as he finished clearing the ground, then turned to Mellik.

"There, I don't think we'll break any ankles now," he commented with a smile. "I seem to recall the Warden saying you weren't bad with that staff. I'm tired of getting beaten up by Warden Hake, so let's see what you've got."

The Lieutenant took his staff in both hands and stood in a lazy on-guard position, obviously waiting for Mellik. Mellik approached very slowly, unsure of why the Lieutenant had brought him out here. Mellik raised his staff in both hands, holding it just above waist level and at the ready, as his father had taught him.

When Mellik had approached to a couple paces away, Aaron lunged forward and swung the staff out awkwardly with one hand. Mellik blocked the attack easily and took a step back.

"Good, I wasn't sure you were ready," commented Lieutenant Aaron. "But you should have stepped in and countered while I only had one hand on the staff. Now, let's go over the basics."

The Lieutenant went slowly through the standard blocks and attacks, and then had Mellik do some attack and blocking patterns with him.

"Good. You know the basics. Now let's see what you don't know. A centime for every strike that lands," and the Lieutenant shook his belt pouch with a provocative jingle.

Trying to catch the Lieutenant with one hand on the staff, Mellik darted in with a jab, but the soldier was quicker and easily blocked the stab and gave Mellik a rap on his shoulder in counter. After that, it was all Mellik could do to keep from having his head bashed in as Lieutenant Aaron waded in with strike after strike. Mellik turned or blocked most, but the taller, stronger man landed enough that Mellik knew he'd be sore all over later on.

Then the Lieutenant tripped. He went down on one knee,

catching himself with one staff point. Mellik saw an opportunity to earn that centime, and swatted quickly at the soldier as Aaron tried to circle around him. Mellik concentrated on light, fast strikes to keep the soldier from regaining his feet, but the Lieutenant was still too quick, easily blocking them all even from his knees. Then Lieutenant Aaron leaned back from a strike and blocked behind it, sending Mellik's body twisting halfway round. Before Mellik could recover, Aaron popped up onto his feet and jabbed the butt of his staff lightly under Mellik's armpit.

"Hold!" the lieutenant called out.

Mellik gratefully lowered his staff and took a step back. Sweat ran freely into his eyes and down the length of his staff; his arms cried out in fatigue and he was bruised in a dozen places.

Lieutenant Aaron smiled and gave Mellik a slight bow as he also took a step back. Mellik noticed that other than dirty knees and the slight sheen of sweat, the soldier seemed barely winded. Mellik returned the bow.

"Not bad," commented the Lieutenant. "Your father was a good teacher, but I can see he was teaching you to fend off wolves or jackals. We need to work on your reach, and using those ends for thrusts."

"What on earth are you doing?"

Mellik spun to see that Mage Arbret was standing a few paces back with his arms crossed. He was very obviously addressing Lieutenant Aaron.

"Just giving the boy a workout," replied Aaron. "Warden Hake said the boy showed some skill with the staff."

"He is to become a wizard, not a shepherd, or worse yet a soldier," said Arbret with scorn. "He doesn't need to learn to fight."

Aaron shrugged, "He seemed idle enough in the evenings. I thought it would do him good to be learning something while we travelled. You know what they say about idle hands."

"If he is to learn anything on this trip, it should be mage craft, not war craft," scoffed Arbret.

"Of course Master Arbret, I apologize," and Lieutenant Aaron bowed to the Mage, but Mellik saw the ghost of a smile flicker across his face. "And, of course if I'd have known that you were starting his lessons in magic, I wouldn't have taken him this evening. I assure you I won't interfere with tomorrow's lesson."

Arbret grunted, "Yes, well, you could not have known I suppose."

Arbret looked up at the sky, "Well, I suppose it is getting late now. Tomorrow is soon enough. You may as well finish up whatever you were teaching."

Arbret turned and strolled away with an air of victory.

"I'll teach you about the art of the feint some other time," and the Lieutenant smiled in a way that was already becoming familiar to Mellik.

"Thank you," said Mellik, and bowed to the Lieutenant again.

"Ahhhk, I'm an indifferent staff fighter at best, and I really haven't taught you anything yet."

"I didn't mean for that."

"I was just trying to avoid an unnecessary injury," explained the Lieutenant.

Mellik just looked at him quizzically.

Lieutenant Aaron smiled again, "I have one of my men on watch all night. If I'm awake, sometimes I'll take that first watch. It's amazing what you're able to see by the light of that full moon.

The Lieutenant looked over at Mellik to make sure he understood. Whatever he saw on his face must have reassured him because he nodded and gave him a clap on the shoulder.

"Remember that sometimes who is witnessing something is more important than what we do," advised Aaron. "Do you want to continue the staff lessons?"

Mellik nodded enthusiastically despite his soreness.

"I'll teach you some basic staff strikes and combinations with a bit more reach that you can practice on your own. I'll teach you some more whenever I can, but I don't want to push Arbret too much.

"Now, get into your basic square stance. Good, now..."

Chapter 4

Mellik swore as a bump in the road sent his vision swimming; the plants he had been looking at blurred in a double image of colors and shapes.

"You need to maintain concentration," said Arbret, sitting next to him driving the wagon. "Do you want to use the mirror?"

"No," replied Mellik, concentrating hard to get his visions in sync again.

"Your normal sight should fade into the background," intoned Arbret for the thousandth time – he sounded mostly sober today. "It is the *second sight* that we need. See the plants, so full of magic that they are like bright points of light in a darkened world.

"There," and Arbret pointed past Mellik's nose, "that red flower with the thick stem. What do you see?"

It was mostly scrub and brush in these arid hills, but Mellik followed Arbret's finger and saw the oddly shaped plant. It might have looked like any other flower, except its stem was as thick as a small tree branch. Then Mellik saw what Arbret was asking him.

"The stem: it's glowing brighter than anything else I've seen," replied Mellik. He'd already seen that humans glowed with more magical energy than animals, and animals more than plants, plants more than rocks and on down to air; but even air had enough mana in it to block a wizard's second sight after a league or so -- like looking through a light fog.

"And what color is dominant there?" asked Arbret.

"White, air mana," replied Mellik, answering Arbret's next question as well. "Why does a plant have air magic stored in it?"

Animals were mostly fire and water, making a purple color.

Plants were fire, water, and earth for a purple-brown with more earth toward the roots and more red out on their leaves. This plant would have looked the same except for that bright patch of pure white at its center.

"That is called a Death's Head Rose," lectured Arbret. "It stores air mana because it creates sharp needle-like seeds just beneath the petal. When it collects enough mana it launches those seeds high into the air, scattering them into the wind. It got its name because if a creature bites off the petals, the plant will launch the seeds with whatever energy it has stored. This is often enough to penetrate the soft tissue inside the mouth and kill the creature. Corpses make for surprisingly good fertilizer."

Arbret grimaced at this last statement and Mellik saw his gaze drift off toward the horizon.

"Don't the animals learn not to eat it?" asked Mellik.

"Animals don't learn the way you and I do, plus the temptation is probably too much for many of them."

"Temptation?"

"Whoa," and Arbret drew in the reigns, halting the wagon.

Arbret turned and rummaged under the wagon's canvas for a moment before coming up with a large frying pan.

"Stay here," he instructed as he climbed down and absently waved off the guardsman coming to check on why they had stopped.

He strode back to the stout little blossom and crouched down next to it. Drawing his belt knife, Arbret held the pan just above the petals, angled slightly away from himself. With a deft cut he sliced off the top of the plant. Mellik heard the staccato dings of the hard seeds hitting the pan. Arbret picked up the flower's bloom and returned to the wagon.

Arbret handed one of the four petals to Mellik as he climbed back onto the wagon's seat.

"Just chew on it," Arbret instructed, putting one of the other petals in his own mouth. Arbret picked up the reigns and got the wagon moving again.

The petal was much coarser than Mellik had expected, and strong for a flower. He sniffed the flower petal experimentally. It smelled something like honey.

"I'll take it back if you don't want it," commented Arbret.

That decided it. Mellik quickly popped the petal into his mouth and bit down. Arbret chuckled at the expression on Mellik's face as the flower's sweetness flooded his mouth.

"Another name for the flower is the love blossom," Arbret told him. "They say that it is because, despite the danger, the sweetness is worth it. A single petal will retain its flavor for hours. As we go further south you will see more of them, but do not get used to them. There is a toxin hidden in that sweetness. Eat too many, even over several years, and your bowels will turn to goo. I have heard it is a most unpleasant death."

"Did you grow up in this area?"

A week ago, Mellik wouldn't have asked the question. Since beginning lessons however, Arbret had become almost pleasant -- at least when he was sober. Arbret took a while to answer, and then looked at Mellik with a sour expression.

"Near here," he finally answered, looking back to the cart path.

The Lieutenant trotted his horse back to ride alongside them.

"We'll be stopping at a slave camp," he said. "I'll want your apprentice to stay with the wagon with most of my guards."

Arbret nodded in return and the Lieutenant trotted back to the front of their line.

"I thought slavery was outlawed by the Emperor?" asked Mellik.

"For everyone but the Emperor, yes," and Mellik could hear the bitterness in Arbret's voice. "To be more accurate, I should say that only the empire may own a person, but as the saying goes, 'The Emperor is the empire.'"

"But we only test the very young. Are children slaves?"

"Technically, no, but a child stays with their parents until their majority at fifteen, so there are children present at the camps. They owe the empire for their food and upkeep for those years, so at fifteen they are conscripted into the empire's service, usually the army, until they repay their debt."

"But that's awful!" spat Mellik. "They must spend their entire lives working for the empire."

Arbret shrugged, "I have heard another fifteen if they survive that long and do not accrue more debt. And where else should they go? Prison work camps are a tough place to grow up. They would end up criminals or in the army either way.

"That is enough law. Back to the practice of magic for you. Now look at me as I gather in mana."

*   *   *

Mellik lay on his stomach on the gravelly ground looking at a small beetle working its way through the sparse grass. The speckled brown bug blended well with the sand and pebbles, but in the second sight it stood out in a blaze of fiery red. A few of the pebbles were beginning to dig into Mellik's ribs, and he was just about to poke the beetle to figure out why it was storing so much fire energy, when he heard the sound of the wagon returning.

Mellik looked around, but couldn't see over a small rise in the ground. Standing up, he absently brushed sand and dry grass from his front. He could see the wagon with the Lieutenant and Warden riding after.

He began walking back to where the other soldiers were already packing up, when he noticed another figure walking behind the wagon. Mellik's pace quickened in excitement. The figure looked tall from where he was, but Arbret had said they almost never tested adults, and from where he was, the person looked and moved like a boy, not a girl. Until that moment, Mellik hadn't realized how lonely he was.

Mellik checked his pace as he realized he was still looking at the group with his second sight. Now that he was closer, Mellik saw that there was something different about the extra figure walking between the horses: he had the usual mix of reddish-blue mana that Mellik associated with animals now, but he shone brighter with it than anyone else except Warden Hake. Arbret had explained to him that the Warden, like all non-wizard adepts, instinctually used mana to heighten their natural abilities and therefore could hold extra mana in their body without danger. Wizards, on the other hand, did not use mana at an instinctual level, and had to maintain concentration and control over any extra mana at all times.

Mellik switched back to his normal vision and could now clearly see that it was indeed a boy. The boy was much taller and broader in the shoulder than he, but Mellik thought he looked to be of a similar age. Mellik jogged forward, smiling.

"Hi, my name's Mellik," he said, extending his hand in welcome.

Mellik didn't even see the boy move, but the air rushed out of his lungs as he landed hard on his back. The boy landed on top of him, holding Mellik's arm twisted uncomfortably over his head. Mellik's other arm was trapped by the boy's knee. The boy's other knee crushed down on Mellik's neck, cutting off his air.

"Filthy rock-head!" screeched the boy. "I should rip your eyes out."

"Pollum," Mellik heard Lieutenant Aaron call out. "Any harm you do to one of my company will be echoed tenfold on the old man. I suggest you let the boy up quickly or I'll take the blind one's ears first."

The boy stood up with a growl, his knee grinding into Mellik's neck as he rose. Mellik was only half aware of the big lad stomping off as air whistled and whined back into his lungs.

"Are you alright?" asked Aaron as he gave Mellik a hand up. "You're breathing and standing: both good signs."

Aaron turned to speak to Warden Hake, "Catch the boy. Make sure that he understands that the old man is only useful as long as the boy is making progress. If he runs away or fails in any of his training, his life and the old man's are forfeit."

"Sorry about that," said Aaron, turning back to Mellik as the Warden strode off. "No one made any mention of the boy having a hatred for Kamori. It might be wise to just keep some distance from him."

Mellik just nodded in reply as he rubbed his neck.

*   *   *

Mellik kept that promise over the next week. He learned that rumor had it that a blind former Warden had raised Pollum and trained him at the prison camp. Other than that, Mellik just knew that the boy stared daggers into Mellik's back whenever he was in sight.

Mellik had heard the term rock-head while growing up. His parents had taught Mellik very early that there would be people who hated him for his appearance, for his race. It bothered him only a little. Far more worrisome was the fact that the boy might kill him given the chance, but as the days passed without incident, even that worry faded.

Mellik couldn't help himself from watching Warden Hake and Pollum spar however. It was like trying to watch a hummingbird's wings. They were a blur of motion. Only their heads seemed to move at a normal speed. The two struck and dodged at the same hyperkinetic speed, but Hake had the reach, and Mellik guessed the experience and strength as well. Mellik thought he saw the big Warden land several blows with the practice swords, but the boy seemed to only swing his swords in defense. Finally, the Warden became angry.

"What's wrong with you?" he yelled at the boy. "I clearly left myself wide open!"

Mellik couldn't hear the boy's answer, but it didn't mollify the Warden: Hake strode in again with his swords whirling even faster, if that was possible. For the first time, Mellik saw the boy wince in pain as Hake's blows landed.

The Warden stepped back with a curse and hurled his swords down at the Pollum's feet before turning and striding away. The boy just stood there glaring at the Warden's back.

Mellik decided it was a good time to return to the wagon.

*   *   *

It was a gloriously hot day and Mellik stood bare-chested gazing off across the rolling hills of scrub. The air wavered and billowed with heat, but Mellik could imagine the great southern desert was just beyond. Arbret had confided that they would be crossing its expanse on their way to the Academy of Magic in a couple of weeks.

"Hey boy, go get some more water," commanded one of the guards.

Normally, the guards left him alone, but Mage Arbret, Lieutenant Aaron, and Warden Hake were all gone. They had stopped early at a village and then those three had brought Mellik back to the camp so they could "investigate" something. That left Mellik to do all the grunt work for the guardsmen.

Mellik picked up the bucket with an internal shrug and ambled off toward the creek.

He loitered at the creek, standing in the cool water and splashing himself for relief from the heat. The air was still and stale, and even the crickets were quiet in the midday heat.

Mellik stopped as he felt the sensation of eyes boring into his back. Spinning around, he found Pollum staring at him from a few feet away with a wide smile on his face. The smile was a painful parody of true happiness, and Mellik knew the boy's opinion of him had not changed.

"You know what they said about hurting me," said Mellik. He was shaking slightly as he began to back away.

"Assuming they ever find out what happened to you?" commented Pollum, the smile leaving his face to be replaced with something even grimmer.

Mellik sucked in air to scream, but Pollum was simply too quick. The air came bursting out of his lungs as Pollum darted forward and brought both fists hard into Mellik's abdomen. Mellik landed hard on his backside. Pollum was on him before he could even start to get up. He was flipped onto his stomach, Pollum's right arm wrapped stoutly about his throat.

There was no breath in his lungs, and Pollum's arm was like an iron rod wedged beneath his chin. Mellik began to thrash and rip at the arm, but Pollum was far too strong. Mellik could only beat harmlessly at the few parts of the boy he could reach.

Mellik knew he only had moments of consciousness left when a strange calmness came to him. He could feel a strength and a patience from the earth he lay on. There was a power buried there as well: a power that wanted to rise up, wanted to move.

Desperate for anything that might help him, Mellik reached out with his mind and his body to that power. As his consciousness stretched out toward that power, Mellik felt a portion of that strength reaching back. Mellik let the strength in the earth join with his own. It seemed to help, as the pressure of Pollum's arm seemed to lessen.

Mellik still couldn't breathe. Probing at the strength in the earth with his slipping consciousness, Mellik could feel another, equal strength opposing the power that wanted to rise up. The two powers were close to balanced, and where they met the earth quivered with the struggle. Mellik's own strength there was minuscule, but he hoped it would be enough. With all the energy left to him, Mellik pulled the energy toward him.

It was enough. The energy rushed up toward him in release and the quiver became a shaking. Mellik was thrown violently upward and he pulled the earth to him even more as he struggled to hang on. A roaring filled his ears, and Mellik squeezed his eyes shut as sand and pebbles battered at his face.

Mellik felt like he had been thrown into a world of chaos, with no up or down and no sound but the angry growl of the universe. Somehow he hung on, stuck against the land beneath him as it bucked and danced in a mad caper. It sounded like a never ending scream from some huge giant, deep and coarse with pain and anger. Then it stopped.

Mellik remained still, his eyes closed in case this was just a reprieve. He heard a groan some distance away, and then the indistinct cursing of Pollum. Mellik quickly decided it was prudent to find out where the murderous boy was.

When he opened his eyes, however, what he saw right in front of him made Mellik pause. Where he had been lying on sand and loose gravel next to the creek, he was now on a rough slab of some dark gray stone. What was more shocking was that the fingers of both hands were sunk knuckle deep in the stone. The stone there was smooth, almost polished, and Mellik carefully slid his fingers from the holes.

A small sob and a curse from Pollum made Mellik spin around, the finger holes in the rock forgotten. Mellik was once more stunned by what he saw.

The slab of stone Mellik rested on jutted up from the earth at a low angle, but rose some twenty feet above where the creek now disappeared into a crevasse. There were other slabs of stone running North and South along the former channel of the creek, but none higher than the one he sat upon. Cracks and fissures riddled the earth where stone did not jut up out of it.

Some fifty yards away in the midst of this devastation was

Pollum. Both of the boy's legs dragged behind him, and his left arm was twisted unnaturally and covered in blood, but Pollum was dragging himself with his one good arm toward where Mellik now sat. Mellik couldn't hear what the boy was muttering to himself, but Pollum never took his eyes from Mellik, and his eyes spoke of death.

There was shouting coming from the direction of their camp. Mellik supposed there was trouble there as well, but his own worries were much more imminent and getting closer with each painful lurch.

Mellik scrambled to his feet and suddenly realized how weak he felt. His legs wobbled and shook as he stood, and there was a throbbing, stabbing pain that came with a sound like a rabbit's death squeal. Mellik's vision began to swim and spin. He desperately tried to stay upright. He took one staggering step forward, felt his foot clumsily catch on the rock and then the stone slab was rushing up at him. Mellik never felt his body strike the stone.

Chapter 5

Mellik woke to darkness. His eyes wouldn't open. Something was covering them, keeping them closed. Mellik reached up to remove whatever was on them.

"Do not," instructed Arbret. "The bandage needs to stay there for a while longer."

Mellik remembered the confrontation with Pollum, and panic seized him.

"Am I blind?" he cried out. "Did he take my eyes?"

"What?" asked Arbret, "Who? Your eyes? You mean Pollum? No, lad, you still have your eyes. You simply overextended yourself. You have not been trained to channel magical energies like that. You drained yourself dangerously. The bandages are just a precaution. Some Mages have done permanent damage to their second sight by opening their eyes too soon.

"And Pollum?" asked Mellik. "Is he . . . okay?"

"No, but he likely will be. He broke both legs, dislocated a hip and his shoulder, broke a couple ribs, and had a rather nasty break that punctured the skin on his right upper arm. The soldiers bandaged him up as best they could. The Lieutenant and Warden Hake are taking him to a garrison town near here that should have a healer."

Mellik could hear Arbret rustling around, and the sound of pewter and tin clinking together, followed by some liquid being poured.

"And you say he'll be okay?" asked Mellik dubiously.

"One of the benefits of the Warden talent is a knack for healing quickly and soundly. Not surprising considering their occupation. Here," and Mellik felt Arbret slip an arm behind his shoulder, "sit up slowly. I want you to drink while you're still awake."

Arbret helped Mellik sit up, and Mellik was surprised to find that he needed the help. Arbret put the cup in his hand. Mellik took a sip, and was delighted to find it was a fruit juice he didn't recognize.

"Am I going to be okay?" asked Mellik in a querulous voice: he'd never felt this weak before.

"You'll be fine," replied Arbret without hesitation. "I wasn't sure at first, but you're building your energy back up nicely now."

Mellik's stomach gave a fierce growl, and he realized suddenly that he was ravenous.

"How long have I been sleeping, and can I have something to eat please?"

"You have been out three days and half of another," replied Arbret. "You can have some more juice and a small piece of flat bread. We need to take it easy with your stomach."

Mellik waited as Arbret refilled his mug and drank the nectar slowly this time, savouring the sweet, tangy flavour. He took his time with the bland piece of flat bread as well, trying to fool his stomach into thinking it was more. Two seasons ago, his village had gone through a blight in the wheat and everyone had learned the trick except the newest babes.

"Will we be going to join them at the garrison?" asked Mellik, a huge yawn escaping him.

"No. Pollum and his keepers are headed to the capital as soon as he is able. You and I will be going straight to the Academy of Magic from here in a few days. So you have likely seen the last of Pollum. Do you want to tell me what happened?"

Mellik thought about Pollum and his hate. He wondered if some kind of revenge could be had by telling the story. Was what he'd done normal for an apprentice though? He was Kamori.

"Nothing," replied Mellik at last. "I just fell. I guess I was luckier than Pollum."

"There was bruising around your neck and a pair of bruises on your stomach," commented Arbret. "Odd placement for those."

Mellik just shrugged in reply, and then a huge yawn escaped him.

"Have it your way then. Now enough questions. Lay back down and let yourself sleep and recharge. And if you wake before me, one rule: no second sight for a while."

Mellik barely registered the act of lying back down before he was out again.

*   *   *

Mellik woke slowly this time. He could hear the faint flap of the tent in a listless wind. A few birds sang their morning songs, and he could see the faint red of light seeping through his eyelids. Wait: that meant he could see.

Mellik cracked his right eye open. He could see the faint brown of the canvas tent above him -- nothing covered his eyes. The light was still very dim. Years with the goats on the hills told him that dawn had only just broken.

Mellik opened his other eye and rolled on his side to look toward the tent's door. Looking back at him with a huge grin on his face was a sandy haired man with a deeply tanned complexion. So startled was Mellik that he shot up in his bedroll with a yelp. Mellik suddenly felt dizzy and the tent began to wobble and spin. Even more disorienting was the fact that the man seemed to be holding a rainbow on his upturned palms. The man was still smiling, but the smile now had a strained, concerned look to it.

"Mellik," called Mage Arbret sleepily from Mellik's other side. "You are awake? Are you feeling okay? Yes, yes: this is Bo. He is with us now. You should lie back down."

Arbret gently pushed Mellik back down on his bedroll.

"Bo?" asked Mellik.

"Yes. He is the boy we went to find on the day you and Pollum had your . . . 'accident'."

Boy? Mellik looked again at Bo. He was big: probably almost as large as the butcher in his village, though not quite as tall. Bo grinned at him widely and openly again and now Mellik could see the smooth face and round features that spoke of youth. If he was Mellik's age however, he was easily the biggest boy Mellik had ever seen.

"His grandmother said he was thirteen," said Arbret, answering Mellik's unspoken question. "You might have noticed he has a talent for illusion."

"The rainbow?"

"Exactly. The villagers said he was a simpleton. He cannot speak beyond the occasional grunt, but he uses the images and some simple hand gestures to communicate. Watch."

Arbret turned to Bo, "Bo, get Mellik some juice."

Bo's brow furrowed and he shrugged at Arbret and covered his mouth and then his ears briefly with both hands, before grinning again.

Arbret pointed at Mellik. "Juice," he repeated.

This time a white puffy cloud appeared just in front of Bo's forehead.

"That is his way of showing he does not understand something," Arbret explained. "His grandmother made us stay and learn some of this.

"Bo, drink," and this time Arbret pointed to Mellik and pantomimed drinking from a cup.

Bo's grin became huge and the cloud was replaced with a pewter cup that floated lower. A long, spiny leaf appeared above it and liquid drizzled out of it into the cup.

"Exactly," said Arbret and gave Bo a thumbs up.

The image disappeared and Bo returned the thumbs up, and then turned to Mellik with his thumb still up.

Mellik couldn't help but return Bo's grin and the thumbs up. At least Bo didn't seem inclined to kill him.

Bo's smile widened once again, and he clapped in delight before turning away, Mellik assumed to get the drink.

"Is that the juice I had last night?" asked Mellik.

"Yes, it is called sword fruit," explained Arbret.

Mellik drank greedily when Bo offered him the cup of nectar.

"So is Bo only able to make the images?" asked Mellik.

"Oh no, he is a potential Mage, just like you," explained Arbret. "The illusions are just what he began using when his talent manifested itself. This may be limiting for him since he has been doing it for a couple of years. When wizards learn on their own, it can often hamper them in learning the broader craft. With his limitations, this may not be such a bad thing for Bo. You, on the other hand, need to get back to full strength so we can delve into your training before this affinity for earth magic stunts your development."

Mellik opened his mouth to protest, but Arbret forestalled him with a gesture.

"Say what you want about what happened between you and the Pollum boy -- I could feel the residue of your magic in the earth where we found you. I also found your hand print in the rock. You did not drain yourself this badly trying to pick flowers. Personally, I would have gone with something a little more subtle; or at least more focused."

"I just tapped into the energy I felt trying to release itself," Mellik felt he needed to defend his lack of control. "I had no idea what it would do."

"You felt the earth line below you?" asked Arbret.

"I guess so. I don't know what an earth line is though."

"A line of high earth energy down below the ground," explained Arbret brusquely. "Earthquakes like the one you started seem to be more common where one is found. More importantly for wizards is that a Mage sensitive to such things can tap into that energy for a huge reservoir of earth mana. It is a rare talent because the lines seem to exist leagues beneath the earth's surface."

This was heady and exciting information for Mellik, but a huge yawn slipped out despite that.

"I'm sorry," said Mellik, trying to cover his yawn.

"Do not be," and Arbret cracked one of the first smiles Mellik could remember seeing. "One of the benefits of sword fruit other than its sweet flavour is that it makes the imbiber quite sleepy. Let yourself sleep. I want you to rest up so that tomorrow we can break camp and make some headway. We need to get you and Bo to the Academy."

Mellik obeyed with alacrity.

Chapter 6

The next day, Mellik was pronounced sound enough to travel and they broke camp. Or at least the others all broke camp. Arbret impatiently explained that even if Mellik felt fine, he was still too weak to help. Mellik was delighted with the diagnosis at first, and revelled in lying about in the wagon's shade as Arbret, Bo, and the guards scurried about packing. After a very short while, however, Mellik found that not only was doing nothing boring, but he felt both guilt, and a strange sort of exclusion from an activity he hadn't thought he'd mind being excluded from.

Mellik's boredom didn't ease once they were on the road either. He was relegated to sitting with Arbret in the cart, not even allowed to drive. He was no longer allowed to practice the little mage craft he had learned, and that seemed to dry up whatever conversational stream he and Arbret had developed.

Bo walked along beside the cart, but was useless for any kind of distraction. Mellik tried to get Bo to make some more of his magic pictures, but Arbret explained that illusions required a very stringent mental focus, and also that Bo lacked the training to use magic efficiently and thus even a small number of images could be very draining: Just as Mellik's tug on the earth line had nearly drained Mellik to a husk.

So after weeks of having no one to speak to, and then having a boy his age whose only interest was in killing him, Mellik finally had someone near his age and station who seemed friendly and they couldn't even communicate. Mellik silently vowed to do something about that. But how?

*   *   *

That evening, as soon as Arbret released him from his duties,

Mellik took Bo aside. Gathering rocks and sticks, he began to teach Bo his numbers. Picking a sandy spot, Mellik placed the objects on the ground and drew the number above them. Mellik made sure to mix up sticks, rocks, and whatever else he could find so that only the number symbols remained the same.

Mellik saw Bo's face light up with delight when he got the concept. Bo's face then quickly took on a look of fierce concentration, and an image of an old woman appeared between them. The bent and gray haired woman held a chicken egg in one hand and held up three fingers on the other. That image was quickly replaced with one of the same woman now with a bucket holding up five fingers. Another image began to form but Mellik waved at Bo and the illusion disappeared. Mellik understood: The woman must have been Bo's grandmother, and she had obviously taught Bo some basic numbers with hand signals. Mellik smiled in relief that he had somewhere to start from. Bo's huge grin answered his own, and Mellik began to test Bo to see how much he knew.

Bo knew one through ten well, so Mellik taught him the symbols for adding and subtracting. Bo picked that up quickly, and Mellik made a game of quizzing Bo on addition and subtraction using just those numbers. Bo's smile at being taught such a simple thing made Mellik feel joy in a myriad different ways that he didn't even completely understand.

Mellik was just starting to teach Bo eleven when he heard Arbret calling for him and realized that it was getting too dark to see the numbers. Mellik hopped to his feet and, motioning for Bo to follow, jogged back to camp.

That night as he lay beside a snoring Bo looking up at the moon, Mellik thought about the joy he'd had in the company of someone he couldn't even communicate effectively with. Mellik realized that for the first time since Arbret had taken him from his home, he wasn't lonely.

*   *   *

Mellik awoke to Bo sitting and looking at him. As soon as Bo saw that he was awake, he popped up to his feet and brought a cup over for Mellik. Curious at this service, Mellik looked down into the cup and saw the same milky yellow liquid he'd been drinking a couple of days ago.

Turning, Mellik saw that Arbret was already awake as well, cooking something over the fire.

"Master, is this more sword fruit nectar?"

"Yes," replied Arbret without turning.

"Do I need to be sleeping today then?"

This time Arbret looked up, "No. That is the juice from an immature fruit. Bo made a point of showing me the husks he had squeezed it from."

"Then why did he get it for me?" Mellik asked half to himself.

"You would have to ask Bo to be sure," commented Arbret, carefully turning what Mellik assumed was the mage's breakfast over the fire. "I assume it is because he knew you liked it."

"Master, what is that you're cooking?" asked Mellik, now curious since Arbret usually awoke Mellik to get a fire going and start cooking the breakfast gruel.

"Young sword fruit is hard to get," said Arbret, and Mellik wondered if the wizard had heard his question. "It starts in the center of the plant and goes to the outside of the plant as it matures. Beyond the thorny leaves of the outer plant, almost all sword fruit will have a nest of dream vipers living around its base.

"This," and Arbret held up the stick which Mellik could now see was a skewered snake, "is the momma Bo killed before getting the young fruit."

The Mage turned back to the fire and his cooking. When Mellik began to ask another question, Arbret held up his other hand in a gesture of silence and then shooed him away without turning around.

Mellik turned back to where Bo was packing away their bedrolls. Mellik walked to where Bo could see him. Bo looked up with a smile. He pointed to the cup and held a thumb up in the good sign and rubbed his belly and pointed to Mellik. Mellik nodded and repeated the tummy rub and thumbs up. Then Mellik pointed to the mug and shrugged to show his confusion. Bo's face crinkled up in a confused frown and then smoothed out in understanding. He motioned Mellik to come next to him and drew something in the smooth soil where his bedroll had been. There in the sandy loam was Mellik's answer:

"1 + 1 = 2"

*   *   *

Bo progressed rapidly through numbers and adding and subtracting. Mellik had never tried to teach anyone something before, but he guessed that Bo was anything but a simpleton. He had just lacked any way of communicating his thoughts.

After a few days, and when Bo had a firm grasp of counting to 100, Mellik decided it was time for some words. Mellik had been given one of his mother's few precious books as a going away gift. Mellik had never questioned before why his family was the only one in the village that could read. It had always just seemed to be a part of being different -- just like his brown, tear streaked skin. Now he supposed it was being a descendant of royalty, and with a magical heritage on top of that. Now the book would come in handy for something other than passing time while tending herd.

As luck would have it, Arbret pronounced Mellik sound enough to walk half of that day. For the half he spent walking with Bo, Mellik would play the addition and subtraction game with him. While he sat with Arbret in the wagon, he skimmed through the book looking for good words to teach Bo.

It was obvious that Bo was frustrated with the lack of attention while Mellik rode on the wagon. Bo tried to get Mellik's attention several times. Mellik would play the game with him for a while, then return to his book. This was almost as frustrating for Mellik, as he knew he was hurting Bo's feelings, but he had no way of explaining what he **was** doing.

By lunch, Mellik had decided that he wouldn't worry about teaching Bo the individual letters, but would just teach him the shorter words. Without sounds, Mellik couldn't see how the letters would have much meaning for Bo.

They never stopped long for lunch, so Mellik rushed around getting the horses fed and watered. Grabbing his hard tack and sausage, Mellik stashed them on the wagon, figuring he could eat while he rode later. Bo caught Mellik's intensity and followed easily when Mellik motioned for him.

Mellik squatted and smoothed the soil in front of him. Bo sat next to him, still busily chewing on his lunch. Making sure Bo was watching, Mellik carefully traced the letters "B O" in the dirt. Mellik pointed at the word and then at Bo. Bo just looked at him with a frown of confusion. Mellik then put a "1 =" on the ground and pointed to a rock, pointed to the equation and a stump, pointed at the equation a third time and pointed to his other pointer finger up in a one sign. Then Mellik very slowly put an "equals" sign after Bo's name. Mellik pointed at Bo's name and then back at Bo.

Bo looked at the finger for a long time, and then down at his name. He stayed frozen that way for a long time. Finally, his hand came out and a shaky finger pointed down at his name. Looking back up at Mellik, Bo brought his hand back up in a fist and thumped his chest hard, letting out a low, growling grunt as he did so. Mellik nodded, and Bo pointed to his name quickly and again thumped his chest. Mellik nodded again, and Bo pointed and thumped himself even quicker, never looking away from Mellik. This time Mellik just kept nodding.

Bo smiled his brilliant smile and Mellik couldn't help but echo it. Bo bent down to carefully trace the letters Mellik had written there, and Mellik saw a single tear roll down his cheek to drop into the sandy soil.

Bo suddenly wiped his name and the "1 =" equation from the dirt. Mellik reached out to stop him, not understanding, but Bo held out a hand to forestall him. Mellik watched as Bo carefully brushed the soil smooth. Bo pointed at the blank earth, his finger shaking again, then pointed at Mellik. Mellik didn't need Bo to repeat the gesture to understand what he wanted.

Mellik reached down and carefully traced his name, "MELLIK.". When he was done, Bo reached down and drew his own name just beneath it. The letters were blocky and angular, but Mellik could clearly make out Bo's name.

When Mellik looked up again, Bo pointed to his name and then held his hand out in greeting. With a smile, Mellik took the proffered hand and pointed to his own name. They shook and Mellik felt that he had never truly been properly introduced to someone before now.

When they returned to the wagons, Mellik found a flat, black board and a small wooden box next to his lunch.

"Master, what is this?" Mellik asked, holding up the heavy black board as Arbret climbed into the wagon.

"That, is a writing slate," replied Arbret without ever glancing at Mellik or the slate. "The box has chalk sticks in it. You use them to write on the board. Be careful to keep them dry."

Mellik opened the box to find it filled with round sticks of a light yellow colour.

"Once you are done with whatever you have written on the board, simply use your sleeve or another piece of cloth to wipe the slate clean and you can write on it again," continued Arbret. "Be careful to hold the sticks near the bottom. They are prone to breaking."

Mellik wrote his name on the board and was delighted at how clearly the white lettering showed on the black slate. Using his sleeve, Mellik rubbed at his name. Although the slate became slightly whiter overall, his name disappeared.

"Is this magic?" he murmured.

"As I have told you before, there is magic in everything," replied Arbret. "But the board and sticks are no more magical than the cart we ride in."

"Thank you so much Master. These..." Mellik trailed off as Arbret turned suddenly toward him.

"Part of my assigned task, along with finding candidates with talents, is teaching any wizard apprentices reading, writing and basic math," Arbret explained in what Mellik now thought of as his strict teaching voice. "Since your parents had already done that, there was no need with you. I honestly did not think Bo would be able to learn, but since you have made a start with him, I feel it would be better if you continued his education. Do you understand?"

Mellik nodded his head in assent.

"Good. Then understand something else: I dislike failure, and your teaching Bo reflects on me. Make sure you do it well."

"Yes, sir. And, Master, thank you again."

Arbret merely grunted in reply and gave the reigns a flick.

Chapter 7

Mellik concentrated on the small tin bowl sitting in the tawny sand. He squatted on his knees in front of the bowl, extending his hands out to just above it. He could feel the excess mana jangling around his body. It was like a low vibration, or a heat, but like neither. He just knew he could feel it as something foreign, but a part of him. Mellik thought of his body in its normal state (Arbret had spent many hours just to teach him what that should feel like.) He thought of it as a sound: a hum. He brought that hum to its normal volume and sound throughout his body, all but his hands. He pushed all that excess hum into his hands. Mellik could see it clearly with his second sight. The usual purplish hue of a living creature was overwhelmed in his hands by the piercing white of pure mana.

Arbret had told him that he could hold that much and more through his whole body.

"But not for a while, and even then only at need," Arbret had said. "You can still learn magic, still be useful to the empire if you burn your hands to cinders or turn them into lumps of stone. Not so for much of the rest of you."

Mellik still wasn't sure if that had been humor on Arbret's part, but Mellik's nervous titter had been met with cold silence.

"Do you remember what to do now?" asked Arbret, almost at a shout he was so far behind Mellik.

He just nodded in reply, concentrating on keeping the mana trapped in his hands.

"You have your focal point?"

Mellik extended his index fingers.

"Remember, it is the point right **after** the mana leaves you, but not a moment later. That can be even more dangerous than manipulating it too soon."

Mellik only nodded in reply again.

"Then any time you are ready."

He heard Arbret shuffle away even further behind him. Mellik had long ago decided that instilling confidence in his pupils was not one of Arbret's strengths.

His body was covered in sweat, but he held down a shiver nonetheless. According to Master Arbret, this was the most dangerous point in his training. This was where every apprentice had to take the drilling and teaching and theory Arbret had been giving him and make magic happen consciously and with purpose.

Mellik went over the steps in his head one last time: push the mana out of his hands by imagining the glow brightening at his fingertips, but darkening at his wrists and then moving down. Change the mana from the white of raw magical energy to the blue of water -- but not too early or the mana would change inside his hands, and not too late or it would be uncontrolled and could do anything. And lastly, make sure his own personal levels of mana remained steady so he wouldn't drain himself like the last time, but were still just below normal so he didn't leave any excess mana inside himself.

He felt like he could do any one of those things with the drilling and teaching Arbret had been giving him. The problem was, he didn't have to do one of them; he had to do all three. And they weren't really steps: he had to do all of it at the same time. On the bright side, the worst that could happen if he messed up any one part was his own death, possibly Arbret's.

"Whenever you're ready," Arbret called, and Mellik could tell he must be a hundred strides away, so it seemed that Arbret at least was out of harm's way.

With a deep breath, Mellik decided he wasn't becoming any more ready just sitting there. He channeled.

*　　*　　*

"Are you sure I'll be alright?" Mellik whined, waving his index fingers, both with swollen tips that looked like someone had stuffed grapes under his skin.

"It's just water," Arbret was still chuckling lightly. "If it's uncomfortable we could pop them. They're just blisters. All in all, it could have been much worse. You only lost concentration right at the end. It's a good lesson for you.

"...snow...," Arbret muttered with a shake of his head and another chuckle.

Mellik would have been insulted, but this was as jovial as he'd seen Arbret -- and the Mage was barely drunk at all. That and the wizard was right: it could have been far worse.

Snow. In between fits of laughter, Arbret had explained it to him; Mellik had made the mana a very light coloured blue, making it produce both water and cold. He'd also released the mana far too slowly, so instead of a steady stream, the mana had trickled out, mixed with the air and produced snow.

From Arbret's vantage, he'd only seen the slow trickle and yelled at Mellik, "Faster, faster." Mellik had complied, but the water still came out too cold, so now he was producing ice. Arbret could see the other problem now, and yelled, "Darker, darker." Once again Mellik had corrected himself, but he'd made the mistake of trying to fix the colour just before where he was currently controlling the mana stream, and his fingers had ballooned up with the trapped water.

As Arbret had stated, that last had happened with so little excess mana left that Arbret was able to simply stop Mellik before any real damage was done.

"Master, you know Bo could really benefit from this training too," Mellik ventured, trying to capitalize on Arbret's good mood.

Arbret stopped and turned towards him, and Mellik knew he had made a mistake.

"I have told you no before, apprentice, and if we were in the Academy such insubordination would warrant a beating," Arbret's eyes practically glowed with anger, and Mellik wondered at the sudden transformation. He'd seen the Mage taciturn and grumpy, but never angry before. "Now that you have channeled on purpose, I will give you an explanation. Hopefully you can understand it.

"You are bright and took my instruction well. You also had the advantage of having channeled, albeit accidentally, before. Despite all that, you managed to err in three different ways while channelling consciously the first time. Luckily for you, none of them to your permanent detriment. Does Bo have the vocabulary to understand what you did wrong?"

Mellik thought for only a moment and shook his head no.

"And if he did start to channel incorrectly, how would you stop him and correct it instantly?" Arbret barely paused for Mellik's shrug before continuing, "Continue teaching Bo, and teach him well, because it is his best shot at becoming more than just an oddity at the Academy, but until someone with authority at the academy decides, he will not learn to channel. Learning that skill incorrectly or incompletely is far more dangerous to Bo than anything else in his life."

Arbret stood looking at him for a moment.

"Did I make myself clear, apprentice?"

"Yes," Mellik answered, pouting just a bit.

Arbret made a circular motion with his right hand. Mellik saw the stream of mana pour from Arbret's palm in a bright crimson: In the blink of an eye, the mana struck the ground around Mellik and sprang up in a curtain of fire.

The fire was a stride away in every direction, and rose well above his head. The fire roared in toward Mellik, contracting swiftly as Mellik covered his face and head, cowering with a yelp of fright at the sudden show of malevolent power. Just as quickly the fire was gone.

Mellik looked up at Arbret in confusion.

"What...?" he began, but was cut off as Arbret made a pushing gesture with one hand and some unseen force barrelled into Mellik's chest - sending him flying through the air to land sprawled on his back.

"You are a Kamori. I know your mother and father taught you what that means in that little village of yours, but we are headed for the Imperial Academy Magica, and there it means something entirely different," Arbret stood above Mellik and though his voice had taken on its droning, lecturing tone, his face was twisted in an anger that Mellik had never guessed lurked there.

"Mages are the most powerful tools and weapons in the Emperor's arsenal," continued Arbret. "Therefore we are also the most danger to the empire and the Emperor himself. Because of the prophecy, every full-blooded male Kamori, and probably most of the half-bloods, were hunted down and killed. Do you know why the women were spared?"

Mellik shook his head mutely.

"It was not because they were not mentioned in the prophecy," explained Arbret. "It was because your forefathers were very smart. Over hundreds, maybe thousands of years they slowly tied the magic in your people's blood to an earth line. A line just like the one you tapped into that day with Pollum, but one thousands of times more powerful: one that runs all the way from the mountains to the sea, one that runs through the heart of the empire and underneath the capital city itself.

"They stabilized that line and locked it tight so that in all the years of history we can find, not one quake or shift has occurred there. But the key to that lock is the life-blood of the Kamori themselves, constantly feeding it to keep it tied off. Remove enough of your people, and no one knows how bad it would be. The Emperor himself? He might risk it, but not his generals, his mages with land and kin and wealth all tied up in it.

"So your people were saved, but not the men - and certainly one little boy at the academy would not make a difference."

Mellik gave a small yelp of fright as fire sprang from Arbret's hands. Arbret just held the flame there however: twin gouts of flame rising a foot from his upturned palms.

"I have been too lenient with you," Arbret almost seemed to be talking to himself now. "All the Masters at the academy will expect instant and absolute obedience from an apprentice, as well as a very high level of respect. Normally that can be taught, even drilled into a student, but there are those at the college who will be more like Pollum, and will simply want you dead. You are not going to give them the excuse they need."

The fires in Arbret's hands suddenly went out and Arbret took a step toward him. Mellik flinched back in reaction, but Arbret merely held out his hand. It took Mellik a moment to recognize the gesture. Tentatively he reached out and took Arbret's hand to be hauled to his feet.

"Good," commented Arbret. "Your first reaction to any Mage should be fear: Your second, suspicion. You could be a great Mage someday. I will not let that kind of potential be snuffed out without a fight.

"From now on, you will address me as Master Arbret or simply Master. You will speak only when spoken to or after receiving my permission. You will answer any question promptly and with respect. Understood?"

"Yes, Master," Mellik answered, still in a daze from the sudden turn of events, and Master Arbret's complete change in demeanour.

"You learn fast. Good. You will need to," commented Arbret, looking to the southwest horizon.

"Tomorrow we will reach Tel'Borune," continued Arbret. "It is an imperial fortress town at the edge of the Col'Borune wastelands. Guard your tongue, your eyes, and even your face."

Arbret looked back at Mellik, studying him for a moment.

"The natives often wear a head wrap and cover their face against the sun and sand. You should to do the same."

Chapter 8

The gates of the fort towered above him. The walls to either side rose up some thirty feet, and the towers at either side of the gate were another ten feet above that. The largest building Mellik had ever seen before this could have fit beneath the iron portcullis that was raised before them. Even the stone blocks that had been used in its construction were huge: each one was easily twice as large as him, and Mellik could not imagine how much each one weighed, nor how anyone had managed to stack the blocks so high.

The fort was built on what seemed to be the last hill looking out over a vast flat plain of cracked and parched earth. Mellik could feel the heat of the plain blowing up the hillside and into his face. The side of the hill facing that desolate landscape was a cliff. The line of the cliff ran in jagged half moons: like bite marks. It was as if the desert was eating away at the hill one swallow at a time. The fort sat perched atop that cliff.

It was neither the heat nor the impressive size of the fort that made Mellik's skin prickle. It was the conversation he'd had with Arbret the night before.

They had arrived at Tol Barud early on the previous afternoon. The fort had been built around the largest spring in the area. Arbret had explained that the town that had occupied the area was destroyed to make room for the fort. Because this was the nearest landward route to the academy, the Emperor had allowed a stream to be cut to feed a small pond outside the fort. This pond then became the center of a trading village of tents.

It was at the edge of this tent circle that Arbret had the soldiers make camp. The soldiers had grumbled a bit at this until one of them had wisely pointed out that if they were to stay in the garrison, they would get real beds, but the food would be army rations, and there would be no local girls allowed inside to share those beds. The grumbling vanished after that.

As soon as their tent was set up, Arbret instructed Mellik to take Bo and stay in the tent until his return. Being the most exotic and largest town Mellik had ever seen. He was tempted to protest, but one stern glance from Arbret was enough to remind Mellik of their new dynamic. Mellik instead gave a meek, "Yes, Master," and disappeared into the tent with Bo in tow.

Mellik distracted himself with teaching Bo some more reading. They hadn't had a chance to sit together and go over words since Mellik had recovered enough to travel. Mellik was surprised at just far he had come. Bo could recognize almost all of the things and actions Mellik could find in his lone book, and Mellik was forced to struggle to explain the meaning of words like "idea" and "victory."

Mellik's head was just beginning to swim from the pantomimes when Arbret returned. Mellik was caught with one leg and both arms held in the air as he attempted to show "slip." Mellik froze in his pose and Arbret studied him for a moment as he let the tent door fall closed.

Finally, the Mage just shook his head. "I do not want to know," he said and threw a bundle down next to Mellik.

The mage sat down on a stool next to a small table with hot tea Mellik and Bo had prepared for his return.

"Is it fresh?" Arbret asked, waving at the pot of tea.

"Yes, Master," replied Mellik.

"Sit, sit," and Arbret waved at Mellik, who sat on the cushion next to where he'd been standing. The pile of black cloth sat next to him.

"Do you know what that is?" and Arbret pointed at the cloth while stirring his tea.

"No Master."

Arbret studied Mellik for a moment before nodding in approval.

"You learn quickly and control yourself better than I had thought," Arbret commented. "Good. You may just live long enough to become a Mage and have the power to protect yourself.

"That," and Arbret waved absently at the pile, "is the native headdress I told you about before. Bo may be able to help you put it on correctly. His grandmother was from the Tol Barud Wastes. You'll also both need to wash out your clothes and faces as best you can. We've been invited to dine with the Governor of the fort tonight."

Arbret seemed nervous to Mellik. There was an unnaturally sober stillness and quiet to him.

"Master..." began Mellik tentatively. He wasn't sure how to ask a question in this new hierarchical dynamic of Arbret's.

Arbret smiled. "Go ahead Apprentice Mellik," he instructed, blowing softly on his tea.

"Should we be worried about going to dinner with this Governor?"

Arbret sipped quietly at his tea for a moment before looking up at Mellik.

"Maybe," he replied. "More likely it is just you who should be worried.

"The Governor is a wizard," explained Arbret. "I don't know of him personally, they only gave me a name, but he must be very loyal to the Emperor to have landed this high of a position."

"So he might not accept my half-blood status?"

"He might ignore it entirely, and do not forget the 'Master'," Arbret reminded him. "Consider this a test before the crucible of the college. Be on your best, most obedient, most loyal behavior."

"Yes, Master."

Mellik wanted to know what a crucible was, but it sounded unpleasant, and he had enough to worry about in his immediate future.

*   *   *

It turned out Bo had never worn one of the head wraps either, but he was able to see one of the villagers wearing one from the tent door. With the help of an image Bo conjured up and a mirror, Bo and Mellik managed to make it look right to both of them.

When Arbret came to collect them later that afternoon, Mellik thought he looked a little flushed with drink, but he stood steady and his speech was clear.

He looked quizzically at Mellik's headdress, but made no comment about it. Then he looked down at Mellik's necklace.

"I suppose you wouldn't agree to leave that here?" Arbret asked him.

"No, Master."

Arbret's forehead crinkled up in a frown.

"I have two talents in magic," Arbret told him. "The first is a strong affinity for fire. The second is a lesser ability in enchanting. That necklace would fool most, but the stone is a very weak earth and water magic. There is a deeper and more complex magic lurking in there."

Arbret looked Mellik in the eyes, and Mellik stopped breathing as he waited for what might come next.

"I do not know what is in there, or where your mother or father got it," Arbret continued. "More, I do not want to know. The problem lies in bringing a young apprentice, supposedly from a poor family but with an enchanted amulet, before a Master Wizard. That is to say nothing of your obvious Kamori ancestry."

Arbret looked at Mellik with an intense frown.

"It's very important to me, Master Arbret. My parents gave it to me. He said he found it during the war and it had brought him luck. I promised my parents not to part with it," all of which was true, if a bit misleading. "Couldn't we hide it in a box, or something I could carry it in?"

"You already know more about magic than that, Apprentice. You have looked at the world enough with your second sight these last few weeks. It would take something dense with its own magic, like gold or another enchantment, to block a wizard's sight. You could swallow it, but your body will try to ingest the magic, just as it draws sustenance from a piece of fruit. The results are likely to be unpleasant at best," Arbret paused and studied Mellik.

"Would you trust me with it?" he finally asked.

"What . . . uh, Master?"

"Would you let me carry it while we are at dinner? I would return it to you as soon as we are back. As a journeyman Mage, having an enchanted piece of jewelry will elicit no curiosity at all.

My belt buckle already has a minor enchantment if you have not noticed, and it has a hollow area in back to further disguise the enchantment, if that is what you are worried about."

Mellik's mind was racing. Arbret didn't know what the amulet was, did he? Did he care if he did? Was he trying to take it away from Mellik? Surely he could have done that any time, even killed Mellik if Arbret had wanted without anyone the wiser. Hadn't Arbret always told him how dangerous that first channelling was, wouldn't that have been the perfect excuse for his death?

"Mellik?" Arbret asked, interrupting his thoughts.

"What? Oh yes, of course, Master. That's very kind of you to offer," Mellik managed to stammer.

"I will take good care of it, Mellik," said Arbret, extending his hand. "I really do understand how important this is to you and your family."

Mellik pulled the amulet out of his shirt, silently pulled the chain up over his head, and placed the necklace in Arbret's outstretched hand.

Chapter 9

They waited outside the great hall's doors. Two of the governor's guards stood in front of them. The soldiers studied Mellik and Bo openly. Bo seemed not to notice, but Mellik fidgeted with the headwrap nervously. Arbret had warned him that Mellik would have to remove the burnoose, as it was called, when presented to the Governor, but Mellik planned to take no chances before then.

Mellik would have liked to look around in wonder at the fabulous palace with its ornately carved columns and doors like Bo was doing. Mellik was afraid the burnoose would slip or reveal too much, so instead he just looked down at the strange white stone of the floor with its swirls of brown and red.

"It is marble," said Arbret.

It took Mellik a moment to understand the Mage was speaking to him.

"What, M-Master?" he blurted, only looking up as far as Arbret's calves just in front of him.

"The stone," explained Arbret. "It is called marble. Specifically, it is fire marble. It only comes from a small town called Miraglay well north of here near the mountains. We would have gone there if not for Pollum."

There was a certain nostalgia to Arbret's voice that Mellik had not heard before. He wondered if that was where Arbret was from.

One of the large doors swung open, and the steward who had greeted them when they had first entered the palace appeared. Mellik had thought him the Governor when he met them at the palace gates with his ornate robes and golden burnoose.

"The Governor is ready to see you now," the steward intoned, and the guards swung both doors open.

Mellik had not been able to see in when the steward had gone in earlier. Now that he could see the great hall, its size and grandeur took his breath away. Mellik had to concentrate to keep his feet moving and follow Arbret into the room. Bo just stopped and stared until one of the guards nudged him into the room with the butt of his spear. Bo didn't even seem to notice, but just started to shuffle into the room, his head spiralling around to take in everything, his mouth open in awe.

Glancing covertly around, Mellik felt the same way, but was determined not to show it as openly.

The room was huge. Fluted columns of white marble rose like trees to support a ceiling easily three times taller than any building in Mellik's old village. The floor was made up of squares of what Mellik assumed were more marble, but in greys and blacks, orange and even green. In between some of the columns and against the walls were tapestries, suits of armour, statues, and some creature with a sinuous body like a snake, but with a mane of fur and an enlarged head that looked like it could swallow a small child. Mellik assumed the creature was a statue of some kind as it sat coiled, its mouth held perpetually open.

"They call it a sand lion," said a sonorous voice that echoed through the room.

Mellik turned to see a woman, dressed in a simple white, standing in front of one of the pillars. Her skin was such a pale alabaster that with the white dress and platinum hair, Mellik hadn't even noticed her.

Arbret made a deep bow and it was only as Mellik hastened to copy him that he noticed the thick gold chain about her neck and an even larger one at her waist.

"Governor Yew?" Arbret's introduction sounded as a question, so Mellik assumed his Master hadn't known the Governor would be a woman either.

The lady laughed, "Yes, and I see my steward has played his favourite joke and failed to inform you of my sex. Among fellow practitioners of the arts, I prefer Master Yew.

"Welcome," and she gestured for them to rise as she sketched a small bow in return.

"I was referring to the animal your apprentice was so entranced by," and she waved at the serpent. "Misnamed by the ignorant natives of course. They are a type of snake. They live in the hills south and east of the desert and rarely come down into the wastelands. Highly venomous and quick as any viper a hundredth its size, plus the hairs of its coat are so tough they can be woven into a cloth almost as strong as steel. Indeed, the only creature that they fear is a larger sand lion. The chance to study the creatures was one of the reasons I agreed to take this post for the Emperor."

The lady's voice had a throaty purr to it, and Mellik was entranced by her passionate description of the sand lions.

"But as usual, I've forgotten my manners," she continued and turned back to Arbret with her hand extended. "As you said, I am Master Yew."

"Mage Arbret at your service, Master," and Arbret took her hand and bowed his head over it, not quite touching his brow with her knuckles.

Bo and Mellik copied his pose as they had been instructed, bowing their heads and bringing their hands to their foreheads.

"Good, Mage Arbret," commented the lady as she released Arbret's hand and strolled over to where Bo and Mellik held their pose.

Bo glanced covertly at Mellik, raising his eyebrows in question. Mellik just shrugged almost imperceptibly. Arbret had told them that the Governor, this Lady Yew, would gesture with her palm up, signalling for them to rise from their bow. Mellik had not seen any such gesture and apparently neither had Bo.

"Their bows are most correct," she continued, "but I don't think this one grew up wearing the burnoose. If he had, he would know that it is very bad manners to keep one's head thus covered when visiting someone's home as a guest."

She was standing directly in front of Mellik now, and Mellik glanced desperately behind her at Arbret for a clue as to what he should do. Arbret replied with a furious pantomime of unwrapping his head. Mellik quickly complied, keeping his head down but using both hands to unwrap enough of the headdress to allow him to lift the rest off and tuck it under one arm. The moment he had, the lady gestured for them to rise.

"Now if you'll follow me, I believe our meal is ready," and she turned and strode away before Mellik had completely straightened. Arbret, Mellik, and Bo scrambled after her.

Lady Yew led them to a corner of the great hall where a set of stairs led down. At the bottom of the stairs was a small landing with a set of double doors on one side. The lady stopped there and turned to them once again.

"Did you know that the name of this castle is the 'Crystal Palace'?" she asked, and then continued without waiting for a response. "It was named thus because the king who built it had just conquered most of this land and his kingdom was at peace. He also found himself with many fire mages and earth mages with a great deal of experience and nothing to do. Knowing that the melting of sand can create glass, he decided that his new palace would be built completely of glass and put these wizards to work constructing it.

"Unfortunately, wizards and kings cannot always also be good engineers, and they found the palace kept collapsing under its own weight. They finally settled on building with old fashioned materials like stone and wood. Luckily, they did not give up entirely on the idea of a crystal palace," and with her last word, Lady Yew swung the doors wide open.

The two apprentices gasped as they took in the room that was revealed. The floor was an almost pure white marble that glowed orange in the day's dying light. That light flooded into the room through the walls and ceiling, which were made almost entirely of glass, with just thin rods of brass holding each one to its neighbour. Beyond the longest wall opposite the door, Mellik could see the Great Southern Desert, the Col'Borune, stretching off to the horizon far below them. The dunes were lit orange and pink in the sunset, with large shadows extending down their sides away from the sun. The shadows played with the sunset, giving off hues of purple and red as they extended their reach. Purple, red and rich white rays of light refracted off the glass panes and danced across the floor and back wall. The room seemed like it resided inside the orange band of light in a rainbow. Mellik didn't need the second sight to see its magic.

They all just stood and watched for moments uncounted as the spectacle unfolded below them. Finally, as the shadow engulfed all but the tips of the highest dunes, Arbret broke the spell.

"Thank you milady, Master Yew. That was a gift beyond price."

"I am glad to give it, Mage Arbret," she replied. "I must say that was one of the more spectacular sunsets I've witnessed since coming here. There are only three of these rooms left now, although I'm told the castle was riddled with them when it was built."

"Why would they get rid of such beautiful rooms?" Mellik mumbled to himself.

"Did you ask something Apprentice?" said the lady.

"Um no ma'am, milady, I mean Master Yew," stammered Mellik. "I was merely talking to myself."

"A habit that makes you sound simple at best, but I will answer the question since it is a good one. The rooms are simply too expensive to maintain and of little or no value. In other words, pretty, but not useful.

"You see, in these sunny southern climes, this room becomes unbearably hot during the day. Hinges and doors have been installed so that air can circulate, but this room and its counterparts are practically unusable for most of the day. Then there are the harsh sandstorms that sweep through every year. Some of the glass panes need to be replaced every year, and the ones that survive can become so pitted and scoured by the sand that they must also be replaced. Maintaining these rooms is a costly indulgence.

"Enough history," and the lady swept into the room. "You'll both be getting enough of that soon. Our dinner grows cold as I stand here lecturing."

Mellik followed Arbret into the glass room and noticed for the first time the table at its center laden with platters of food. The table itself was made of glass and Mellik wondered at such extravagance. There wasn't a single glass window in Mellik's village.

Three servants entered from another door on cue and escorted the guests to their seats. Mellik and Bo were seated to either side of Arbret, and the lady sat across from them. There were a lot of rules to a formal dinner, but Mellik did as Arbret had instructed and carefully copied everything Arbret did. This took a great deal of Mellik's concentration, but he was thankful that the lady seemed completely uninterested in the two apprentices and directed all of her questions and comments to Arbret.

After a while, Mellik's nerves subsided enough that he began to actually taste the food. The dishes were delicious. A few were too spicy for his taste, but there seemed an almost endless supply to choose from -- far more than they could possibly eat.

Mellik heard Arbret and the lady begin to talk of life at the academy and tried to listen in. Mellik was disappointed to find that their talk was so full of people and places he didn't know, it was almost unintelligible. Mellik went back to simply savouring his food. He was getting quite full and was just nibbling at his favorites now.

"And that brings us to your apprentices," the lady commented.

Mellik looked up and wiped his mouth, remembering just in time to use the piece of cloth he had placed in his lap at the start of the meal.

The lady glanced at the two boys and then back at Arbret. "Have you taught them anything yet?"

"The big one is named Bo. He is deaf," explained Arbret. "I judged it too risky to begin any training, but he does show a natural affinity for illusion, Master Yew."

"Oh, delightful!" exclaimed the lady. "May I see something?"

Bo had also noticed he was being talked about, and was looking back and forth between the lady and Arbret. Mellik noticed that Bo had not thought to wipe the grease from his face. With his friendly grin, it made him look simple and Mellik was ashamed to think the lady might think him so.

"Of course," said Arbret, and turned to Bo. Arbret made the shape of a rainbow with his two hands.

Bo nodded and his grin got even wider. Mellik knew that grin. It meant Bo was up to something.

Bo spread his hands and instead of the perfect rainbow Mellik had come to expect, a dark little cloud rose up from his palms. The cloud immediately began to rain down on Bo's hands. Bo lifted his left hand up and to the side of the cloud and a sun rose out of it; but this sun had a face and even from his angle, Mellik could make out the Lady Yew's likeness. The smiling sun shone down on the cloud and it dissipated to be replaced by the familiar rainbow.

"Oh, how delightful!" exclaimed the lady as the rainbow and sun faded from view. "I'd say he has more than just an affinity for illusion.

"Illusion can be more than an entertainment you know. I served with a wizard in the Eastern Campaign who was a master illusionist. He disguised a box canyon as a field and led a superior force right over the edge of it. Several hundred died falling over the side before they even realized it. In the ensuing confusion we were able to envelope and overwhelm them. We didn't have to take one prisoner."

The lady smiled wide at the memory.

"And your other apprentice?" She asked. "A Kamori?"

"A half-blood of course, Master Yew," the lady nodded in acceptance of that. "He has only just recently begun to channel mana. We've done some of the initial water work, but I suspect he'll have a natural affinity for earth magic from his half-Kamori ancestry. Would you like to see something?"

"Have him channel? No of course not: no reason to take that chance for my amusement," she replied. "It does beg the question of whether **he** is worth the risk."

"I'm sorry Master. What do you mean?" asked Arbret.

"Well, as you said: he's Kamori."

Mellik's whole body began to tingle and he felt as if he was floating just above himself, watching this conversation from afar.

"He's **half**-Kamori," pointed out Arbret. "I have the paperwork and sent a copy to the Emperor."

The lady waved away the argument. "Paperwork, and proof can be forged and faked. I'm sure you are positive about your own investigation, but even the greatest Mage can make a mistake. What I'm asking is whether he's worth the risk."

"And that is why I'm taking him to the College of Magic, Master," Arbret stated. "They will have many more qualified wizards to judge his worth and risk."

Lady Yew waved this statement away as well, like an annoying fly.

"Baah," she said. "They are a committee paralyzed by politics. They will avoid making any decision until forced to, and by then it might be too late. No, you were given an opportunity to make a decision on your way here. I do not fault the decision you made, Mage Arbret, but now it is my turn to make that decision."

"But it is the Emperor's own law, Master," protested Arbret. "Only he may pronounce on a wizard or adept except in defence of your life or the Emperor's."

"And that is exactly what we are talking about," replied the lady. "If he is the prophesied one, his death would be in defence of the Emperor."

"But I have proof that he's not," said Arbret.

During this entire conversation, the lady had been staring a hole into Mellik. Now, she turned back to look Arbret in the eye.

"Master," she pointed out Arbret's omission.

"Master," repeated Arbret, bowing his head to the lady's hard gaze.

"And so we're back where we started from. We must trust our fates to whatever proof you garnered. I choose not to," she turned back to Mellik. "Are you loyal to the empire and the Emperor?"

Mellik was shocked from his reverie at being addressed.

"Uh, milady, I mean Master," Mellik stammered. "I am a loyal citizen."

"Of course you would say that. Mage Arbret has stated that if I were to kill you without proof of some threat you might pose, my own life would be forfeit. Yet I would willingly make that sacrifice if I believed it was for the good of the empire. Would you do the same?" she asked.

Mellik paused, trying to consider what the lady asked of him.

Arbret jumped in, "He is very young, Master. I am not sure he understands all that you are asking of him."

The lady paused, considering this, before nodding.

"True enough," she said, turning back to Mellik. "The empire, which cannot exist without the strength of the Emperor, has brought stability and peace to millions. With that stability, we can bring medicine, farming advances and protection to all our people. If I told you the safety and well-being of your family was at stake, would you be able to put your life at risk for them?"

Mellik thought hard about what she asked. He knew the answer he should give, but the intensity of her gaze and the seriousness of her questioning made him second guess himself.

"I, I think so, Master," he finally stammered out.

"A good answer," she said, leaning back in her chair and studying him now over steepled fingers. "I think I believe you as well. The seriousness of your situation requires more than words and beliefs however. Do you know about talents among mages?"

"A little, Master. Aren't they just things that you can do with magic that you're particularly good at?"

"Oversimplified, but yes. My primary talent is healing. A rare talent, and useful in these violent times, but I've always thought it could do more than just heal the sick and wounded. I've managed to unlock a way to keep tissue from dying even when removed from the host.

"You're probably wondering what this has to do with you," the lady smiled at Mellik, but there was no warmth there and Mellik did not return the smile. "I require proof of your commitment to the empire. I also need to see something in you that makes me believe that you will be more than another middling wizard in the Emperor's arsenal. You must be more than that or I don't believe it is worth the risk of allowing you to live."

The lady's gaze was locked with Mellik's and he could not look away.

"Are you afraid?" she asked.

"Y-yes, Master."

"Good, then at the very least you are no fool."

The lady held out her hand and one of the servants came forward with a silver tray. The lady took a dull grey disc from the white linen on the tray and held it up for Mellik.

"Do you know what this is?" she asked.

Mellik studied the disk for a moment. Although the center of the disk was grey, the edge of the disk was of polished steel, and there it was ground to a fine edge with several small teeth protruding from it.

"No, Master," replied Mellik, "but it looks like some kind of weapon."

"A good guess," she replied, "and its origins lie as a weapon, but I have modified it to serve me as a tool. Do you know what it is made of?"

"No, Master."

"It's made from something called a lodestone. Look at it with your second sight."

Mellik easily slipped into that other sight and looked at the disc. The brown of earth was very visible, but unlike most other metals Mellik had seen, this tool seemed to hold too much earth energy. A fountain of brown earth energy shot out in a constant stream from both sides, only to loop around and be absorbed by the piece of metal. This looping earth energy passed right through the lady's hand even -- unhindered and unchanged.

"Amazing isn't it?" said Lady Yew. Mellik saw the energy in the lady flow to her hand and turn to the dark brown of earth mana as it left her hand to flow with and push against the cascading energy of the lodestone. The disc rose from her hand and began to spin.

"I call it a cutting disc," explained the lady, looking Mellik in the eyes again. "Here is your test and your service to the Emperor rolled into one. I've studied Kamori, but you can only get so much cooperation from a live one, and a dead one is useless for my research. So what I'm asking from you is a piece of your skin. It's the only physical dissimilarity I can find between our two species."

"Master!" exclaimed Arbret.

"Silence!" roared the lady, and only her echo and a soft mewling whine from Bo could be heard in the chamber.

Her tone modulated back to the soft, polite one she had used all night, "The test is not only your agreeing to give me this piece of flesh, but your self-control as well. You will assuredly be able to feel the earth magic from this disc as it gets closer. If your ability with earth magic is anything like your forefathers, you could likely wrest control of it from me easily. If you don't, if you pass my test, then just maybe you're worth the risk of letting you live for a while longer. Will you give the Emperor a piece of yourself?"

Everything stood out in stark relief to Mellik. The sky had gone dark in the window behind the lady. Mellik could see the slight sheen of perspiration on her face and the enlarged pupils in her grey eyes.

Mellik stared into those eyes wondering why she bothered to ask if his other option was death. He had to assume that this was all part of his test now. Fail one part and he would fail them all.

Mellik clasped his hands tightly beneath the table to stop their shaking and tried to swallow and force some saliva into his parched mouth. He didn't trust his hands to grasp the cup in front of him. He looked Lady Yew in the eyes again.

"I will, Master," he replied, gratified that his voice quavered only a little.

"Good," she said, and the disc rose and travelled towards him. "Try not to move, or you will lose more than just a little skin."

It seemed to be aimed straight for Mellik's right eye, but he tried not to flinch or draw back. He would pass this test: he had to.

Almost beneath his eye now, the disc began to spin even faster, emitting a high pitched whine. Mellik could feel the mana of the disc. He could feel it travelling through his cheek and jaw. It called to him, sang a song that drowned out the whining of the air around it. Mellik knew that, with a thought, he could wrest control of this small disc and send it against this lady of cold and emptiness. Mellik resisted.

The next moment he felt the disc in truth. He felt pain.

There was a tugging and cutting and Mellik could see a mist spraying from just below his eye. He could feel something wet coursing down his cheek.

Mellik tried not to see, not to feel. He wanted to close his eyes, but refused to give her the satisfaction. Instead he stared at her face, concentrated on her cold grey eyes.

Mellik heard a soft, mewling whine and realized it was coming from his own throat. He was powerless to stop it.

The tugging stopped.

"It is done," pronounced the lady.

Mellik heard no more as the last light, Lady Yew's face, went dark.

Chapter 10

"Wake up," commanded Arbret.

Mellik blinked his eyes open and winced at the bright light pouring through the open tent flaps. His hand shot up to his face as biting pain to shoot out from his right cheek. Memories of the night came rolling in as he felt a cloth bandage wrapped carefully around his face.

"Master Yew agreed to do a little healing after she had what she wanted," commented Arbret. "The chance of infection should be slight, but keep the bandage on as long as you can. We can't afford to wait for the wounded today."

As Arbret finished saying this, the soldiers began removing the tent walls. Mellik saw that they were now camped out in the dunes.

"How long was I out this time, Master?" asked Mellik.

Arbret followed Mellik's gaze out into the dunes.

"Since last night," he replied. "Master Yew said you had passed her test, but I don't trust her to stick with that assessment. I thought it prudent to move our camp before the sun rose and she started thinking about you again."

"But if she said I passed, won't she leave me alone?"

"Maybe," replied Arbret with a shrug. "People like that don't worry about following rules, not even the ones they make up. Now get yourself ready to go. No sense wasting our head start."

Mellik did as he was instructed. He was surprised to find that if he kept himself busy, he could even forget about his throbbing cheek.

When they were all packed and ready to go, Arbret offered to let Mellik ride in the cart. Mellik politely declined, explaining that the sudden motions of the wagon would make his cheek hurt.

"Fair enough," replied Arbret. "But before we get going, Master Yew wanted you to have this."

Arbret held out his hand, and lying there was the cutting disc from the night before.

Mellik reached out and gently took the disc between his thumb and forefinger. He turned the disc back and forth in his hand. He supposed he was searching for some sign it was the same disc -- a trace of his blood perhaps.

"She said it was something to remember her by," Arbret said. "I'm guessing she wanted to make you fear her, remind you of last night. I suspect you don't need the disc for that. If nothing else, that wound on your cheek will likely be a reminder for the rest of your days.

"You could throw it away if you like. Me, I would hang onto it. Just like fear, you can use that as a tool or a weapon . . . or so I have often been told."

Mellik looked up at that last part. It sounded more like Arbret was talking to himself than to Mellik anymore, but Arbret was already looking away, urging the wagon mare on.

There was no road through the dunes. Mellik could see how any such road would soon be buried in sand. They had stopped in the morning shadow of a large dune. They quickly left the shelter of the dune and Arbret led them back to the grassy scrub at the edge of the dunes where a road ran just above the sand's reach.

"We just spent the night there to get out of sight," Arbret explained without being asked. "The wagon could not have made it through the deep sand."

Mellik could well understand, as he could feel it in his calves after just a few hundred paces.

Bo largely left Mellik to himself that day. They pantomimed out that Mellik felt okay, and that his scar didn't hurt too badly. Bo plodded along next to him in companionable silence.

After a while, Mellik carefully pulled the cutting disc out of his breast pocket and looked at it again. Mellik noticed that the blades were a different metal than the body of the disc. Most of the disc was a dull grey, but right where it flared out into the sharp razor edges, it was the polished silver that Mellik thought of as blade material. So cunning and fine was the joining that Mellik could see no ridge or seam where the two metals met. Mellik pulled out his belt knife to see if he could scrape away anything that might hide the joining. He was surprised and alarmed when the disc twisted in his hand and stuck to the blade.

He must have cried out because Arbret spun around in his seat and glanced down at him.

"The lodestone of the disc does that naturally with metals," he said and then turned back around.

Mellik opened himself to the second sight to study the disc that was now attached to his knife. He could see the waves of earth mana flowing out of the disc just as he remembered them, but now the waves had shaped themselves to include the knife. Although he couldn't see it, he was pretty sure the stream of mana from the disc was pulling at the mana in the knife.

He didn't want to, but Mellik forced himself to think back on the night before -- to remember what the lady had been doing to manipulate the disc. He could remember her spinning the disc above her palm. She had created several waves just like the ones coming out of the disc. These waves had been in opposition to the disc's, pushing against each other and keeping each other apart.

Mellik could see how this would be very efficient with mana, as once the stream was created, it continued to flow out of the wizard and then cycle back in again. That didn't sound right though. Arbret had said to never let mana that had been changed back into his body: that it was dangerous.

Mellik studied the disc again. The streams of mana looked different from other earth magic Mellik had seen before. Mellik leaned in close, practically touching the disc with his nose. For the first time, he saw there was a form to mana, and not just color. Everything else he had studied with the second sight had been like translucent vessels filled with a colored liquid: the colors might swirl and separate, or blend and settle, but they took the shape of whatever thing they occupied. This earth mana was different. It was more like smoke wafting out of the disc, but fast, like it was blown in a fierce wind. It was also a smoke that could travel through a knife blade or a his hand, never disturbing the mana that filled either vessel or the vessels themselves. It passed through unhindered.

Mellik stumbled in a rut in the path but barely noticed. He pushed at the disc from one side, being careful to avoid its sharp blades. With only a little resistance, it slid toward one edge of his knife. Still being careful, Mellik grabbed one edge of the disc and pried it off of the knife. Once again, the disc gave some resistance at first, but then came away quite easily.

Mellik put his knife away. He would have liked to study how the blade and disc interacted more closely, but that would have to come at another time.

The disc now lay quiescent in Mellik's palm. He could feel it; not just the cold metal in his hand, but the earth energy racing from it, calling to him. The lady had said that this would be an easy, almost natural magic for him.

Mellik thought back again to the lady's multiple waves of energy. He thought maybe she had only needed that many to make it spin. Mellik had only channeled one wave of energy at a time before, he wasn't sure he could do that many at once. He would try just two.

"Apprentice Mellik, you have my permission to channel," said Arbret.

Mellik jumped and looked up. Their small caravan had come to a halt with everyone looking back at him. Mellik had no idea how long he'd been just standing there.

"However," continued Arbret. "You shall do so from the back of the wagon. Channeling should take all of your concentration right now. We can at least relieve you of the burden of walking."

Mellik obediently climbed into the back of the wagon. Thinking about the disc had made him forget his wound. He didn't even notice the much wider berth the guards were now giving the wagon.

Once again Mellik brought his focus down to his palm. The lurching and swaying of the wagon seemed to find a rhythm and faded into the background. Mellik thought about what he wanted to do, what the mana threads should look like. He brought a small amount of extra energy into himself. He channeled.

The disc flew a few fingers above his hand and then tumbled off the back of the wagon. Mellik heard the distant sound of a guard's sarcastic applause. He didn't bother to look up. Bo scrambled to pick up the disc for him.

Mellik frowned and then winced as the expression pulled at his tender cheek. Schooling his face to a calm neutral, Mellik took the disc from Bo, and with a nod of thanks tried again.

It took Mellik several tries, but eventually he got the disc to hover, spinning above his hand. Mellik found that the spinning, at a moderate pace, actually made the disc easier to manipulate. It wanted to wobble and bob otherwise. Even the mana threads were odd. They absolutely required being in motion: when Mellik tried to stop them, they would collapse and disappear.

Mellik was surprised when Arbret halted and told him it was time for lunch.

"You need a break and some food," Arbret said. He studied Mellik closely for a minute. "Does not seem to use much mana at all does it? You look okay, but no channelling until after lunch.

"Here," and Arbret shoved a waterskin into his hands. "Make sure to drink all of that and then come find me for another after lunch. You're getting dehydrated."

Bo was glad to have his friend back during the meal. He entertained Mellik with images of plants and animals Mellik had missed that morning. Mellik wasn't sure if Bo was adding details to a couple of the more fantastic ones. Who ever heard of a black and white striped horse?

Lunch was a nice break despite being painful to chew, but as soon as they started out again, Mellik hopped back into the wagon to resume his study of the disc. He was determined to be able to protect himself other than with a random ability to sprout big rocks out of the ground.

Mellik could make the disc hover above his hand and spin, albeit in a slow and wobbly fashion, but he was frustrated. It took so much effort to watch the threads of mana and try to change, correct and re-correct them constantly. He had no time or brainpower left to make the disc do anything else. Mellik remembered the look of intense concentration on the lady's stony face and supposed it just took months or years of practice, not just one day's worth. It had seemed like it would be so natural and easy when he had first felt the disc's energy.

That was it! He'd felt the disc's energy, not relied on his eyes to see what the disc itself was doing. The earth energy flowing from it should tell him what was happening before he could see it -- or he hoped it would.

Mellik closed his eyes. He could feel the disc's energy flowing through his hand. What's more, he could feel the energy flowing above his hand as well. Mellik didn't trust himself to channel with his eyes closed. He opened them and was relieved that now that he had isolated the sensation, he could still feel the earth energy coming out of the disc.

Holding on to that sensation, Mellik channeled again. This time, even as he saw and created his own streams of earth energy, he could feel their flow, feel them merge and bend with the disc's mana. Just like that, manipulating the disc became as natural as wiggling his fingers. Mellik flipped it, spun it, sent it tumbling high into the air, only to catch it again a finger width above his palm.

Bo clapped in appreciation. Mellik looked up and was pleased that he could feel the interactions well enough to keep the disc spinning without even looking.

Mellik experimented with the disc. Spinning, hovering, moving; all these things proved easy now that he could feel the ebb and flow of his own streams interacting with the disc's. The hard part was having any significant distance between himself and the disc. His ribbons of earth mana had to be under or over the disc to keep it in the air, and the further out it was, it seemed to double and redouble the amount of energy to make his streams extend that far.

"Enough, Apprentice," Arbret ordered. "Cease channelling and let go of the second sight."

"But..." began Mellik.

"Now Apprentice!" thundered Arbret as Mellik turned to plead his case.

Arbret's look and tone jolted Mellik back from his mental

wandering, and he barely had the wherewithal to check his own mana levels before releasing the second sight. It hit him like a rock how tired he was.

"It is hard to measure one's own mana levels while concentrating on channelling," commented Arbret. "Make sure to take regular breaks to assess your own reserves in the future. No more channelling for today."

"Yes, Master."

*   *   *

Mid-afternoon brought them to a small cliff with a trickle of water forming a pool at its base.

Arbret instructed the guards to prepare camp. It was very early to stop travel for the day, and Mellik's surprise must have registered on his face.

"This is the last water until we get to the college," Arbret explained. "We'll use one horse as a pack animal and send the other back with the cart and a couple of our guards. It's only two days walk from here, but we'll need plenty of water and rest. We'll camp here tonight and leave before first light."

Mellik began to help with the unpacking. He was surprised at how tired and weak he felt. He remembered the effects of draining himself the first time, but Arbret had stopped him well short of that this time.

Mellik stumbled while unloading a crate of food from the cart and immediately felt a hand on his shoulder, steadying him.

"Magic use can be exhausting even when you do not use up your mana," Arbret said as if reading Mellik's mind. Arbret spun him around and studied his face.

"You are exhausted and maybe a little dehydrated," Arbret shoved a loaf of bread and a wedge of cheese with one bite taken out of it onto the top of Mellik's crate.

"I'll trade you," he said, taking hold of the crate. Mellik took the cheese and bread.

"Find Bo," instructed Arbret. "That is enough for two, and that boy is always hungry. Grab some waterskins and fill them on the other side of the pool where it is shady. Make sure to drink plenty while you are there too."

Those instructions likely saved Mellik's life.

Chapter 11

Mellik woke confused. He opened his eyes to see bright stars in a moonlit sky. It took his mind a moment to realize that that meant he wasn't in a tent. He had to pee -- likely what had awoken him. Propping himself up on his elbows, he found that he had been covered in extra blankets against the desert night's chill. Bo lay next to him breathing softly, and he also had a thick swaddling of blankets.

The night was beautiful. They lay in the shadow of a pair of palms, but the cliff face and the rest of the area around the pool was bathed in the light of a glorious full moon. The tents of their camp were dark pyramids against the moonlit sand on the other side of the pool. The silhouette of a lone sentry sat on the seat of their wagon.

No, there were two men. The unknown man sprang up, grabbing the guard with one hand, and swung violently into the sentry's neck with his other. The sentry slumped. The assassin laid him gently down on the wagon seat. Mellik had heard not a sound above the gentle trickle of the water.

Mellik sat there in stunned silence. He wondered if he was dreaming, some heat induced nightmare.

The assassin moved away from the wagon, and now other shapes began to rise up from the sand around the campsite, other men cloaked in the night's shadow.

Mellik reached out and quietly shook Bo. Bo's eyes blinked open, and he looked up at Mellik. Bo's face transformed instantly into its usual wide smile. Mellik held a finger up to his lips for silence and pointed toward the camp. Bo sat up and looked across the pool. His smile vanished.

There looked to be eight men, and after some hand signals from one of them, four of them went toward the tent with the guards. The other four headed for Arbret's tent, where Bo and Mellik would normally be.

It happened so fast that Mellik never thought to open his mouth in warning. Swords were drawn in one swift motion, and the tents were slashed open. The bandits jumped into both tents, and the sound of screams and a few metallic clashes could be heard.

Mellik looked back at Bo, who was getting up from his blankets in a crouch. Bo held up one finger to his lips, and then vanished.

Mellik stifled a gasp, and realized that Bo's eyes still looked back at him from a blur of shadowy darkness. One of the eyes closed in a wink, and then Bo turned and was almost impossible to see against the palm's shadow on the sand.

Bo's shadow moved off toward the tents with only the soft churning of the sand to give him away. Mellik thought the whiter glow of the moonlit sand might give him away, but a heartbeat after exiting the shadow of the palm, Bo's faint but discernible shape changed from black to the hazy silver of the moonlit sand.

The sound of battle ceased, and Mellik looked up to see three of the bandits emerge from the guards' tent. Four others came from Arbret's tent, two of them dragging the Mage between them.

Mellik huddled back down in his blankets as he tried to watch Bo's shape move slowly around the pool. Fear kept him rooted next to the palms. He had nothing to fight with. His staff was at the wagon, he had no shadow magic to hide his approach like Bo, and he feared his earth magic would be nothing more than throwing sand.

The bandits threw Arbret roughly to the ground. Arbret moved painfully, getting up on his knees to face his captors.

"Release me," commanded Arbret, but even from his seat across the pool, Mellik could hear the quaver in his voice. "I am a Battle Mage of the Empire. I will allow you to run from me in your ignorance, but do not try my patience."

A couple of the brigands took a step back as Arbret brought his hands up in a threatening gesture, but the one directly in front of the Mage simply laughed. That man took a stride forward and kicked Arbret under his chin, lifting him from his knees and sending him sprawling on his back.

"We know about you, Mage," said the bandit, drawing his knife. "You're the one who's afraid, not me."

The man bent down and grabbed one of Arbret's arms, twisting it violently and flipping Arbret onto his stomach. Arbret's arm was brought up to the nape of his neck, eliciting a squeal of pain. The man put his knee into Arbret's back, pinning him and trapping his arm there. He yanked Arbret's head back with a handful of hair and placed his knife at the Mage's throat.

"You know you're going to die anyway," growled the man. "So it can be quick, or slow and painful. We don't care about you, but where are the two boys?"

At that moment a thump caught everyone's attention. Mellik looked to where the other three brigands had been rooting through the tents. One of them now lay face down in the sand.

"What happened?" asked the man kneeling on Arbret.

"I don't know," replied the bandit closest to the body, walking over to inspect it. "Looks like he got stabbed in the neck. No bolt or anything. We got all the guards."

"Watch him," said the brigand on Arbret, getting up and motioning at the prone Mage. "It must be one of the apprentices. Not as helpless as we were told. You other three make a square with me. He can't sneak up on us then."

The four men arranged themselves around Arbret. Mellik wished there was something he could do. Bo would be found if he approached again now, and they would be hunted down if they didn't do something. Mellik shifted and felt the metal cutting disc press against his side in the leather bag he had found for it. He knew the bandits were too far away for it to be helpful, but he pulled it out anyway since it was his only weapon other than the small eating knife on his belt.

Mellik was surprised to feel sand stuck to it. He switched to the second sight and saw that the earth mana of the sand on the disc more closely resembled the hue of an iron pot than the dirt and sand he was used to seeing. Looking down at the sand around him, it didn't seem to match the sand on the disc.

Mellik held his hand out over the sand and channeled as if he was making the streams of mana to manipulate the disc, but reversed it to attract instead of repel. Mellik saw and felt the grains of sand pop up from the ground to stick to his palm.

"Come on out apprentice boy," called the bandit leader. "Don't make us hurt you. You're worth more alive, but I can't let you hurt any more men. Come out or your master here will die."

Mellik had to do something. He knew Bo couldn't have heard the threat, and he couldn't let them kill Arbret. Mellik closed his eyes and imagined himself a piece of metal like the disc, giving off ribbons of earth mana from everywhere. Mellik could feel the sand begin to cling to the exposed parts of him closest to the sand. He quietly slipped out of his clothes and burrowed and rolled slowly in the sand. Mellik could feel the grit attach to his eyelids and copied Bo's trick to exclude his eyes from the effect so he could see.

Opening his eyes, Mellik could see that the five men in a circle were now slowly inching outward, eyes scanning and heads swivelling to try and catch Bo. Mellik had run out of time. He fervently prayed that the sand coating him was the same color as the rest of the sand to normal vision.

Mellik got into a low crouch and tried to slink quickly down to the edge of the pool.

"There he is!" exclaimed the nearest bandit as soon as Mellik left the concealing shadow of the tree.

The man was pointing directly at him. Mellik could see the bandit on the right of the circle reach down and pull up a crossbow. Everything slowed down. Mellik noted that the crossbow was already loaded. He wondered if it had belonged to one of the guardsmen. The bandit brought it up and pointed it at him. Mellik thought maybe he should try for the pond, or maybe just move to make a harder target -- but those thoughts were distant. Mellik stood frozen, like a sheep cornered by a wolf.

The bandit took aim, and then a shadow reared up and struck the man. Mellik felt the wind of the bolt's passage a few fingers from his cheek. The other men were now turning toward the shadow that was Bo, and Mellik had control of his legs again and was sprinting around the pool. The black sand dropped from him as he released the weave of earth mana ribbons.

Someone cried out. Mellik tried to run faster through the loose sand. Another scream - this one agonizing, and Mellik saw a flair of bright orange light from the midst of the bandits circling Bo. The next instant Mellik saw flame erupt from the four remaining brigands. It seemed to sprout from their very skin, singeing and disintegrating the clothes from their bodies. They opened their mouths to scream, and a torrent of flame spewed forth. No sound but the roar of flames issued forth, but Mellik could hear their tortured screams in his head. They seemed to burn forever, until they were nothing more than blackened husks that toppled to the ground -- the flames slowly subsiding to sputter and die out.

Mellik sprinted to the top of the dune. There, amongst the charred bodies and savaged tents, Bo sat cradling Arbret. A trail of blood trickling down from the Mage's abdomen to stain the moonlit sand.

Chapter 12

Arbret looked up as Mellik approached.

"Good, you're alive," Arbret said, wheezing in pain.

"Master, are you alright?"

"No, you idiot. I am dying," Arbret said with a little more strength. "We do not have time for an eulogy. Go find my writing desk."

"Master?"

"My writing desk! Quickly: did I not just say I was dying?"

Arbret winced in pain and Mellik scrambled to obey. Their tent was ripped to shreds, but the bandits had only just started to tear up the inside for loot. The small portable writing desk sat with its lid open, but the contents seemed undisturbed. Mellik closed the lid and quickly scampered back to Arbret.

Bo had gathered sleeping rolls and supply sacks to prop Arbret into a sitting position. A large piece of tenting was wrapped around Arbret's midsection, but Mellik could see the dark dampness already soaking through in the moon's pale light. Arbret sat drinking from a skin of brandy, but for once Mellik did not begrudge him the vice.

"Good, bring it here," instructed Arbret.

Mellik set the small lap table gently next to the Mage.

"Is there anything else," Mellik asked.

"Yes," replied the Mage, slowly sliding the table up onto his lap. One arm seemed to not be working. "Go find my belt. The one with the gold buckle. Check the soldiers if it is not in my trunk."

Mellik scampered off. He assumed Arbret needed it to tie the bandage around his waist tighter. When he found the Mage's trunk, it had indeed been ransacked, and there was no belt or buckle to be found. Mellik glanced up at the charred remains of the bandits. Studying them from close up for the first time, Mellik was repulsed by their blackened skin, their mouths drawn open in an unending scream, even their limbs seemed twisted and warped in some unfinished agony. Arbret had said he was dying, so Mellik had to overcome his squeamishness.

Standing up, Mellik saw that two of the bandits, the ones Bo had stabbed he assumed, were untouched by flame. Mellik decided that he might as well start with them: after watching the brigands burned alive, the cold corpses seemed preferable.

Mellik was lucky. The corpse of the bandit just outside the tent, the first one Bo had killed, still clutched the belt. The buckle gleamed warm gold in the moon's cold light. Mellik used a nearby tent stake to pry the fingers loose and returned to Arbret with the belt.

Arbret was busy writing with his good hand. Bo sat next to him, holding the page still on the lap desk. Arbret saw Mellik's approach, and peremptorily motioned him to silence. Arbret finished by signing it with his flourish. Arbret's head immediately tilted back in exhaustion, and Mellik saw tremors take over the hand with the quill.

"Read it," sighed Arbret.

Mellik knelt next to the Mage, not wanting to disturb the still wet page.

Arbret had a neat hand, and it took Mellik no time to discern that this was Arbret's last will and testament. It was short. Arbret was leaving all his worldly possessions to Mellik and Bo as his "only apprentices." The only two items that were spelled out explicitly were his ring to Bo, and his golden belt buckle to Mellik. It went on to say that Mellik was a Kamori half-blood, investigated by Arbret and confirmed by the village priest.

"I have the paperwork proving your heritage here, as well as both of your recruitment papers," Arbret said, tapping a bone scroll case next to him when he saw that Mellik was done.

"But Master, we can get you back to the city. The lady can heal you," protested Mellik.

Arbret slowly rolled his head back and forth in the negative.

"Who do you think sent these men? Look at their boots, Mellik. All the same type and in good repair. These are soldiers, not bandits. I'm guessing the lady had a change of heart, or perhaps she felt another test was in order. Who can know with someone like that?

"Besides, I can feel my life pouring out. I would never make it even if it were an option. You will have to leave tonight. There are likely more of them, and they will come looking when these men do not return."

A fit of painful coughing gripped Arbret then, and it took him a few moments afterwards to gather himself and continue.

"The college of magic will be somewhat safer," Arbret said, almost whispering now. "It is about two days walk south and west of here. Travel in the morning and evening. Keep going west from here, but watch to your south. From the north, it will look like the tip of an uneven crown pointing up out of the desert."

Arbret paused to draw a crude sketch of the front of a simple crown.

"There is a tower on the top of that point," he continued, "and at night it is always lit up with a blue light. So you can look for that in the early morning and evenings as well. If you have not seen it by your third evening, head due South. The college sits in the middle of an inland sea. The water is not drinkable, but if you follow the shore you will come to one of the boat houses that can take you across to the college.

"The desert is harsh, so pack as much water as you two can carry. The horse will only slow you down so leave it, and rest during the midday heat. Hide from the sun if you can. Do you have any questions?"

Everything Arbret had said swirled around in Mellik's head. He thought it was all there: it had certainly seemed like simple enough instructions. Mellik would have liked to have questions about the journey, the desert, the college; but only one question kept rising up.

"Why did you wait so long?"

"Eh?" queried Arbret, looking up at him out of only one eye.

"Why did you wait?" repeated Mellik. "I've seen you torch trees with a flick of your wrist, and what you did to those soldiers just now. Why did you wait, why let them do this to you?"

Arbret seemed to deflate even more, sinking into the carpets and tenting bundled beneath him. He closed his eyes.

"Did you ever wonder why a Mage with that kind of power was wandering around testing children for talents instead of out with the army?" asked Arbret and then opened his eyes to look up at Mellik.

"It is because I am a coward," and Arbret looked down again. "I freeze during battle or any conflict. I cannot think straight, I even have trouble just switching to the second sight.

"They tried counselling it out of me, gave me second, third, fourth chances, even tried beating it out of me. My talents were deemed too valuable to waste. But nothing worked. The fear was always more powerful. Then they thought to use me as an instructor, but I failed miserably at that too. This was my end. The only way I could be useful to the Empire. To be truthful, teaching you has been the only thing I have succeeded at in a very long time."

"But what about just now: those soldiers?"

"I do not know," and Arbret paused, his eyes went unfocused as though thinking back to that moment. "I think at last I was not afraid. You are my only apprentice, my only success, and they were about to take it away. Finally I became angry, and for the first time it was stronger than the fear."

"You saved Bo and my lives. Thank you, master," and for the first time Mellik felt the respect of the title Arbret had been insisting on. "My father always said that everyone is afraid except for fools. Bravery is doing what you have to despite the fear."

Arbret took another long draughts from the bottle of wine. He looked down into its open mouth as if divining the future there.

"There are a few masters at the college you can trust," Arbret said finally without looking up at Mellik. His voice was slurred and soft. Mellik had to lean in to hear him even in the quiet desert air. "Wendess, Jacoby Vai, and Sagato. Jacoby is a master of enchantment, Wendess is a fire Mage, and Sagato is a summoner. Do not write those down, and do not go to them right away: it might look suspicious. Once you have settled in, and if the need arises, I think you can trust them. Now give me your necklace."

"What?" asked Mellik, startled by the request.

"Your necklace, apprentice," and Arbret's gaze at least was as strong as ever. "I told you before, a true enchanter would be able to see through that ruse in minutes. You are going to the center of magic in the empire, likely the world: you will need some way to keep it hidden."

Arbret held up his buckle. With a snap, the front popped open to reveal a hidden compartment.

"It is small," commented Arbret, "but I think it will hold whatever is in that rock. It is also already enchanted with a little bit of magic to hide the catch and the lid and make them look seamless. Before you leave, I will put as much fire magic into it as I can to further hide the magic in that amulet. None of that will matter, however, if you do not let me see the amulet because it might not fit inside."

Arbret put the belt in his lap and held out his good hand.

Mellik took the heavy amulet from about his neck and gently laid it in Arbret's palm.

Arbret studied the stone for a moment and held it to the hidden compartment. It would fit. Arbret held the amulet in both hands and Mellik changed to the second sight to watch what Arbret was doing. Arbret held the stone up to the moonlight, pinched between his thumb and forefinger. Then Mellik noticed that the mana coloration of the stone was becoming darker, bluer. It took Mellik a moment, and then he realized that Arbret was slowly drawing all the fire mana from the stone: making it cold. Mellik wondered how long this would go on when Arbret brought the stone swiftly down on the writing table. The stone shattered, and the ring inside was revealed.

"Pretty little thing for so much trouble," commented Arbret, "but then it is the pretty ones that always are."

Mellik had thought the ring rather ugly and misshapen the first time he had seen it, but now he looked with his second sight and understood what Arbret meant. Where before he had thought the ring crudely shaped and rough, he now saw that the ridges and curves had been created to highlight and enhance the magical energies that swirled and pooled in the ring. Mellik could see the magic in the buckle as well, but it was a dim, hazy star to the ring's golden brown sun.

"Enchanting is the most taxing of the arcane arts," Arbret explained, and Mellik felt a lecture coming. "This is because in order for magic to stay and continue to charge itself over years and ages, a Mage must permanently invest some of his own essence in the enchantment. This magic never comes back to a Mage, and in this way, every enchantment slowly kills the enchanter, until there is not enough essence to sustain the caster and they simply wither away, bereft of the will to live.

"I am telling you this because in order to set a ward on the buckle so that only you or those who share your essence will ever be able to open it, I will need the tiniest bit of your essence."

"But I know nothing of enchanting," protested Mellik.

"You do not need to. An enchanter can use the essence of another, but it must be freely given. Enchanting with essence forced from someone is almost impossible, and never works as the enchanter wanted because that victim's essence fights against the enchantment forever after. So you must freely give this essence.

"Understand that I do not ask this lightly. I could set the enchantment to respond to a word or an item, but those things can be stolen, your essence cannot. I believe with what is at stake, this is the only way."

"Okay, master. I trust you."

"You will need to. Your body will fight to hold onto its essence. You will need to keep that trust foremost in your thoughts. Do not try to force your essence out, but try with all your might not to fight my pulling a small bit from you.

"Are you ready?"

Mellik nodded.

Arbret pulled Mellik's hand out and placed the buckle in his palm. Arbret covered the buckle with his own hand.

"Embrace the second sight but do not concentrate on or think about your own mana levels. Concentrate on what I am doing instead. Do not resist, but make sure not to push your essence out either."

Mellik watched Arbret channel. The Mage brought only the smallest amount of mana into himself. Mellik felt Arbret draw from him. His own response was primal, almost uncontrollable. He wanted to fight against that tug, to run from it. He could feel fear and anger welling up inside himself. He fought it all down, forced himself to try and relax, to trust Arbret. In the end, he simply thought of the only other enchanting he'd ever seen, even though he hadn't watched with his second sight. He thought of his mother being the one tugging at his being and finally his body let go and something of himself flowed into the buckle.

"Well done," Arbret said, slowly sinking deeper into the pile of cloth. "I need to place my own enchantment on the buckle now: something to hide the ring's magic mostly. When I am done you need to make for the open dessert immediately. Do you remember how to find it, the names of the mage's you may be able to trust?"

Mellik thought a moment, "It's two days West of here, I might see the crown tip to my south. Wendess, Sagato, and Jacoby Vai."

"Good," and Arbret looked up into Mellik's face, his eyes shining in the moon's light. Mellik could barely hear him. "This enchantment will offer a bit of protection from both heat and cold, but its power is limited, so do not rely on it too heavily. Mellik, you are the one thing I have done right in this sorry life. Apprentice: do not let them take that away from me."

Arbret looked down before Mellik could think of a reply and began to channel. Mellik watched in fascination this time as the enchanting went on. Arbret wove fire into the buckle, but far more of it was a raw mana. Mellik guessed that to be the essence Arbret had spoken of.

The enchanting went on, and the buckle grew brighter and brighter as Arbret became dimmer. Mellik began to become concerned.

"Master?" he asked tentatively, but Arbret gave no reply.

Pure blazing white mana continued to pour from the Mage into the buckle. Mellik sat still in fear as Arbret's glow grew dimmer and dimmer. Finally the last glow of mana left the Mage and he collapsed like an empty sack.

"Master?" but Mellik knew there would be no response: Arbret had killed himself to create the enchantment.

Chapter 13

Mellik sat looking at the buckle still cradled in Arbret's lifeless hands. No thoughts ran through his head, he wasn't even seeing the buckle or hands. Finally a nudge by Bo brought him back to life.

"Huh?" he said, not even remembering for a moment that Bo couldn't hear him.

Bo shoved a sack and some water skins into his hands, laying Mellik's favourite quarterstaff beside him. The water skins were full, and looking in the sack, Mellik saw flat bread and cheese. Mellik wondered if Arbret had given instructions to Bo as well, or if Bo had just figured out what they'd need on his own. Arbret.

Mellik looked down at Arbret's still hands again, and the golden belt buckle lying there. Arbret had done this for him, had even asked Mellik to not make his sacrifice in vain.

Mellik reached out and took hold of the belt, being careful to avoid touching any part of Arbret's body. The buckle lifted easily from the open fingers of Arbret's clutch. Mellik hesitated a moment and then shot his other hand out to grab the buckle.

It was warm and heavy in his hand, but otherwise Mellik could tell no difference from any other belt buckle. Mellik pushed at the hidden catch on the buckle's back and the secret compartment sprang open. Mellik carefully stowed the ring inside, adding a scrap of cloth from his shirt so the ring wouldn't rattle, and then closed the compartment with a snap.

Mellik buckled the belt on and was surprised to find that Arbret had not been much bigger around the waist than he. Mellik would need a new belt for the buckle soon.

Mellik stood and turned to find Bo patiently waiting for him.

Mellik didn't need any hand signs to read the expression on Bo's face.

Mellik nodded to Bo. "I'm ready."

Bo nodded in reply and turned away from the oasis, the bodies, and the waterfall to shuffle off into the sand. Mellik looked back once as Arbret's body began to meld with the shadows of their camp. He wondered briefly if they should have buried Arbret's body, but Arbret's voice echoed the mage's opinion in Mellik's mind and Mellik turned back around to trudge away into the softly glowing night.

*   *   *

The sun was coming up behind them. Mellik and Bo made long shadows that shuffled and slid along the dunes in front of them. Mellik could feel the sun's warmth on his back. He supposed it would get hot soon.

Mellik glanced over at Bo. During the night Bo had donned a burnoose and a piece of tenting he'd fashioned into a poncho. Mellik had assumed the other boy was cold, but the exertion of walking through the shifting sand had been enough to keep Mellik comfortably warm. Now Bo had taken the burnoose and poncho off and was sweating.

Mellik stopped. Bo stopped as well, looking over at Mellik with questioning eyes. Mellik motioned for Bo to wait. Mellik unbuckled his new belt and slid it from around his waist. He held it out to Bo. Bo shook his head in refusal, but Mellik shook the belt at him and Bo tentatively reached out to take the belt.

The moment he let go, Mellik could feel the difference. The sun at his back was hot, not just warm, and his feet in the sand on the shadowed side of the dune could feel the cold seeping in through his tattered leather shoes.

Mellik looked over expectantly at Bo, but Bo just stared back in puzzlement. Arbret had said he would key the lock on the buckle to Mellik. Mellik suspected he must have done the same with the buckle's other enchantments.

Bo's sweating now made sense. They would need to find some shelter before the sun desiccated him.

Mellik gestured at the sun and then made a roof with his hands.

Bo nodded his understanding and handed the belt back to Mellik.

They ended up sleeping at the base of a dune in its shadowed evening side. Bo fashioned a small shelter from the two large pieces of tent he had packed. Mellik's quarterstaff served as the lone tent pole, and there was just enough room for their heads and upper bodies beneath it.

Mellik wondered if he would be able to sleep: too many thoughts rattled around in his brain. He closed his eyes nonetheless, and the thoughts vanished like shadows in the noonday sun.

*   *   *

They spent the day dozing fitfully under their small makeshift canopy. Mellik was warm and gritty: too warm to sleep comfortably after his initial exhaustion wore off. Mellik could only imagine how Bo felt without the benefit of the buckle warding off the worst of the searing heat.

Near noon, with the shadows at their shortest, Mellik took off the belt just to see. The heat was stifling. Mellik thought he could actually feel his skin tightening up and his mouth drying out. Mellik felt a twinge of guilt, but he quickly picked the belt back up and put it on. There was no reason for both of them to suffer, after all, and this way he could save some of his water for Bo.

By mid-afternoon, Mellik knew that sleep had abandoned him for a long spell. The sun was now making its way under their canopy, and soon they would need to find a different dune's slope. He was restless, and glancing over at Bo, Mellik could tell the other boy was too.

In silent accord, both boys got up out of their nest and packed up their meagre camp.

They took their time: staying in the shade of the dunes as much as possible, stopping to rest and drink before going up into the sun when they had to. Mellik studied the belt buckle during these breaks. He was pretty sure it was protecting him from the heat by absorbing the fire energy around him. It was a slow process, but he thought that it glowed just a little brighter at each stop they made.

They made better time once the sun went down. It was still

slow going over the hilly dunes and through the sand, but they stopped less often. Mellik gave Bo his piece of tent when he saw Bo wrap himself up with his poncho. Mellik could actually see the belt slowly giving off the fire mana it had absorbed earlier to now keep him warm.

They were both tired, but once again by silent accord they pushed on. Time spent idle with the sun down was more time in the blistering heat. Even with the belt, Mellik was sweaty and his lips chapped. Bo was in much worse shape: his lips were cracked and where bare skin peaked out at his neck, nose and wrists, his brown skin had a distinct red cast.

By the time the first light of day glowed behind them, Mellik's legs burned and ached with the effort of every step. He sank gratefully into the cool sand of a big dune and helped Bo erect their small shelter.

Mellik awoke once more to heat and sticky sweat coated in fine sand. His hand itched, but when he went to scratch it his other hand recoiled from the pain. Looking down, he saw that his hand must have strayed out from the shade of their little tent. It was red and puffy with whiter blisters. Now that he was aware of it, he could feel the heat sinking in from the inflamed skin.

Mellik's movements must have awoken Bo. Bo looked up at Mellik, who was propped up on his elbow holding his other hand. Mellik showed him the hand in explanation.

Bo's eyebrows furled in concern. Bo pointed at Mellik's waist. Mellik raised his hand palm up in confusion. Bo reached over and tapped Mellik's belt in explanation. Mellik couldn't figure out how to explain to Bo that that wasn't how the belt worked, so instead he just unbuckled the belt with his good hand and placed the buckle lightly on the outside of the burnt hand. The relief was instantaneous.

Taking the buckle away again, the hand still looked red and blistered, but Mellik no longer felt the stinging, burning heat. Now the hand just itched. Mellik wished he'd been watching the interaction with his second sight. Mellik nodded his thanks to Bo and the two drifted off into their fitful sleep again, Mellik's burnt hand curled tightly about the belt buckle.

Mellik woke to the lengthening shadows of late afternoon. Getting out from their shelter, Mellik looked to the West and saw that it was even later than he had thought, as the sky was beginning to blaze a brilliant orange and the sun had already ducked beneath a high dune.

Mellik realized he was still dragging his belt around by the buckle. The hand was looking even better now. The blisters were receding. There was still a slight tingling ache there, but the hand felt no worse than his legs, which ached from two nights of shuffling and sliding through the sand.

Mellik reached out and gently shook Bo awake. He saw the same realization cross Bo's face as Bo saw how late in the day it was. Mellik put his belt back on, and they quickly took down their small tent.

As they were packing away their meagre shelter, Mellik could hear the soft sound of the sand blowing across the dunes. The sound tickled something in Mellik's mind. It was wrong somehow. The sound was wrong.

There was no wind.

The sound stopped even as Mellik turned and stood.

It was bigger than Mellik remembered the two from the diamond palace. It was slightly below them at the base of the dune, but its head swayed back and forth almost level with Mellik's. Its golden mane of fur looked softer and fuller than the statues as it waved about in echo to the sand lion's movements.

Fear took hold of Mellik, but the weeks of drilling by Arbret made him instinctually switch to the second sight and begin to gather mana to himself.

Mellik had no clear idea what to do with the mana once he had it. Luckily, the sand lion did not seem inclined to attack him right away either. It wasn't even really looking at them, but had its head pointed up toward the sky, its forked tongue flickering in and out as it continued to sway. The thought came to Mellik that it looked like a hound sniffing for the direction of a fresh baked pie.

If so, the sand lion found what it was looking for. The head came down and its black eyes locked onto Mellik. It opened its huge mouth and what came out was not the hiss of a snake, but the scream of some primal bird of prey. Mellik was rooted in fear as he saw the sand lion coil to strike. It was still some twenty long strides away, but it seemed far too close.

Mellik reached out with his senses to the earth, to find that power buried there that had saved him before. Instead he found only sand. There was some power there, but it was weak and fragmented. It had no direction or purpose like he had felt before.

Then there was no more time for thinking as the sand lion bared its fangs and struck. Instinctively, Mellik did the only thing he could. Already holding the feel of the sand in his mind, he channeled. He tried to form the large earthquake he'd summoned before, but each grain of sand acted independently, vibrating and shaking to their own rhythm. The effect was unexpected.

The sand beneath the maned snake suddenly collapsed downward in a large sinkhole. The sand lion fell with it, and more sand poured into the newly formed whole.

Mellik quickly turned and scrambled up the dune and away from the settling sand. Turning near the top, Mellik saw that Bo had been forced to one side of the sinkhole and was now near the base of the dune.

Movement in the hole quickly squashed any vague hope that the giant snake had been buried permanently by the sand. The sand lion slithered out from the sand and up the side of the hole. It was making a bee line for Mellik, and moving faster than any horse he'd ever seen.

Mellik fumbled for his belt knife, with echoes of the Lady Yew's description of its impenetrable hide telling him that here approached his certain death.

As the sand snake came up out of the sink hole, three dirty urchins seemed to pop up out of the sand in front of it. It took Mellik a moment to realize that the urchins were identical, and that they were images of him.

'Good thinking, Bo," Mellik thought to himself.

The sand lion reared up above the images, then opened its maw and struck down in a fearsome blow on the middle one. The snake flashed through the illusionary Mellik and rammed its open mouth in the sand. The sand lion reared up and let loose its raptorous scream to the sky.

The snake looked down again, and again there were three Mellik's in front of it. This time it struck like lightning: once, twice, three times it lashed out and bit down on the heads of the illusory Melliks. Each time the illusion would disappear, and then reappear a moment later in a different spot. This time the snake hissed at the Melliks like a frustrated cat.

Mellik still stood rooted in place, afraid any movement by him would tip the snake off.

Now the snake seemed to pause, almost like it was thinking. It lifted its head to the sky again, but no sound issued forth. Its tongue flicked in and out again and again when its head came down, its eyes locked on Mellik.

It began to slither up the slope toward him, but slower than before. Fake Melliks popped up in its path, but the forked tongue flicked in and out and the sand lion slithered right through them.

Mellik backed away. He wanted to run, but he knew to run would be to die. This was just a big snake: if he could get lucky with his knife, it would die just like a smaller one.

Mellik finally stopped and gripped the knife with both hands, reversed like he would to gut a deer.

Just as the sand lion neared, a new set of Melliks appeared, this time encircling Mellik himself. Once again Mellik silently blessed Bo. If the snake chose the wrong one, Mellik might just have a chance to plunge his knife into its skull.

The sand lion paused again, its tongue flicking in and out as its head swayed side to side surveying its prey. Then it surprised Mellik again. Bringing its head down, it flipped its long tail around in a swipe at the whole group of Melliks.

This was much slower than the lightning fast head strikes and Mellik saw it coming and had time to bring his knife down hard on the sand lion's tail. Mellik saw the sharp point barely scratch the hardened scales and then twist and bend out of his grip from the impact as the huge tail continued on, sweeping Mellik and his doppelgangers from its path.

Mellik was thrown sprawling face down in the sand. His ribs burned with pain and he could barely seem to breathe. Mellik managed to roll himself over and saw the giant maned snake once again slithering cautiously toward him. Mellik looked around, but his knife was lost: Mellik was lost.

The sand snake was almost upon him when an image popped up around him. It took Mellik a moment to realize that it was the image of another sand lion. This one was even bigger than the real one, towering up above Mellik, its illusory body completely engulfing him.

The real sand lion stopped. For a moment Mellik thought it might actually back down and flee. Then he looked into its eyes. Its body was now coiled in a more defensive posture, its mane puffing up like a scared cat's, but its eyes spoke of malice and hatred and an unfulfilled violence that could not be turned aside.

Mellik remembered the small cutting disc and pulled it from the pouch at his side. The sand lion's mane might be like steel, and the creature's hide was stronger than boiled leather, but all creatures had soft spots. Mellik started the disc spinning.

Mellik could see Bo behind and to one side of the sand lion, waving furiously for Mellik to run, but both Mellik and the giant snake ignored him.

Mellik knew that Bo could only maintain these images for so long: and then what, hope he had run far enough as his friend died? The disc rose higher, steady even as Mellik's hands trembled with fear. It rose up until it was above Mellik's head, just below the mane of Bo's illusion. Mellik didn't need to see it any more. He could feel it.

Mellik didn't see the sand lion coil or bare its fangs so fast was it. It was hurtling toward him, its mouth wide and turning sideways in the air. Mellik had the barest of instants to fling his small disc at its open maw before it struck him, spinning him and pushing him through the sand. Pain blossomed from his neck. Mellik tried to find the disk, make it spin faster, make it dart about inside the snake. Then the sand lion struck him again.

*   *   *

Bo ran up the dune, his tired legs screaming in protest, but like any other cry, he didn't hear it. He'd known that Mellik was still inside his illusionary sand lion when the real one had struck. The image was too complex to maintain as the real snake plummeted through it. Bo had even seen a glimpse of Mellik falling beneath the giant snake.

Now there was no sign of Mellik: just the sand lion thrashing about. It's convulsions were dying down to mere twitches now. It was dying or more likely already dead. Bo had seen his grandmother's chickens do the same thing.

By the time Bo reached the snake, only it's tail flicked fitfully back and forth. Bo scanned the pile of snake but there was no other movement. Then at last he spotted the soles of Mellik's worn shoes sticking out from a coil of the giant snake.

Bo clambered up to the snake and saw Mellik lying face down in the sand beneath the giant snake - one arm twisted unnaturally above his head. Bo leaned over the sand lion to feel Mellik's face. The other boy didn't feel cold like Bo remembered his grandfather being, but then the snake felt warm too, and it was definitely dead. Bo poked at the limp boy and slapped Mellik's face, but there was no response. Tears streamed down Bo's dusty cheeks, leaving marks like the ones permanently on the only friend Bo had ever known.

Not knowing what else to do, Bo set about freeing Mellik from beneath the dead snake. Bo was big and strong for his age, but even he could barely budge the big coils of sand lion, so Bo began to dig out the sand from beneath Mellik as best he could.

It took far longer than Bo had thought. He was tired, and the snake and sand both wanted to sink into whatever trough he started. The sun set and the sand and the snake became cold to the touch. His friend, Mellik, stayed warm however, so Bo kept working with a lighter heart.

At last, Mellik's body had sunk low enough that the sand lion only barely rested on his hips. Bo's arms ached and burned from the effort so he decided that must be good enough. Bo grabbed Mellik by the ankles, and with a mighty heave he pulled Mellik free and backpedalled down the dune.

Something must have jostled Mellik's arm as he came underneath the sand lion. Mellik rolled over, yanking his ankles from Bo's grasp. He sat up, clutching the injured arm to his chest.

Bo saw his mouth fly open, and felt the vibration of his cry. Bo had always wondered what those vibrations felt like to other people. He'd always thought it would be like the warm touch of the sun at times, and at others like the scorching heat of a kettle over the hearth fire.

Bo crouched down next to his friend, afraid to touch him again. Mellik sat holding the arm, rocking back and forth. After a few moments the rocking ceased. Mellik looked up at Bo with the tears of pain still in his eyes. Mellik nodded to Bo and then carefully set about standing up.

Bo scrambled back to the sand lion. Climbing about and tugging at the thinner end of its body, Bo found Mellik's meagre bag of gear and easily freed it from the snake's corpse. Bo returned to his friend to find Mellik staring off to the south.

Bo followed his gaze and saw a blue star shining low in the distance: too low to be a star really, so some man-made light. Mellik turned and said something to Bo. Bo didn't understand the words, "We made it," but he understood the expression on Mellik's face and smiled in return.

Book 2:

HEAT

Chapter 14

Mellik drifted in and out of consciousness. Memories and dreams collided and mixed but it made little difference to him. There was a beautiful woman who healed and soothed him, or perhaps she cut him cruelly. Sometimes the healer was his mother. Sometimes the cruel one turned into a giant snake of fire. He remembered a desert, a boat, and men with swords. Even in his dreams a boat in the desert made no sense. Just like the woman, sometimes the men with swords helped him, and sometimes they attacked him. Both types of men looked at him the same way however. The one constant was pain. That always seemed real.

Mellik woke to a room of muted daylight. The ceiling was a pale stucco. Mellik moved his head slightly and saw that the light came from a window with dark, heavy brown curtains covering it. He assumed he was awake. The pain of his head and shoulder were too real, and this seemed too . . . boring for a dream.

Movement caught his eye. Mellik recognized the large, square frame of Bo, along with his huge smile. Bo's grin grew larger as he approached and looked into Mellik's open eyes.

Bo gave Mellik a thumbs-up and then cocked his head to one side to show it was a question. Mellik somehow knew that nodding his head was a bad idea. Instead, he moved one hand out from the soft sheet covering him to return Bo's thumbs-up. Mellik was surprised at how tired he felt and how much effort that small gesture took.

Bo smiled and held his hands out, palms up. A rainbow appeared between them, and Mellik couldn't help but smile in return.

He remembered coming out of the desert now: seeing the academy of magic's bright blue beacon and finding the small hut with the guards and their boat. There'd been a fight with a giant snake -- a sand lion. Mellik remembered seeing the snake dead. He thought he might have had some part in that. That was probably where his injuries had come from.

Mellik was parched. He raised his fingers slowly to his lips. Bo immediately understood. Trotting over to a table, he grabbed a clay pitcher and filled a tin cup. A reed straw stuck out from the cup, and Mellik greedily sucked down the sweet, fruity contents. He consumed a second cup after that but waved away a third. He wanted to find out what was happening, but Bo's vocabulary was still very limited even with the slate writing board. Plus, he was so tired; so very, very tired...

It was darker when he woke again. A dim yellow glow lit the room. Mellik's head felt better, and he looked about him. The window was dark. Looking the other direction, Mellik saw the outline of a door, and a figure slouched in a chair next to it. The figure looked too small to be Bo, so Mellik subtly cleared his throat.

"Oh, I'm sorry. You're awake," the figure said with a soft, young feminine voice.

The figure rose, and Mellik could see a short, slender woman with long hair. A step forward brought her face into the light of the small oil lamp sitting on his bedside table. Mellik could see now that she was a girl, probably no older than he. She had sharp, chiseled features softened by youth and a look of gentle concern. In that same instant, her features changed and hardened as the sleep retreated from her eyes. Now her face reminded Mellik of Lady Yew. This girl had the same alabaster skin that was so rare in the South, but a few freckles broke up the purity of that skin, and her hair was a midnight black compared to the lady's platinum.

Mellik's own face tightened and as it did, it pulled painfully at the scar on his cheek where the lady had removed a piece of him.

"Where's Bo?" he gruffly asked.

The girl didn't answer or even look at him at first. She poured a cup from the same pitcher Bo had used and set it on the small table next to him.

"Is that the deaf boy?" she finally asked after retreating into the shadows again.

Her tone and demeanor made Mellik want to be rude right back, but his mother had taught him to act otherwise, and he had faced worse attitudes than this before.

"Yes," he answered in a neutral tone. "Where is he?"

"He did not leave the room for the two days you were unconscious," her tone seemed less combative now. "He ate little and slept less. Last night was the first time he'd gone to the dining hall. He gorged himself on stew and then passed out at the table. The healers thought he might sleep better in his own room. He's next door."

"Are you a healer?" asked Mellik.

"No," and the brittle, superior quality had returned to her voice. "I am apprenticed to them this season as I have shown some aptitude for it. They were pleased enough with your recovery to deem me capable of watching for any signs of trouble."

"Trouble?" a slight tremor of fear crept into Mellik's voice.

The girl let out a sigh of exasperation, "You'll be fine, else the healers would be watching over you and not me. You broke your collarbone, and the shoulder came out of the socket. They fixed those, and they're strong enough as long as you don't do anything stupid."

She sounded doubtful of Mellik's ability to pull that off.

"You were also dehydrated, and a bruise on your head made them wonder if you had been concussed. I'm to ask for signs of dizziness, headaches, nausea."

Mellik saw the shadow of her head tilt to one side, and he guessed that had been a question.

"Nausea?" he asked.

"Do you feel like throwing up?" she said slowly, as if he were stupid.

"No," and he couldn't keep the anger from his voice.

"Good," and she did indeed sound pleased now. She turned as if to leave.

"Excuse me," Mellik called. The girl paused without turning. "I've been teaching my friend Bo to read. If the college had a piece of slate and some chalk sticks I could borrow, I would greatly appreciate it."

"You're teaching the deaf boy, your friend Bo to read?" the girl still didn't turn, but her tone was strangely neutral now, less combative.

"Yes, and I know you don't owe me anything, but I would consider it a great personal favor."

The girl nodded, "I must stay here until morning. Such things are common here, so I may be able to get them for you."

Mellik relaxed back into his pillow. He hadn't even realized he was tensed up.

"Thank you. My name is Mellik, by the way."

The girl turned slowly and straitened before giving him the barest of nods. Mellik knew the brittleness in her voice would be back before she even spoke.

"I am Keyessa Dravidian. Please drink your juice. If you require anything else, I will be right here."

Mellik drank as instructed. Having one more random person hate him shouldn't bother him too much. He just hoped she didn't hate him so much she wouldn't get the chalk and slate.

The next day Mellik felt much better: less tired and only a little achy around his right shoulder. No one was in the room, and Mellik felt disappointed. The odd part was that it wasn't just Bo that he had hoped to see.

The pitcher and cup sat next to his bed. Mellik sat up and poured himself some of the sweet juice. He was just finishing his second cup when there was a soft tap at the door. Before Mellik could think to reply, the door cracked open, and a thin, old man stuck his head in the door. He had white hair, a fair complexion, and a close-cropped beard.

"Ah, good, you're awake," said the man, stepping inside and softly shutting the door behind himself. "And you've drank some, yes? Good. My name is Mygammeen. Do you remember me?"

Mellik slowly shook his head, trying to think back, but not remembering the tall man in yellow robes.

"I was one of those who helped treat you when you came in," the man explained. He hooked the stool by the door with one long arm and came to sit by Mellik's bedside. "Let's take a look at that shoulder."

The man twitched aside Mellik's sheet and gently pulled aside the loose shirt he was wearing.

"Any pain? Sharp or just tender? Can you sit up? Slowly raise your arm above your head. Any pain there?" Mellik responded to each question and request. "Now, how's the head? No aches or dizziness there? You've drank? feel like you could do with something more substantial? Have you needed to relieve yourself yet? More juice then. Empty that pitcher, and I'll have some water brought with some porridge. There's a bucket just beneath the bed if you need it. How was Keyessa?"

"Very nice," replied Mellik.

The old man leaned in and stared into Mellik's eyes.

"You're a lousy liar," he pronounced and then chuckled. "Not a skill usually encouraged in the young, but one you might find handy nonetheless."

"Uh, yes Master," replied Mellik, belatedly remembering his late Master's instructions.

"Ah, very good," and the man winked at him. "Some Masters might not be so absentminded as to have missed your earlier omissions. We're easy to spot by the way. On the island all journeymen are to wear black, and the apprentices are dressed in various shades white, and yes I know there are no shades of white, but apprentices manage it anyway. Since no Master would ever want to be mistaken for a journeyman or, heavens forbid, an apprentice, we'll be the more colorful ones."

The man gestured at his own pale yellow robes.

"You may address me as Master Myg or Healer Myg."

"Thank you, Master Myg."

"You're welcome, Apprentice Mellik. Now, can I answer any questions for you?"

"Is Bo okay, Master Myg?"

"Your deaf companion? He's fine. He was a little dehydrated as well, but he's already recovered from that. Since he finally got some sleep and food, the other Masters are prodding at him to see where he fits here at the academy."

"He won't be sent away will he, Master?"

"Not likely. I've heard he has a talent for illusion. At the very least he'll be trained as far as necessary to avoid being a danger to himself or others. The Emperor does not lightly let an asset as powerful as a budding wizard go to waste. Anything else?"

"Why does she hate me?" Mellik had not meant that question to be voiced allowed.

Master Myg chuckled and shook his head.

"And that is why I've stayed here at the Academy. But, to answer your question, I think you know why she dislikes you: you're a Kamori.

"To be more specific, she's likely been brought up to hate you, or at least your people. She was born and raised in the Empire's capitol, to a family that has been at the right hand of power since before the Emperor. She would have been born right near the end of the Kamori war.

"The Empire has fought and conquered many nations since the Emperor came to power. Some nations killed even more of the Empire's men than your own people, and in perverse and wicked ways. But your people did something no other people or nation had done before: they made the people of the Capitol know fear. People hate what they fear. You do know the curse your people laid on the empire?"

Mellik nodded.

"So every Kamori that dies at the hand or intent of someone of the Empire adds to the power that is destabilizing the earth beneath the city. Too many such deaths will cause the city to be destroyed. The people of the Capitol still fear and hate your people. The laws which protect your life make them hate you even more."

"So she'll just go on hating me."

"Most likely," and something about that amused the healer as he chuckled. "Don't worry about it too much though: at least you know why she hates you."

"Now make sure to eat and drink as much as we give you.

You'll likely need your strength tomorrow," and with that heartening comment the healer swept from the room.

Mellik needed to get up. Even though he had slept through it all, he felt like he had been in bed too long. Bright light shone out from the edge of the curtains, and Mellik wanted to see what was outside his window. As he slid from the tall bed, Mellik was pleased that although he felt a little weak, he otherwise felt fine -- even his shoulder barely hurt. Mellik looked down at the loose smock he was wearing. He glanced around, but couldn't see anywhere they might have stored his things. 'One thing at a time,' he thought to himself.

Mellik had just reached the window when the door clicked open behind him. Mellik spun around and almost lost his balance.

"Good, you're up already," commented Keyessa. "Can you manage the curtains, or do you need a hand?"

She sounded as if she doubted Mellik had ever even seen curtains before, let alone knew how to operate them.

"I think I can manage," Mellik said, making a sketchy bow to the girl, "but thank you for your concern."

Mellik's stumble when he turned had shown him that he wasn't completely recovered yet, but he'd be demon-damned if he let her see that. Mellik had faced crazed wizards, assassins, and a sand lion: he wouldn't let a spoiled girl beat him. Mellik turned slowly back and very deliberately pulled one side of the curtains away.

It must have been mid-morning or mid-afternoon, and the bright light of day came streaming in the open window. Mellik's eyes were so adjusted to the dim light of his room that he was momentarily blinded. Mellik stood there blinking in the bright sunshine, trying to pretend like he'd meant to open only one side while his eyes adjusted.

"Would you like to eat your breakfast by the window, milord?" asked Keyessa sweetly.

"That would be nice," replied Mellik, not acknowledging her mocking tone, and then he gasped as the view outside his window finally came into focus.

"Did you not see the bowl when you came in?" asked Keyessa archly as she brought a chair for him to sit in.

Mellik forgot his defensive mood and sat lightly on the edge of the seat while never taking his eyes from the view.

"No," he replied automatically. "At least, I don't remember it."

The window gazed out over a lush, tropical forest. Birds and butterflies flew about the tops of palms and fig trees. Around the outside of this jungle rose a steep cliff face. Mellik could see it curve around towards him on either side. Keyessa had said it was a bowl, so Mellik assumed that the cliff continued all the way around to where they were. What was most remarkable were the windows, balconies, towers and spires that spotted the entire face of the cliff that Mellik could see. They were everywhere, and Mellik could not fathom how many people it would take to fill all that space.

"It's wasn't always **just** a college for wizards you know," said Keyessa.

Mellik was startled to see that the small bedside table had been set before him with a glass of juice and what looked to be a bowl of creamed wheat. Keyessa had brought up the stool she had been using the night before, and now she opened the other curtain so she could sit and look out the window as well.

"The historians tell us that some two hundred years ago, early in the Emperor's reign, he came down the coast to conquer the desert kingdom of Ya'Sul. His armies easily marched across the coastal towns and villages. The Capitol was the city of Mar'Tuk, the volcano crater we now sit in.

"Ya'Sul was a kingdom ruled by sorcerers, and they were more powerful and numerous than the wizards of the Emperor's army, though none approached the power of the Emperor himself. The Emperor's army would have eventually taken the city, but at great loss of life on both sides. The rulers of Ya'Sul offered to surrender to the Emperor, but in return, the city and all in it except the ruling council would be spared. Also, the Emperor would make Mar'Tuk his college of wizardry, and the college would train and send him warrior mages so long as all apprentices were sent here first. This treaty was signed in blood and sealed by magic."

Mellik waited, but there seemed to be no more of the story forthcoming. He turned his attention to the creamed wheat. It was not his favorite food, but someone had fortified it with a healthy dab of butter and a dollop of honey. He ate as if he might never see food again.

Mellik was scraping the dregs of the bowl when he looked up to see Keyessa looking at him with a mix of disgust and loathing. He could feel a sticky clot of the cereal slowly dribbling down his chin and thought he must look like quite the bumpkin to this refined young lady. Mellik's mother would be mortified, he was sure. Mellik could not think of a way to rescue himself, and then it dawned on him: Mellik wiped the food from his face with his hand and then slowly and deliberately licked his hand clean before cleaning his bowl out in a similar manner. Mellik watched Keyessa's face twist into an even more disapproving frown, and he grinned in return. The girl finally just turned away.

At least Mellik's father would have been proud: "Never show your enemy weakness," he'd told him.

Mellik finished his food and then looked over at his bed. He instantly regretted his boorishness, as there on the bed was a square piece of slate, a book, and several sticks of chalk.

Mellik went to the bed and looked at the items. The chalk was largely the same as he'd used before, but the slate was much finer than the one Master Arbret had lent him. It was smoother and framed in wood.

Mellik picked up the book. It was far thicker and heavier than anything Mellik had seen before. The cover simply had an open hand embossed on the leather cover. Opening it, Mellik found pages filled with pictures of a person's hands with arrows and a caption under each one. The page he was open to seemed to be about animals. The captions read; cat, chicken, cow, and dog.

"What is this?" asked Mellik.

"It's called hand signs," replied Keyessa. "I talked with Bo after I got the slates. His vocabulary is very limited, but he told me you'd taught him all of it in a few short weeks. This is a way of speaking with your hands. If you can teach him this, he can communicate even without the slates to someone else who knows it."

"Thank you," and Mellik forgot her earlier attitude. "This is amazing."

"I didn't do it for you," and her condescending tone was back.

Mellik chose to ignore it this time.

"I thank you none the less," he said.

"If it is at all confusing, send Bo to me." Meaning it was not okay for Mellik to come find her.

"The healers say you should rest," she continued. "Tomorrow will be a long day. I'll be in the hall if you need anything."

Keyessa quietly closed the door behind herself without waiting for a reply.

Chapter 15

There was a tapping on Mellik's door.

"Come in," he mumbled, sitting up and rubbing at his eyes.

Healer Mygammeen poked his head inside.

"Ah good, you're awake," the wizard said as he slipped into the room. The healer had a canvas bag hanging from one gnarled fist, and he once again grabbed the stool and came to sit by Mellik's bedside.

"Still feeling good? No headaches, no dizziness?" he asked. "Feeling a little stronger than yesterday?"

Mellik answered the questions appropriately.

"That's good, because the masters will not wait another day, so your testing will be today." There was disapproval in Healer Myg's tone.

He opened the canvas bag onto Mellik's lap. Mellik's clothes, including his threadbare shoes, came tumbling out.

"Normally you should only wear a set of apprentice whites for this, but you've been in the healers' ward, so I must have forgotten to get you some. Hopefully it will remind the pompous bigots of what you've been through, and they'll take it easy on you. I've been told you can read?"

"Yes, Master."

"Good. Can you read this?" and the healer handed Mellik a slip of paper.

Mellik found that it was a list of simple directions: go out his door to the left, take the third corridor to the right, etc.

"Yes, Master."

"Good. I don't have the time this morning, and Bo is being tested elsewhere already, coincidence of coincidences. Keyessa has been assigned elsewhere this morning. You would almost think someone at the college already dislikes you," and the wizard gave Mellik a pointed look.

Mellik wasn't sure if he was supposed to understand what the healer was referring to or not, so he made no reply.

"Well then, I shall wish you luck," and Healer Myg bounced to his feet. "Hopefully you won't need it. Don't rush as I made sure to wake you with plenty of time, but don't doddle either. Better to arrive early and wait there."

The healer swept from the room, closing the door softly behind him before Mellik could think to ask him about the testing.

Mellik dressed quickly despite Myg's instructions. He was too nervous to do it any other way. As he was dressing, Mellik thought for the first time of his belt: it wasn't there.

He scanned the room, but it was as it had been: sparse of furnishings and no belt or buckle in sight. Mellik squatted down to look under the bed, but it was bare of even dust on the smooth stone floor. He tried not to panic. He hadn't asked for it after all. Maybe they were just holding it for him. Arbret had told him the compartment would only open for Mellik, because it was magically keyed to him. They wouldn't have healed him just for his execution, after all.

Mellik started to calm down. Glancing at his bed, he noticed for the first time the small table next to it had a small wooden drawer. It was the only closable thing in the room. Mellik walked to the table, and with a hand still shaking from nerves he opened it.

There, coiled neatly in the small drawer, lay his belt. Mellik reached in and gingerly lifted the belt out by the buckle, letting the leather unwind beneath it. Mellik studied the buckle with his second sight, his wizard's vision. It looked as he remembered it: full of bright red fire mana and slim traces of earth and spirit.

Mellik glanced around the small room, as if some spy might have hidden behind the small stool in the corner. Mellik went to stand with his back to the door, just in case. He pressed his thumb into the back of the golden buckle, and it sprang open. Inside was a rough gold ring. It hardly looked shaped at all, as if pulled from the ground whole in this crude circle. Viewed with the second sight, however, and it swirled and danced with earth and spirit magic, a thing of rare beauty. Mellik snapped the hidden compartment closed again and released a breath he hadn't realized he was holding.

Mellik wrapped the belt about his waist, pulling the loose shirt tight. He supposed that made him as ready as he could be.

Opening the door, Mellik found a board with salted pork, a white cheese, a thick slice of bread, and a mug of fruit juice waiting for him. Mellik's stomach rumbled. He gulped down the juice and hastily made a sandwich to take with him. He would eat it on his way.

Mellik had only the vaguest memories of coming into the college. He remembered a large tunnel that he thought had been the entrance and a jungle that he now knew was the bowl of the crater. The smaller passages he now traveled down were entirely unfamiliar to him. Not only that, but having grown up in a rural village, he had never seen a place of this grand a scale, let alone one that tunneled through dark stone with no view of the outdoors at all. Even the crystal palace had been studded with windows to the desert and bright blue sky.

Sunlight did filter through high slits in the hallway, but they were too high for Mellik to see out of them. His first turn took him down another hall, and Mellik could feel the weight above him increase as he moved deeper into the crater's rim. It felt like he might be going down, but if so, it was too gentle for him to tell for sure. The hall was getting darker. Looking back, Mellik could only just see the last white light coming from outside. Looking ahead, he could tell the light there had a greenish tinge to it compared to the light behind.

There were no halls branching off of the one he was in, and his next direction was to a door on his right. Opening it, the first thing Mellik noticed was a strong sulfur smell. He realized that he'd been smelling sulfur since he'd awoken at the college. It was so pervasive yet subtle that he hadn't noticed it. Here the smell was strong and distinct.

The walls here were much more brightly lit with the green light. As Mellik stepped into the hall the door closed softly behind him, and he saw that he had been mistaken. The walls were not lit with green light, they were giving off that light.

Looking closer, he saw that the stone here was almost completely covered in some kind of moss or lichen that glowed with the eerie green hue. Mellik reached out to touch it, but then thought better of it. What if this was already part of his test, or worse yet, what if the plant was dangerous? Lady Yew's test had been painful, cruel, and could have been deadly if he had failed. Could he assume the wizards of the college would be more benign?

Mellik switched to the second sight and looked at the fungus on the walls again. It looked no more or less dangerous than before. There was a slightly greater concentration of fire mana in the plants, but only barely enough to be noticeable. He had expected that. Mage Arbret had explained that anything that gave off light or heat would have fire mana. The glowing algae came all the way down to the floor, even creeping out from the wall in places. The floor was otherwise bare of the stuff, however.

Mellik assumed that the wizards wouldn't allow anything to grow along the walls that might be dangerous. It would be too easy for someone to stumble into it. However, he stayed to the middle of the hall just to be safe and didn't touch the glowing green walls. The hall ended at a stair that spiraled down into the depths of the stone.

The stairs went down and down. Mellik wondered how far beneath the ground he was. The air was damp and warm. The lack of anyone else in the halls combined with the green lighting made him feel like he had entered some other world and had been there for ages, though he knew it had only been minutes.

Another door sat at the bottom of the stair. Mellik pulled it open to reveal another stone hall, brightly lit with a more familiar orange glow. The hall echoed with dim voices. The presence of other people made him less apprehensive. He pulled the door closed behind him, as the instructions explicitly stated.

Glancing around, Mellik saw that the dull orange glow came from the ends of sticks in the ceiling. They were attached evenly down the hall, and their downward ends smoldered with a bright orange glow. Mellik surmised that they slowly burned upwards, as they were of varying lengths. The hall extended in both directions as far as Mellik could see, with doors dotted along its length on either side.

Mellik turned right and headed down the hall, counting doors on his left. The hall ahead was not completely straight. It curved slightly to the left and disappeared.

At one point a figure popped out of a door ahead and to Mellik's right, but the boy dashed away without a glance at Mellik. Even that one boy in the apprentice whites made Mellik less apprehensive. He was not alone in these deep tunnels.

As he approached the door the boy had come from, he could hear that the echoing voices were coming from the doors ahead. Behind the first door, there was a muted cacophony of conversations. The next door contained a lone, deep male voice in a lecturing tone. The lecturer reminded Mellik of Master Arbret, though his voice had not been nearly so bass.

Mellik was tempted to knock at a door and ask if he was headed in the right direction, but he did not know if he should intrude on whatever was happening on the other side. Plus, he had only two more doors to go on his left, so he was almost there.

A tone went off. Mellik thought it might have been a bell, but the rich sound reverberated through the halls and seemed to emanate from the walls themselves. The sound of voices took on a different pitch, and multiplied in number and volume. A moment later the doors on his right burst open, and people flooded out into the hallway.

Mellik had never been amongst so many people crowded into such a small space. He hopped against the door on his left to avoid the press of bodies. The vast majority of the people were young, some younger than him. They were also mostly dressed in the drab whites and tans of apprentices. A few black clad figures dotted the crowd, and Mellik caught a glimpse of one bright flash of red, but otherwise it was a sea of cream cloth. They were almost all headed the direction he had been going.

Mellik began to follow the crowd in that direction when a tall boy a couple of years his senior stepped into his path. Three other boys and a girl stood behind the tall boy. Mellik glanced up, and his initial fear disappeared as he recognized the girl as Keyessa.

"Oh good, Keyessa," began Mellik, "Would you take a look at these directions and make sure I'm headed in the right direction?"

The big boy pushed Mellik's outstretched hand away with a hard slap. He was tall and lean with sinewy muscles and the deep brown, lustrous skin of the southern people. His clothes were of fine silk, cut trim and fashionable to show off his muscular frame.

"Ya da not talk ta her," he said with a thick southern accent. "Lady Keyessa is ta far above ya."

"It's okay Brin," Keyessa took a step forward and lightly laid a hand on the big boys shoulder. "He only knows me from the healers' wing."

"I, I'm sorry if I've done something wrong," stammered Mellik. "I didn't mean to give offense."

Mellik lowered his head in a small half-bow, hoping that that would suffice.

"There, ya did it again," commented Brin.

He reached out and shoved Mellik by the head. Mellik reeled backwards, only keeping his feet by running into the far wall.

"Ya dat Kamori apprentice I heard a aren't ya. No one wad miss one less of ya. I shad da Keyessa *and* the Emperor a favor and just finish ya now."

Brin held out his hand, and a blindingly bright light pulsed in his palm. Its strobing light was accompanied by a staccato popping noise. Small white and blue sparks gyrated and flew from the globe of light. Brin took a menacing step forward, and Mellik attempted to retreat, sliding along the wall away from the large boy.

"Brin!" boomed a tenor voice from behind the group.

Brin's light disappeared, and the group turned as a portly red faced man with scraggly grey hair haloing an otherwise bald head came striding up. He wore a vibrant purple that only a Master would dare.

"I assume Journeyman Suggs will tell me you were practicing something from his class?" asked the man, who stood a full head shorter than Brin.

"Uh," began Brin.

"Let me put it another way," interrupted the man. "If you were all to disperse rather quickly, and you became model students for the next week, perhaps I will forget exactly what it was I just saw and even what I just asked."

"Yes, Master Vai," mumbled a couple of the boys behind Brin as they turned tail. Keyessa and Brin were right behind the rest. Mellik drew breath to thank the Master but was interrupted before he began.

"And I assume you have something to do as well?"

Mellik released his breath, at a loss for words.

"Well, do you have somewhere you should be going?" asked the Master.

Mellik just nodded, his brain still reeling.

"Good, then I suggest you get to it before I decide you were at fault in that confrontation."

With that, the Master turned and marched back the way he'd come.

Mellik took a moment to collect his wits. He should have thanked the wizard, but it was too late for that now. Pushing off from the wall, he looked around again to orient himself with his directions.

Mellik forged on down the hall. A couple more students popped out of open doors ahead of him, but they didn't spare him a second glance.

Mellik found the door he'd been looking for on his left. He hesitated a moment, wondering if he should knock or something, but the directions explicitly said to go in upon arriving. Mellik gave the plain iron handle a shove, and the door swung open.

Inside was a small, dimly lit room. A tall, broad shouldered man stood inside. He wore dark blue robes trimmed in silver and had a neatly trimmed beard gone to salt and pepper, though his hair was still a deep midnight black.

"Mellik Ackins," he intoned as he strode forward to take Mellik by the shoulders and firmly guide him into the room. The door swung shut, and Mellik heard a latch click loudly. "You are here to be judged."

Chapter 16

"W-what?" stammered Mellik.

"The hour of your judgment is upon you," intoned the wizard. "In this room you shall be weighed, sorted, and measured. From this point forward you shall not speak unless in answer to a question or specifically instructed to. Do you understand?"

Mellik sorted through that in his mind and decided it was safer to just nod his head in understanding.

"Good. You are now allowed one question of me before we begin. Ask quickly."

Though the Mage had stressed that he should be quick, with only one question to ask, Mellik looked around to assess the situation.

The room was very small. There was just enough room for him and the wizard to stand comfortably facing one another. There were only two doors: the one he had come in by, and another opposite it. A small bench stood against one wall with a plain tin box sitting on one end of it. The most interesting thing Mellik noticed was that other than the wall with the door that he had come through, the other three walls and even the ceiling were built from a whitewashed wood. They were the first wooden walls Mellik had come upon, and the ceiling seemed lower than the rest of the complex.

"Do you have a question?" prodded the Mage.

Mellik did, but even in the face of the wizard's impatience, he still took another second to word it correctly in his head.

"How do I succeed here at the College of Magic?" Mellik asked as the wizard opened his mouth to say something else.

The Mage closed his mouth with an audible snap. For the first time Mellik felt like the Mage really looked at him. The tall man gazed down at him with eyes like the blue sky after a heavy snow: deep and beautiful, but cold.

"A very good question, neophyte," and the wizard smiled, but without warmth or humor. He bent down to look into Mellik's eyes, his face mere inches away. Mellik could not meet that cold blue gaze.

"A better question might have been: 'How can a Kamori survive the College?' But I will answer your question instead. **Obey**," the tall wizard glared into Mellik's face a moment longer and then straightened quickly.

"Behind that door are a series of rooms," intoned the Mage. "Each one will have at least two doors leading from it. None of the doors will open until the door you have come through is closed behind you. Once closed, the door you enter through will not open again. Just as in life, you must always go forward. Do you understand neophyte?"

Mellik nodded, wondering what neophyte meant.

"Good. Now, study each door carefully. I am told that you are proficient with the second sight?"

Mellik nodded again.

"Then you will need to use it. Many of the doors will glow with mana. Choose the door that seems to glow brightest. If you can't tell which is brighter, choose one that seems right to you or find some other way to decide between them. Once a door is opened, no other doors will open until you pass through and close the door behind you: so choose carefully."

The wizard looked down at Mellik like he smelled something foul in the air.

"Are you ready then?"

Mellik thought back through the instructions, trying to ignore the Mage's tone of imminent failure. Mellik couldn't think of how to ask a question without speaking, and then realized he couldn't think of a question to ask anyway. He nodded his readiness.

"Then begin," and the wizard gestured grandly at the door in front of Mellik.

Mellik reached for the handle and then briefly paused. What if this was part of the test? If it was, Mellik could see no other choice but to go through or disobey and ask another question.

The door swung open with a gentle push, and Mellik stepped through. Once again, he paused before closing the door behind him. Its hollow click sent a shiver up his spine. He was in a small, square room with a door centered on each wall, including the one he had just come through. The door he had come through had no handle or latch on the inside. The other three were plain, whitewashed wood, identical in every way, including the dull black iron handles.

He looked again at the identical wooden doors in front of him and to either side, and realized with chagrin that he had yet to embrace the second sight. Switching to the Mage sight came easily, and Mellik immediately saw the difference. Everything took on a brighter aspect. The normal look of the room was now overlaid with a sheen of glowing color. Each door had a distinct hue. The one across from him glowed with the deep blue of water mana. The door to his left was the golden amber of earth magic, and the one to his right shone with the shimmering grey haze of air mana. The door behind him also had a subtle glow of magic about it, but its color was a motley brew of many manas.

The doors to his right and left were definitely brighter. After a moment's study, Mellik decided that the golden earth door was the brighter of the two.

Opening the door, Mellik found a room similar to the one he was leaving. The room on the other side was probably twice as long, extending off to his left with a door at the end and two more doors on the wall across from him. He was tempted to look back one more time to make sure he had chosen the correct door, but the Mage had said his choice couldn't be undone. He stepped into the new room and shut the door behind him.

This time the doors across from him glowed purple and silvery grey. The one down on his left was brown flecked with gold, similar to the one he'd just come through. It was by far the brighter of the three. It was a relief to have the decision be an easy one, and Mellik strode down and went quickly through the glowing brown door.

More rooms followed the first two. All were similar, though some had two doors, others three, and once there were four. The rooms were small and uniformly rectangular in shape. Mellik lost his dread of picking the wrong path somewhere around the fifth or sixth room. Soon after that the choosing became routine. Mellik stopped in the middle of a bare, whitewashed room and tried to remember how many doors he'd come through. He couldn't remember. It seemed like he'd been choosing doors for a long time.

This testing seemed odder and odder. Great effort had gone into setting up this maze of doors and rooms. What did choosing one door over the next prove, and why make some doors glow so obviously brighter. Mellik hoped someday he might understand the reason and logic for this test. For now he could only keep moving forward, keep obeying.

Mellik moved through another door, barely noticing that it glowed a muddy green. The next room was different enough to make him pause. The doors were all laid out on the opposite wall, and there were five of them. This was the first time Mellik had faced a choice of more than three. To add to the uniqueness, the middle door shone brightly with a shimmering red.

Mellik reached out for the door shimmering just in front of him, and then stopped. It was definitely the door shining most brightly with mana, and therefore the one he should pick. Still, he hesitated.

It seemed wrong. The mana almost pulsed to his eyes, but with a movement that was more spiritual than physical. The image of a trapped lynx a neighbor had caught years ago gashed through Mellik's mind. Mr. Hoxil, their neighbor, had heard that rich people at the Capitol were paying good money for live lynx as pets, so he had put it in a wooden cage. Mellik had gone with the rest of the village kids to look. Most of them had seen a lynx before, but not from up close.

The animal had just laid there, perfectly still with its eyes barely open. But there had been a pent up energy, a contained violence waiting to happen. Mr. Hoxil had wanted to entertain the kids with his prize so he poked at the cat with a stick. The lynx still wouldn't move.

Finally tiring of his game, Mr. Hoxil bent over to pick up the cage. The lynx must have been waiting for just that. It twisted around and grabbed his index finger in its teeth. Hoxil straightened up with a howl, and the cage went flying through the air to crunch down against the hard-packed clay. The lynx squirmed out through the wreckage and sped off into the hills.

Mellik's mother treated Hoxil's finger. It had festered, and eventually she had to cut it off below the first knuckle. Mellik's father told him in private that it served Hoxil right: you never poke at a wild animal. "Kill it or leave it alone," he'd said.

This door was that lynx: wild and full of pent up energy waiting to explode in violence.

Mellik remembered something Master Arbret had told him. They had almost reached the desert, days before Arbret was killed. He had grown more stern and yet more open with Mellik those last few days. They'd been riding on the cart, with Bo walking along side. The only sound had been the cart's wheels and the horses' hooves on the rutted road.

"Magic is not a science," Arbret had announced into that silence. "It is not like adding rocks and sticks or learning to spell. It is an art form, by which I mean it is different every time for every person.

"Magic is making the impossible real. To do that we tap into the very stuff of chaos and bend it to our will. But chaos does not follow any rules, and when it acts the same, you will not know for how long. There is only one way to become an old wizard: trust your instincts."

A lone cricket began to chirp out in the sparse grass.

"You, more than most, will have to feel those instincts and get to know and trust them quickly," Arbret never looked over at Mellik as he was telling him this. His eyes were distant and focused on something beyond the path ahead. "Many of your teachers at the college will not care if you fail. Some may actively try to discourage your progress. A few may even wish you dead."

Arbret looked over at Mellik with bloodshot eyes, "Be careful, be suspicious, and trust your instincts."

In Mellik's memory, Master Arbret looked like some crazed soothsayer. Maybe he had been. Two men he trusted were telling him not to open the door. The only voice telling him to go through it was a man he'd barely met who obviously had a dislike for him. He would trust his instincts and the men who had taught him most of what he knew.

Mellik walked down to the end of the room, where a door shone a cooler, more welcoming sapphire that was brighter than all but the red one With a deep breath, Mellik turned the latch and pushed open the door.

On the other side, Mellik could see a long table in a C shape with seven people seated on the outside. Two were looking toward him. Mellik recognized one as the man who had come to his aid in the hall. Another was the man who had met him inside the first room.

Then a warm wind that roared and billowed lifted him from his feet, throwing him towards the wizards. Mellik's head snapped back, and he saw no more.

Chapter 17

Master Myg looked down at him and smiled.

Mellik felt the soft pillow under his head and recognized the look of the ceiling behind the healer.

"How long was I out this time?" asked Mellik.

Myg chuckled, "Less than a day this time. There's hope among the other Masters that you may go an entire week without needing my care."

"What happened, Master?" Mellik asked. He remembered stepping out of the last room in that odd maze, and then nothing.

"You will have to ask someone that was there," replied the tall, lanky wizard. "There was a fire, and you were very lucky to come out of it virtually unscathed. You are burned, but it's a very light scalding, not much worse than a moderate sunburn in most places. You have a few spots of blistering, and there is a cream by the bedside that will help soothe any pain. It will also help the skin recover, so use it liberally -- we have plenty.

"The one thing I want you to especially tell me about is if you have any dizziness or headaches. You punched your head through a wall. That's what actually knocked you out. Now, how do you feel?"

Mellik took a moment to think about it.

"Not bad, Master. Stiff, thirsty."

Myg laughed again. "I'll take that as a good sign. We'll keep you abed today and keep an eye on you. I suspect by tomorrow you'll be up and around. We've got to get you on your feet for more than half a day if you're ever going to learn anything here."

"Yes, Master. Thank you."

"Now, one of the other Masters has some questions for you. I'm afraid we can't put this off, but I'll send him in with some soup and that fruit juice you like so much."

Mellik thanked the Master again as he stood to go, but Myg waved away his thanks.

Mellik only had a moment to wonder who this other Master was when the door swung back open, and the portly, red-faced Master who had come to his rescue in the hall walked in.

"Hello," the Master said, sliding a tray with soup, bread, and a glass of juice onto his lap as Mellik scooted himself into a seated position.

"My, your face is as red as mine," the wizard commented before Mellik could return his greeting. The Mage leaned in closer. "I think the color might suit you better.

"I am Master Jacoby Vai," and the wizard held out his hand.

"Master Vai," said Mellik, taking the proffered hand with his own. "Mellik Ackins."

Jacoby Vai -- the name sounded **so** familiar to Mellik.

"I am the head Master of the School of Enchantment.

The name suddenly clicked for Mellik. Jacoby Vai was one of the wizards Arbret had told him he could likely trust at the college. Mellik relaxed a little.

"Go ahead and eat, Apprentice Ackins," the wizard waved at Mellik's food as he grabbed the lone stool in the room to sit by Mellik's bedside. "Ostensibly I'm here to ask you some questions, but as my students will tell you, I'm likely to do most of the talking."

Mellik gulped down most of the juice before taking a large bite from the roll.

"What would you like to know, Master?" He asked around the chunk of bread.

"Well, let's start with that last room in our little maze. Tell me what you did and noticed right up until you blacked out."

Despite the wizard's earlier statement, he listened attentively as Mellik described coming into the room, the bright red door, and some of his reasoning for not going through it. He told about the feeling of being lifted up off his feet by a warm breeze and then blacking out.

"Humph," the Mage commented at the end of Mellik's tale.

"Probably not much you can add to what we know. Did you see the door at all as it released its energy?"

"No, Master," he replied with a shake of his head.

"We'll, that's as it is. I suppose you're probably curious as to exactly what happened?"

Mellik nodded his head around a mouthful of bread too big to talk around.

"It seems someone set a trap for you. They assumed correctly that you'd follow the doors with earth mana to that side of the maze. We're not sure if they fudged the results by making some doors more magical than intended. Much of the room was destroyed in the fire.

"From what I saw, two things kept their plan from succeeding. The first was you choosing the wrong door. They'd layered on enough magic they must have been sure you'd go through the middle one. The blast alone likely would have killed you if you'd have stood right in front of it. The second was that little trinket you have at your waist."

Mellik reached under the covers and found that he was indeed still wearing the belt and buckle Arbret had enchanted for him. It had saved his life twice already.

"That little buckle is actually why I'm here," continued Master Vai. "I convinced the other Masters that it was continuing to protect you from the heat of the burns that got through its protections. They agreed to leave it with you until you awoke and appeared out of danger. Now obviously that time has come."

Mellik's hand clenched protectively around the belt buckle beneath his sheets. Arbret had enchanted it with fire magic because that's what the Mage had been good at, but he'd done it to hide the magic of the ring of his forefathers. If they studied it, Mellik knew they'd find the ring inside. The ring of Kamori kings that would surely mean his death.

"Oh, don't worry," said Vai blithely. "The belt and buckle will be returned to you. But all such things must be studied by the enchanters. Some items can be dangerous in untrained hands.

"You still look like you doubt me," commented the wizard, frowning down at Mellik. "I trained Arbret in enchantment you know. If the empire hadn't needed combat wizards so desperately, I could have made a decent enchanter out of him. They ruined the boy, if you ask me. I'm glad it was him that found you. They always underestimated his potential."

"He saved me and Bo's life."

"You should say Bo and I, and as I said, he was underestimated. Now, about that buckle..."

Mellik gripped harder at the buckle, wondering what to do. Should he try to run? Master Vai held out his hand, and in it was a small bag of black leather.

"This is a deadwood bag."

"Deadwood, Master?"

"Yes. You see, this leather was stripped of all its mana in some catastrophic event. When a material or item is stripped of mana, we call it dead. Take a look with your second sight."

Mellik switched to his third eye and looked at the bag with his mage's vision. Where the bag should be, there was only blackness. Mellik had taken for granted how much color and light everything contained when viewed with the second sight. This was the first thing he'd ever seen with absolutely no glow of mana about it. Even the air glowed with a thin, fog-like mana. This bag seemed wrong: out of place in this view of the world.

"I inherited this silly bag with my position," commented Master Vai. "Dead wood, stone, and especially metal are highly valued because they can ignore any magic they are brought up against. Highly effective against that enemy Mage with a shield of air or an opposing general with enchanted armor.

"But this leather bag is too small to be used for protection and too light to be any kind of effective weapon. Really, its only possible application would be to put some small magic item in it. In all my years with this bag up on my shelf, I have yet to find a situation where that would be useful. First you would need a reason to hide a magical device, and then it would have to be small enough to fit inside. Plus, any properties of that object would not be useable while in the bag.

"Now, I know it doesn't seem like much, but I thought I could offer you this bag," and Vai stretched out his hand with the bag to

Mellik. "Call it payment for letting me borrow that belt of yours for study."

Mellik still clutched the belt with one hand, but with his other he reached out to gently grasp the small bag. Arbret had told him he could trust this man. Was the Master really offering him an even more secure way to hide the ring of his people?

"Looks like you could use some more juice and bread," the Master commented, picking up the mostly empty tray. "I'll go find you some while you think it over. You can pull that belt off while I'm gone."

Master Vai left, closing the door softly behind himself.

Mellik sat staring at the door, assuring himself that he was indeed alone. Finally, he turned his back to the door and pulled his belt out, letting his body shield both buckle and bag from anyone coming back in.

Feeling along the back of the gold buckle, Mellik found the small seem that marked out its hidden catch. With a gentle push, the back of the buckle popped open, and the ring of Kamori kings rolled out onto his palm.

Mellik had never released the second sight, and he was struck again by how beautiful the chunky globular gold ring looked with his third eye. The warm brown gold of its mana almost seemed to flow and pulse through the ring.

Mellik stopped admiring the artifact and slipped it into the small leather bag. Cinching the leather drawstring, the warm life of the ring disappeared in blackness. Mellik turned the bag over and over in his hands, but no hint of the ring's magic leaked out that he could see. The bag was only a bit larger than the ring itself, and Mellik wondered what small piece of magic it had originally been made for.

By the time Master Vai returned, Mellik had placed the small deadwood bag with his ring beneath his pillow, and the belt and buckle lay on his bedside table, the buckle's hidden compartment now closed again.

Master Vai glanced at the belt and buckle.

"I take it you have decided to accept my offer?" he asked.

"Yes, Master."

"Excellent. Then I have one more gift for you. That bag of black nothingness shows up just as obviously with the second sight as that red ball of energy you call a belt buckle. I made this little pouch to make it a bit more inconspicuous."

Master Vai pulled a small, white silk bag out of his pocket and held it up for Mellik's inspection. Mellik switched back to the second sight again to see that it was a mix of manas: primarily water and fire.

"Remind you of anything?" asked the Mage.

Mellik slowly shook his head.

Master Vai languidly twirled the small bag about his index finger and then brought it to rest against his right cheek.

"And now?" he asked.

Now Mellik saw it.

"It's like the mana of a person." Mellik said in delight.

"Yes, but if you look at it carefully, you'll notice it lacks the flow and pulse of a living creature, so it will only stand up to a cursory examination. Not that you'll likely need to hide anything here at the college, but something fun for you to have in exchange for your help nonetheless."

Master Vai placed the small bag on the tray with the bread and cup of juice he'd brought in. He picked up the belt with his free hand and slid the tray in its place.

"Now, one last thing before I go."

"Yes, Master?"

"You killed that sandsnake north of the college?"

"Yes, Master."

The wizard was turning the belt buckle over and over in his hands, not really looking at Mellik now as he spoke.

"The armorer here at the college has the remains. By law, whoever kills a sandsnake has rights to the carcass. The skin, teeth, mane, and even the bones are worth quite a bit. Master Myg has excused you from lessons today, but he made no other restrictions on your activities. If it were me, I would pay the smith a visit."

The Master turned and slipped from the room so quickly that Mellik had no chance to even ask him where the smith might be located.

Chapter 18

Mellik had to gather his courage to ask an apprentice for directions to the blacksmith's. The directions had been very simple. After finding the exit from the healer's wing, Mellik had simply to follow the path downhill through the lush gardens and then find the large cavern that served as the gate to the crater and the college.

Mellik stood just outside the small shelter to the left of the gate where the smith was at work. He wasn't sure how to approach this ox of a man. The smith had been striding from one side of the smithy to the other, turning this and checking that. Now he had finally pulled something out of the large forge full of orange coals and was beating at it on a small anvil. Mellik could see what he thought must be the skull of the sandsnake he had killed hanging to one side of the forge.

The big smith wore a thick leather apron that covered his neck down, but his arms and back were bare. Mellik could see sweat dripping from the muscles rippling along his shoulders and neck. Reaching some juncture with the piece he was hammering on, the smith gave it a cursory examination, then shoved it back into the forge with a grunt. The man took off his apron with a practiced flip. Grabbing a rag and a large pitcher from a table, he turned toward Mellik.

"I know there must be more entertaining things to watch up at the college, so I assume you're here for some other reason," he commented and then he took a long swig from the pitcher as he toweled off his chest with the rag. The man spoke with an accent that Mellik didn't recognize; all sharp edges and thick vowels -- like he was spitting out gravel.

"Uh, yes Ma..sir," stammered Mellik. "Uh, I'm the one that killed the sandsnake."

Mellik gestured at the huge skull hanging from the rafters.

"Congratulations," the smith commented. "Was that it?"

"I was told that the carcass was mine; by law," explained Mellik.

"Is that so, apprentice?" The smith said apprentice like it was a bad word, looking Mellik up and down. "Were you also told that the price of skinning, curing, and hauling the beast must be negotiated ahead of the work being done? Not many men know how to properly cure a sandsnake, and it's expensive work. On top of that I had to hire a crew to haul it here and help me skin it, plus I ruined a dozen good blades in the process.

"If you're claiming the beast, then you owe me for all of those expenses, plus my fees. Do you have those monies, *apprentice,* or should I report you as a negligent debtor and have the imperials haul you off?"

Mellik took a step back, stunned by the smith's threat. Something about this didn't seem right. Surely Master Vai wouldn't have sent him here if he didn't have some rights to the sandsnake skin.

Something about the smith's tone tickled a memory in Mellik. The smith's attitude and words didn't seem to fit. He didn't look angry or threatening, and he stood casually, the hint of a smile on his face. Mellik remembered. It was like when a tinker came through town, and his mother would barter for things she wanted. The words and even tone might seem heated at times, but there was a good-natured play about it that Mellik had always found fascinating.

Mellik took a step forward and extended his hand, "I'm Mellik Ackins."

The only bit of advice on bargaining he could remember was that his mother would always introduce herself and pour a cup of tea. She had said it was harder to cheat someone you knew and had showed you a kindness.

Mellik became worried when the smith just looked at his outstretched hand for a moment. One blow from that huge arm would cause Mellik's head to come tumbling off his shoulders.

Finally, the smith strode forward and accepted Mellik's outstretched hand.

"Fainar Kaleed."

"This is obviously thirsty work. I have some fruit juice back at the college if you'd like."

The smith gazed across the crater bowl and shook his head, "I might die of thirst before you returned. Good to meet you, Mellik." The smith turned and headed back into his smithy.

"It was my master that sent me to talk to you," Mellik called in desperation.

The big smith turned only his head.

"And who is that," he asked.

"Master Jacoby Vai."

"The enchanter eh? Prove it."

"Well, he gave me this pouch, but..."

"Okay then," and the Smith motioned for Mellik to follow him. "I've got to finish this piece, or I'll have to start over. You can talk to me while I work."

Mellik hustled after the big man.

"Sit there," and Kaleed jabbed a finger at a stool. "Don't move, and don't touch anything."

Mellik sat and watched as the smith put his apron back on and pulled the twisted piece of metal out of the coals.

"So what do you want?" asked Kaleed. He began hammering on the piece with a smaller hammer, twisting and spinning it as he worked.

"How did you know the pouch was enchanted?" asked Mellik, unable to control his curiosity.

"I can see it," and the big man paused his hammer to glance back at Mellik.

"So you're a Mage?"

"You don't have to be a Mage to have the third eye. Granted, most who can see it can use magic, but there are plenty of others like me, that can't. Now, are we going to discuss the sandsnake carcass?"

"Well, what do you think would be fair?"

"I did all the work. I'll tell you what: I'll give you that skull as a trophy. The teeth and fangs are some of the most valuable pieces. I'll take the rest as payment for my work."

Mellik was in a quandary. He had no idea what any part of the giant snake was worth or what he should be asking for. Even if he knew what the snake was worth, he didn't know what the services of a smith cost.

"I want half," Mellik finally announced. "Half of each part of the creature. Half the hide, half the mane, one of the fangs - everything that you kept from the animal. That is more than generous since without my friend and I there would be no sandsnake to skin."

Mellik had an idea and plowed on before the smith could interrupt, "Further, you will fashion each of my parts of the creature into an item of my choosing."

"Bah, I don't need to do none of that," guffawed Fainar.

"When my father has the thatcher fix the roof, the thatcher doesn't claim the house as payment," commented Mellik. "Nor does the thatcher come over without asking and then expect to be paid. That sandsnake was mine and my friend's."

Mellik stopped, as the smith was staring at him from beneath his brows, the piece of iron laying forgotten on the anvil. Mellik was afraid he might have gone too far.

"Good, apprentice Mellik," said Fainar. "No one deserves anything they are not willing to fight for.

"Now, for someone who obviously doesn't know the law or what a sandsnake is worth, that was generous. On the other hand, you have no way to sell it or keep it from decaying into uselessness, so I could probably rob you for far worse by making you pay me later for those services. So I accept, but with a few additions to the agreement.

"You are new to the college, I take it?"

Mellik nodded his head, wary of what the smith might be leading to.

"And another apprentice helped you kill the snake and will be sharing in your portion?"

Mellik nodded again.

"What's their name?"

Mellik thought for a moment before deciding not giving his name would be rude. "Bo."

"I do not have an apprentice right now, and I have plenty of work to do for the college. If you want finished items that you can sell or use, then you will have to make them. You will work for me here until you are skilled enough to work the materials properly. You and this Bo if he wants his share."

"But we are apprenticed to the college of magic," protested Mellik, sliding off the stool onto his feet. "We can't apprentice to you too."

"I don't need an apprentice to help out around here," grumbled Fainar. "Just hands willing to work and do what they're told. The college always gives a couple hours of each day to physical labor for the apprentices. I'll tell them I want you and this Bo to do your work here. And it's work you'll be doing here, make no mistake. You look like a farm boy, and that can be hard work. This will be harder. You've got some muscle on ya - this will grow 'em bigger. We got a deal apprentice Mellik?"

Fainar held out his thick, calloused, and scarred hand.

"We've got a deal, Master Kaleed."

*   *   *

Mellik worked at Fainar's forge for more than two hours that day. Mostly the smith had Mellik work the bellows, which was plenty hard enough. The big man rambled on about exactly what he was doing and why he was doing it. Fainar was an easy man to work for, with generally mild corrections, and he was patient as Mellik learned to work the bellows to produce coals of just the right color. Mellik rested in between pumping the big bellows. His arms, legs, and back all ached from trying to keep the orangey-yellow glow Fainar wanted. The heat stung at the burns on his face and arms, but the smith kept him working so hard he would often forget about them.

"I could use a break," Fainar announced, just as Mellik was wondering if his arms would last much longer.

Fainar dropped the pick head he had been working on in the barrel of water to quench it. From another barrel of water, the smith scooped two wooden mugs and brought them sloshing over to one of his cluttered work tables.

"Sit," he said and slid one mug toward a stool opposite him.

Mellik resisted the temptation to simply collapse on the sandy floor and stifled a groan as he climbed up onto the stool.

"Is this Bo as strong as you?" asked Fainar.

Mellik blushed slightly at the compliment.

"He's much stronger," replied Mellik, thinking of Bo's large frame and tireless, upbeat attitude. He wondered if he should mention Bo's deafness, but decided he'd tackle that when he had to.

"That's good. Sometimes you apprentices can be worthless. You don't happen to have a talent for fire do you?"

"I don't think so. My testing was kind of interrupted."

"I heard there was a fire. I take it that was not of your making," and the big man gestured to Mellik's arms.

"No," Mellik rubbed at his arm, remembering. "There was some kind of accident, I guess."

Fainar reached a long arm up to the rafters above the table and brought down a small clay jar. He slid the jar over to Mellik.

"Here. The healers keep me supplied with burn ointment. In this heat working the forge, you'll need it to keep the skin from drying up and cracking even with the work they've put in healing you up."

"Thank you, Master Fainar. I do seem to have an affinity for earth magic, if that's helpful. It comes from my Kamori heritage."

Fainar leaned in and studied Mellik's face. "So that's what those lines are. I thought they might be some kind of tribal tattoo, like the Errity wear. Earth magic? . . . Stay here."

The smith popped up and jogged through a leather curtained doorway into the crater wall. Mellik heard steel and wood being shuffled about, and then Fainar returned with a pair of daggers clutched in one big hand.

"What's the difference between these two blades," asked the smith as the weapons tumbled onto the table in front of Mellik.

One was longer than the other, and the shorter one had a handle of horn, while the other was wrapped in metal wire. The way Fainar had asked made Mellik guess that the real difference lay deeper.

Switching to his second sight, Mellik picked up the two blades and held them up, away from the table and all the tools and paraphernalia of the forge.

At first, both daggers looked the same. They had the dark, golden brown that Mellik had come to know as good blade steel. The blade with the wire-wrapped handle seemed just slightly brighter than the horn handled one. Mellik tried to look closer, trying to see what gave that blade its brighter glow - the greater concentration of earth magic.

"The knife with the wire handle is brighter," said Mellik, finally giving up.

"But why?" asked Fainar. "And don't tell me it has more earth magic in it. I can see that for myself."

"I don't know," Mellik admitted after briefly looking again. "I've never really studied metal that much."

Fainar harrumphed in exasperation.

"Well, just hang on to both of those," the smith said. "Maybe you'll eventually see something I can't. Don't lose that wire wrapped one though, or I'll be taking its price out of your share of the sandsnake."

Fainar was looking behind Mellik as he said this. Mellik turned to see Keyessa walking into the smithy.

"Has he been bothering you, Master Fainar?" she asked without even glancing at Mellik.

"On the contrary, he's been helping me," replied the smith. "I take it you magicky people need him now."

"Yes," replied Keyessa. "Master Myg wants to check him one last time before he's put into the apprentice dormitory."

"We're done for now," said Fainar, turning to Mellik. "You might be busy over the next couple of days before they send you back to me. If you have some time, bring Bo by so I can meet him. And don't forget to study those knives."

The smith turned and walked back to his forge without another word. Mellik smiled. Myg and Vai had been friendly, even kind, but they were both master magicians: exotic and so far above him as to be unapproachable. Working with Fainar had felt good in a way he hadn't felt since leaving his family months ago.

"Well come on then," huffed Keyessa. "You can't keep a master waiting."

Mellik plucked up the two daggers and turned to Keyessa.

"After you milady," he said and swept her his best courtier's bow.

Keyessa snorted and stomped off back toward the other side of the crater.

Chapter 19

Mellik dressed with a grin on his face. The second thing he'd found when Keyessa had shown him his new room was a stack of three new or well mended sets of clothes in apprentice tans and whites. There had even been a new pair of leather sandals.

What really put a smile on his face, however, were the splashes of stars and flowers that kept popping up from the other side of the room. He had a roommate: Bo. He had assumed since waking up at the college that he and Bo would be split up.

Mellik had almost been able to excuse Keyessa's condescending tone yesterday when she had patronizingly explained that new groups of apprentices were always put together, and since he and Bo had arrived months ahead of any other recruits, they would be roommates.

There was also a slate board on the wall just inside the door with their daily schedules. Mellik was both nervous and excited to finally begin his formal instruction. Mellik and Bo had different schedules, and Keyessa explained that a bell would announce the hours. She herself would be guiding Bo his first few days to make sure his lack of hearing didn't become an issue while he was becoming orientated.

There were two more slates with rough, hand-drawn maps showing the main areas of the school. Keyessa had explained that the color of doors was very important. White doors were apprentice rooms. He and Bo could only enter their own room, which had "A211" carved into it. Grey doors led to common areas like the dining hall, the apprentice communal area, and most of the classrooms. They could enter any of these areas, but they should have a reason for being there. All other door colors were off limits to Mellik and Bo unless invited or instructed to enter by a Journeyman or Master. Bo asked about a rainbow door, which made Keyessa laugh, and Mellik quipped about a polka-dot one, but apparently that wasn't nearly as funny.

Only the hall names were on the map, but Keyessa had explained that the doors were in numerical order with even numbers on one side and odd numbers on the other. Once he had the right hall, it should be easy to find the room he needed.

Mellik took one of the maps down and studied it. He'd looked over the map and planned out his route at least twenty times the night before, but he did it one more time this morning. Mellik was sure he'd memorized the map by now, but when the 7 o'clock bell rang, he still felt unprepared.

Mellik got up and looked over at Bo. Bo smiled at him and cupped his palms where a prickly red fruit appeared. The sword fruit was one of Mellik's favorites, so he was sure Bo meant to reassure him, but Mellik couldn't help but remember that the stalks of the sword fruit were sharp and dangerous, and the base of the plant was a favorite home to the deadly dream vipers.

Mellik heard the bell-like tone ring out from the hallway seven times. It was time to go. He turned to Bo and tried to make a smile he didn't feel. Bo returned a more genuine one and made shooing motions with his hands. Mellik guessed Bo was right - not that he had any choice.

The hall outside was empty. The rest of the dormitories in the hall were empty, waiting for the new apprentices. Mellik could hear the muted sound of feet and voices from the direction he should be heading. Keyessa had said the complex was large and apprentices were allowed ten minutes to get to their assigned class or duties. Mellik had only the chalk map to go by so squandering those minutes on hesitation was foolish. Putting his head down, he walked quickly toward the hall's intersection.

There were other apprentices walking by that intersection now. Mellik ignored them, keeping the directions he'd memorized in his mind: left at the first intersection, passed two more crossings and a right at the third. Mellik knew he was being looked at. He also knew that more than one of the jostlings he suffered were likely intentional.

The hall he was in now seemed to be a main one, wider than the others. The corridor forked, and he took the path on his right and then went down a wide set of stairs. At the bottom, four corridors led away and Mellik took the one to his right again. A slight curve reminded Mellik of the hall he'd been in the other day. Had it really only been two days ago? Mellik idly wondered if this was the main area of classrooms, or if there were this many apprentices elsewhere. They skipped, jostled, and laughed their way past him on either side. Today, Mellik saw no black clothed journeymen, or brightly colored masters.

The door he wanted was the second on his right, number: 21. The doors here were all grey, so Mellik entered. A short hall led to three more grey doors; 211, 212, and 213 -- one on each wall. Mellik tried not to think of the similarity to his testing as he opened door 211.

A big room lay within, and then the smell of charred wood struck him. Mellik looked in and saw a line of doors, in a wall interrupted by a large area of charred and splintered debris.

"I apologize," said a familiar voice, and Mellik looked over to see Master Vai standing a few strides away from the rubble.

"I meant to meet you in the hall, but got caught up in my examination of the accident and lost track of time."

The master strode over to Mellik.

"Are you alright?" he asked

Mellik had to drag his eyes away from the charred rubble where he had had been knocked unconscious the other day.

"Healer Myg said I was fine. Do you really think it was an accident?" asked Mellik.

"Don't ever forget the 'Master', apprentice Mellik. If Arbret taught you nothing else, he should have taught you that."

"I'm sorry, Master Vai," and Mellik gave a deep bow. "He did, and I should not have been that distracted . . . or rude."

"Apology accepted, Apprentice. Just remember that many of the other Masters will not be so forgiving."

Vai looked sternly down at Mellik, his eyebrows furled and his face scowling, but a smile couldn't help but twitch at the corner of his lips, and Mellik was forced to smile in return.

"Good," said Vai on seeing Mellik's smile. "Now as I was saying, I'm sorry, but it was decided that you should be interviewed about the incident here while it was still fresh in your mind. Since the trap was set with an enchantment, that job has fallen to me.

"And to answer your question, we here at the college may sometimes be blind and opinionated, but we are only rarely stupid. Of course we don't believe this was an accident. A cursory examination of the magical residue has already established that much," and the tall master waved at the rubble. "What we have to find now is the how, the why, and most importantly, the who.

"Now, as I said, I'll be conducting the interview, but for something this important, it was agreed that I would not be the only witness to your answers."

Vai reached into his robes and pulled out a cube slightly larger than his fist. It was shiny, like a piece of glass, but it was a pitch black that allowed no light to shine through.

"This is a scrying cube," explained Vai, holding it up to Mellik. "When I activate it, a larger cube in another room will show everything you can see from this cube, and they will also be able to hear us. Do you understand?"

It almost sounded like Vai was trying to warn Mellik of something. He would be careful.

"Yes, Master," Mellik replied, looking Master Vai in the eyes.

"Good. Then we shall begin."

The tall man strode to a small table set in the middle of the room with two chairs set in front of it. He motioned for Mellik to sit in one of the chairs, and he set the cube at the edge of the table. He must have done something with magic to activate it before coming to sit across from Mellik.

"Now, let's start with the very first thing you remember from that morning."

Mellik went through his day, trying not to characterize anyone too harshly while sticking with the truth. Master Vai prodded him along and made him explain more as needed. The explosion in the maze was something of an anticlimax to the interview, because all Mellik could remember was the heat and pressure of it along with a sense of being picked up and flung by a large hand. Vai wanted to know more about the mana he'd seen in the explosion and the mana in the door, but Mellik had seen so many doors that day. He could only recall a vague memory of earth mixed with fire magic.

"Okay, I think that's all," said Vai, leaning back in his chair with a sigh. He turned to address the cube on the table. "Do you have any other questions for the apprentice?"

Mellik fidgeted and tried not to look at the cube.

"No, I think that's all for now." The voice coming out of the cube made Mellik jump. For some reason he'd assumed the cube's abilities were one way.

"Well, that's done then," commented Vai, scooping up the cube and sliding it back into some interior pocket.

"Master, do you think you'll catch whoever did this?"

"To be honest, it's hard to tell at this point. There are a lot of people involved in setting up this room, and since you came earlier than expected, there were even more than usual. This was a fairly rudimentary temporary enchantment, so anyone beyond the most junior apprentices could have acquired the knowledge to place it, and because it was only temporary and caused a backlash of magical damage, it's impossible to see any kind of magical signature in what mana residue remains. On the bright side, when they try again, we'll be ready to catch them."

'**Again?!**' Thought Mellik.

Vai laughed, "I'm sorry. I've been told many times that I have a terrible sense of humor. We have already put safeguards in place to prevent a repetition of this event. The masters are all in agreement: it's bad precedent to allow anyone to kill the apprentices other than ourselves."

Mellik wasn't sure if that last comment was a joke either.

"Don't worry about that. We will take care of the attacker. **You** need to capture the attention and respect of the other Masters, or no one will care about keeping you safe.

"Now, follow me. I've had enough of the smell and look of amateur enchantments."

Vai turned and strode away so quickly that Mellik had to scramble to catch up. They exited by the same door Mellik had come in through, and Vai turned and went through the door to their left. He stood holding the thick wood door and motioned for Mellik to join him.

It was dark on the other side, and Mellik guessed it to be a very large room since he could not see the other side, and his footsteps echoed and bounced about the chamber. The footsteps had an odd, hollow sound, and Mellik looked down to see that they stood on a floor of metal lattice. He could just make out the dark stone of the wall behind them curving away beneath the metal floor.

"Let me show you our practice room," commented Vai, and a flair of brilliant blue light sprang from his palm.

It wasn't the size of the room that was impressive. Though large, Mellik had seen larger on his journey to the college. What took his breath away was its shape and makeup.

The room was the inside of a giant stone globe. The black gabbro rock had been carved into a perfect sphere. Looking at the wall closest to him, Mellik saw that the stone had been etched with runes and symbols that covered every inch of the rock's surface.

"This room is one of the greatest achievements in the history of magic." Mellik could hear the pride in Master Vai's voice. "Artisans and wizards worked for most of two generations to create this room: driven by the vision of a man who theorized what we could do here: Theorly Zelkin.

"That was back in the grand age of wizardry, when mages weren't too proud to work alongside blacksmiths, and they could make things like warm steel," and Vai tapped the floor with one booted foot.

Mellik looked down and saw that they stood on a walkway of woven metal that gleamed sharply in the magic light. The steel had patterns with runes worked into its latticework frame. The small metal bridge forked left and right immediately inside the doorway, and each fork ended at a gleaming metal globe. The globes were even more intricately laced with runes and patterns of gold. They stood out in stark contrast to the dark rock. Each cage had a round door hanging open on a hinge.

"The globes are a protection for those who use this room," explained Vai, following Mellik's gaze. "They allow mana to flow out, but not in. I'll tell you more about those in a moment."

Master Vai reached back and closed the door behind him, shutting them inside the huge room.

"First, we must speak frankly," and the master locked Mellik's gaze with his own. "There are people and forces that want you dead: and not just among our apprentices and journeymen."

Vai looked at Mellik expectantly.

Mellik thought of Lady Yew. She probably had only let him go, because she was sure he wouldn't make it to the college. Perhaps it had all been some sick game to her, and one she'd been sure she would win.

"Uh, yes Master."

"This room is magically shielded. No one can eavesdrop on us here," and Vai gestured at the rune carved walls. "So we may speak freely for a little time. Did Mage Arbret die trying to get you here?"

Mellik nodded.

"Lady Yew?" asked Vai.

Mellik nodded again.

"Then by now the Emperor knows you are here," Vai scratched at the small patch of hair on his chin thoughtfully, speaking as much to himself as Mellik as he paced back and forth on the short catwalk. "Not that it matters. Now or later, he would have heard of you eventually.

"Did Lady Yew think you were the prophesied Kamori?" and now Vai spun to face Mellik.

Mellik closed his eyes and tried to think back on exactly what she had said.

"Not exactly, Master" he answered. "She just said it was possible, and that she wanted to find out if I was worth the risk."

"Since you are here, I assume you satisfied whatever criteria she set?"

Mellik shrugged, "Maybe she changed her mind, Master."

Vai chuckled, "Maybe, but she's not here, so we will deal with what is obviously a more immediate threat that **is** here.

"Try not to go out alone. Some of us think it's possible you could be the one prophesied to defeat the Emperor. Do you know the prophecy well?"

Mellik nodded in reply.

"Good. Then you know that if the Emperor learns of you and thinks the same, he will attempt to destroy you. Your best defense is probably to stay beneath his notice, but that may not be possible.

"Be careful in all you do and especially what you say. His ears and hands infect this place. You can come to me if you must, but only in great need, otherwise you put us both in danger. Do you understand?"

"Yes, Master," Mellik replied as earnestly as possible.

"There are a few others who are also on your side, but they will reveal themselves in their own time."

Mellik decided not to tell the Master that Arbret had told him two of the other Masters who might help him.

"I advise you to never tell anyone that there is a possibility that you could be the prophesied Kamori," continued the Mage. "You need to stay alive, which means staying defensive. This brings me to why I've brought you to this room. We use this room as a safe place to teach and test students. The twin cages block most incoming magical energies while still allowing the slow absorption of mana.

"I'm supposed to be seeing what you already know so we can place you at the appropriate instruction level. I also want to try and teach you a little defensive magic while we have this time.

"Enough talk. We're wasting the little time we have. Enter the globe on your left and make sure to close all three latches."

Mellik walked to the globe. He could hear the tromp of his boots on the iron grating echoing from the stone. A softer set of footsteps mirrored his own, and he knew Master Vai was going to the other steel globe.

The door was ornate and designed to seamlessly blend into the surrounding magical patterns and symbols. It swung smoothly closed, and the three simple latches closed to secure it with gentle clanks.

"Now, look with your second sight if you haven't already. Pull in a comfortable amount of mana, but don't try to hold anywhere near your maximum."

Mellik no longer had to visualize his mana levels. He could feel the extra mana as a tingly warmth suffusing his body. He was a little surprised when he felt the warmth come in and spread out from his feet. He was used to it coming from all over, like his skin was absorbing it through the air.

"You might notice this room's mana is different," commented Vai. "The globes hold and convey a great deal of it, as do the stone walls, but they suck most of the mana out of the air around us. This makes channeling magic easier. You'll learn the theory behind it later.

"You will have to look past the cage of symbols and ignore them. They won't interfere with magic going out. It's very similar to looking at something far away and letting the closer things blur into nothing with normal vision. Can you do that?"

With the second sight the cage of symbols glowed like the sun off of water in the afternoon. Mellik couldn't even see the other globe. Mellik tried to do as Master Vai said and relax his vision, looking further out. He was surprised to find that it worked. The glow was still there, but with his second sight now focused elsewhere, it was like looking through a haze of golden fog. He could now clearly make out the other globe with Master Vai standing inside it. The room seemed even larger than he had first thought now that he was looking across it. He nodded to Master Vai that he had could see him.

"You can see me with the second sight?" asked Vai.

"Yes."

"Good. Some apprentices can struggle with that. Now, the globe blocks magic from entering, so you will have to project your defenses out through it and not just form a shield about your body. Some students find it helpful to put their hands right up next to the cage."

Mellik nodded his understanding but decided to try and project his defenses from where he was at. He had been told he would need to prove himself. Now seemed like a good time to start.

"There are more types of magic than there are colors in one of Bo's rainbows. If you know what type of magic is being used against you, you can block it with the correct counter magic. That's assuming of course that you're quick enough, that you know what the counter is, and that you can work the type of magic required to counter the attack. That's a lot of ifs.

"What I'm going to teach you today is the standard counter. You still have to be quick enough to use it of course, but it will work against most magics. What you need to do is form a shield of the five elements: earth, air, fire, water, and spirit in quick succession, over and over. You'll be slow at first, and some shields will be easier than others. I'll warn you again and again, but remember, don't go too quick too soon. Many an apprentice has died or been maimed by letting the pattern get out of his control, and has ended up releasing undirected, raw magic. I assume Arbret told you the danger of uncontrolled mana?" Master Vai didn't wait for an answer. "It might block the spell, but it could just as easily amplify it, not do anything, maim, or even kill you all on its own.

"Now, since we know you have a talent for earth magic, we'll start there."

Chapter 20

Mellik walked a few paces behind Master Vai down the crowded hall. He should have been frightened and wary from the Master's warning, but he was too excited from learning new magic to heed that small voice. He was having trouble obeying Master Vai's admonition to walk a few paces behind him like an apprentice should. He wanted to skip ahead and run. He hadn't realized how much he had missed Arbret's teachings. To be honest, Arbret hadn't been much of a teacher compared to what Master Vai had coaxed out of him in a few short hours.

Earth magic came to him naturally and he had called it up almost at will. He was surprised at how easily air came to him once Master Vai had demonstrated. Water was the first thing Arbret had taught him, and he was able to draw on his study of the belt buckle Arbret had enchanted with fire magic to channel fire. It had been spirit magic that made him struggle the most. They had spent most of the session just getting that right.

The magic globes had made it much easier. As long as he projected the mana just outside the globe he was protected from any mistake. That allowed him to relax and experiment until he got it right. In the end they had only enough time to go through the magic blocking sequence one time. Master Vai had let him use earth magic to block a few spells so he could get a feel for how quickly he needed to respond.

They were on their way now to the great hall. Master Vai told him that all meals for apprentices were served there except when a student was in the infirmary. The only time Mellik had ever eaten with anyone other than his parents was during the spring and fall festivals. He wondered if it would be like that.

There was a crowd of people around them now. Raucous laughter and conversation enveloped him. Mellik was swept along through an archway in the stone.

If the young apprentices in the hall had seemed boisterous, the din in the great hall was cacophonous. Dozens of long tables were arranged in neat rows, with benches on either side. The long tables were the only things in the room that seemed orderly. Boys jostled and joked with each other; some stood at the tables, while others sat. Mellik saw one young man standing on a bench proselytizing about something to those around him. Even the line to get food was a snaking, bulging, living thing that refused to maintain its form.

Mellik was almost knocked from his feet by a large boy coming in the door.

"Sit down or get in line, but get out of the doorway," the blonde boy commented. He glanced at Mellik's face and gave a start, but moved on without saying anything else and joined the food line. Mellik moved to join him.

There was so much going on in the room that Mellik was having a hard time focusing on any one thing. A different boy gave Mellik a light shove as he got behind in the line, and from then on he stuck to watching the boy's back in front of him.

The line moved quickly. Mellik copied the boy ahead of him and soon found himself holding a trencher with a piece of bread, chicken, a wedge of cheese, and an orange. A wooden cup of water completed his meal.

Mellik followed the boy to a table and was about to sit down when the boy rounded on him.

"What do you think you're doing?" The boy asked. "Go find your own table, weirdo."

The other boys already at the table snickered. Mellik turned away as he felt the blood rush to his face.

Motion caught his eye, and he looked up with relief to see Bo frantically waving to him from an almost empty table.

Only one girl sat across from Bo at the table, her back to Mellik as he approached. Mellik came around to sit next to Bo and saw it was Keyessa.

She looked up as he approached. Seeing it was him, she rose without a word and left. Her trencher had been empty, but Mellik didn't think that was why she'd left. Bo looked up at him and shrugged his shoulders to say that he didn't know the reason for her abrupt departure either.

As Mellik bent to place his trencher on the table, someone gave him a shove, and his meal went tumbling from the wooden board. The orange fruit and cheese wedge tumbled off the far side. Mellik heard the cruel laughter and knew who it was before his antagonist spoke.

"Stupid rock heads are clumsy too," commented Brin.

Mellik heard Brin's cohorts chortle appreciatively. Mellik ignored them as he slowly and carefully went around the table to collect his lunch.

He grabbed the fruit, which had rolled to one end of the aisle. He was just bending down to retrieve the cheese when a white booted foot came down and crushed it on the floor.

"Very cute," Mellik commented as he looked up.

Instead of one of the apprentices he had expected, it was a white haired man with a long, pointed beard in flowing silken robes of powder blue so light he had mistaken them for white.

"Do you know how to address a Master, Apprentice?" the man asked in a deep rumbling bass.

"Uh, sorry, I mean ye..."

"Stupid or ignorant makes no difference to me. You will report to my classroom after lunch for proper instruction. I am Master Pelliery. Clean this up."

"Yes, Master," Mellik managed to say as the man strode away.

He gathered all the crumbled cheese he could in the front of his shirt and sat down where Keyessa had sat a minute before, dumping the dirty cheese bits on the table.

Mellik quietly dug into his meal, not wanting to look up at the grinning faces he was sure to see. He wished, not the first time, that he could communicate more effectively with Bo.

Bo slid a slate tile in front of him. Written in chalk it asked, "Magic?"

The question brought back some of the wonderful feelings he'd had just moments before. Mellik grabbed up the piece of chalk next to the slate and wrote back, "MAGIC!!" with a drawing of a smiling face.

Bo grinned at him, and Mellik wondered where he'd learned the word. He was sure it wasn't one he had taught him.

"Is this where we freaks are sitting now?" chirped someone.

Two people walked up and slid their trenchers onto the table to either side of Bo. Mellik looked up and froze. One of them might have passed for a tall, thin human with sharp features, pale skin and platinum hair, except for the sheen of his skin. His face almost glowed with a diaphanous quality that seemed to catch and refract the light in the room. Mellik thought he could see the faint lines of muscles play under the boy's skin as he smiled down at him.

The second figure was the shadow to the other's light, and he could not have been mistaken for human. Fine scales the color of pitch covered his body, and he had an almost flat face except for a slight bulge and slits for a nose. Small ivory spikes shot back from his forehead like a flattened crown.

"You're a goblin," Mellik blurted out as the description from a story came to mind.

The creature opened his mouth to show a double row of needle-like teeth.

"Yesss, but I prefer be called Fesskah," and he extended a black clawed hand to Mellik.

The stories gave goblins a bad reputation as underworld lurkers who would rob, kill, and even eat a person. On the other hand, Mellik himself was an evil, stupid rock-head with enemies all about and few allies to speak of.

Mellik extended his hand and tried to ignore the smooth, cool feel of the goblin's hand and the claws at its fingertips.

"Pleased to meet you. My name is Mellik."

Fesskah's expression changed subtly and Mellik heard a chirping, fluting sound from the light-skinned boy. Mellik looked over and realized he was laughing.

"I'm sorry," said the boy, trying to contain his bird-like laughter. "That's Fess's little joke and you've turned it around on him for the first time I can remember."

"Mosst Humanz won't touch a goblin. The handsshake confussess them," explained Fesskah as he sat down next to Bo.

"Well, apparently most humans around here won't sit with a Kamori either," Mellik replied.

Fesskah showed even more of his teeth, "I may like you Kamori Human Mellik."

"My name is Querin," the other boy said, sitting and extending his own hand.

Mellik took the proffered hand and was surprised at the strength of the delicate fingers, but there was a lightness to the handshake as well. It was like gripping a butterfly that could bend iron.

"You won't get bothered for sitting with me?" asked Mellik.

"Mellik, my dear new friend," responded Querin, "With you here as a new and apparently favored target, I daresay our troubles will likely lessen considerably merely by your presence."

Mellik smiled, "You should pay me for my services then, just to make sure I stick around."

Fesskah reached over and delicately placed his wedge of cheese, pinched between two claws, on Mellik's trencher.

"That was a joke," Mellik commented, turning toward the goblin.

Fesskah gave a guttural, grunting laugh.

"I know. I do not eat cheeze. Conssider it a down payment on future prankss you will be enduring for me."

"If I thought it would keep them away, I'd give the cheese back," said Mellik, looking at his meal mournfully, and thinking about what had just happened.

"Don't let them perceive that it gets to you," Querin said. "It will only encourage them to do it more. Ignore them, and they will get bored and move on. It's what you humans do."

"You're not human?" asked Mellik.

Querin placed his hand over his heart, and his mouth went wide in shock, "You wound me, sir. I, as any intelligent and educated being could tell you, am an elf."

"Really?" asked Mellik. "I didn't think elves were real."

"So the goblin is recognized without comment, but I am left to defend the very existence of my race? No wonder you are ill liked."

There was a smile and a twinkle in Querin's eyes, and Mellik could tell he was being teased.

"I apologize from the depths of my soul, sir elf," Mellik said, trying to imitate the elf's manner. "I had read descriptions of goblins and Fesskah is so . . . well, I didn't know what else he could be. I am afraid I am less familiar with elves."

"I told you Goblinz were more famouss," commented Fesskah.

"Well, I suppose you can be forgiven," Querin said with a wave of his hand. "And as a gesture of good will, I will even foretell your future in these cheese crumbles."

Querin made a show of brushing the crumbs around, occasionally grabbing a few and letting them fall artfully in the midst of the swirled spatter of cheese. Finally, he looked up with a dour expression on his face.

"I see pain and humility in your future."

Mellik had been sure he was kidding, but his serious tone and bleak look made Mellik unsure.

"He's joking right?" Mellik asked Fesskah.

"No. Masster Pelliery iz a ssadisstic basstard. Let him ssee you cower and cringe, and it will go quicker."

"And do not be late," added Querin. "Master Pelliery will punish you again for any slight to his status. Grovel a little and suck up to him. He's a pompous, egomaniacal bastard as well. Now, who is your silently gawking friend here?"

Bo was sitting, staring at Fesskah. Mellik snickered slightly as Bo's mouth hung open slightly in awe. Mellik waved at him to get his attention.

"This is Bo," and he grabbed Bo's slate and wrote Fesskah and Querin's names on it with arrows to show who was whom.

Bo looked down and smiled, writing his own name in two big letters with an arrow pointing back at himself. Then he made his customary rainbow above his hands.

"Excellent," said Querin. He held out his own hands, and a fog sprang up above them, and then a small sun rose up from behind the mist, and the fog turned a golden hue.

Bo chortled and clapped noisily.

"You can do illusions too!" exclaimed Mellik.

"Apparently, I need to find you a tome on elves," commented Querin with a playful roll of his eyes. "It's the most common magic among the fae. Almost every elven wizard has some talent in illusion."

"Was that foggy place where you're from?" Mellik asked, thinking of the rising sun scene Querin had produced.

"No, that was my name."

"Querin means fog, or is it sunrise?"

"Both, and neither my new, uninformed friend. My full name is Querin dosh Mangank Fellicipole mo Kellientis. Roughly translated it means 'the sound of a forest meadow awakening to a new dawn shrouded in mist.'"

"Thatss why we call him Querin," commented Fesskah.

"It's beautiful," said Mellik.

"Maybe you will be worth defending, young Mellik," said Querin with a broad smile.

Mellik looked around the dining hall. "Are there other elves here?"

"No. In conquering our people, the Emperor required that there be at least one Elven Mage in attendance at his academy. I am currently the sacrificial fae for them to poke and prod."

"Is that why you're here also, Fesskah?" asked Mellik.

"No. External magicss are rare among my people. I came to be trained. They agreed to take me if I let them sstudy my people'z magicss."

"Your people have a special magic?" Mellik asked.

Fesskah showed all his sharp teeth as he pushed back the bench and stood. Suddenly he began to grow. His slim frame began to grow huge, bulging muscles. His snout elongated, and the small, needle-like teeth became huge, jagged canines in row upon row. He stood towering above the table now, almost twice Bo's height. The loose grey robe he'd been wearing now looked like a shirt coming down just to the tops of his thighs. The monstrous Fesskah looked down at the slack jawed Mellik and Bo, and gave a low, guttural laugh before shrinking down to his normal size and pulling his bench back up to the table. A hush had fallen around them, and the other apprentices seemed to make a point of not looking at Fesskah.

"Some goblins have a limited talent in self-transmogrify," explained Querin. "Not only is Fesskah particularly gifted in this area, he also can perform the external magics which are more common here at the academy."

"Thatss what I'm here for," added Fesskah.

Querin glanced at Mellik's empty trencher. "Say, if you're done eating I should give you directions to Master Pelliery's office. You don't want to be late."

Mellik glanced nervously up at Bo.

"He iz ssafer with you gone," commented Fesskah.

"Don't worry. We'll keep him company," added Querin. "We'll compare non-verbal notes on illusions . . . maybe show him what a naked female elf looks like."

Chapter 21

Mellik stood and fidgeted outside Master Pelliery's door. He was afraid he might interrupt the Master's lunch and dared not enter until he knew lunch was over. Fesskah and Querin had been very nice, but their concern over this master and their obvious reticence in coming with him had Mellik beyond worried.

The strange ringing tone announced the end of lunch, and Mellik immediately reached out for the door handle, yanking the door open in his nervous state.

"Master Pelliery," he said as soon as he was inside. "I'm extremely sorry."

The master looked up slowly and studied Mellik for a handful of heartbeats.

"You'll have to learn to be more specific, Apprentice," he finally commented. "Are you sorry for your rudeness in the dining hall? Are you sorry that you barged in like the bumpkin you were raised to be, or are you sorry you're late?"

"But Master, I'm not late. The bell just rang."

"And I told you to be here by the end of lunch. Since that bell signals the end of lunch, you are late."

"But you said to be here after lunch. I waited outside so I wouldn't interrupt your meal," explained Mellik.

Pelliery's bushy eyebrows came up as his lips curled down. Mellik knew he'd made a mistake.

"You have a problem with authority. You would stand there and tell me what I myself said, and you still obstinately refuse to use the title I deserve. You need a lesson in silence."

A strange crackling noise and a blue light threatened to draw Mellik's attention. Thinking it might be some king of test, he steadfastly looked at the Master's pristine blue-white boots and meekly said, "Yes, Master."

Pelliery did, however, look up at the sound.

"You've met my apprentice?" he asked, gesturing toward where the sound had come from.

Mellik looked up to see Brin grinning at him from across the room. He lounged in a chair, blue lightning playing about his fingers and lighting his face with a shifting azure glow.

"A showy thing, but not that useful since we have to touch someone with it. Only nature can make bolts shoot across the air," Pelliery said in a lecturing tone. "Of course, air magic has much more to offer. An unseen force to most, it's more malleable than water or earth, and more controllable than fire.

"For instance," and the master flicked a finger in Mellik's direction, and Mellik found himself flung up against the stone wall behind him. His head struck the wall painfully, but did not rebound off of it, as something held both his head and hands firmly against the stone. A heartbeat later, and Mellik realized something much worse: something held his mouth open, and that same something wasn't allowing breath in or out of his mouth or nose.

Mellik thrashed at his bonds for a moment, but though his heels slapped hard against the wall, and his hands clenched spasmodically, his head and arms were held tight.

"This will give you some practice in keeping your mouth still," commented Pelliery. "Interesting that air seems so soft and forgiving, and yet when held still, it's as firm as the hardest stone."

"Don't panic," Mellik's first teacher, Arbret whispered in his mind. "Focus and react."

Mellik went to his second sight and absorbed some mana. He tried to focus on absorbing the mana from his mouth, but nothing happened. He wasn't' surprised. Arbret had explained that you couldn't absorb what someone else controlled. He couldn't see the mana in his mouth, and couldn't turn his head to see his wrists, so he closed his eyes. Brin's smirking face had been disconcerting anyway.

"Now that could be dangerous, Apprentice," he heard Pelliery say. "How will I know when you pass out?"

Mellik ignored him and concentrated on the mana in his mouth. He could feel it sitting there, still like a rock, but it felt different, light, and like it wished to move and stir. Mellik could feel his lungs desperately pulling at the block of air. He fought the panic down, putting it away in a pocket of his mind, and instead thought furiously on how to wrestle control of the air from Master Pelliery.

The Master would be more skilled and more powerful, obviously, but the air wanted to stir and move. Only Master Pelliery's will kept it still. Mellik was closer to the air: he could feel it there, where the Master could only see it from across the room. That was it!

Mellik slouched down against the bonds on his wrists and face, letting them take his weight. He kicked his right leg up in front of his face, while pushing at the air mana in his mouth with his mind. He didn't channel to change it. He added to it and it started to move.

Mellik gasped in a huge gulp of air, flinging his head to the side so Maser Pelliery couldn't see his mouth. He felt the hold on his head and wrists disappear. He crumpled to the floor in a heap, wheezing and coughing; his face buried in the wall, his arms and legs twitching and flexing spasmodically.

"Not what I expected," commented Master Pelliery.

"Shall I return him to ta wall, Master?" asked Brin.

"No, Brin. I have a few questions for the Kamori. Please stand and face me, Apprentice Mellik," Pelliery instructed.

Mellik shook a little in fear. He stood and quickly scrubbed the tears from his cheeks.

Master Pelliery still sat, looking at him impassively. "Describe what you did to remove the gag," he ordered.

Mellik had thought the wizard would have already known.

"Uh, Master, I blocked your view with my foot."

"Obviously, you idiot, but what did you do after that?"

"Master, I, uh, just pushed on it a little."

"With what?"

"With magic, Master."

"For the love of chaos!" yelled Pelliery. "Are you a simpleton? Of course you used magic, but what type of mana did you push on it with? Do you understand the question?"

"Y-yes, Master," stammered Mellik. "I used air mana."

Pelliery stared at Mellik for several moments.

"Show me," he finally said.

"Yes, Master," and Mellik opened his mouth as it had been before.

"No, no, simpleton, just push some air around from your hand or finger, idiot. Unless Kamori can only channel looking like fools."

Anger began to overlay Mellik's fear. He clenched his jaw and held his hand out. He was tempted to try something fancy like Master Pelliery had done or something impressive like Brin's lightning, but he'd only channeled air a few times. Mellik settled for a simple stirring of the wind as he'd done before. This was much easier, as he could see the mana gather in his hand and then visualize the change to air mana as he expelled it from his palm. He was rewarded with a nice gust that billowed Master Pelliery's platinum hair and threatened to blow papers from the master's desk before the wizard calmed them without looking down.

"Interesting," Pelliery commented, steepling his hands in front of his mouth. "Today is the first time you have worked air magic?"

"No, Master. I channeled it one other time while testing my abilities with Master Vai."

"And I've heard you have some talent with earth magic. Have you done anything with fire or water magics? Healing?"

"I started with water magic, Master. I also tried fire and healing for the first time with Master Vai."

"Well, perhaps your initial teacher wasn't a complete dolt even if you are. You will report here every day after lunch for instruction. Come in after the bell as you did today."

Mellik's jaw hung slack in surprise.

Brin's surprise was more audible. "What, uh Master?"

"Even though he is addled, or simply prefers to look that way, this Kamori needs instruction in air magic. I will make sure he receives that training most thoroughly."

Pelliery smiled coldly, and a shiver ran down Mellik's spine. Brin echoed his Master's smile.

"Of course, Master," he said.

Pelliery turned back to Mellik. "Close your mouth and leave my room, Apprentice. I'm done with you for today."

Chapter 22

In some ways this had been an easy day. Mellik thought this as he held a water soaked rag up against his swollen cheek. He casually pulled some of the heat out of it and stored it in the belt buckle Arbret had left him. The cold rag took some of the sting out of the bruise, and Mellik had taken to keeping one on him for just such occasions.

After six weeks, he still dreaded his sessions with Master Pelliery. Though painful, today had at least been straight forward: just block or dodge the bludgeoning fists of air Master Pelliery had directed at him. Mellik could feel bruises on his shoulder, thigh, and hip, but the one on his cheek hurt the most, and he had learned from Master Myg that the cold would keep the swelling down around his eyes.

At least Brin hadn't been there. The big apprentice had gotten bored with not being allowed to participate or even talk while Master Pelliery "instructed" Mellik and had stopped coming regularly after the first week. Mellik didn't know if he still occasionally came out of boredom or cruelty, but those days were always worse. Master Pelliery saved his worst lessons for those days to entertain his apprentice.

In one way, Master Pelliery's ministrations were a good thing. Mellik didn't think the Master had ever truly meant to teach him about air magic, but the desperate use of it every along with watching the Master's deft magics rapidly advanced Mellik's skills. His ability with air magic was now almost as good as his earth magic.

He practiced with his cutting wheel whenever he had time in his room. Technically, apprentices at his level weren't supposed to channel without supervision, but Querin had told him the prohibition was more about not getting caught than truly avoiding the act. Understanding the way air worked and being able to control it had vastly improved his control of the disc. His movements with it were more precise and its spinning speed was noticeably faster. It was a very unimpressive weapon compared to Brin's lightning or the balls of fire he'd seen apprentices juggling, but it was what he had.

Today at least hadn't involved the air restraints or the gag. Whatever way Mellik found to supervene Master Pelliery's control, the Master would fix the next time. Twice Mellik had passed out from the lack of oxygen. Those days were the worst. Mellik would take the sharp blows over the helplessness any day.

One thing that kept Mellik going during those sessions was that he got to come out into the courtyard afterward and work at the smithy with Bo and Master Kaleed. As a bonus, Keyessa was teaching them all hand language to communicate with Bo. Mellik was constantly playing make-up because of his sessions with Master Pelliery, but it gave him and Bo something to do in the few minutes before succumbing to exhaustion and sleep at night.

Mellik was going through his vocabulary as he came up to the smithy. He looked up to see both Bo and Master Kaleed waiting for him: Master Kaleed with his habitual frown, and Bo with a smile even wider than normal.

Mellik looked around, "Master, where is Keyessa?"

Kaleed's face opened into his teasing grin.

"I gave the girl the day off. Today is between the three of us."

"Okay, Master Smith Kaleed," and Mellik returned the grin. "What is our secret task for the day then?"

Kaleed made a gesture with his hand that meant, *"bring."* Bo bounced over to a table and brought out a bundle wrapped in hemp linen.

Mellik suddenly knew what this was, or at least what it was made of. Whenever Master Kaleed didn't have an urgent order to finish, the three of them had been working on the sand snake skin. Bo had turned out to be handy with a needle and thread, so Mellik's part in the process had been relegated to the curing of the hides under Master Kaleed's directions. Since he wasn't even allowed to cut the pieces of sand skin for the pattern, Master Kaleed had gotten the cruel notion that "someone" had to be surprised by the finished product. Mellik didn't even know what they'd been making.

"*Done?*" Mellik signed.

"*Done.*" Master Kaleed signed back.

Mellik slowly, almost reverently unwrapped the bundle. The first thing he saw was the silky, golden hair of the snake's mane. Mellik took a moment to gently stroke the fine fur. It was the first thing they'd worked on, and Mellik had forgotten just how soft it was.

"Ruined five good blades just working with that fur. That something so soft could be so demonically strong; amazing."

Mellik nodded and lifted the rest of the material out of its wrappings. It was a cloak. It was a beautiful cloak. The golden tan of the sand lion fur covered the hood and the shoulders of the cloak, giving way to the snake's skin below. Master Kaleed had placed the burnt orange that ran down the snake's spine at either edge of the cloak, which ran from orange-yellow, to corn-silk, and finally to pale tan at the cloak's center. One of the snake's smaller teeth was set as the clasp.

"It's beautiful," murmured Mellik.

"It's more than that," replied Kaleed with pride. "Try it on, lad."

Mellik swung the cloak up over his shoulders and pulled up the hood. It was heavier than the wool one he'd left home with and just a little large.

"I made them big on purpose," said Kaleed reading his mind. "Boys your age often have some growing left in them. Also, you want room underneath for when you go someplace colder than here.

"The mane is stronger than all but the finest steel, and watch this," Kaleed grabbed a stick lying on a nearby work table and swung it at Mellik's head before he could do more than turn slightly away.

"Hey!" Yelled Mellik and then realized that he had barely even felt the stick's impact.

He looked back up, and Master Kaleed's grin was broad as the desert as he held the broken stick up for Mellik to see.

"The hairs stiffen when struck sharply," he explained. "I only had enough to do the top of the cloak, but it gives a stylish look to it. Even the snake's skin is tougher than the best boiled leather. Neither will keep your bones from getting crushed, so wear something underneath if you end up in a real fight.

"Sand snakes like to stay warm, so that cloak is as warm as any you'll find. Not good in this heat, but we're at the ass end of the Empire, so you won't be here forever and won't need a cloak while you are here.

"I had more of the skin, so I made up a couple of jackets for you and Bo," Kaleed gestured, and Mellik turned to see that Bo was holding a snakeskin jacket and modeling one of his own already.

The jacket wasn't as pretty as the cloak. Without the fur trim, the beige and yellow snakeskin seemed subdued by comparison. There were also beige pieces strapped to it in curved lines everywhere but the seams.

"I used the snake's rib bones to reinforce the jacket like brigandine armor," Kaleed explained, reading Mellik's mind again. "The bones become brittle when dry, so I coated them with goat tallow. I'll give you some tallow to reapply when you need to keep the bones from drying out too quickly. It'll stink, so I wouldn't keep those in your room."

"You made us armor, Master Kaleed?"

"I know. It doesn't fit the image of a grand imperial wizard, does it? You'll be a while before you can bend blades away with a thought, however, and the Empire is always managing to be in a war with someone. You can always sell them if you want. Some lord will pay a heavy coin to give this to their second son before he rides off with the cavalry."

Mellik looked at the lumpy jacket again. "I've never had money. Nothing to spend it on here anyway. If they make us battle mages it will be nice to be dressed in better armor than the lord commanders."

Master Kaleed gave him a slap on the shoulder that sent him stumbling forward.

"Good lad. And money's hard to spend if you end up a corpse. Don't let the tales fool you into false confidence: wizards die just like any other man."

An image of Arbret lying lifeless in a pool of his own blood on a moonlit dune came unbidden to Mellik's mind.

"Now, I've got a little surprise for ya," Kaleed said and pulled something from his pocket.

Mellik saw that it was a small sack made from the snake skin. He could tell that something heavy was inside. Master Kaleed held the bag out to him. Mellik took the bag and, with a glance at the smith, pulled open the draw string to look inside.

Confused, he carefully pulled out a piece of steel. Actually, it was several pieces of steel stacked together with sharp edges and points sticking out in a circle.

"Pull them apart," instructed Kaleed.

On a hunch, Mellik switched to his second sight and instantly recognized the cascading loop of earth mana that signified magnets. From experience with the material, Mellik gingerly slid the top-most piece of metal from the stack. It was a triangular flat blade, sharpened at each edge, and about the size of his palm. He could now see that there were five more triangles still stacked together.

Mellik put the stack back in the pouch and rested the last one on his right palm. He pulled in the smallest bit of mana and channeled at the triangle, not enough to push it up and into the air, but just enough to feel it rock back and forth in his hand as he tested the magnetic pull. It was different than the cutting wheel he had: it was larger and heavier, and the magnetic pushes and pulls were less centered. When he thought he had a decent feel for the thing he popped it into the air above his hand and started it spinning. To his surprise, controlling the magnetic blade was very similar to the small discs, once he had it spinning.

Mellik raised an eyebrow at Master Kaleed. The big smith gestured at a round of wood set on a work table near him and then moved out of the way. Mellik pushed the triangular blade away from him with a flurry of earth mana, and it shot across the space to bury itself a couple of finger widths into the center of the wood. Master Kaleed and Bo clapped.

"Very good," Kaleed commented. He grunted as he tried to pull the blade out. Grabbing a corner of his leather apron, he braced the round with his other hand and yanked the blade free. "That will be most effective."

"It's amazing," Mellik said. "But it's so different from the one Lady Yew used and gave to me."

Mellik's cheek ached a little with the memory.

"Hers was meant as a tool, not a weapon. Also, only a very few smiths are allowed the secret of making steel into a magnet. It is rare, and she likely didn't need it made that way so she used a lodestone instead."

Master Kaleed held the three edged knife in his hands, studying it like he'd never seen this thing he had created before.

"I've only heard of these before," he commented. "First time I've ever made one. In the capital they are called throwing stars. Some have four or more points. I thought three to be the correct number."

"They are wonderful, Master Kaleed. How much do I owe you for them?"

"And what would I do with gold or silver here, apprentice Mellik?" Kaleed echoed Mellik's earlier thought as he gestured around the crater. "They are a gift."

"Thank you, Master, I hope to someday repay you."

"A gift does not require repayment, but we are not done," and Kaleed motioned him to another workbench.

The big smith pulled a cloth away from what looked like a row of eight short spears. Each one was identical, with a square steel shaft that flattened to a short blade. Each little spear was a little longer than his arm and had a hole in the end opposite the blade.

"What are they?" asked Mellik. Bo had come up to look too, and made a questioning gesture with his hands.

"Nothing yet," Kaleed signed.

"Come, work," he gestured to both of them. He grabbed up all eight spears in his big scarred hands and strode over to toss them in the forge.

Both boys knew what to do and quickly donned their leather

aprons and gloves. Bo began to work the bellows, and Master Kaleed gestured to Bo that he wanted the metal spears as hot as Bo could get them. Mellik began gathering tongs and gloves for the smith.

"On the stump, not the anvil," Kaleed directed him. "And I'll need those throwing stars."

Mellik handed the pouch to Master Kaleed and then watched as the smith pulled them out of the pouch and set them on one end of the huge round of oak. Mellik had only helped the smith work metals on one of the anvils before, and had thought the big piece of oak just a convenient work bench for things like leather. Master Kaleed brought out a rough grey stone larger than his hand and a short, thick metal rod. On a hunch, Mellik changed back to his second sight. Both items were magnetic. Master Kaleed let the stars, the rod, and the lodestone snap in place as Mellik watched their earth mana mesh and then expand in strength. Master Kaleed took the jumble and carefully set them at one end of a line that had been seared into the top of the wood. Realizing he had work to do, Mellik turned to help Bo at the forge.

"No," commanded the smith. "Come here."

Kaleed walked to the other side of the oak round and squatted down, sighting along the burnt line. Satisfied, he stood and brushed off his hands. He walked up to Mellik and put a heavy hand on his shoulder. It was Kaleed's sign that he wanted you to pay attention.

"I will put the spear arms on the line. When I begin to hammer on it, you need to cool it quickly, but still keep the steel from getting brittle."

"I'm ready, Master."

They had been working on this exact thing for much of the last six weeks. Master Kaleed was not a Mage, but his ability to see magic allowed him to guide Mellik in the way steel reacted to heat, cold, pressure, and compression. Master Kaleed showed Mellik how to use magic to heat and then cool the metal.

Heating and cooling the metal had been easy. It had even helped just watching the way his belt buckle reacted to heat and cold. The buckle also protected him from excess heat if he got it wrong.

It had been much harder keeping the metal soft when it cooled quickly. It had taken weeks of watching to be able to see the difference in the metal's mana when it became hard and brittle versus soft or springy. Mellik didn't have words to describe it to Fess and Querin when he'd finally seen it. It was like a texture to the mana, but inside of it, not on the surface.

"Our people call it the Valinary properties of magic," Querin told him later. "There are five Cardinal Valinary directions. I don't know which one you are describing. Few wizards can see that deeply into magic. Maybe it's part of your Kamori background," explained Querin.

When Mellik asked Master Kaleed the next day, he'd shrugged and explained it as he worked.

"I didn't know if you would be able to see it, but I thought it worth the trying. The Valinary property you're seeing is called Bellkrum. All Valinary properties are either North or South. In this case North is hard, South is soft. It's said some fae can see all five and all dwarves can see Bellkrum. To answer your next question: yes, I can see it, and no, that's the only one I can see or know about. Now get back to those billows."

Mellik had worked for weeks to be able to change the Bellkrum properties in metals. It was almost impossible when the steel was cool and set in its form, but when Master Kaleed was working the metal and it was still hot, the steel's Bellkrum was in flux, allowing Mellik to nudge the piece in the direction he wanted; North or South, harder or softer, or keep it stable.

They had just started practicing the cooling and controlling of a piece's hardness the day before, and then only on scrap iron and small, cheap knives.

Kaleed glanced at the forge where the small spears were glowing almost white hot as Bo worked hard at the bellows.

"Are you ready?" he asked.

Mellik licked his lips and nodded in reply.

Kaleed grabbed one of his lighter hammers and a pair of tongs.

"When I raise the hammer, begin to cool the spoke. Remember

to keep its softness."

Mellik nodded again.

Kaleed grabbed one of the hottest spears and placed it along the line charred into the stump. There was a click as the magnets latched onto it. Kaleed raised his hammer just slightly over the piece and nodded to Mellik. Mellik pulled at the fire mana, absorbing it into himself. His belt buckle already wanted to pull at that mana, and it was easy to simply redirect it into himself. The trick was changing it to raw mana and then to earth mana, which he then streamed back out at the piece. He could change to earth mana's Bellkrum to slightly South, counteracting the metal's desire to stiffen as it rapidly cooled. Mellik kept an image of the piece as they wished it to be fixed in his mind's eye, overlaid on the actual metal.

Mellik had just enough attention left to notice that Master Kaleed was using a firm, but light stroke to tap at the metal. With each strike, the earth mana sprouted from the spear and then flowed back into it, getting thicker each time. The spear was becoming a magnet!

Kaleed continued to lightly hammer at the piece until it had fully cooled. He looked up at Mellik and grinned.

"Now don't be telling anyone what we just did. That's a craft secret and the master smiths guard it most jealously."

Mellik grinned back, "Yes, Master."

"Seven more to go. We'd best be at it before Bo's arms fall off and ruin the coals."

The rest of the spears were the same and got so easy that Mellik had to remember to use up the excess mana from the spears' heat. He used it to stir a breeze around Bo in between pieces. Bo smiled a thanks at him, and Mellik thought how nice it was to use Master Pelliery's lessons for something other than cruelty.

When they were done, Bo joined Mellik and looked down at the work bench with the eight short spears spread out on it far enough that they're magnetic fields didn't disturb their neighbors.

"But what.." Mellik began, but Master Kaleed shushed him with a gesture.

From his apron pocket Kaleed pulled out two small, metal half-moons hinged together. There was a deep groove running along the round edge of the half moons and four sets of holes on each one. Kaleed took a ball-peen hammer and some brass rivets and secured the small spears to the contraption by their short hafts. The smith checked that all the spears were secure and could pivot on the thick rivets and then held the completed device up to Mellik.

"Spin it," he said.

"Um . . . what, Master?"

"Spin it like your cutting disc, but can you spin it so it's spinning vertically in front of you?"

"I'll try, Master" and Mellik eyed the bunched spears dubiously. "Maybe I should hold it."

Master Kaleed handed Mellik the spears, and Mellik was surprised to feel that the smith had arranged their magnetism so that each one was pushing away from the two next to it. Eyeing the device more carefully with his second sight, Mellik also saw that the two half moons were magnets also. Experimentally, Mellik folded the half moons together and they snapped together with a click. The whole thing seemed more balanced and solid now. It was also **so** much bigger and heavier than his disc or the stars.

Mellik glanced around at the cluttered smithy and strode out from its shade to the clear path leading up to it. Mellik faced away from the smithy and balanced the thing in his right palm.

"Vertical," Kaleed called from the edge of the smithy.

Of course he was right. If he spun it this way he'd likely cut himself, even if he got it right. Mellik grabbed hold of the round center between the spear shafts to hold it in front of himself. The spear points flopped down on either side of his hand, pushing off from each other just enough to create a small fan. The balance was far more awkward than his disc or the stars. He felt the currents of mana running through the thing and absorbed some mana from his surroundings. He usually spun the cutting disc above his hand and pushed it away, letting gravity keep it down. This would be different.

Mellik channeled at the round center of the device and let go. It fell to the sand with a clatter, as Mellik had expected. He'd briefly felt the tug of his earth mana trying to push the object up and spin it. He'd almost done it right, he would just need to put more oomph behind it.

Mellik picked it up again and arranged the spears on either side of his hand. He channeled again, this time unleashing far more earth mana at the contraption.

The spears went spinning into the air. They shot straight up, and Mellik marveled for a moment as the spinning spears spread themselves out into a twirling disc of metal against the noonday sky. Mellik realized too late that the disc of metal with its razor sharp points was heading straight back down at him. Mellik ducked and covered his head with his hands.

The spears hit him on the shoulder, but it felt more like a hard shove than the sharp strike of metal he had expected. Mellik straightened and looked down at the spear contraption and then at the shoulder of the snakeskin cloak he was wearing. He looked up to see Bo and Master Kaleed looking at him with the wide-eyed look of those who had just seen disaster narrowly avoided.

"Well, they work," Kaleed commented in a pitch slightly higher than his usual rumbling baritone. "You might consider putting the hood up."

Mellik nodded and put the hood up as he bent to retrieve the spears. He tried not to think about the look on their faces. He had felt the weight and spin of the device, and even the way it shifted as the spears fanned out. He hoped he could at least not hit himself with it this time.

Mellik held the spears out in front of him again and really studied the play of the magnetic fields. He channeled just a little at the disc in the center and watched the magnetic field push against it, and felt it tug against his hand. Experimentally, he made the center of his palm exude magnetic mana to attract the disc to it. He could feel the disc pushing against his hand and he spread his fingers, letting go. He smiled as the central disc stayed stuck to his hand. Now it was much easier to start the spears spinning with mana from his fingers. The device was spinning smoothly, the spears spread out and forming a blurred saucer in front of him.

"Turn around so we can see," called Kaleed.

Mellik turned slowly with a big smile on his face. Out of the corner of his eye, he saw something flying through the air toward him, and the smile vanished. Mellik tried to duck his head out of the way, but he had to keep his hand steady. He wasn't used to the spinning magnets enough to trust moving them quickly.

The object smacked into the spinning spears and was thrown harmlessly to one side. The disc hardly jerked on Mellik's palm.

"It works!" yelled Kaleed. "It's a shield."

Something was making his palm uncomfortable. Mellik stopped the spinning spears and looked at his hand. A blister was already welling up there.

"Are you alright?" Asked Kaleed, striding quickly up to him.

"Just a blister, Master."

Kaleed grabbed his hand and looked at it.

"Not bad," he commented with a grunt. "A snake skin glove will take care of that."

"Master, what's it for?"

Kaleed grinned like a child, "I told you. It's a shield. One you can see through. The mages tried magic hardened glass long ago, but the glass mana gets in the way, even without the enchantments blocking your magic sight. This one you don't see through, you see around the spokes."

"That's not what I meant, Master. The shield, the armor, the weapons: What are they for?"

Kaleed's smile dissolved, and he stroked his chin thoughtfully.

"The first of the other new apprentices arrived this morning," he said cryptically.

Mellik remained silent, assuming there was more. The big smith looked at him thoughtfully, concern creasing his brow.

"The rest will arrive soon, and you'll begin more formal training as a wizard. They've never had a Kamori apprentice here," Kaleed continued. "You have paperwork that shows you can't be the one from the prophesy, and the Emperor doesn't like to kill Kamori casually because of the curse, but what if your paperwork is wrong? What if there was a mistake? A Kamori wizard would be the obvious fulfiller of the prophesy, wouldn't he? Can the

Emperor take that chance? Will he want to?"

Kaleed was now gazing north, looking through and past the crater walls as he spoke.

"You're only hope is to make yourself useful. Give him a reason to keep you alive. And what does the Emperor need? He needs weapons. The Emperor has been conquering the world one piece at a time for hundreds of years," Master Kaleed looked back at Mellik, his eyes more intense than Mellik had ever seen them. "You must make yourself into a weapon. A weapon he trusts and comes to rely on. I don't know how you do that without making yourself a threat to him, but you must."

Chapter 23

"But Master Marran, if magic is the force of chaos, how can we learn it? Won't it just change?" asked a boy at the front of the room.

This class on basic magic theory was the only one Mellik shared with all the new apprentices. His reading and writing had been deemed good enough that he'd been put in the advanced class with some apprentices from this group, and more from the year before. His last class was in advanced earth magics with Master Tanay. Mellik had decided that he hated all of the apprentices. The ones who hadn't known what a Kamori was adopted the animosity so many of the people at the college showed towards him. His hopes of finding friends amongst the new apprentices were quickly dashed on the rocks of ostracism. If anything, they seemed intent on proving just how much they visibly despised him to the Masters and older apprentices. Mellik's shins now had permanent bruises, and his white apprentice clothes were a dingy, mottled brown from all the food stains he couldn't quite scrub out. On the bright side, Master Pelliery had declared he was too busy with the new students to continue Mellik's private instruction.

"You're right," said Master Marran. He was incredibly good looking. All the girls were already in love with him. It was hard to dislike him for it, however. He didn't seem to know how good looking he was, and he was one of those nice, funny, smart guys that are impossible to resent. His reaction to Mellik was to simply ignore him: Mellik was never called on in his class, nor would Master Marran call on him if Mellik had a question. Mellik had entertained the idea of cornering Master Marran to ask his questions, but he was afraid of antagonizing the only person in the class who wasn't overtly hostile to him. Instead, Mellik sat at the back of the class, and paid rapt attention to everything Master Marran said, trying to memorize it all.

"That's exactly right, Geof," continued Master Marran. "Magic is chaos, and the rules governing it can change at any time. Now, we've talked a little about this. Can anyone tell me why the rules governing magic and its use might be relatively stable, why large changes in its governance and control rarely happen?"

Mellik raised his hand. He didn't really have an answer in mind, but he'd decided that he wouldn't meekly go away in this or any other way. He knew his life might get easier if he'd just fade into the background a little, but something inside him refused to let them win.

Master Marran ignored him, as usual. He looked around and finally another hand wavered upwards.

"Yes, Bekka?"

"Because then we couldn't control it, Master," the mousy girl said with some confidence. She was from the Capitol, and Mellik hated them more than most, because they hated him more.

"Well, that's right in that if it were to change often we would have much less control of it, and there is a little something else in there that I'll come back to," Master Marran glanced around the room but apparently didn't see sudden inspiration coming on. "The truth is, we don't know for sure why magic doesn't change more often, but there are three main theories.

"The first theory is that the chaos of magic is balanced by the laws of nature. We can access worlds through the art of summoning that have vastly more magic or vastly more natural law. We've seen that creatures from worlds far more magical than ours use magic almost on an instinctual basis. We call these beings demons. When we summon a demon to our world, we choose a magical plane of existence we know to be more magical than ours for two reasons. The first is that they usually have more raw magical power than we do. The second is that we've found they are even more bound by the laws governing our world than we are. Whether it's because they aren't used to working with those laws, or that the laws themselves become more rigid because of the demon's magical nature, we're not sure, but it makes them easier to control."

Mellik wanted to know more about demons and apparently so did others as almost half of the class raised their hands. Master Marran waived the hands down.

"We'll talk more about demons and summoning another day. For now let's stay on the nature of magic and its relationship with law and stability.

"Now, on the other end of the spectrum from demons, too much law can cause things to cease to change, locking them in a static state. We call these objects dead matter, because they have been stripped of all magic and become locked in their form and appearance. Take this piece of wood for instance." Master Marran held up a small chunk of wood from his pocket about the size and shape of his thumb. "Please switch to your second sight."

Mellik did so and the piece of wood stood out starkly in the room, just as the bag Master Myg had given him had.

"I'm sure you can see the difference between this piece of wood and everything else you've probably ever looked at," Master Marran continued. "If you ever come upon a piece of any dead matter, keep it. They are incredibly valuable because anything that magic can no longer effect, magic cannot defend against. Also important to remember if you ever see that soldier with a dead blade stalking toward you. There is a theory which proposes that life becomes impossible where chaos and law become too imbalanced. So law keeps magic from changing too quickly, but magic facilitates the change necessary for life to flourish."

"The second theory on why magic doesn't change rapidly is that magic does change, but human perspective doesn't see it. An average human lives maybe forty years. A master wizard might live three or four times that long. The Emperor is almost three hundred years old. The elves have written histories going back twenty thousand years and believe that this world was created far earlier than that. Now, let's assume that the world is only fifty thousand years old, and that it will end in another fifty thousand. That would mean that a given piece of magic might cease to function the way we know it somewhere in that one hundred thousand year range. The chance of a given piece of magic failing during any wizard's lifetime becomes minute."

This wasn't anyone's favorite class. The sessions were entirely taken up with lectures with that showing of the dead magic wood probably the most interactive thing they'd done, but Mellik honestly enjoyed it. It could get boring at times, but there were stories here. If one of Mellik's classmates asked the right question, Master Marran would sometimes share one. Mellik also liked fitting Master Marran's teachings on magical theory with what he already knew about working magic. He'd been surprised by how far ahead of the other new apprentices he was in that area. He'd thought they would all have started their instruction on the way to the college, but apparently his situation with Arbret had been unique. Mellik found he owed Arbret more all the time.

"The third possible reason is what you were eluding to, Becca: that we are actively keeping magic from changing because we don't want it to. Any guesses on how we might do that?"

Mellik reflexively raised his hand. Master Marran glanced at him before looking away.

August raised his hand in the front row. August was from one of the Royal families. He had arrived without any other prospective apprentices, escorted by his own family's guardsmen and a wardrobe of dozens of silk outfits in various shades of white and cream. Brin's group had immediately taken him in. He was also the smartest of the new apprentices. Mellik hated him more than the rest.

"August?" Master Marran pointed to the boy.

"Subconscious group cooperative magic, Master Marran."

"Very good, August. For those of you who do not know what that is, a subconscious action is an action that your mind performs without you actively having to think about it. Breathing for instance." Master Marran took in a deep, loud breath to demonstrate. "I was just thinking about breathing right then, but you continue to breathe even when you're not thinking about it. So subconscious group cooperative magic is when a group of beings use magic to do something without actively thinking about it. Most of you are probably under the impression that only mages can use magic, because we can see it and use our will to manipulate it, but magic is constantly being used without conscious thought or effort. Animals and plants instinctually use magic all the time. Similarly, human adepts, like the Wardens, use their magic to enhance various abilities without conscious control of it."

A hand came up from a big farm boy who tripped Mellik in the halls whenever possible to fit in.

"Yes, Wesley."

"But those are all internal magics where they're using mana within themselves."

They had talked about internal and external magics a few days ago. Wesley had a tendency to assume every lesson had something to do with the last.

"That's correct, but remember that mana used from within can still be projected out from the host to create external effects. In this case, many mages believe that we can't see this mana, because the amount being exuded from any individual is too small for us to see it with the second sight. The basic principle is that if an individual believes in a certain thing, they release a small amount of magical energy to help make that a reality, or in this case, to keep it a reality. If there are enough people believing the same thing, there will be enough magical energy to actually create or maintain the thing they believe in."

"So we create our own fairy tales?" Blurted Mellik, and then hastily added, "Master Marran."

"We raise our hands in this class, Apprentice Mellik. Do not make me remind you again."

Master Marran was as easygoing a teacher as you could find at the college, but the warning in his voice was explicit.

"Yes, Master Marran," Mellik replied meekly, looking at Master Marran's feet.

"That is one possibility, if this is true," Master Marran continued in his normal tone. "Another is that we expect certain magics to react a certain way, and because enough people hold that belief, it remains true."

The bell announcing the end of class vibrated through the

stone walls. Everyone looked at Master Marran expectantly. It was the last class of the afternoon for many of them.

Master Marran grinned, "I guess that's as good a place as any to leave off. You're dismissed."

The room burst into chaos as everyone popped up out of their seats, jabbering and jostling each other, except for Mellik. He'd learned quickly that he was elbowed and shoved far less, if he stayed seated until everyone else had left. Being at the back of the room helped too - his foot was only stomped on once today.

When the back of the last girl was disappearing through the door, Mellik stood to leave. Only he and Master Marran were still there, and the tall master had already gathered his things to leave as well. Master Marran looked directly at Mellik's eyes and held Mellik's gaze as he very slowly and deliberately slid a folded piece of parchment off the edge of the small lectern he stood behind. The paper fluttered to the floor. Master Marran turned and left, his usual open smile wiped away.

Mellik walked up to the lectern and picked up the piece of paper. Parchment was too valuable for the apprentices to use in most cases: it wasn't just thrown on the ground. It was a very small piece of paper, carefully cut and folded, barely bigger than Mellik's thumbnail. Feeling guilty for having the paper, Mellik retreated behind the door where no one passing by could see. Unfolding it, Mellik saw two words written in careful block letters. It said, "Be careful."

Chapter 24

Mellik was still worrying over what the scrap of paper meant as he came out into the blistering heat of the afternoon sun. Most of the crater was planted with large trees and shrubs that provided shade as he made his way across to the smithy. It was a tropical paradise that Mellik usually relished, but not today.

He wished Master Marran had been more specific, assuming he had written the note. Mellik had a feeling that he should destroy the note, not that it would tell anyone anything more than it told him. "Be careful." Something, anything more would have been helpful: careful when, of what, or whom? Mellik knew he had enemies, he even knew who some of them were. Was this something more, or just more urgent? Did Master Marran know something he didn't, or was he just now blithely learning what Mellik already knew?

Mellik entered the cool shade of the small rainforest. Something struck his ankle hard, and he was sent sprawling into the dust of the path. His foot felt tingly and numb, but Mellik ignored that and pushed himself up off the dirt.

"Uh, uh," said a voice Mellik recognized. "No ya don't."

Something jabbed into his shoulder, and pain blossomed outward. Mellik felt his limbs convulse, and he went crashing back down into the dirt. A boot came under his shoulder and rolled him roughly onto his back. He stared up at the smugly smiling face of Brin.

"I wanted ta make shar ya saw me," said the older boy. There was a leaf jutting oddly from the boy's thick, black hair. He must have been hiding in the dense brush, waiting for Mellik.

Mellik flipped to his second sight, but Brin jabbed something into his gut, and the pain blossomed, scattering his thoughts and making channeling any kind of magic impossible. The pain withdrew, and Mellik noticed half a dozen other apprentices gathered behind Brin: his lackeys.

"Ya'r not ta only one dat can have a toy," and the big apprentice held up a slim sword unlike any Mellik had seen before. Long and straight, it was far too thin and didn't seem to have an edge. Mellik saw Brin channel into it and understood as air and fire raced along its length, crackling with the energy of lightning.

Brin delicately brought the rapier down against Mellik's groin. Some dim part of Mellik's brain wanted to scream but nothing came out. Brin began to jab him in various places without pause. Mellik's vision became fuzzy, and a little voice in the back of his mind was glad he hadn't had time to draw in any mana, because it would have gotten loose inside of him and likely killed him.

"I'm gonna kill ya," Brin muttered over him. "Gonna kill ya, and no one will care. Tey'll reward me."

The sound of two bodies colliding interrupted this litany, and the pain receded. Mellik blinked to clear his vision. Someone was on top of Brin, thrashing wildly with his arms, beating at him.

"It's the dummy!" yelled one of Brin's cohorts. All six of them piled in to drag Bo off of Brin. They were barely enough, and it took a boy on each limb to finally pull Bo off of Brin and get Brin to his feet.

Brin stood. His face was scratched, and blood ran from his nose and lip. One eye was already swelling. There was a look of hatred and anger that Mellik hadn't seen since Pollum had almost killed him. His hatred for Mellik had looked cold and still: this was raw, and feral. Brin still had the rapier clenched in his fist.

"All ta better," he spat. "We da ya bote now."

Brin jabbed Bo in the gut with the sword, and Mellik could see the magic energies flash from his hand, down through the rapier, and out into Bo's body. Bo's big frame jerked with the pain, and his mouth flew open, but only a gurgling groan escaped.

Mellik's head was fuzzy. He couldn't concentrate on the mana in his body or reach out to the mana around him. He could feel the earth beneath him, but couldn't find the means to grasp it with his mind. His limbs were similarly useless. His hands scrabbled at the dirt in front of his face, but he couldn't control them. Even his voice had left him as he watched Brin shock Bo over and over, and the only scream he could muster was in his mind.

"Brin, stop!" yelled a girl from above Mellik.

The girl stepped over Mellik, and he recognized Keyessa's tan boots as she strode between Brin and Mellik. Brin half turned to look at her.

"What the demons are you doing?!" Keyessa yelled.

Through the blur of his mind's eye Mellik could see that she was holding mana, a lot of mana. It was so bright that it formed a halo around her.

"I was taking care of ta Kamori for all of us when tis dummy got in ta way," spat Brin.

"He's not a dummy," said Keyessa. Mellik could hear the controlled anger in her voice, and the mana she held pulsed brighter. "He's just deaf. Now let him go."

"I can't Key. He saw what I was doing wit ta Kamori."

"Then I guess you'll have to let them both go."

Brin turned to fully face her, his face a bruised contortion of anger and confusion.

"Are ya on tere side den?" He asked, his own mana flaring.

There was a pause, and then Keyessa answered in a softer voice, "I guess I've already made that choice."

"Now let them go," and her voice was strong again. "You know I'm stronger than you, and they'll find out if anything happens to me."

Brin looked at her and then looked down at Mellik, and the hatred in Brin's eyes seemed to grow: both the cold hatred and the feral rage. Brin looked down at the rapier, lightning coursing and arcing to the ground next to him.

"Let ta dummy go," Brin ordered to his cronies without turning from Keyessa. "We'll finish tis later."

The group holding Bo up let him crumple to the ground. Bo was crying, sobbing from the pain. Brin turned and trailed casually after the others. On his way by, he dragged the rapier along Bo's body, letting lightning crackle through it. He never slowed or looked down as Bo twitched and spasmed.

Keyessa ran over to Bo, telling him with words and gestures to calm down and lie still. Mellik finally managed enough control to scrabble up onto his knees. He crawled over to Bo. His crying had grown less violent, but there were bright patches of blood all about his body.

"Is he all right?" Mellik asked.

"I think so," replied Keyessa. She was checking the small wounds all about his body and doing something with magic that Mellik couldn't follow. "No thanks to you."

A part of Mellik was incensed that she would say that any of this was his fault. Mellik was still too groggy to voice his objection.

The rest of Mellik thought about what she had said as he watched her and Bo flash through hand language too quickly for him to register more than a few words here and there.

He shouldn't have needed Bo to come to his rescue. He knew he had enemies. He'd already met people who would do horrible things, even kill, because of who and what he was. He'd even been warned: not just today, but also by Arbret with his dying words. Arbret, Vai, Kaleed, and even Myg had talked to him about these things. They couldn't watch over him. He needed to start taking care of himself. Master Kaleed was right - he needed to be a weapon.

Chapter 25

The big oak door opened, and a dour journeyman clad in a black robe stuck his head through.

"Apprentice Mellik, you may come in now," and the journeyman disappeared, leaving the door standing ajar.

Mellik's hands were sweaty from nerves, and they shook slightly as he reached out to open the door. Inside was a room larger than the apprentice quarters he and Bo shared, but smaller than the all of the classrooms he'd seen.

Five masters sat behind a long table on one side of the room. The journeyman sat to the side behind a small desk. He motioned Mellik toward a lone chair facing the masters.

He knew four of the masters. Master Myg was one. He had treated Mellik and Bo after the attack the day before. The wounds had all been small punctures, mostly cauterized by Brin's lightning magic. Master Myg had kept them overnight, just to be certain.

Three of the others were Master Marran, Master Pelliery and Master Tanay: a willowy woman with short, corn silk hair who was his earth magic teacher.

"Apprentice Mellik," said a large bald man with a thick salt and pepper beard. "I am Master Samuels. Would you please tell us what happened yesterday afternoon?"

Mellik was nervous. He took a deep breath and briefly described the attack, omitting only the note of warning he'd received from Master Marran. There was a significant pause after Mellik finished.

Master Myg finally broke the silence. "You realize that Apprentice Brin came to us with a different story? He said that you and Bo attacked him."

"What?" exclaimed Mellik in shock. Master Tanay arched an eyebrow at him, and Mellik reflexively corrected himself. "I'm sorry, Master. I don't understand. Brin said that I attacked him?"

Master Samuel replied, "Yes, Apprentice. He said you ambushed him in the forest. He said he was able to hold you off until your friend Bo jumped him, and the two of you beat him almost senseless before his friends dragged you both off. All six of them witnessed your attack. This story won't help you."

"But Master, Apprentice Keyessa was there. She saw what happened as well."

"We have already interviewed her. She said that she did not witness the brawl, only the end where Apprentice Brin and his friends had already subdued you and Apprentice Bo. Also, her romantic involvement with you diminishes her credibility as a witness. Apprentice Brin has already admitted to getting carried away in anger, and he will be punished for that. We are interviewing you to establish your punishment."

Mellik was so stunned by hearing that he and Keyessa were romantically involved that he had to go back over what had been said in his mind. Something about Master Samuel's pronouncement rattled around in Mellik's head. "Establish your punishment." They had already decided that he was guilty.

"But he had a sword! He used magic and said he was going to kill me!" Mellik cried in desperation.

Master Samuel turned to Pelliery. The master of air magic leaned forward and gazed at Mellik pitilessly.

"I have watched Brin practice with both his rapier and his lightning magics. He easily could have killed you with either one. I believe he showed remarkable control with both, under the circumstances. Master Myg has concurred that the wounds were shallow and precise, designed very specifically not to kill, but to administer moderate shocks through the weapon."

Master Samuel also leaned forward, steepling his hands on the table in front of him. "Lying to us will only make matters worse, Apprentice. Do you want to tell us what really happened?"

"I did," Mellik whispered. Hot tears threatened the corners of his eyes. He scrubbed at them with a sleeve when they began to fall. He looked up at the masters, but there was no help there. Only Master Myg showed any emotion, looking saddened but resigned.

"Very well, then," said Master Samuel, leaning back in his chair again. "The tribunal has no choice but to find Apprentices Bo and Mellik guilty of assault on another student and lying to this court."

"Wait," Mellik called out reflexively. He remembered Bo's tortured face as Brin shocked him over and over. Would Keyessa be able to make Bo understand what was going on? Did Bo deserve whatever punishment was coming just for defending Mellik? "Masters, Bo didn't know what was going on. He saw Brin with his sword and came to my defense. He had nothing to do with starting this."

Manuel gazed at Mellik thoughtfully.

Master Myg spoke up, "Brin did say it was initially just he and Mellik - that Bo jumped him afterwards."

"It **is** consistent with all the children's statements," added Tanay thoughtfully.

"Is that your official statement?" asked Manuel, staring intently at Mellik. "That you attacked Brin, and Bo only became involved to defend you?"

Mellik gritted his teeth. He wouldn't lie for these people, but he wouldn't let Bo be punished just for being his friend either.

"Masters, Bo was just defending me after Brin and I were already fighting, yes."

"Alright then," and Manuel looked around at the other masters. "Being confused and defending someone are not offenses, but I think we can all agree that any type of fighting amongst the apprentices needs to be discouraged. For Bo, I propose one week of confinement to his room outside of classes and bread rations."

It wasn't a bad punishment. Mellik had heard of apprentices getting a day or two just for forgetting to use the honorific with a master or for being late to class. Bo would be hungry and bored, but Mellik was glad that that was the worst of it.

Some of the other masters seemed surprised at it though. Tanay's left eyebrow shot up again, and Master Myg's came down in a frown. Mellik even thought he saw a surprised look in Master

Pelliery's eyes.

"All those in favor?" asked Manuel.

If some of the masters were surprised by the sentence, none voiced an objection.

"Now, for Apprentice Mellik here," Manuel gazed coolly at him. "Six lashes for attacking another student. Three more for the vicious nature of the attack. Six lashes for lying about the incident. Three more for refusing to apologize or fully admit his part in this."

"That seems a bit harsh, Manuel," offered Myg.

"Bah!" injected Pelliery. "Not harsh enough! This type of thing shouldn't be tolerated. He'd make a good example to the other hooligans."

"You see," Manuel spread his hands. "I merely strike a balance. Tanay, Marran: what say you?"

"If he were to recant his story now, could he reduce the lashes?" Tanay asked.

Manuel shook his head. "Confession merely to avoid a sentence already given hardly counts."

"Then I suppose it is as fair as the circumstances allow," Tanay agreed.

Master Marran, looked at him with a steady gaze, no expression registering in his eyes. Their gazes locked for a moment, but Mellik could read nothing there.

"I will agree on one condition," said Marran.

"And that is?" asked Manuel.

"As a neutral party, I should be the one to carry out all martial punishment in this case."

Manuel glanced at the others and received thoughtful nods in return. Only Pelliery scowled before giving his ascent.

"Done," announced Manuel. "Public lashings to take place this evening after dinner."

*   *   *

Mellik didn't feel hungry. Fesskah and Querin had given opposing advice on eating before a public lashing. Fesskah thought he should eat to build up his strength, but then Fesskah thought you should always eat. Querin was worried that Mellik might throw up and embarrass himself. They seemed more concerned with his food consumption than his imminent whipping. They were still better than the other apprentices who were laughing about it and telling him people had died from that many lashes. Mellik set his knife down. Everything tasted like ash in his mouth right now anyway, and his stomach felt like it might not even make it to the lashing post.

Querin and Fesskah looked up, and Mellik turned to see if Bo had been allowed to come to this one last meal. Instead, he was surprised to see Keyessa standing there. Surprise turned to shock as he noticed the black eye and bruised jaw.

"What happened?" he blurted out.

Keyessa neither looked at him nor answered his question.

"May I sit with you?" she asked. There was a note of pleading in her voice.

"Of coursse," replied Fesskah. Querin stood and gestured at the seat beside Mellik, giving the hint of a bow as he did so.

"Yeah, yeah," mumbled Mellik belatedly.

Keyessa gingerly stepped over the bench, leaning on the table to take her weight as she did so.

"What happened?" Mellik asked again.

There was a pause, and Keyessa still didn't look at him as she pushed the sausage around her trencher, but eventually she answered. "What do you think?"

The bitterness in her voice finally made it sink in and made his mind start working again. It had been Brin. Sharp rage made Mellik's face flush, and he could hear his heartbeat begin to throb in his ears.

Keyessa glanced around nervously and slid a bundle of cloth over to him.

"Here," she said. "Don't let anyone see. There are leaves inside. Eat them, and they will help with the pain."

"Make sure to eat something with them," she added with a glance at his untouched dinner.

The anger must have burned away Mellik's upset stomach, as he found himself now hungry. He took the flat bread and added the greens on the trencher, slipping the dried leaves from the piece of cloth in amongst them. The sausage went on top, and then he rolled the whole thing up. There was a bitter, acrid taste that he assumed was from Keyessa's leaves, but the spice of the sausage covered most of it.

Across from him, Querin rolled a silver penny across to Fesskah.

"That was cheating really," commented Querin.

"No cheating," responded Fesskah. "Not my doing. Jusst luck and unforesseen ssircumsstancess."

"You guys bet on whether I'd eat?"

Querin looked at him with innocent confusion. "It seemed cruel to bet on whether you'd pass out."

Keyessa sputtered as she contained a laugh and then put a hand to her bruise with an, "Ow."

Mellik didn't think he'd seen Keyessa smile before. Even with the bruises, it made his face feel flush and warm.

"I heard about you defending Bo," she said without looking at him.

"He's my friend." Mellik didn't know how he was supposed to respond to that.

Keyessa finally looked at him; looked him right in the eyes. There was a something in her eyes at that moment: Mellik thought it was a look of both understanding and confusion. She nodded once and went back to her dinner.

"Make sure to come to the medical office right after," Keyessa said toward her food. "The leaves will only numb the pain for a while, and you'll need to get your back cleaned and stitched up."

Everyone at their table became quiet then. Mellik appreciated that no one said it wouldn't be that bad or that he'd be fine. They were there for him in the silence, and he took what strength and courage he could from that.

The bell rang for meal's end. The tables and benches clattered and banged with raucous jostling as apprentices rushed out to get a good spot to view the whipping. There was a festival atmosphere that Mellik had failed to notice earlier.

Mellik rose slowly to his feet, and his friends stood with him. Even Keyessa gathered with them as they walked from the dining hall. No one commented on her quick inclusion in their group.

The hallways were deserted as they made their way out to the crater bowl. Mellik could hear shouts and whoops and the occasional pounding of feet echoing back to them. There was an otherworldly feel to the walk. Mellik wasn't sure if that was just in his head, or if the leaves he'd eaten had something to do with it.

They neared the doors out to the crater, and by some unspoken agreement, Fesskah took the lead with Querin and Keyessa to either side of him. Querin adopted a stride and demeanor Mellik had never seen before. There was a regal bearing and an emanation of power. On his other side, Keyessa had also taken on an aura of command that made her seem taller than her five foot frame should allow. Mellik wondered at both their abilities to transform their bearing so completely.

Fesskah needed no such demeanor to seem larger. His skin turned shiny, and the scales became larger and more pronounced. He grew and stretched even as he pushed open the big oak double doors. When he'd demonstrated his abilities before, he'd just gotten big and muscular. This time he stretched, growing to nine feet tall or more. Fesskah's muscles and skin grew taught against his bones, which began to jut gruesomely at his ribs and face. Fangs extended and multiplied in his mouth until it couldn't close, and his eyes sunk deep into their sockets becoming beady black dots. His arms and fingers elongated to almost drag upon the ground, and his claws extended into vicious curved blades. Barbs sprang from his spine and along his legs, arms, and hands. A low, hissing growl burbled from his throat, and yellow-green fluid dripped from his fangs as his head swiveled back and forth at the gathered students.

The apprentices lined either side of the path, and their raucous jostling died out in a wave down the line as they each caught sight of Fesskah. Small stones and sticks fell from some of the boys' and girls' hands. Others held onto similar objects, and Mellik noted clinically that they had probably meant to throw them at him. Mellik and his escort walked in spreading silence down the jungle path. Some of the apprentices lining the path looked horrified as they caught sight of Fesskah, and Mellik thought a few might have run if not for the students knowing who and what Fesskah was.

In the center of the crater was a clearing with a hump of stone that rose up out of the sandy soil. Many of the students used it as a gathering place after classes and in the evening. Mellik had never lingered there, and after his first couple of weeks, he had gone to lengths to avoid the area. Now, two stout wooden poles rose up from it with a crosspiece running at chest level. Surrounding the platform of stone stood the masters with their spectrum of clothing. There were easily thirty of them. Mellik had never seen that many gathered at once. Standing near the wooden beams was Master Marran, Brin, and three journeymen swathed in black with deep hoods pulled up over their heads.

Brin stood naked down to the waist. He was tall and muscular, with a wiry physique and short, dark body hair. Mellik was strong for his age, but he wasn't tall, and he'd gained a little padding since coming to the college. He'd keep his shirt on as long as possible. Brin must be here for a lashing as well; that, at least, made Mellik feel a trifle better.

"We'll be waiting here when you're done," Querin whispered when they reached the circle of masters.

Mellik nodded in reply as his legs took him woodenly up the small stone hill. One of the journeyman motioned for him to stand on the opposite Brin with Master Marran in the middle.

"We are here to mete out and bear witness to the punishments of Apprentices Brin Sarkosian and Mellik Ackins," intoned Marran as soon as Mellik was in place. "Brin Sarkosian has been found guilty of using magic without permission or guidance. The penalty for this is six lashes."

A small gasp came from the assembled students.

'Wait until they hear my punishment,' thought Mellik.

"For admitting his fault and being truthful in his testimony, we reduce this punishment by two lashes."

Mellik's jaw popped open, and he shut it with an angry snap. Brin was being rewarded for lying!

"Because he acted out of self defense, his punishment is lessened by an additional two lashes."

Mellik's hands tightened into fists.

"And finally, because he showed restraint in his actions and only used magics a master had already approved, we reduce his punishment by another lash."

Brin grinned at Mellik as he was led to the post by two of the journeymen.

One lash! For attacking him and Bo, Brin would get only one lash. For torturing Bo, Brin would get only one lash. For beating up Keyessa, Brin would not get any punishment!

Mellik didn't know if he had ever hated someone before. If he had, then his feelings for Brin now went beyond hate. In his mind, he thought of all sorts of punishments and deaths for Brin, but none of them were harsh or horrible enough.

Brin put his hands through a pair of leather loops attached to the horizontal post, and the journeymen tied leather chords around his wrists and hands to keep them secure.

The last journeyman handed Master Marran the whip. It had a wooden handle and half a dozen leather chords hanging from it. It was horrifying. Mellik tried not to focus on it.

Out of the corner of his eye, Mellik saw Marran walk up to Brin. The murmurings of the gathered crowd hushed, and then there was a crack that sounded impossibly loud in the sudden silence. Mellik looked up. There were angry red lines on Brin's back, but Mellik had received worse playing swords back in his village.

The journeymen undid Brin's bindings. Mellik began to take off his own shirt as the master declared his crimes and punishment. The journeymen took him to the posts, and Mellik gripped the beam hard to keep his hands from shaking. The journeymen stepped back after binding him and Master Marran came forward to check the leather bonds

"I will do what I can, but it must be real to satisfy them," Master Marran whispered to him. "Some prefer to kneel."

Brin had stood.

"I'll stand," Mellik replied. He was pleased that his voice was steady.

"Put this between your teeth," and Master Marran put a thick piece of boiled leather up to Mellik's mouth. "It will keep you from breaking teeth or biting off your tongue."

Mellik didn't remember Brin getting a piece of leather, but he opened his mouth to receive it anyway. Master Marran stepped away behind him. Mellik had just time enough to wonder when it would start when the first blow landed. He let out a surprised grunt, but as he'd suspected, it wasn't much worse than getting hit with a wooden sword. The second was the same as the first but lower on his back, and this time Mellik made no sound. The third was even lower, but it just managed to overlap the flesh still tender from the second lash, where his burned and cried out in protest. Now Mellik understood. He only had so much back, and each lash would become worse than the one before.

The fourth lash lit his shoulder like blades of fire. The fifth and sixth did the same for the rest of his back. On the seventh strike, Mellik felt his flesh tear open. A small whimper escaped him, but Mellik resolved not to cry.

More gashes were rent in his back as Mellik lost count of the strokes. Tears ran from his eyes, and soon sobs wracked his breathing. At some point, he had fallen to his knees.

His mind sought escape, and just as it had with Pollum, it reached down into the earth and found strength there. This time it wasn't two forces pushing against each other, but a more powerful, yet dormant force seething with heat and pressure. He knew he could reach out to it to end his pain and take his tormentors with him. The power was there, just waiting to be tapped. It simply needed releasing.

With a sobbing cry, Mellik tore his mind back to the pain and fire of his body. Another lash sent a spasm through his body, but Mellik kept his mind on the pain. They couldn't stop him. He would learn. He would become a weapon to keep himself and his parents safe.

Mellik didn't even realize when the whipping stopped. Someone untied his hands. He would have fallen, but someone else was holding him up. They brought him to his feet. A twisting of his tattered skin wrenched a whimper from his throat.

"Get him to the infirmary," Master Marran commanded. "They can't stop Myg from treating him there."

Chapter 26

Mellik carefully pulled the shirt on. He did it as slowly and gently as he could, but he still hissed as it scraped against his raw back. Master Myg had cleaned and stitched him up, and had given him something to help him sleep the day before.

"Healing magic has to take power from the one healed," he'd told Mellik. "I've gotten the skin to close, which will keep infection at bay and get your body started toward healing itself, but it's better to leave your body to do the rest and leave as much of your energy with you as we can."

He'd been asleep as soon as Bo, Fesskah, and Querin had lowered him to his pallet.

There was a small clay jar with some dried leaves of the type Keyessa had given him the day before. Mellik remembered Master Myg lecturing Keyessa on why the drug hadn't worked as well as she'd hoped.

"Undried, the drug absorbs much quicker in the system. The dried leaves are also more potent by weight so you likely gave him too small a dose. Add to that that Mellik was probably nervous, and we've found stress and agitation make the body burn off the drug much faster than normal and sometimes hold its properties at bay.

"Having said that, you do not know nearly enough to be giving out medicines. If you do it again, I will have you whipped to match Mellik's back here. You could accidentally poison someone. Do I make myself clear?"

The rest of their conversation had been quieter and Mellik couldn't make it out. He'd drifted into sleep. He only vaguely remembered his friends lowering him to his bed, and now he'd woken up, too uncomfortable to sleep.

The two long holes that let light into their cell were glowing dimly, so it was still well before the general wake up call. He finally got up. His stomach growled at him, and he wondered if there would be food in the great hall yet.

Mellik finished his slow, painful process of getting dressed and glanced over at Bo. The big youth was sprawled on his pallet, limbs akimbo and snoring softly.

Mellik backed out of their room and quietly closed the door.

"Good morning."

Mellik jumped and then stopped in mid-motion as his back screamed at the sudden movement.

Querin sat on the floor of the hall, half an orange in his lap.

"I'm sorry," Querin said, rising smoothly to his feet while nibbling at a piece of orange. He held out another piece. "Want some?"

Mellik took the offered piece and barely chewed.

Querin laughed and held out the rest of the orange, "Master Myg said you'd be hungry when you woke up."

"I don't suppose you have anything else?" asked Mellik as he wolfed down the last piece.

Querin fished in his pockets and came out with a roll in one hand and a slice of cheese in the other. Mellik took both.

"Okay. I guess you can still be my friend," Mellik commented around a mouthful of bread.

"Yes. I can imagine the crush of people clamoring to be your friend in this place must be quite a burden."

Mellik thought of how lonely and awful he would feel without the few friends he had and felt grateful and embarrassed.

"Thank you," he said, thinking of more than the bread and cheese.

Querin put a warm hand on the front of Mellik's shoulder. "It's what friends are for. Since you're up so early, care to take a walk with me? I have an errand to run."

"I don't know if I'll have time before Master Tanay's class."

"You've been excused from your morning classes for today by Master Myg."

He'd miss breakfast, but that might be safer anyway. He certainly owed it to his friend.

"I've brought some extra breakfast," and Querin held up a sack that had been leaning against the wall behind him.

Mellik grinned. "I hereby promote you to Third Best Friend."

"Like you have three," Querin replied, slinging the sack over one shoulder and motioning Mellik to come with him. "You're too much trouble, so Bo, Fesskah, and I take turns being your one friend."

Querin set a slow pace, but Mellik found that his legs worked just fine, and if he kept his walk carefully smooth, it didn't irritate his back.

"Where are we going?" He asked as they came out into the crater bowl.

"It's a surprise."

They had come out a different door than the main one from yesterday, but their path cut through the clearing with the raised stone. The memory of pain made Mellik's stomach turn. The whipping post had been removed, and a man in red clothes stood there going through slow, dance-like movements. A dozen people faced the man mirroring his movements. Querin stopped for a moment, watching. Mellik watched with him.

It wasn't a dance that Mellik was familiar with. No movement ever seemed to repeat, and the rhythm was slow enough that Mellik had trouble finding it at first. No words were spoken, and the only sound was the soft rustle of clothing and the occasional scuff of feet across sand. It reminded Mellik of watching Warden Hake work with a weapon, but in slow motion.

Querin silently touched his arm, and Mellik followed him along the path back into the jungle.

"Who were those people?" asked Mellik.

"The school of transformation."

"What?"

"Transformation," repeated Querin, and he shot Mellik a look like he should know this already. "Wizards who can change themselves."

"What, like Fesskah?"

"Some are like that. Others are somewhat like the Wardens, making themselves faster and stronger. Some can take animal shape. Some can do really exotic things like turn themselves into liquid or smoke or even stone."

That seemed pretty fantastic to Mellik, but he supposed summoning lightning or holding someone captive with air would have seemed the stuff of legends not so long ago.

"So, what were they doing?"

"It's called the Kigana. It's derived from an exercise elven warriors developed centuries ago."

Mellik waited, but Querin didn't say anymore. Mellik could see Querin's self-satisfied smile.

"And why were they doing that exercise thing?" Mellik asked with an exasperated sigh. Querin loved knowing things and liked sharing his knowledge even more, but what he loved most was having information you wanted and making you ask him for it.

"The exercises were designed to use every part of the body. Some movements stretch, some balance, others use strength. The transformation wizards use it so that students can learn about their own bodies. In some ways, turning yourself into something else is relatively easy. If you can feel the mana in your own body, and know the feel of water mana, then poof! - you're a puddle of water. However, the first problem is that water doesn't think or remember, at least not the way you and I do. So let's say you solve that problem and keep your head."

Querin paused, and Mellik gave the required polite laugh.

"Secondly, how do you change back? Your mind automatically knows the feel of your body deep down somewhere in your subconscious, but you are using your conscious mind to will yourself back into your body. For that you need to really know yourself. Having a mirror and a picture might help, but you could easily look correct and then find you can't move because you fused all your bones together or put the muscles in backwards for instance."

"So shape-shifters have to learn their own bodies and the bodies of animals on top of that?"

"Very few elves have ever mastered that talent," replied Querin.

"I think it's because we live too long in our bodies. Our minds have trouble imagining another. Or perhaps we are merely too proud of what we are. Some of the other fae have a knack for it, however. I've heard it helps if you can project your mind into another being using telepathy. You can ride around and get a feel for things that way. Master Ibreem, who was the one in red leading the exercises, has two familiars you might see: a cheetah and an owl. I've been told that knowing the form you're shifting into is less important. As long as you don't forget something important like a heart or brain, you can always try again.

"Here we are."

They had come to another wall of the crater. The jungle wasn't kept clear of the wall here, and vines crept up and then hung down over a large doorway. Mellik had never been to this part of the crater bowl before. The path was clear but narrow, and though the vines hung about the doorway, the door itself was unobscured.

Querin stepped forward and opened the door, which swung out silently. Inside, a hall led off into darkness. Querin motioned for Mellik to step inside.

The darkness and quiet were a bit eerie, but Mellik didn't want to seem afraid, so he stepped in. Querin followed, and the door swung quietly shut behind them.

Querin strode slowly forward without a word. Mellik wanted to ask what this place was, but something about Querin's demeanor told him to wait.

Mellik realized the hall was not as dark as he had thought. Light filtered in from holes like the ones at the college. The hall should have seemed more familiar to Mellik: it was the same size and shape as the ones at the college, had the same workmanship, and even the torch sconces along the wall were the same, if empty. The college felt lived in. There was a feel to it, almost a buzz that this area lacked...or almost lacked.

The whispered echo of a sound came from down the hallway. It sounded like the soft trilling of a tentative bird heard from under water. Mellik wouldn't have even heard it if he and Querin weren't moving so silently down the hall. Mellik looked over at the elf and saw the knowing smile on his face. Querin picked up his pace slightly.

They strode down the dim hall, and the sound grew slightly louder, but was still muffled and indistinct. Querin passed by other halls and doors without a glance. Finally, a large set of doors loomed up in front of them from the gloom. Mellik could hear that it was music now. It sounded like a flute, but it was different than the ones he'd heard back home.

Querin stopped at the doors. "Be respectful," he told Mellik. It was not a phrase Mellik had expected to hear from the brash elf. Querin opened the doors.

Sound flooded out of the doors like water released from a dam. Now that he could hear the richness and complexity of the tune, Mellik would have thought there were two flute players, but he could see only one man sitting in the middle of the huge room playing.

This room was similar in size to the common room of the college, but the tall ceilings in this one gave it a cavernous air. There were a few tables scattered about the room, and musical instruments sat atop each table or leaned up against walls. There were flutes and horns, lutes and pipes, and others that Mellik didn't even know the name of. The man playing sat on one of the tables with his back to them, and next to him, a bright lantern sent shadows of instruments spilling across the floor and walls.

The man continued to pour strong, delicate music into the room. Querin stood just inside the room, still holding open the door. Mellik stood next to him in wondrous delight. After a moment, the man looked up toward the ceiling. The notes died off, and he turned toward them, shielding his eyes from the lantern's light.

"Querin? Is that you?" the man called. He had an odd way of speaking. His vowels were all stretched out, and it was like he was tasting each word before he finished it.

Querin waved and strode forward, but made no reply. Mellik trailed after him.

The man was tall and spare, with silver white hair and a prominent nose and chin that gave him a hawk-like appearance.

"Good morning, Master Babbayannek," and Querin gave a

respectful bow. "May I introduce my friend, Mellik."

Babbayannek looked at Mellik. "So this is the troublemaker I've been hearing about? How dare you be born a Kamori." He smiled and winked at Mellik.

Mellik grinned. "It's an honor to meet you, Master Babbayannek." Mellik bowed to the man.

"Oh? And has Querin told you much about me?"

"Actually, Master, he's never mentioned you before."

Babbayannek smiled at Querin. "Honestly, Querin. I'm the only other elf on the island, and I don't even get a casual mention?"

Mellik was surprised by this. He should have seen it. They had the same glowing skin, the same eye shape and fine features, but something about Master Babbayannek had kept Mellik from guessing his heritage.

"Do not all elves have the prominent ears?" Mellik asked as he realized what the difference was. Querin had ears easily three times as large as most people Mellik had met. Master Babbayannek's were longer than they were wide, but they still stuck out too far to be hidden by his hair.

Querin grabbed Mellik's arm in warning, but Babbayannek just smiled at both of them.

"It's alright, Querin. It is of my choosing, and the years have made it lighter than it once was."

Babbayannek pulled back the hair on one side of his head to reveal a bald patch with a small puckered scar where his ear should be. The sight was disconcerting to Mellik, but even more, it was confusing.

"But, Master, you can still talk...and hear me."

"I've learned to read lips," explained Babbayannek, "and I can still remember the shape of words in my mouth and how to make them."

"I'm sorry, Master."

"No need to be. As I said, I chose this for myself a long time ago."

"Why, Master?" Mellik heard himself ask.

Babbayannek studied him for a moment before answering. "Do you know the history of this college before the Emperor conquered it?" Mellik shook his head. "It was one of the first things the Emperor took control of. The college was independent for hundreds of years before that. Wizards came here to train and exchange knowledge from all of the kingdoms. It was a huge coup for the Emperor to gain all of those powerful Mages for his army, and no histories tell how he took control of the college, only whispered rumors of demons and blackmail.

"During the time before his conquest, there was another college of learning and knowledge established in this crater. It was the bardic college, and they taught and studied not just music, but history, oratory, and much more. Musicians have always been attracted to knowledge, as well as the stability and safety necessary to pursue their art. The college of magic provided both of those, and soon both colleges thrived side-by-side.

"I was a member of that college when the Emperor came. He disbanded the college of bards. One of my masters told me he said he could write his own histories and he wanted them to be accurate and consistent. I believe that meant he wanted them to say what he wished, and only what he wished. We were told that we could leave for our own lands and take word of his offer of fealty to our sovereigns. He told us our other option was to "die here." I was young: even younger than Querin here. I knew there were too many instruments for the bards and musicians to take with them, and some instruments could not be carried. I have always been fond of the instruments and impertinently spoke up to ask what would become of them. He told me they would likely be burned or melted down with no one to maintain them. He cared not. So I asked if I could stay to care for them.

"He laughed at me, and I can still hear his reply, "You may stay and care for your toys, but I have already pronounced that if you stay, you will die here, and so you shall. The bard's college is done, and no one will come to learn to play them, nor will they come to take these instruments away. One more thing: you will never hear the sound of these precious instruments of yours again." Then he held me fast with magic as he pulled my ears from my head."

No one spoke. Mellik didn't know what to say. Mellik knew the

Emperor had killed thousands of his own people, but he'd always been some far off bogey-man. Now he was more real. It was almost like Mellik had watched all those long years ago as he tore off Master Babbayannek's ears.

"I'm sorry, Master," Mellik finally managed.

"Thank you, but again, it was a choice I made. I don't know if I'd make the same choice now, but still, I don't regret it. Some things are worth suffering for."

"But the music, Master," Mellik said as the thought came to him. "How can you make music like that without hearing it?"

Babbayannek turned to Querin, "Do you think this one has the eye for it?"

Querin shrugged, "There's only one way to find out, Master."

"Would you mind helping out? It's easier to see with the interweaving."

Mellik had no idea what they were referring to.

"Shall we play a string duet?" asked Querin.

"No, the winds are easier for me to follow and easier to see as well."

Querin nodded and looked about. Going to a nearby table, he picked up a silver flute. It was much like the one Babbayannek still held, but easily twice as large. Babbayannek nodded his approval. Querin returned to the table and sat next to Babbayannek.

"Now use your third eye and see the magic around you," Babbayannek told Mellik. "Do not try to look for anything though: just let your wizard's sight unfocus and listen to our music."

Mellik did as he was instructed, or at least tried to. From the beginning he'd been trained to use the second-sight to see things and focus on them. To do the opposite seemed frustratingly hard.

Querin began to play. The large flute had a deep throaty sound that Mellik could feel behind his ears. The notes were long and sad, and the tune had the feel of rain on an autumn evening. After a few moments Babbayannek joined in. There was an air of dancing light to his higher melody, but it also echoed and complemented the lower tune Querin still played. Now it was like the flicker of a candle or a hearth fire burning on a cold, wet eve. There was a warmth to it, and a feeling of protection: home.

Querin's deep tones changed. They became hushed and slow, like the hills after a deep snowfall. Babbayannek paused as Querin's tune seemed, though beautiful, to offer only the cold and desolation of a long winter. Babbayannek began to play again. So soft and in harmony with Querin that Mellik didn't even notice at first. The higher melody gradually changed. It still echoed the cold beauty of Querin's notes, but now there was more, or the promise of more. It hung somewhere between the earlier hearth fire and the cold of winter. The image came to Mellik of a crocus peeking up through the snow. It was the promise of spring. It was slightly discordant to Querin's deeper part and the two parts pushed against each other.

Mellik had been watching with his second sight, the slow swirl of air magic blurring as he listened to the complex weave of music. Suddenly he saw it: there was more than just air mana swirling about. Spirit magic that twined, joined, and parted from the air magic. It was like two dim currents flowing from Querin and Babbayannek. The streams twined and bobbed, and eventually ran together in a complex weaving and then dancing together through the air. Mellik gasped as he saw the spirit mana flow not just around Querin and Babbayannek, but around himself as well. He glanced at the two elves and saw delight and merry laughter sparkle in their eyes and faces.

The music had changed again. The two parts had merged and no longer played against each other but played off each other. It was spring, and there was dancing, fires, and laughter in the night air. The two elves were animated in their playing, and Mellik noticed that the spirit mana moved about the room differently as well. The music wasn't faster, just more joyous in its movements. Babbayannek trilled his instrument in a vibrant crescendo, and Querin followed. They finished, and the music echoed about the room. The air mana dissipated quickly, but the spirit mana faded away slowly. Mellik burst into applause.

Babbayannek bowed politely and then waved away Mellik's applause.

"But did you see it?" he asked.

"The spirit mana? Yes, I saw it, Master."

Babbayannek's face split into an even wider grin, and he pounded Querin on the back.

"Good job! Well done bringing him here. But he'll need an instrument." Babbayannek's voice grew a little harder to follow with his excitement, the words slurring and clipping. He began to rummage about on the tables, reaching out to one instrument and then shaking his head to grasp another. Querin waved in front of him to get his attention.

"He won't have much time for learning with all his other studies, Master," Querin explained when he had the older elf's attention.

Babbayannek stopped and looked intently at Mellik. One finger tapped idly at his chin while the other hand rolled out a rhythm on the table.

"So be it," he finally said, coming back to the table with the lantern. He lit a smaller lamp off the lantern, and then strode off with the lantern.

"Stay here. I'll be right back," he called over his shoulder.

"You're very good," Mellik said with a gesture at the flute in Querin's hand.

Querin waved away the compliment. "Master Babbayannek is better. He can't play as quickly anymore since he can't hear the notes, but being able to see the magic between himself and his audience the way he does . . . Have him play you a ballad on the harp some time. It will have you weeping."

It was darker in the hall with only the small lamp for light. The hush of the room seemed wrong now. It made Mellik want to speak.

"Querin, why did you bring me here?"

"Master Babbayannek gets his powers of music by drinking the blood of mortals."

Querin said it with a straight face, but Mellik knew him too well. "No, really. Why?"

Querin sighed and fiddled with the flute for a moment. "You have seen enough ugliness the last couple of days. I wanted to remind you that there was beauty here too. Not everything... Not everyone is cruel and ugly."

"I know that, Querin."

"Yes, but could you feel it?"

Mellik bit back his reply as the intensity of his friend's gaze made him really think about the question. He tried to remember how he'd felt yesterday or even earlier that morning. There'd been rage. It was still there, along with pain and a sense of loneliness. Now there was room for other things; joy at the music, wonderment at the magic he'd seen coming from it, curiosity about what Master Babbayannek would bring, even a desire to play that well.

"Thank you," he said.

More light jumped into the room as Babbayannek opened a door with his lantern bobbing before him.

"Found it," he announced, almost jogging up to Mellik.

The elf handed Mellik a narrow wooden case that looked about the right size for a flute. Babbayannek was bouncing from foot to foot. Mellik carefully undid the clasp and opened the wooden case. He was slightly disappointed to see a wooden flute-like instrument. He'd had thoughts of something grand like the silver and brass instruments he saw scattered about the room with their large bells and shiny keys. He should have known those weren't for beginners.

"It's a recorder," Babbayannek told him.

Mellik looked again. Indeed, it wasn't a flute. It had a more bulbous mouthpiece that tapered, and the other end flared slightly where the flutes were straight. Looking closer, Mellik saw that it was also beautifully carved, with a pattern of vines and lilies outlined subtly in the wood.

"It's beautiful, Master Babbayannek," he said. Mellik glanced at Querin and saw a look of disbelief on his face that quickly dissolved into a smile.

"Here," and Babbayannek reached over to take out the instrument. "Let me show you how to play it."

*   *   *

Mellik strolled along the path back to the college of magic with Querin at his side and the recorder tucked under his arm in its case. He was going to be late to magic theory class with Master Marran, and would likely have to work the kitchens as punishment, but he didn't mind. To be truthful, Mellik was taking his time sauntering back, not willing to let go of the joyous feeling of the music. Mellik was amazed that he had been able to play anything in such a short time. Granted it was only a few notes and a couple of short tunes, but it had still been music. He was a long ways from making spirit mana flow through the air like the elves, but Master Babbayannek had said that he was a quick study, and he would get there someday if he promised to practice every day: which he had.

Querin did most of the teaching since Babbayannek could hear Mellik, and Mellik's skills weren't good enough to produce the magic the elves had shown.

Mellik remembered Querin's startled expression when Babbayannek had first brought out the recorder. "Querin, what is special about this instrument?"

Querin smiled and looked up at the trees around them.

"Have you heard of a heartwood tree?" he asked.

"No."

"There are trees called heartwoods in the southern forests. They call them that because the wood is a deep crimson in color, but that's not a real heartwood. True heartwood trees grow only in the forest of the elves. They are larger than any other tree in this world. Many people believe that this is because of elven magic, but the trees were there before the elves and before anyone. They are also the smartest and wisest of trees, though like all trees, their thoughts are slow."

Querin smiled at this like a subtle joke. Mellik was trying hard to believe a tree could think at all.

"The elves protect the trees, and in return, the trees give us a home. We don't cut them for wood like human houses, nor do we shape them with magic. The trees watch the lives of the elves and then provide what they believe we need: not just the structure of the house, but things like tables and chairs and beds. Most of the time all these things that the heartwoods create are attached, living parts of the tree. The tree can slowly move them, change them, or even reabsorb them depending on the changing needs of the elves living there. On a rare occasion, however, a tree might make a gift of something that it splits from itself. Think of making something from your flesh and then cutting it off."

Mellik thought of the act of enchanting, and he fingered the belt buckle that contained much of Arbret's essence now.

"That is where your recorder came from. Elves can name every heartwood tool that has been made and probably tell you some of its history. They are rare and precious to our people."

Mellik stroked the case under his arm. It was made from some kind of animal skin, but it was hard and bumpy.

"Then I should give this one back."

"That's not what I meant at all. It was a gift. Elves do not hoard these things like a dragon's gold. Understand how rare and precious it is, honor Master Babbayannek for the gift, but do not insult him by giving it back."

"But why would he give it to **me**?"

"Master Babbayannek has been giving instruments away to any student who had an interest in learning since the Emperor took his ears. As to why he gave you that one? It's hard to explain, but elves are more in touch with our other senses than you humans. In addition to taste and touch, smell and hearing, we have a sense that goes even deeper than the third eye of a wizard. Call it intuition, instinct, or premonition. Master Babbayannek had a feeling that he should give it to you, and I could tell by his look when you opened the case that it felt right to him. It's hard for you humans to accept this, but you need to trust Master Babbayannek. He probably can't even tell you why, but it was the right thing to do.

"Besides, I heard you try to play that flute. We're going to need all the help we can get making you into a musician."

Querin dodged Mellik's backhand. Mellik smiled as he jogged to catch up with his friend.

Chapter 27

Brin was promoted to senior apprentice a few days after Mellik's whipping. Mellik figured if Brin had managed to kill him the promotion would have been immediate. Senior apprentice was just a step below journeyman. Querin had explained that senior apprentices were deemed to have all the knowledge necessary to achieve journeyman, but they had to prove they had the necessary skill and control out in the real world. That should have been good news to Mellik, since Brin would be leaving. In reality, it could take weeks or months to find him the correct posting. In the meantime, he now officially had rank over Mellik, and could even wear his rapier around the school. Which, of course, Brin did: giving it a slap and smiling every time he saw Mellik.

Mellik didn't go anywhere alone. He took different routes to and from all his classes every day. He knew more of the school's unused back corridors than probably anyone else.

At the same time, Mellik was busier than he would have thought possible. He woke early now so he could learn Kigana. Querin had come with him at first, but after he'd helped Mellik learn the basics, Querin started having Bo go with him. Mellik didn't really have any interest or talent in the transformation magics, but after getting beaten up by Brin, he figured anything that might give him some martial training was worth the hour of sleep. The group did everything in slow motion, but every few days Querin would show he and Bo how one of the movements could be used for actual fighting.

After that came breakfast and his assigned classes. He still spent his afternoons at the forge, but now he rushed over to practice music with Babbayannek and Querin before dinner. After dinner he would go to an unused classroom he had found during his explorations to practice and study. Bo, Querin, Fesskah and even Keyessa would usually join him. Having such experienced apprentices made studying easy. Being such good company made it pleasant.

"Why aren't you a journeyman?" Mellik asked Querin at one such gathering. The elf was so knowledgeable and skilled at magic, it was impossible to imagine he had anything left to learn for the rank.

Querin shrugged, "If you asked the masters, I'm sure they would tell you that though I am surpassing skilled in some areas of magic, my knowledge and abilities are lacking in others."

The room was lit by a warm yellow light that seemed to come from everywhere at once. Mellik had been surprised to find that illusion magic was really just the use of light, which made Bo especially competent at lighting their gatherings. He'd been experimenting each night with something different. The yellow was one of the best he'd come up with: it felt like the light of sunset. The lack of shadows was a bit eerie however.

"But that doesn't make sense," commented Keyessa. She kept a running interpretation with her hands for Bo of any conversation when she was there. "All journeyman and even the Masters aren't skilled in all areas of magic."

"I didn't say it made sense, I said it is what they would tell you," Querin stated with another shrug. "They had to raise me to senior apprentice years ago, but they've never sent me out to earn journeyman. "Still looking for an appropriate position," is the official line."

"No elf will make journeyman," said Fesskah. "No goblin either."

"How do they decide who makes Journeyman?" Mellik asked.

"That'ss jusst it: they deesside. No tesst or sstandard criteria; your Masster ssayz you're ready, the other massterz assk quesstionz, then they vote."

"It's all very political," added Keyessa. "They don't even say how the voting went. They'll tell you things to work on if they vote against you. That rarely happens though because a Master won't put his apprentice up for promotion unless he's sure he'll pass."

"There must be some way..." Mellik mused.

"Don't be naive," Keyessa snorted at him.

Mellik ignored her. She rarely spoke to him unless it was sprinkled with subtle derision.

"Could you do something that made it impossible for them to ignore your skills and knowledge?" Mellik asked.

Querin up at him with his bright green eyes, "Like what?"

"I don't know," Mellik admitted.

Keyessa snorted condescendingly again.

"Like what the Massterz have to do," chimed in Fesskah, his head popping up.

"What do you mean?" asked Mellik.

"The requirement for becoming a Master Wizard," explained Querin. "There's no testing or politics. You have to come up with an entirely new magic. Something that no one has ever done before."

"They call it, "Advancing the art of Magic," Keyessa's tone was dismissive. "Good luck doing that. Most Masters spend decades researching and experimenting to come up with a new magic. Most journeymen never make Master because of how hard that is. That's not even mentioning finding the time or getting the space to do this research as an apprentice."

"She's right," Querin acknowledged with a hearty sigh. "The elves have been practicing magic since before humans came. An elf who broadens our knowledge of magic is revered and remembered, but there are so few of them in this millennia that I can list their names. You'd have better luck changing the Master's minds."

Querin's tone left no doubt how dim the chances of that last coming about were.

"Still, there must be some way," Mellik muttered.

Keyessa began to hum a tune Querin had taught them all. It was called, "Fool in the Well". Mellik opened his mouth to defend himself, but Fesskah cut him off.

"Let'ss work on your tranzmutation," the goblin ordered. He didn't give Mellik time to protest. "Concentrate on the sskin of your arm. Look at the mana of it right at the ssurfass. Memorize it; feel it. You need to be able to conjure up that image always on a momentss notiss.

"Oness you know the sskin - the layerz, the texture, the way it interactss with the resst of your arm - we will talk about how to make it thicker and tough: like leather."

"I still think turning a small bit to stone would be easier for him," commented Keyessa. "It's his talent and would come more naturally."

"Yesss, but if he does not learn hiz body well enough firsst, he will not be able to change it back."

"If it was just a small spot, even if he failed we could cut it out and heal the wound," she argued. "The body is complex, even the skin. Changing it without a natural talent for it or a deep knowledge of the type of leathery skin you are talking about could be worse."

Mellik had had enough. He wouldn't just let it go this time.

"Ignore her, Fesskah. She just wants to cut me open like Lady Yew."

Mellik said it to hurt her. He had told them the story of the scar on his face. He remembered her disgust and anger when she heard of what the lady had done. It was one of the few times he could remember her not looking at him with scorn.

A small gasp issued from Keyessa. Mellik saw her jaw work in an angry retort as her pale cheeks flushed. She turned and stomped from the room. The door slammed shut behind her.

"That was illy done, my friend," commented Querin.

"A Goblin would have just eaten you," added Fesskah.

Bo asked what had happened.

"*Later,*" Mellik signed at him. The last thing he needed was to explain this to Bo. The big apprentice fawned over her like his long lost love.

"I'll go apologize," he added out loud and headed for the door.

Mellik didn't actually feel like apologizing. Keyessa constantly made him feel like he didn't belong, or wasn't good enough to be a part of this group that she herself was the newest member of. She had never said anything outright, but it was always there in her tone, or the way she would fail to ask his opinion on things. These were his friends. How dare she wedge herself between them.

Mellik went to the door and formed a small ball of light in his palm. It was far dimmer than Bo's or the one Keyessa would have made, but it had taken weeks of hard work and was the best he could manage with illusion. You could see in the dark with the second sight, but the glow of mana blinded you to anything more than a few feet away.

As he trudged off toward the used parts of the tunnels, Mellik became angry. It was just like Keyessa to manage to make him seem like the bad guy in front of his friends. She probably hadn't even been upset. First she had made him look stupid, and now she was trying to make him look mean. She was the one always making snide comments and putting him down. He'd been nothing but nice and polite to her. He couldn't be expected to put up with that forever could he?

A muffled thump and a girl's sharp cry made him pause. Then Mellik began to run. He dug in to the pouch at his side and pulled out three of the throwing triangles Kaleed had made for him.

"You stupid demon whore," a young man's voice echoed down the hall. "Brin will be very pleased to see you."

Mellik heard Keyessa cry out in pain again. He slid around the corner to see Keyessa standing facing him, August stood behind her, one hand pulling her head back by her hair, the other holding a belt knife to her throat.

Mellik brought his hand up to throw his discs but was brought up short with a warning from August.

"Those discs go in the air and she dies."

Mellik could see a drop of blood trickle down Keyessa's throat.

"Drop the discs," August commanded. "And I can see if you channel, so try anything and the bitch dies."

The fact that August needed to tell him he could see channeling made Mellik suspect August couldn't himself channel yet. It was small consolation as Mellik let his cutting discs clatter to the floor. Anything Mellik did would be slower than the knife.

"Now turn around. If I see your eyes again I'll slit her wide open."

"August, my family will see you well rewarded if you release me." Her voice was steady, but Mellik could see the fear in her eyes before he turned around.

Keyessa gasped, and Mellik had to restrain himself from turning around.

"Bitch, I know who your family is. I could buy them to lick horse's asses if I wanted to. Brin and his masters on the other hand can give me power, teach me things you'll never get to know."

"Take me instead," Mellik said without turning.

"What?" asked August.

"I'm the one Brin really wants. You can't take us both, so take me."

"You think I'm stupid?" growled August. "I know the demon whore knows more magic than you. Hold still bitch."

August let go of Keyessa's hair and grabbed her blouse by the shoulder. With a yank, he ripped a large piece of the long sleeve off all the way down to her wrist.

"Tie this around your eyes. And no tricks, I want the cloth all the way up over your eyebrows and down over your nose."

Keyessa complied, her hands shaking as she tied the knot.

"Rock-head: up against the wall with your nose right up to it. And put your hands flat out against it where I can see them too."

Mellik took a couple steps forward and pressed his nose against the hard stone. He could see the steady glow of its mana right before his eyes. Oddly he noticed that the mana didn't blur up this close as something with his normal vision would have. He placed his palms out to the sides, feeling the cool steadiness resting there.

"Remember, one twitch and the she-demon gets it. Bitch, you're going to go right next to your rock-head boyfriend there and do the same thing he's doing."

Mellik saw her movement to his left and felt her fingers brush his arm as she placed her hands against the wall. An instant later the cool steel of August's knife was pressed against his own throat.

"Now it's you that gets it if you try something," August

whispered in his ear. "You better hope she cares for your life as much as you do for hers. You're almost as good to me dead, so don't tempt me.

"You start counting slowly to one hundred," August instructed Keyessa in a louder voice as he pulled Mellik away from the wall. "Turn around and rock-head dies and then you're next."

Mellik only had a second to think about it while August's attention was on Keyessa. Brin would kill him. Mellik's best chance was now. At least Keyessa should be able to run away...

Mellik concentrated on his skin laying cold beneath the knife. He thought of the look and feel of the stone's mana on the walls. He changed the magic within himself. Just below the blade of the knife he stilled it, cooled it; made it solid and patient like the stone. Mellik took no time to ponder what he had done, but channeled again. This time he lashed out at the air around his neck and shoulders. He captured it in place first, made it as immobile against his body as stone, then he poured more and more into it as quickly as he could. He could feel August begin to pull at his arm and the knife in reaction.

"Run!" Mellik yelled.

August pulled hard and Mellik felt the knife slip and heard it grate against the stone that used to be his skin. August yanked Mellik off balance and he felt himself falling backward into the bigger boy. Mellik's body reacted instinctively to keep him upright, scissoring backward, while his mind was desperately working on solidifying the air around the knife. It was hard enough working on a space he could not see, but keeping the image of himself and his internal mana in his mind was difficult now that he had a chunk of something in his neck that his mind fought with him to correct.

They caromed off the wall behind them with a satisfying grunt from August, but Mellik lost his balance and was launched to the floor with August on top of him. Mellik had the wind knocked from him. He managed to keep his mind on the air trapping the knife, but he was losing. He could feel the knife sliding and scraping along the stone of his neck. It was only a matter of time before it found skin. Mellik fought on, keeping the air as solid as he could. He would give Keyessa every second he could.

Suddenly August's weight slumped against him.

"You can let go of the air around the knife now," Keyessa told him.

August seemed lifeless against his back, but Mellik could hear the boy's breath whistling behind his ear. Mellik released the air mana and reached up to carefully move the hand with the knife away from his neck. The knife slid easily from the boy's grasp, and Mellik wiggled out from beneath him.

"Are you alright?" asked Keyessa.

Mellik just nodded: the adrenaline and his labored breathing too much to speak through.

"Did he cut you?" she asked, reaching out to tilt his chin up. Mellik felt guilty noticing how soft her skin felt. She felt at the patch of skin that was now stone. "Demon shit! You idiot!"

"Didn't...have...choice," Mellik managed to gasp out.

"But your neck? Stone?" Keyessa held a hand to her forehead as if in pain. "I know, I know: You didn't have a choice. "Okay, quickly before your body gets used to that stuff -- If you can remember what your whole neck used to feel like you can use that image. If not, you can try to copy the feel and look of the skin around it."

Keyessa reached out again to gently push and tug at the patch of stone.

"Okay. It doesn't feel like it's attached to anything, so you only transformed the skin itself. That's good. When you try to change it back, make sure you don't do anything deeper. If you're not sure, it might be safer to go the infirmary and just cut it out."

Mellik could remember his mind rebelling against the stone of his skin. He could almost see what it had tried to do against his will.

"I think I've got it," he said, his breathing coming more easily.

Keyessa took her hand away. It was almost the opposite of channeling. Mellik simply thought of his body's mana levels as normal, releasing a small amount of the mana he'd absorbed as a light breeze. It was relatively easy since Arbret had drilled him for weeks on just this. He thought his neck felt slightly different, but it was hard to tell.

"Well?" he asked.

Keyessa reached out to poke at the spot on his neck. It felt normal to him.

"It feels normal," Keyessa echoed his thoughts, stepping back. "Even the teardrop mark on your neck is back. What do you call them."

Mellik smiled at the memory. "My mother called them, "Tears of the Mother"."

Keyessa looked down at August, who had begun to snore.

"Come on," she said. "We should get back in case his friends come looking for him."

She turned and stalked back toward their abandoned classroom.

"What did you do to him?" Mellik asked, jogging up next to her.

"I put him into a light coma. Basically, I put him to sleep. A Mage skilled in healing can put you to sleep, or even kill you. If he touches you, you can't even stop the magic unless you're holding an image of your healthy self in your third eye. It's one of the reasons apprentices are always sent to a beginning transformation class as soon as they can channel. It's the most basic skill a mage needs to survive." Keyessa stared hard at Mellik for a moment.

It took Mellik a minute, but then he got it. "And they were never going to send me to that class..."

"Exactly. And that's why Querin and Fesskah have been working with you."

And that was why Arbret had drilled him so hard on that very thing for weeks and weeks.

"They're good friends," Mellik murmured.

Keyessa stopped and Mellik turned back to see why. She was looking down, one hand on her hip, the other shading her eyes.

"Are you alright?" Mellik asked. "Did he hurt you?"

Keyessa turned away without answering. In the glow of the ball of mage light hovering in front of her, Mellik couldn't see how deep the cut on her neck was. She slumped against the wall. She turned and slid down to sit against it. It was only then that Mellik realized she was crying. He didn't know why she was crying or what to say, and he felt awkward standing above her. Mellik slid down to sit next to her, an arm's length away.

She was upset, likely scared. Mellik tried to think of something to say.

"August is just a demon dangle. What he said didn't mean anything.

Keyessa began to laugh. Mellik was even more confused. It wasn't what he had expected, but it seemed better than the quiet crying.

Keyessa looked up at him finally, the dust and tears mingling on her face. "You really make it hard to hate you."

That statement was almost as confusing as the laughter.

"August was right." Keyessa waved away Mellik's protest. "I've been a right demon bitch and you can't possibly deny that. Do you know they teach us to hate you?"

The confused look on Mellik's face must have been answer enough.

"In the Capitol," she continued, "they teach us that Kamori are heartless killers. Elves can't be trusted, Goblins should be feared, and Kamori are to be hated. We hear stories of suicidal Kamori who attack citizens and soldiers just so their spirit can add to the curse that might one day kill thousands of innocents in and around the city. A whole race so bent on vengeance they refuse to become a part of the great and benevolent empire."

Silence stretched out between them, and the light seemed to dim as it awaited his response.

"That's not how it was told to me." His voice sounded weak and inadequate breaking that barrier of quiet.

Keyessa chuckled again, but it seemed forced this time. "Of course not. I've read the Dwomin Prophesy you know: a couple of weeks ago. Querin filled me in on some of the history when I asked. I've managed to not be afraid of Fesskah, and I trust what Querin has told me as truth, so why have I gone on hating you? I think it was easier than admitting I was wrong, that I was just like August. I followed Brin because it felt safe to be a part of them. My father would say I forgot my duty."

"But you came to our defense out in the crater."

"I came to Bo's defense. My little brother is deaf too. I think I've defended him from bullying so much it was a reflex. You just happened to be there too."

"I think you might have stepped in even without Bo being there. You took out August just now even though you could have run. Demons, I even told you to run. You risked yourself for someone you've been taught to hate. That says something."

Keyessa looked at him with an honest smile for the first time he could remember.

"Thank you, Mellik. I am sorry for the way I've treated you, and I'll try to be a better friend if you'll have me as one."

Mellik grinned and stuck out his hand, "Heck, anyone who can kill me with a touch I want on my side."

Keyessa gave his hand a brief shake and then stood, brushing off the hall's dust. "Speaking of which, we should get going. August could wake up any time."

Mellik stood and they strode off together.

Book 3:

WIND

Chapter 28

". . . The art of transmogrification is almost as dangerous to learn as teleportation," Master Marran lectured to the class. "Many people believe the goblins are the masters of this art, but in truth, their own mastery is due to an instinctive affinity for it. This instinct gives them a powerful advantage in transmogrification, but it also limits their ability to mimicking different aspects of other animals, mostly reptiles. The pinnacle of the art of transmogrification is considered to be the complete transformation of one's body into the semblance of another creature."

The bell rang for the end of class, and Master Marran paused.

"I'll be leaving in a couple of days, so class will be canceled during that time." A happy murmur went up in the class, but Master Marran raised his hands with a grin to forestall it. "To make sure you have something to do, I'm assigning you a report on your choice of the magic specialties. You'll be presenting the strengths and dangers of that magic specialty to the rest of the class."

The murmur turned to a groan.

"We'll get started tomorrow," he continued, "but start thinking about your choices now. Class dismissed."

The class broke up amid a buzz of discussion.

"Mellik, can I speak to you a moment," Master Marran said as Mellik was getting up to leave.

"Yes, Master?"

"Walk with me a moment would you?" Marran gestured for Mellik to come with him as he left the classroom.

Master Marran's classroom was the last one deep in the volcano's walls, and the halls were already deserted. The echoes of the retreating students gathered around them like happy ghosts. Marran turned to head even deeper into the caverns. Mellik took his place just behind Marran.

"You've had some trouble here at the college?" Master Marran asked.

They'd never talked of the attack, and Mellik had never

mentioned Master Marran's warning to anyone. He wasn't sure if this was an invitation to broach the subject or not.

"Yes, Master." Mellik would let Master Marran be more specific if that was what he wanted.

Marran smiled at his response. "And you've found allies?" he asked.

"My friends are a great help, Master."

"Friends, yes. Friends can be a great boon, but sometimes their motives are less pure than a true ally."

"Yes, Master." Mellik had no idea what Master Marran meant by that.

The hall echoed only their footsteps now.

"Here we are."

Marran stopped at the only door on the wall. It was sheathed in steel with a lock and no handle.

"Well, Mellik, what do you see?" Master Marran gestured at the door.

"It's trapped, Master." Mellik had already been studying the door as they approached.

"I wouldn't call it a trap," Marran said, looking thoughtfully at the door. "If it were a trap, it would be hidden, wouldn't it? This is more of a warning for those who shouldn't be entering this room and a protection for those who do. Shall we see what's inside?"

Master Marran pulled a small key from his pocket and turned it in the lock. There was a barely audible click and the door swung silently open. Master Marran swept to one side with his arms spread and exclaimed, "Ta-da!"

The room was impressive. It had ten walls that formed a decagon, and each wall was painted a different color: red, aquamarine, black, yellow, silver, green, purple, white, blue, and gold. The floor and ceiling were the natural black stone in the rest of the tunnels, but inlaid in the floor was a golden pentagram inside a silver circle with runes placed inside each point of the pentagram. Mellik recognized them from his studies as earth, air, fire, water, and spirit. There were five more runes that Mellik didn't recognize on the outside of the pentagram, and another at its center.

"It's beautiful, Master. What are the runes?"

"Ah, come in and shut the door," Master Marran said, striding into the middle of the room. "Do you remember any of them?"

Mellik followed him into the room and shut the door, but stayed at the edge of the circle.

"Yes, Master. I know the runes for the five elements, but I don't remember the rest of these."

"You're a good student, Mellik. We haven't learned these others. This one in the center," and Master Marran stepped aside to gesture at the rune he'd been standing on, "is a different symbol for earth. In Old Tequin the literal translation is "great mother," but it refers to our world. The other runes are highest, knowledge, center, power, and magic."

Marran pointed at each symbol as he said them. "Do you know what this pentagram is for?"

"Master, is it a teleportation circle?"

"Very good, and the runes allow a mage to teleport something or someone to this unique spot."

"But Master, what if someone else made a pentagram with the same symbols?"

"Excellent question," Master Marran beamed at him. "First, we mages are very careful to not duplicate teleportation circles. Each one has to be approved by the Emperor himself. Second, that's what the walls are for."

Marran walked over and rapped his knuckles against the blue wall. It echoed woodenly in the chamber.

"These walls are moveable. The Emperor occasionally has the walls rearranged for security. If we want to teleport anywhere, we have to send a message and get the correct wall order for our destination. We also get a timeframe for when we are allowed to make the teleportation. The college has three teleportation circles."

This was sounding like one of Master Marran's lectures, so Mellik stood patiently and waited for the rest of the information.

"The smallest is used for sending messages. That circle is in a room the size of your head. The walls don't move, but it's isolated and buried in rock, so there's little chance of using it as a weapon. The second is our main teleportation circle. It's roughly half this size. It has the moveable walls for security. Its main use is the transporting of people and small amounts of goods between locations. Due to the hazards inherent in teleportation, the immediate presence of the person or objects being teleported needs to be deemed critical by the Emperor. This is the largest of the three, and we're one of only a few locations with a teleportation circle this large. The palace has one, of course, but the others are all military forts strategically located around the Empire."

Master Marran paused, and Mellik could tell he was supposed to inquire further.

"Why is that, Master?"

Marran grinned. "You **are** a good student. Well, this circle existed before the Emperor, a relic of the circle's original use. Do you know what it is?"

Mellik shrank back from the edge of the circle. "Is this a summoning circle, Master?"

Marran chuckled. "Summoning circle, teleportation circle - they're all the same until you put them to use. Some rumors persist that this is the very circle where the Emperor started his conquest of the Western realms. Personally, I believe he must have used the one below us."

"The one below us, Master?"

Marran chuckled again. "Yes, and actually there are two circles in the tunnels below us. I know that makes five, but the caverns down there aren't considered part of the college. That's actually one of the reasons I asked you here. You see, the two circles below us are used for teleportation practice by senior apprentices when they are deemed ready. Now, you're not ready for that, but Master Tanay says that you show remarkable ability with earth magic. We are bringing a small handful of her students with us on this trip as well. As the Mage in charge of this little expedition, it's up to me to determine if you would be an asset or a liability to us."

Marran paused significantly, as if waiting for a response. Mellik couldn't think of anything to say on his own behalf, so he kept silent.

"You've made some enemies - both within the school and without," Marran finally commented. "You could use some allies as well."

"Of course, Master. I would take any allies I can find. I **have** made friends with Querrin and Feskah."

Marran sniffed and rolled his eyes. "An elf and a goblin? You could hardly have managed to ostracize yourself any further. You need human allies."

Mellik bristled at the implied slight to his friends, "Master, some would argue that I am not human."

Marran grinned slyly at Mellik, "and the Emperor would argue that your friend Bo isn't a human either, but a genetic mutant; a mistake, a 'sub-human'.

"You're familiar with the Regidion Prophecy, I take it?" Marran continued without waiting for Mellik to respond.

Mellik nodded while he tried to decipher the reason for the change in conversation.

"Of course you are:

His power will be brought forth from the place of great magics and fools.
Like a great wave he will cleanse the lands,
A reflection of himself made with his hands.
Hate and love feed him, but fear will be the most effective tool.
A reign longer than man's life, immortal seeming.
A doom will be sewn in the enemy's victory.
Mother of all singing her song, she creates her vessel.

True blood of the earth blood will mark him.
The love of family, sustain and nurture,
While friends protect and guide to mature.
He will bring the cure for all that feeds the grim.
Above their bitter loss and mourning,
A powerful light is seen in its gleaming.
Power found, beyond the vessel's brim.

The vessel's victory, brief.
The cure will still be the way.
Its lack of power will sway
Defeat into hope through grief.
Some will fall to the world's ill
That nations throw off its will
And be free of magic's thief."

"I'm only half Kamori, Master," Mellik said reflexively.

Marran's smile was ironic. "Of course you are. It says so on a piece of paper: a piece of paper half the people choose not to believe, and the other half are merely 'unsure' of its validity.

"There are those who oppose the Emperor's rule; people who would protect you if you would erase any doubt and proclaim yourself the prophesied 'true blood of the earth.' True or not, you have an opportunity to help stop the brutal oppression your people, your mother has endured."

Marran's smile was gone from his eyes as he stared at Mellik, replaced with a zealous entreaty. His face looked almost lupine in its hunger. Master Marran was one of the few masters at the college who had showed kindness to Mellik. He'd been as fair in class as he could. He'd tried to warn Mellik of Brin's attack, and he had done what he could to ameliorate Mellik's punishment afterward. Master Marran was circumspect and inconspicuous, and if there was a Master he could trust at the college, it was Marran. Yet, it was that avid look in Master Marran's eyes that made Mellik pause. It was the same look he remembered in Master Yew's face - a look of selfish need and desire.

"I'm sorry, Master Marran," Mellik managed to mumble. "I don't think I'd be very good at lying."

The look of deep yearning dissolved so quickly into Master Marran's usual beatific smile that Mellik blinked in surprise.

"I'm sorry that I had to do that," Master Marran said, reaching out to squeeze Mellik's shoulder. "There are those who are still unsure of your origin, or whether you might use your Kamori heritage in aid of those opposed to the Emperor. I'm afraid a further test was required before I brought you with us."

"What if I had failed, Master?" Mellik pulled his hands behind his back as they began to shake.

Marran's smile was almost melancholy now.

"No sense in wondering or worrying about 'might have beens,' Mellik. We must all act on what is now in front of us and make the best use of it we can. I'll see you in the courtyard after breakfast tomorrow."

"Yes, Master," Mellik replied.

Mellik was so flustered by the abrupt dismissal and Master Marran's last comment that he was halfway back to the Master's classroom before he realized he didn't know what kind of supplies or clothing he should be bringing. Mellik turned and headed slowly back toward the teleportation chamber. Master Marran should be coming the same way, and Mellik wanted a moment to think about what he should ask about the trip. He came around the corner and saw Brin's cloak and legs disappear into the summoning chamber. Mellik had spent so much time watching for Brin around bends and in dark corners that his silk cloak and silver tooled boots were unmistakable. The door clicked softly closed behind Brin.

Mellik should have just turned around. He could have gone to Master Tanay with his questions. He could have waited until later to talk to Master Marran. Instead he crept quietly up to the closed door and placed his ear against it.

"What was his answer, Master?" There was a note of respect in Brin's voice that Mellik hadn't heard him use even when speaking to Master Pelliery.

"He won't be helping us, not yet anyway," Master Marran

replied flatly. The room echoed a bit, but their voices were distinct even through the door.

"Then the plan, Master?" asked Brin.

"We go ahead as originally planned, and we'll do it your way. We can get someone else to play our savior, and we don't need one right now. Mellik may yet be of use to us."

"Yes, Master."

"And the other apprentice?"

"He is taken care of, Master"

"Good. Keep an eye on your crew. Stay close tonight and keep them quiet. Young men can get nervous at times like these."

Mellik pushed himself away from the door and began to walk quickly, but quietly, away from the chamber. He couldn't help looking over his shoulder, afraid at any moment to see Brin or Master Marran come out into the hall and spot him. As soon as he was around the corner, he couldn't control his legs any longer, and he broke into a run.

Chapter 29

"It's obviously a trap," stated Keyessa, hugging herself and looking at the floor. Mellik signed what she had said to Bo when he looked at him.

"We don't know that," replied Querin as he paced around the perimeter of the room.

"Well, we don't," he reiterated as he saw Keyessa glare at him. Keyessa took up the sign interpretation when she saw Mellik trying to do it. "Master Marran said Mellik might still be useful, so they haven't given up on him joining them. On the other hand, if Mellik backs out, it will look like he suspects something. They can't afford to leave him behind if they think he might know something about their plotting."

Mellik shrugged, "I don't have any choice in the matter then, do I?"

Bo signed, 'Mellik sick.'

"No," Mellik signed back as he spoke aloud. "This is an important opportunity. Sick or not, any other apprentice would go. Plus, they'd likely know I was pretending to be sick."

"I could probably get something to make you truly ill if you wanted to," Keyessa added.

Mellik only thought about it for a second. "No. I'm still not sure it would fool them, and it still might seem too coincidental. Besides, Master Myg already warned you about stealing medicine."

"You are not a normal apprentiss. Thiss iz ssusspisshuss. There iz danger either way." Fesskah was looking slightly more muscular and predatory than usual. Mellik wondered if it was an involuntary reaction, or if he was doing it on purpose.

"The lizard is right," and Querin stopped pacing to look at the goblin, "and please, never use the word suspicious again. I think my ears are wilting. The majority of the other senior apprentices going to learn teleportation are Brin's cronies. Adding a few apprentices with a talent for earth magic at the last minute would seem odd enough, but Mellik will be the most junior apprentice going by far. We haven't heard anything about rebels or a plot against the Emperor, but we're isolated here. They might have a safe place Master Marran is planning to teleport his chosen apprentices to. They could kidnap Mellik and work on turning him into their puppet at their leisure."

'Why are the circles so deep underground?' Bo asked.

"They're teleportation circles," replied Querin, mimicking Charl's lecturing voice. "Teleportation is one of the most dangerous magics. Elves rarely practice it, not just because of its connection to summoning, but it requires the commitment of your entire being the very first time you attempt it. Most magics are external, so mistakes are rarely deadly and can be defended against. Even internal magics like transmutation can be learned gradually. Teleportation is an all or nothing endeavor from the first. Even practicing with inanimate objects is risky. Imagine accidentally teleporting a rock into someone's head. It's almost universally fatal.

"One of the safeguards you can put in place is to surround the teleportation area with something solid, like stone. It's hard to squeeze a body into something solid like stone, and a big piece doesn't want to be moved, so magic takes the easiest route and moves the body to the closest open area. With the practice circles below us, the only things around them are rock and a couple of tunnels that they can keep clear. It's the safest place the college has for teaching this skill."

"I will go," announced Fesskah.

"Can you do that?" asked Keyessa.

"I am a printss of the goblinz. It would be a grave inssult to refuze me in thiss."

"That is a good idea. As the representative of the elves, I will ask to be included as well."

Bo waved his arm, signing, 'Me too!'

Querin shook his head. "I'm sorry, Bo. Fesskah and I are skilled enough and certainly within our rights as senior apprentices to ask to go. You and Keyessa don't have the skills and standing to back up a request to come."

"You ssaid they were meeting tomorrow?" Fesskah asked.

"Yes. After breakfast in the clearing," replied Mellik.

"Good. We will make sshure we get invited right now."

Fesskah motioned for Querin to follow and swept from the room. Querin grinned and made an elaborate bow before following.

"We could be over-reacting," Keyessa commented as she stood to go too.

Mellik and Bo stood as well. They would be her escort back to the girl's wing of dormitories.

"But why would they invite me?"

Keyessa stopped and eyed him for a moment. "Are you serious?"

"I mean, unless it's some kind of trap, yeah."

"Okay, brace yourself, because your head is about to get really big. You've been here just a little over half a year. Haven't you noticed how far ahead of the other new apprentices you are?"

"Well, yes, but Bo and I got here early."

"Six weeks. Six weeks of informal training. In six weeks of being pummeled by Master Pelliery, you mastered as much air magic as an average apprentice might gain after a full year of classes with him."

"Journeyman Arbret started teaching me on our way down too." Part of Mellik wondered why he was protesting so vehemently. She was complimenting him, after all.

"A journeyman mage taught you to channel in a couple of weeks while traveling through the desert and scrub. Haven't you noticed that some of these apprentices still aren't channeling after four months with nothing else to do but learn? And that's normal."

And there it was: the reason he didn't want to be exceptional as an apprentice. He was already Kamori, a pariah. He didn't need anything else setting him apart. He wanted to be normal.

Chapter 30

Many of caves they passed through on their descent into the depths beneath the crater were just that, natural caves. Here and there, a passage had been dug or made taller. Occasional beams of wood held looser rock formations steady, but these were rare; the stone was solid beneath the college. Mellik didn't need the beams or pick marks to tell him when they were in a section hewn by mortal hands. He could feel it. It was like running your hand along your skin and coming across a scar that was rough and hardened - except it was the opposite for the stones. The natural caves felt hard - the man-made tunnels soft. He could feel this without using his second sight. They had been admonished to not use their second sight unless instructed to. Many a student had gashed their head on a protruding rock, because they did not spot through of the wash of mana in the stones around them, according to Master Tanay.

They had been traveling for hours already. Mellik was surprised by the scope of their undertaking. He wore a pack with a week's worth of rations: one day to get to the teleportation circles, five days of instruction, and then a day to return. At least their packs would be lighter on the return trip.

It was slow going through the caves. The man-made tunnels were easy enough, if a bit narrow, but much of the natural caverns had little more than ropes attached to the most precipitous of climbs. They had to hoist each other up smaller walls and scramble across large beds of rock falls. Master Tanay was leading the expedition, with Querin, Mellik, and the other earth apprentices behind her. The senior apprentices who would be studying teleportation brought up the rear with Master Marran.

Fesskah acted as a buffer between the two groups. Mellik was glad his friends had insisted on coming along. If there were senior apprentices along who weren't Brin's toadies, Mellik couldn't tell who they were. Brin's status as a noble and a favorite among the masters counted for a great deal even among the senior apprentices. That made Mellik unlucky, and Fesskah and Querin stupid for befriending him. Mellik was thankful for stupid people.

Master Tanay seemed far too nimble as she scrambled up the current pile of huge, jagged boulders. She was taller than Mellik, which helped, but Mellik had been watching her, and the smaller rocks didn't seem to shift under her like they did for the rest of them. Mellik suspected that there was than mere physical skill and ability in her ease crossing the rocks.

No one would be able to tell if he switched to his second sight if he didn't absorb any mana, and the cavern roof was well above them here. Even with the enchanted glowstones strapped to most of their heads, the ceiling was only dimly visible. Mellik decided to risk it.

With the second sight, the cavern changed. The glow of the stones about them overpowered the light given by the glowstones. It gave Mellik a strange sense of not being able to see the top layer of rocks as well as those beneath. It made the perspective off. Mellik found himself floundering as he reached for gaps instead of stones.

"Are you alright?" Tanay asked, turning to frown at him.

"I'm fine. My mind just wandered for a moment, Master Tanay."

Her frown deepened. She was holding extra mana: not a lot, but Mellik could see the difference.

"Pay attention, then. A slip even in the seemingly benign portions of the caverns can be injurious."

Tanay turned back to the climb, and Mellik watched where she stepped and grabbed, trying to copy her movements with his shorter limbs. As he became better at seeing in the second sight with the lower light levels, he was able to watch Master Tanay more closely. It was a subtle bit of magic. She was channeling a trickle of earth mana into each rock while she touched it. Mellik could barely tell she was channeling at all. It was even harder to tell what the earth mana was doing to the rocks. Mellik couldn't see what she was doing under her hands and feet. He needed to study the rocks before she touched them to see the difference in their mana makeup while she was channeling into them. Then he would have to figure out how to do the same thing, and do it while not looking at the rocks.

Mellik felt the stone beneath him shift. The shift became a roll, and he was airborne before he could even cry out. He landed hard on his side and felt something dig into his shoulder. Mellik levered himself up to a sitting position with a groan. A blaze of light made him look up.

Master Tanay stood on the precipice of a large triangular stone looking down at him.

"Are you injured?" she asked.

Mellik thought about it and rolled his shoulder experimentally. "I think I'm okay, Master."

She crossed her arms, and Mellik noticed she stood on only one foot. The stone was too small to fit the other. She let it dangle in the air, her posture straight and unwavering on the slim stone.

"Excellent. Then might I suggest that you use your normal vision as you were instructed?"

"Yes, Master. I'm sorry."

"If you are obedient and can keep from injuring yourself, perhaps I will show you my trick with the rocks on our return trip."

Tanay turned and hopped to a wider rock, continuing the climb.

"Need a hand up?" said a voice by his shoulder.

Mellik turned to see Joribhy, the youngest apprentice in their group besides himself. He was a pleasant, sandy haired young man with an easy smile who seemed to get along with everyone. Mellik hated him a little.

"Thank you," Mellik said as Joribhy hoisted him to his feet.

"I'll let you and your friends plot revenge on Master Tanay in private," Joribhy said with a wink as he continued his climb.

Mellik looked down the broken slope to see Querin and Fesskah converging on him. Querin made the rocks look like a dance floor, jogging up them with a skipping waltz. Fesskah was even worse. He'd scout the area ahead, and would then take great ten and fifteen foot leaps between the largest boulders.

"Show offs," commented Mellik as they both arrived at the same time. He felt a little better when Fesskah had to catch his balance briefly, as the smaller scree he stood upon shifted.

"Are you alright?" Fesskah asked.

"I'm fine. Does everyone have to be better at climbing this than me?"

In answer, Fesskah gestured back the way they had come. The other apprentices were strung out in a ragged line. With a quick glance, Mellik could see the tentative, uneven progress they were making.

"Okay fine, I'm just another human."

Querin sighed, "We wouldn't be going through all this if that was true."

Mellik laughed, "Brighten up, grumpy. You get a week off from studying."

"You mean a week stuck in a hole with nothing but trail rations and you two for company?"

"Fressh meat if you will eat rat," commented Fesskah.

"Uggh, no thank you," Querin made a face at the idea. "I'd rather keep them alive to improve the quality of my companions."

Fesskah snorted gustily.

"Come on you three," Tanay called from ahead. "Lunch is the other side of this rubble field."

Mellik turned with a smile and a clap to Querin's shoulder.

*   *   *

The rubble field ended at a level spot. The stone was knurled and pocked from cooled magma, but the edges were not sharp, so it was comfortable to sit on. Tanay had found a stone at the edge of the debris that was just the right height to sit on. It lay next to a larger piece of stone she was already using as a table. The other three earth magic apprentices were settling as a group to enjoy their lunch. Mellik would be part of that group for future meals, but this first lunch had been packed individually. By silent accord, he, Querin, and Fesskah chose a spot between the apprentices and Master Tanay.

Fesskah glanced around. "Masster, iz it warmer here?"

Mellik realized that Fesskah was right, he was warmer than the climb over the boulders should account for.

"Yes, Fesskah Gah-anole Gorfindal, it is. I will explain more after lunch."

The three of them dug into their flat bread, cheese, and smoked pork. Or, at least Mellik did. Querin gave his pork to Fesskah, and the goblin did likewise with his cheese.

"Why does Master Tanay call you that?" Mellik asked Fesskah.

"Becauze it iz my name."

"But no one else uses your full name. She's the only person I've ever heard refer to you that way."

"I believe Masster Tanay iz a proponent of the little formalitiez. Alsso, I think it iz ssomething of a joke for her."

"How is that a joke?" asked Mellik. Querin was grinning, but trying not to laugh.

"In my language, Fesskah meanz little tongue," explained the Goblin. "Gorfindal meanz grassland, or place where grass growz. Gah-anole is like to prinsse. So if you don't know it iz name, you might ssay, 'prinsse of little tongue in grass.'"

Querin began to howl in laughter. Mellik grinned at his laughter, but couldn't join in.

When Querin had calmed enough to be heard over, Mellik commented, "I still don't get it."

Querin doubled over, and his laughter became even more intense than before.

Fesskah smiled and reached over to pat Mellik on the shoulder. "You are a good person, Mellik Ackins."

Neither of them ever explained why it was so funny.

"Quiet down a minute, apprentices, so that I can tell you about the next chamber," Master Marran called out. Querin managed to get his laughter down to a soft giggle. "This shouldn't be particularly dangerous, as long as everyone is careful and does as instructed. The next cavern has a large fissure we must cross. There is a stone bridge across it, but it is narrow, and much of the old railing has fallen away. The warmth several of you have noticed is caused by steam coming up out of that fissure from deep inside the volcano. This causes algae to grow on the rocks and the bridge, so it is slippery. If you take it slow, it should still be a very easy stroll across. Just in case, however, we will be going across one at a time, and each person will be roped up."

Marran held up a stout coil of rope for everyone to see.

"I will lead us across," added Tanay. "Master Marran and I have already decided the order, so he will arrange you in a line and show you how to tie into the rope when we get there."

"Is anyone still finishing lunch?" asked Marran.

The sound of food hastily being stuffed into mouths and backpacks answered him.

"Excellent. Master Tanay, after you."

Everyone shuffled into position and got into a ragged row behind the lanky master.

The cavern with the boulders narrowed quickly, and they funneled into a man-made tunnel. A warm breeze blew past them from the tunnel's other end.

Mellik felt the slickness of the stones beneath his boots. The next instant, Joribhy grabbed reflexively for Mellik's pack as his feet slid out from under him. They both would have gone down if the tunnel had been wide enough to allow it. As it was, Mellik banged one set of knuckles painfully on the wall steadying himself.

Tanay glanced back. "The stone is already becoming slick," she said loud enough for everyone's benefit. "Take small measured steps and be sure of your footing. It will get slicker closer to the chasm."

They proceeded at a more cautious pace after that. The narrow passage opened up, and Tanay stepped to one side, motioning for Mellik to follow her.

They were in the largest cavern Mellik had yet seen. It stretched off in either direction past where their light could reach. The inky black algae covering the rock seemed to swallow their light. The chasm could be dimly seen stretching across the cavern's length in front of them, a deeper black than its surroundings.

"Stay near the walls," Tanay instructed as more students

emerged from the tunnel.

They kept in a line walking along the face of the cavern wall. Tanay stopped them when she saw Master Marran had emerged at the back of the group.

"You can take your packs off, but stay here," she said as she walked back to Marran.

The two Masters conversed, and then Master Marran raised a hand to quiet the murmuring apprentices. He held up the rope for them to see.

"As she said earlier, Master Tanay will go across first. You'll each take a turn holding the rope from this side before you cross. We'll start with Fesskah and Querin, and then I'll let you know who is next. Walk carefully up to where I'll be standing with the rope team, and I'll show you what to do when you get there."

The two masters walked slowly out toward the rift with Querin and Fesskah in tow. As their lights got closer to the chasm, they began to see the faint mist in the air, and then the bridge emerged from the darkness. Covered in its own algae, it was a shadow against deeper shadow, like a cloud against a starless, moonless sky.

The four figures stopped a few paces away from the bridge, and Tanay tied herself to the rope while Querin bent down and adjusted something to set their feet. The rope formed a large loop with Tanay at one end and the apprentices holding it with just a little slack, and the rest lying coiled at their feet and then stretching back to Master Tanay. Tanay looked to see if the apprentices were ready. They both nodded their assent. Tanay walked across the bridge. Mellik thought it was a slightly more measured pace than her usual swinging gait, but otherwise she might have been walking across any mountain meadow. She never once even reached for the broken stone railing to either side as the rope trailed behind her.

On the other side she looked for something on the stone floor as she untied herself from the rope.

"Joribhy, you're next," called Master Marran.

Joribhy took Querin's place, and Querin tied into the rope, which now formed a long loop between Master Tanay and the two apprentices. Querin managed to look even more casual than Tanay had. His stride didn't seem to slow at all as he crossed the narrow stone bridge.

One of the other earth apprentices, Kirk was called, and Mellik watched as Joribhy crossed with no difficulty.

"Mellik."

He hoisted his backpack and carefully walked to where Marran and the other two apprentices stood.

"Stand in the impressions and lock your feet in," instructed Master Marran.

Mellik looked down to see two depressions carved into the stone floor that were free of the dark algae. Rough grooves had been cut for traction, and there was an indentation at the front to brace your toes in. Four black plugs of the right size to go into the depressions sat near Marran. Mellik guessed they kept the slimy algae out of the holes.

"Hold on tight, but if you get pulled out of the holes, just let go of the rope," continued Marran. "You'll slide like a greased pig on that algae, so no point in making it worse. We've been doing this for over a century and haven't lost anyone yet, so don't let yourself be first. Right, Kirk?"

Marran had been tying the rope onto the lanky apprentice while he talked, and now he gave him a slap on the shoulder.

"Yes, Master."

"You ready?"

"Yes, Master."

"Remember, slow and easy with little baby steps. Don't look down past your feet on the bridge, and don't lean on those railings."

"Yes, Master."

Kirk was probably the slowest across the bridge Mellik had yet seen, but he made it without a slip. Mellik moved up to take the front position.

Mellik was disconcerted to hear that Brin was the next in line. He tried to ignore the big apprentice and just kept his eyes on the rope. Brin said nothing as he took his place behind Mellik, and the next apprentice was soon safely across. It was Mellik's turn.

Mellik handed the rope to Breanne, the next apprentice and carefully walked up to Marran, who began tying Mellik onto the rope, as the master went through his instructions to the new rope holder.

"You ready?" he asked Mellik.

"Yes, Master."

"Remember, slow and easy with little steps. Don't look down past your feet on the bridge, and don't lean on the railings."

"Yes, Master."

Mellik set off. He copied the pace of the last two apprentices: small little steps taken at an easy pace. He concentrated on the bridge ahead and tried not to notice the gaping maw to either side with the lightly swirling steam coming from it. The rope gently jostling his waist was a comfort. It seemed to take forever, but he finally arrived at the foot of the bridge.

His steps became a shuffle as he stepped out onto the bridge. It didn't look nearly as ominous from up close. Two people could have almost walked across it side by side, and there were only a few spots where the railing had collapsed. There was a gentle arch to it, and Mellik realized as he gazed down at his feet that there were intricate carvings in the stonework obscured by the algae. Complex geometric patterns could barely be discerned near the edges of the bridge and up the banisters. As he shuffled along, he noticed that the patterns changed subtly at each banister he passed, and the geometry was now entirely different than when he'd first noticed it. He was heading down now, and he glanced up to see Querin and Fesskah watching, so he gave them a grin. That's when the world lurched sideways.

Mellik was thrown hard against the stone railing. He heard his hip collide with it over the groaning keen of the stone around him. It kept him from falling over, but then the bridge heaved, and he felt the ground toss him over the railing. He flailed desperately at the railing as he plummeted past it, but it slapped against his fingertips on his way by. The rope tied around his waist and legs snapped tight, and he bounced once and then hung in the air.

Mellik grabbed hold of the rope and pulled himself upright. Looking up, he could see one end of the rope had slipped between the pieces of remaining railing and came down from the bridge above him. The other trailed off at an angle and over the edge of the rift in front of him.

"Mellik! Are you alright!?" Fesskah bellowed from the other end of the rope.

"Yeah," Mellik said, trying to keep the high pitched terror from his voice. "I'm fine."

"Just hang on," called Tanay. "We're going to pull you up to this side."

"Okay."

There was a muttered conversation from both sides of the ravine, and then Mellik was pulled with a lurch a few inches toward the closer cliff wall. Tanay began chanting out the pull, and inch by inch he crept closer to the top of the rock face.

When he was almost there, he looked up to see Master Tanay standing above him.

"Don't try to pull yourself up," she instructed him. "It's too slick. Just brace yourself against the rock, and let us pull you over with the rope."

"Yes, Master."

Tanay nodded and stepped back from the precipice. "One, two, three, pull!" she called out.

They pulled Mellik up over the edge of the crevice and slid him a few feet across the slick rock, away from the edge.

"Make sure you're alright," Tanay said as she untied him. "We can stop here if we have to."

Mellik took stock now that he felt calmer. His right hand throbbed painfully from hitting the stone railing, but it had gripped the rope just fine, and he couldn't see any bleeding or swelling. His back and neck were sore from bouncing on the end of the rope, but nothing debilitating.

"I think I'm fine, Master."

"Okay. Just take it easy. If you feel something, let us know. I need to check the rope and the bridge," she called to the rest of the apprentices on their side. "Querin, Fesskah: see to Mellik. Everyone sit tight."

His two friends helped him up and back to where the other

apprentices stood huddled. Mellik was feeling a light-light headed. He sat down against the wall.

"Brin just saved your life," Querin whispered, squatting down next to him.

"What?"

"When you fell, Breanne came flying up out of the foot holds. Brin was yanked off his feet as well, but he hooked his toes in and managed to hang on until they could magically stabilize the rope."

"That seems out of character."

"I know. Maybe he really likes that rope." Querin said. Mellik grinned. "Anyway, I thought you should know."

"Yeah, thanks."

Mellik put his head back against the cold stone and wondered why.

Tanay returned and declared both bridge and rope sound. The crossing started again, but with renewed vigilance on everyone's part, and an even more tentative pace by the apprentices. Tanay said she would monitor for any more tremors, although aftershocks rarely occurred because of the magic used to stabilize the volcano.

Mellik's face flushed as he realized the earthquake might not have been a random event. If he could cause one with almost no training, Master Tanay or one of the other earth apprentices must have similar knowledge. Marran was a full master as well, but just because he was a teleportation master didn't mean he lacked skill in earth magic, or maybe he could do something similar with teleportation. The same could be said for any of the senior apprentices. Mellik knew far too little about what was possible with magic. The only people he truly knew hadn't just tried to kill him were Querin, Fesskah, and absurdly, Brin.

Chapter 31

The earth apprentices were luckier than the others: they had furniture. Carcarose, a stout apprentice with a surplus of back hair that made his shirt seem to hover above his skin, was a stone shaper: a rare sub-talent of earth magic. He could shape the stone with his hands like it was clay. Carcarose said that stone shaping could be learned, but was not deemed worth the time and effort by most mages. The Masters had made use of his talents that first night to customize stone furniture from centuries earlier, but after their first day of studying with Tanay in the caverns, Car had managed to shape them a table and four stools to cook and eat their meals on. The furniture was simple, but the shaping had retained the swirling spiral pattern of the cavern's black rock, and the sparkle of obsidian gave it a netherworldly beauty. Car could do much subtler work, given time. He said the bridge had been shaped by Dwarves who were masters at the art of stone shaping.

They would need to destroy the furniture when they left. One point of this excursion was that the apprentices were expected to use magic freely while they were away from the college. They had brought very little other than food and bedrolls, and the caverns were stripped bare of anything useful when each group left. They were judged a safe distance from the less experienced apprentices and it was thought to be a good test of their abilities while affording them the chance to work as a team.

Cooking turned out to be something of a redemptive task for Mellik. He was the only one of the earth apprentices with the skill and power in fire magics to give them a reliable heat to cook with.

"Did you hear we're going to get to watch Master Marran's teleportation demonstration after dinner?" asked Jorhiby, who was helping Mellik cook their stew.

"Really? Why do we get the honor?" asked Mellik.

"I heard Master Marran thought it would be a good idea to let us see teleportation since we were already down here."

Mellik glanced up and saw that Brin was perched against the wall a few strides away. One of his friends, Sidarth, was just walking away.

"Can you watch the stew?" he asked Jorhiby.

"Sure."

Mellik got up and walked over to Brin.

"I wanted to say thank you," Mellik said, extending his hand.

Brin ignored Mellik's hand and stared with a rictus smile at Mellik's face.

"I want to be able to look into your eyes while you die," he said, and then walked away.

Oddly, this made Mellik feel better. Not only had he done the right thing, but the world made sense again. Brin was still the backside of a demon. If anything, he was even more of a sadistic narcissist than Mellik had thought. Mellik hummed a tune Babbayannek had been teaching him as he strolled back to the stew.

* * *

The teleportation room was intimidating. A circle with a pentagram roughly 12 feet across had been inlayed in gold in the middle of the floor. The floor itself was the pitch black of the surrounding rock, but it had been flattened and polished to a reflective gleam. Mellik could have easily watched Master Marran give his instructions in the mirror of the floor.

"This particular room was originally used for larger summoning rituals until the Emperor wisely banished such magics," began Marran.

The master paced in a circle as he spoke. The apprentices sat a pace outside the circle with its pentagram and golden runes. The walls of the tall, circular room were another pace behind them. The only entrance was a thick stone door behind Master Tanay. The black stone surrounding them seemed to suck in the light from the single magic globe of light far above Master Marran.

The even polish of the stone seemed to make it even darker somehow.

"Now," continued Marran, "I've already explained this in much more detail to the senior apprentices, which is why I've scattered you earth apprentices amongst them. If you have a question, they can likely answer it.

"In brief, teleportation is the displacement of an object from one place to another. Notice I didn't say the moving of an object from one place to another. What you're doing is creating an image of the object in the place you want and then forcing your will on reality via magic in order to make the object appear there. The object doesn't move, it simply ceases to exist in one place, and simultaneously becomes a reality in another place. Two things you need to ensure is that the object you're teleporting is very unique and that the place you're teleporting it to is equally unique. The reason for this is simple: magic is a lot like an apprentice, it will take the easiest way to accomplish a task every time unless you're very specific."

The apprentices chuckled.

"For example, I could imagine my staff in my hand, but if my image was vague, I could end up with the closest stick around, or perhaps I would just end up with an illusion of my staff or even a brown snake. Now," Marran held out his hand, and a staff appeared in it. A low gasp of appreciation came from the apprentices. "Take a look at my staff."

Marran held the staff out in front of him and slowly walked around the perimeter of the circle.

"You'll see the runes and diagrams inlaid in the wood. This is in part to make my staff unique so that I can pull off the trick you just saw from a vast distance. The farther you're pulling from, the more unique the item has to be as magic will try harder and harder to find something similar that's closer. I can summon it to my hand because I know my hand... well, like the back of my hand."

This got another chuckle from his audience. Mellik was starting to like Marran.

"Now the other role some of these markings on my staff play, is to remind me of the unique sigils and patterns on other tools I might want to summon to me. For instance," Marran looked at the middle point of his staff and slowly turned it in his hands. "Here it is."

A square oak chest appeared in the middle of the summoning circle. A pattern of black circles and lines was burnt into the wood on both sides of the wood that Mellik could see.

"You can see the markings I've put on this chest to make it unique," Marran tapped the side of the chest with his staff, "but what was the other thing I needed?"

"Yes?" Marran pointed to Carcarose with his staff.

"A unique place to teleport it to," responded Carcarose.

"Exactly. And this," Marran emphasized with a sharp rap of the bronze shod staff on the floor, "provides that unique place. I could have summoned the chest to my hands, but I like my arms in their current condition."

Mellik grinned, but as he looked around he noticed several of the senior apprentices looked tense, grim even. He wondered if these jokes were that old, or did they not like Marran for some reason?

"Now, what do we have in here?" Marran took out a key and unlocked the chest, lifting its lid.

"Ah perfect," Marran reached in and pulled out a sandwich with ham and fresh greens spilling from the sides. He took a large bite and sighed in pleasure. The apprentices laughed in appreciation, but once again, Mellik thought some of the laughter sounded forced. Marran carefully set the rest of the sandwich back in the chest.

"One thing a Mage versed in teleportation magic has going for him is surprise. Teleportation effects are really only limited by the creativity and preparation of the wizard. Master Tanay, will you hold this for a moment?" Marran tossed his staff across the circle to her. She smiled in appreciation of Marran's showmanship as she reached up to catch it.

A crossbow appeared in Marran's hands and in the same instant there was the thwap of the bolt being released. Mellik looked across to see the bolt buried in Tanay's chest. The ghost of her smile lingered, but now there was the hint of pain and confusion before all expression disappeared, and she slumped to the floor.

Fesskah was the first to react. He leaped into the air, growing larger and longer in mid-air. The two apprentices at his sides grabbed for him, but reacted too slowly, their hands sliding from his smooth black scales. Fesskah bounded toward Marran, when an armored knight appeared in front of him. Fesskah careened off of it, the suit of armor wobbling on its wooden base. He came around the armor to be met by a stream of knives flying from Marran's hands.

Mellik began to rise, and something hard struck him on the back of the head. He pitched forward onto the floor. Mellik tried to roll, to rise up again, but his limbs were bound in air and couldn't move. He could still see Fesskah, now smaller, dancing and darting about to avoid the knives, but unable to reach Marran.

He could hear other fighting going on. He heard Querin yelling for Fesskah to flee. Mellik could break the bonds of air, he'd learned how the hard way from Pelliery. He embraced the second sight, and felt at his bonds for where they attached to the earth beneath him. A boot connected with his face. Mellik struggled to concentrate on his bonds through the pain. A second kick snapped his head back, and Mellik felt his jaw break. He couldn't feel the magic through the pain, couldn't think of his arms or legs; a third kick, and it all went away.

Chapter 32

Someone was crying. It wasn't the howl of rending grief, or the staccato outburst of sudden pain: it was the soft susurration of despair and loss. It was someone he knew.

Mellik struggled against his own body to regain consciousness. Was that Querin crying? He needed to help. His body slowly bent to his will as he cracked one eyelid open. Jagged rock, blurred because of its proximity, was all he could see. He couldn't get the other one to open. His face hurt. Mellik managed to make his arms respond and gently rolled himself over.

Querin sat on the other side of a small alcove. His knees were drawn up, and his face was buried in his arms. His shoulders shook gently with his muffled sobs.

Mellik tried to call out to him, but it came out a groan as pain shot out from his left ear all down his jaw.

"Mellik, is that you?" asked Querin, his head popping up. A thick band of cloth was wrapped around his head in front of his eyes. It was stained a deep red in color across the front.

"Querin," Mellik was careful to only open his mouth a little, making the pain bearable. "What happened to your eyes?"

Querin brought his hands up but then stopped them, clenching them into fists and then bringing them to rest in his lap.

"They took them."

"They took them?"

"Yes, I was considered too dangerous, so they gouged my eyes out." His voice was tinged with pain and anger, but also with a sorrow that echoed his earlier weeping.

"Demons, are you okay?" Mellik immediately regretted the question, but Querin actually smiled.

"No, but I know just enough healing that I was able to stop the bleeding and keep from going into shock. I wasn't strong enough to let myself die."

"What are you talking about? We need to get out and tell the college what has happened. Of course you can't let yourself die."

"You don't understand. They're going to summon a demon."

"What?"

"Brin bragged about it. Master Marran found some records somewhere. They said that this island wasn't one of the first cities the Emperor conquered, it was **the** first. They said the Emperor summoned a demon, one powerful enough to kill or capture every wizard in the city. The wizards had no choice but to submit to his rule. With the wizards of the college and the demon he was able to conquer the other nations and give himself immortality. They plan to duplicate the feat and kill the Emperor."

Mellik glanced around the small alcove. It was almost a perfect globe, more than twice as far across as he was tall. Light came from a jagged opening to his left, and reflected from large hexagonal crystals that shone a milky purple.

"Did anyone escape?"

Querin laid his head down on his arms again.

"Fesskah," he finally replied. "It is the one thing I managed before they subdued me."

"Where are the others?" Somewhere inside Mellik knew the answer, but he needed to hear it.

"Dead if they're not one of them."

A slow creep of dread crawled up Mellik's spine as he asked his next question.

"Why didn't they kill us too?"

Querin's head came up and tilted just slightly to one side. Mellik could imagine his missing eyes studying him, weighing him through the blood soaked bandage.

"I always forget how much knowledge they keep from you. You know what a demon is, where they come from?"

"They're beings from another realm of existence," Mellik replied, trying to remember the brief lecture Charl had given on the subject. "It's a reality with much greater levels of magic than our world. The magic inherent there makes it easier to summon from across the planes."

"Yes, more magic, more chaos. They are inherently more magically powerful and skilled in the use of magic. We believe they have to be to survive in a realm with that much magic. The one advantage we have when we summon them is that they aren't used to the laws of our own world, and can't gather the magical energies they need to survive, let alone break free from a summoning circle to harm us. It is in those first brief moments that we can exert control over them, but we must also feed them magic for them to survive - a great deal of magic. There are various ways of doing this. The most effective is to feed it a wizard, or in our case two."

It took a moment for that to sink in.

"What?" Mellik finally managed.

"From what I've been told, demons can't seem to absorb mana from their surroundings when they are first summoned here. They can, however, pull it from another creature or object, if that thing is sufficiently overcharged with mana."

"Overcharged? But, what if we just refuse to absorb mana?"

"They can still suck it out of us. Intelligent creatures have more mana by nature. As the mana is pulled from you, it's instinctual for us to react by drawing in more. It takes an incredible amount of calm reserve to allow your life to slip away without a fight. There are tales of wizards doing it, but precious few."

Mellik remembered when Arbret had drawn a tiny sliver of his essence away to create his belt, and what a force of will and trust it had taken to allow that. Thinking of his belt, Mellik reached down and felt for the buckle. It was gone. He reached up to the pouch at his neck, and let out a sigh of relief as he felt the ring still nestled there. They must have missed it, because of the bag made to hide it.

"Don't channel," Querin said.

"What? Why?"

"These crystals around us are mana gems. They're probably why tunnels were dug here in the first place. They hold an incredible amount of mana by slowly drawing it in from their surroundings as they grow. Wizards use them as an easy emergency supply or to power a magical apparatus. The problem with them is that if a sudden burst of magic energy happens near them, they explode in uncontrolled magic. With this many around us we'd surely die."

Mellik switched to the second sight. The crystals shone with an almost blindingly bright amount of mana.

"How..." Mellik wanted to ask how Querin knew they were there but stopped himself.

"How do I know they're around us?" Querin smiled bleakly. "They told me, just like they told me about the demon. I'm trapped by my hope of survival, and it makes me weak in the face of my doom. So many ways to kill myself, yet coward that I am, I wait for them to come do it for me."

"No, we'll get out," Mellik said reflexively. "Is there a door or a guard?"

"Both a trap for a door and a guard to warn us of the trap."

"What?"

Querin sobbed gently before continuing.

"It's almost funny. They gave us so many ways to die, yet they want us alive. It's like they want to see what we'll choose."

Mellik scooted himself over to Querin and rested his hand on the elf's shoulder.

"Querin, maybe there's some way out of this, but I need you to help me. What's this trap?"

Querin steadied himself with a deep breath. He straitened and crossed his legs, taking another deep breath. It was stillness, the position they began each day of Kigana practice in. Querin took one more breath, and his face seemed to calm and transform. The pain was still there, but it had been pushed from the surface.

"You're right," Querin stated. "An elf should be better than that. I will help as I can, and if we fail, I will try to be strong in my failure."

"Well, you'll at least be pompous in your failure." The words were out before Mellik could censor them.

Querin's jaw fell open. Mellik could feel his incredulous stare despite the bandages and even lack of eyes.

Then Querin laughed. "So be it. Let it not be said that Querin the elf went to his death without a pompous, pithy comment on his lips."

The laugh wasn't the free, full one Mellik was used to hearing. There was bitterness and pain reverberating through it, but it was a start.

"Okay, so what's this trap?"

*   *   *

Mellik peaked around the corner at the swirling vortex of blue/white mana that sat at the entrance to their cavern cell. Querin called it a mana converter: a failed bit of magic that originally was supposed to turn anything passing through it into breathable air. It had been intended to allow someone to breath underwater, but it had an unfortunate effect of creating explosive bursts of air when actually used this way. That wasn't its purpose at the entrance to the cave. It would vaporize their flesh or anything else they tried to move through it.

"I can see you, mice," called Guy. He was standing a few paces back from the mana converter, channeling to keep it working. A large light globe was perched next to him. Mellik ducked back around the corner.

"Why don't you come try it out?" called Guy after him. "Stick a finger through, or how about a hand? How about your manhood? Or do Kamori have one? Better yet, why don't you try your earth magic tricks?"

Mellik ignored him and scuttled back to Querin. There was only a slight bend to the cave's entrance, and the spot where the elf sat was in full view of Guy. Mellik sat next to the elf with his back to the blustering apprentice. Guy was powerful, but not the brightest of Brin's cohorts; likely why they had left him to power the mana converter.

"You say it converts the mana of objects passing through it to air?"

"Yes, but as I said, it's neither perfect nor all-powerful. Move something large enough or fast enough through, and not all of it will be changed. Water might turn to mist for instance. I could take a run at it. Maybe enough of me will splatter on him to make him lose concentration."

"No, I want both of us out. Besides, I'd miss your positive outlook." Querin managed a smile. "And this mana conversion won't disrupt the mana crystals?"

"No, it's very efficient, and they put it just far enough away from the crystals to be safe. Make sure none of the crystals get stuck in your shoes if you go near it."

Mellik dug around at his feet, pulling loose stones from the floor. There were surprisingly few to choose from, but he found a few good palm sized stones that were roughly round in shape.

"What about dead matter?"

"What?"

"Matter with the mana stripped from it. I've got a small dead matter. Will the mana converter work on something inside?"

"How did you get a pouch of dead matter?" Querin sat up straighter.

"It doesn't matter, would the contents of the pouch get through?"

Querin sat back, his head tilted up in thought. "If there aren't any holes for the magic to get through, then yes. Magic can't affect or pass through dead matter."

Mellik pulled the pouch from inside the mana-camouflaged one around his neck and looked at it. A draw string held it tightly closed but he wondered if it was tight enough. Charl said any gap large enough for air was more than large enough to let magic through. Of course, directed magic didn't meander, but generally went in a straight line. The mana converter swirled from the middle outward, so as long as the sack opening wasn't facing the middle...he wasn't sure. He'd just have to take the chance. It was the only idea he had.

Mellik pulled his shirt off and began ripping long, thin strips from the sleeves.

"What are you doing?" asked Querin.

"I'll tell you if it works. Here, hold this," and Mellik placed one of the strands in each of the elf's hands.

Mellik took the other end and twisted first one and then the other strand of cloth into a length of chord. He moved Querin's hands close together and then twisted the two strands together in the opposite direction. A small knot at either end finished the length of chord. Mellik did another long length with familiar motions. Not having to hold one end in his toes made this easier. He did another, shorter length of chord and then wove and knotted it into the middle of the other two lengths. The shirt had still been in good shape. Mellik was used to having to knot lengths together to reinforce weak spots. He put what was left of the shirt back on.

Mellik picked up the sling and placed one of the stones in its split cup. He gave the sling a swing and was pleased at the stiffness of the chord and how it didn't twist or flip as he increased the speed of rotation about his head. He sped it up and noted the familiar whooshing whistle. Querin's ears and forehead came up in curiosity, but he didn't comment.

He stopped the sling and looked at the smaller entry cave. It was still tall enough, but not as wide. Mellik had made the sling shorter than he would have liked, but he'd still have to swing it at an angle, launching the rocks up instead of from above his head. He'd done it before, but it worried him.

Mellik opened up the dead matter pouch and placed the golden ring on his finger, replacing it with the best of his rocks. He had eight more of the same size in his pocket.

"Stay here," he told Querin.

Mellik walked around to where he could see Guy. The senior apprentice's face lit up when he saw Mellik.

"Hey, rock head, you gonna try it? Go ahead and give it a poke. Use your smallest digit," Guy rubbed his crotch suggestively.

Mellik ignored him and careful began to spin the sling, watching as it barely cleared the ceiling and floor.

"What the demons do you think you're going to do with that...hey!"

Guy instinctively ducked as the rock came whistling toward him. The rock hit the swirling mana converter and disintegrated into dust that harmlessly floated down just on the other side of the magic.

"You really are stupid, aren't you?" Guy asked as he straightened up. Mellik loaded another stone. "You're not even a very good shot."

Guy was right. The first stone, at best, might have hit his shin even from such close range. Mellik released the second stone. Guy barely flinched as this one hit near the top of the converter.

"Demon piss! This is pathetic. The demon probably won't even take you."

Guy flinched but kept from ducking as Mellik's third stone flew true. It disintegrated like the first two, but it would have struck him square in the chest, if not for the magic.

"You can't possibly be this stupid. Your blind elf should have explained it better. Nothing can get through this but air."

Mellik's fourth stone flew straight at Guy's head before disintegrating. Guy didn't even flinch.

"You're the one who's stupid," Mellik taunted, loading another stone.

"Yeah, why don't you try something useful and channel some air at me. That might work before you turn into a puddle of muddy water." Guy took a step forward, his hands clenching.

The fifth stone flew right at Guy's eyes. Guy was almost close enough to get the dust on him, but he didn't even blink.

"I'm going to enjoy watching you struggle as you die. Brin said he wanted to see your eyes as you die, but I bet he'd let me take your little rock manhood as a souvenir first. It killed him to save you from falling into the chasm, but we need you for the demon."

Mellik had turned just slightly sideways as he loaded the bag into the sling. He was afraid too many tries and Guy would get bored or step away. Mellik spun the now familiar weight.

"You're so stupid you probably think...gah!" Guy was interrupted as the weighted bag struck his neck.

Guy's hands flew to his neck, and the magic barrier instantly disappeared as his magic link to it died. Guy sank to his knees. Mellik sprinted up to him, landing a kick straight to his cheek.

There was an audible crack, and Guy crashed backward to the rough stone floor. His body began to spasm, and Mellik could see the mana in him course and spark before it began to dissipate. Guy laid still.

Mellik stood for a moment, stunned by his success, stunned by the violence, and stunned by the death of this boy not much older than he. He shook himself out of it and grabbed his pouch before going to retrieve Querin.

"Come on, before someone else comes," Mellik grabbed Querin's hand and helped him to his feet.

"What happened? How did you free us?"

"Later, let's get out of here first."

Mellik guided Querin up the rough stone path and around Guy's motionless body. He chafed at the slow progress. He was filled with mana - too scared and jittery to know what he'd do with it if someone popped out in front of them. The tunnel leveled off into a broader cavern, and there by the tunnel's entrance was a pile of their things. Someone had even been thoughtful enough to place one of the light globes right next to the pile.

Mellik stopped and took a good look at the pile and the light globe with his second sight. There, peeking out from the pile of spare clothes were his throwing blades. Mellik pulled Querin along, reaching for his weapons.

Chapter 33

Something stopped him. If Querin was right, and they were to be used in the summoning ritual, why were they so lightly guarded? And Guy had been watching their cage, not the entrance from this cavern. If Fesskah had escaped, wouldn't he have been more concerned about that?

"What's wrong?" asked Querin.

"One second, I need to figure this out." Mellik scanned the cavern around them.

"Maybe I can help if you tell me what's going on."

There on the ground, in the shadow of their pile of things, was a ball of mana. Equal parts fire and air, it was a simple enchantment. It had just enough mana to keep it going for several hours before it unraveled.

"Querin," Mellik whispered, "what would take fire mana and bind it with air mana, like a cage, as an enchantment?"

"Almost equal parts air and fire?" Querin whispered back. "Does the fire strain against the cage of air?"

Mellik looked more closely at the enchantment. The fire did indeed seem to strain against its cage, almost pulsing as it pushed against the ball of air holding it captive.

"Yes."

"It's probably a light trap. They are made so equally balanced that a small thing like some extra light or heat will set them off."

"So you could place one in shadow, and then it would explode with fire when exposed to more light?"

"Exactly."

"Exactly," repeated a voice from the dark depths of the cavern.

The shape of a man emerged from the gloom. The man's skin

lightened from a deep pitch to a light tan, and Mellik recognized Jopin. Jopin was in their morning Kigana practice. He was slight and short. He could easily pass for a young apprentice at first glance with his boyish face, but his eyes held something darker and more violent. You could see the sinewy muscles rippling his chest and legs as he stalked across the cavern. The darkening of his skin and his overly sharp hearing were tricks of the trade for transformation mages, but what made Jopin deadly was his mastery of speeding his body up past what even a Warden could match. He wore only a pair of dark short pants held up by Mellik's belt.

Jopin saw the look on Mellik's face and grinned.

"You like?" He asked, grinning as he fingered the buckle. "It looks far better on me."

Mellik suppressed his rage. "You can keep it, just leave us alone."

Jopin snickered, "I told Brin to leave you your tongue. What is a jester who can't speak? The only shame is that I'm not to kill you: less satisfying, but maybe slightly more of a challenge."

"Querin, follow the wall right, and try to get out of here." Mellik guided Querin to the wall as Jopin slid closer. Querin hesitated a heartbeat before shuffling away.

"You expect the blind one to escape?"

Mellik didn't respond. Jopin was getting too close. Mellik ripped the remnants of his shirt off and threw it over the light globe. The cavern grew dimmer, but enough light spilled out from where Guy lay dead that Mellik could still see. He hoped it wasn't too much. He squatted and threw the clothes from the top of his belongings. He grabbed up his throwing stars and started one spinning.

Jopin smiled widely, "Excellent," and he dashed forward.

Mellik shot a star at him. Jopin dodged out of the way, but another was right on its heels. Jopin dodged again, but this time Mellik kept control of it and made it follow him. Jopin scowled as he casually reached out and plucked the spinning blade from the air. Jopin threw the blade back at him, but Mellik easily stopped its momentum and sent it back at its target again. This time Jopin grabbed the star and held it.

"This will be more fun than I thought," he commented, grinning wide at Mellik.

Mellik started two discs spinning. He could maintain three, but he needed to be wary of the one in Jopin's hand. He shot the two stars to either side of Jopin. The small apprentice ducked down and twisted to one side as they passed, but Mellik merely had them circle back, spiraling around Jopin. The lithe apprentice crouched low, hands out, and Mellik's stars circled him outside his reach; at first slowly, then faster and faster. Mellik had hoped Jopin would make a lunge for one, but he just crouched and watched. Mellik fainted in with one, and Jopin spun away as it came closer, but he pivoted back too quickly for Mellik to take advantage.

Mellik fainted with one again, but this time Jopin was ready, and as he spun he snagged the star from the air. Mellik was ready too, and a third star shot out from his hand toward Jopin, and at the same time Mellik cut in with the second orbiting blade. Quick as a cat, Jopin swung back around and deflected the second blade with the one in his hand, the metal chiming and echoing through the cavern. Without slowing his turn, he released that same star toward Mellik and caught the third one Mellik had shot at him. Mellik caught the approaching blade with his earth magic a few feet from him, but then felt something rip into his shoulder as a second star came hurtling right after the first, so close Mellik hadn't seen it.

Mellik had no time to think on the injury, as Jopin was barreling towards him, a star poised to throw. The star whipped from Jopin's hand, and Mellik managed to stop it and send the other back at him. Jopin slid beneath the oncoming star. He closed on Mellik too fast for him to do anything more. Jopin's right hand came up under Mellik's chin, forcing his head up, and the left hand chopped down severely on his wrist, scattering the rest of Mellik's stars as his hand became numb from the blow. The smaller apprentice drove him backwards, and Mellik felt his head and back strike the wall simultaneously, driving the air from him and dizzying his vision. Jopin's hand tightened on his throat, and Mellik struggled to pull a breath into his empty lungs.

"Don't worry, I won't let you die," Jopin told him. "You'll just pass out and wake up to a demon sucking out your soul."

Mellik choked and sputtered. He lashed out at Jopin with air, but it slid off the barrier of air the apprentice was maintaining. Mellik could feel his own belt buckle digging into his thigh as Jopin put his arms in a lock and twisted his legs into a pincer hold. Mellik flashed back to being attacked by Pollum. He wanted to reach down into the stone, but knew what he would find there, and knew he couldn't use it. He would kill himself just as surely with the fiery earth straining to be released here. Worse, he would take his friends with him.

The image of the light globe covered by his tattered shirt popped into his head. He hadn't moved except for being slammed up against the wall, so it couldn't be far. Mellik's hands were pinned facing down, so he simply sent a massive stream of air straight down against the floor. It was hard enough to push back against his palms, and he felt it rush by his ankles. The cavern ceiling became lit by a crescendo of light accompanied by a sound that could be felt in their bones.

Mellik was thrown sideways to the ground. Someone was screaming. Dazed, it took Mellik a moment to realize the screaming voice was not his own. He took a ragged breath of dry, warm air that smelled of burnt flesh.

Mellik found the source of the screaming. It was Jopin. He laid face down a stride away, twitching as he screamed. He was horribly burnt with bright red blistering across most of his body, and his left side was charred black. He twitched and screamed and then slowly the twitches became movement as he brought his hands beneath him and began to lever himself up. The blackened flesh cracked and bled as he moved, and he turned his head to look at Mellik, one eye burnt away. Why couldn't they just die?

"You'll die," Jopin said in a hoarse wheeze, a twisted echo of Mellik's own thoughts.

Jopin managed to get his shaking legs underneath him. A throwing star buried itself in the side of his head with a meaty thunk. He stared at Mellik, his eyes wide as he toppled forward almost into Mellik's lap.

Now Mellik began to shake. He couldn't look away from the charred boy with the blade buried in his temple. He finally turned away as he began to retch and heave, bile dribbling down his chin to drip on the cold stone floor.

"That doesn't sound like Jopin throwing up," Querin called from across the cavern. "I take it we won?"

"Yeah, we won," Mellik replied, still out of breath. He stayed looking down at his puke rather than turning and seeing Jopin's charred remains. "Do all elves have such a dark sense of humor?"

"Only the best ones."

Mellik smiled despite himself.

"Should I come back there?" There was concern in Querin's voice.

"No, no. I'm fine."

After saying it, Mellik wondered if he really was okay. There was a tingling along his right side, and the skin was a little pink there, as if he'd been in the sun too long, but otherwise he did indeed seem to be okay. Mellik looked up at Jopin's body but avoided looking at the face and head. His belt was still wrapped around the corpse's torso. The cloth around it was singed and tattered, but the belt looked untouched.

Trying not to think about what he was doing, Mellik stood and grasped the belt to turn the body over. The déjà vu was hard to avoid as he pulled the belt loose. It was a mighty gift that had likely saved his life twice now. He put on the belt and gathered up his scattered throwing stars. He had all but the one lodged in Jopin's head when he stopped. The idea of pulling it from Jopin's skull almost made him throw up again. He began to heave and had to turn away from the sight of the body. It had been a gift, and he might need it. Mellik finally gave up. He couldn't make himself touch it.

"Come on," he said, going over to take Querin's hand. "Let's go find Fesskah."

Chapter 34

Mellik had no idea where he was going. Slowly guiding Querin up the steep tunnel didn't bother Mellik at all. It just delayed the inevitable moment when Mellik would be forced to make a decision. He had told Querin that they were going to find Fesskah, but he didn't know where Fesskah would be. Would he be looking for them, trying to get back to the school? Even if Mellik had the answer to that, he still had no idea where they were or how to get where they needed to go.

A light appeared ahead of them. Mellik noticed in that light that the tunnel opened up into another cavern. A figure stepped into the mouth of the tunnel carrying the light.

Sidarth didn't bother to talk like Jopin had. Instead, a magic shield instantly popped up in front of Sidarth. Mellik shot one of his stars at the same moment, but he was too slow. The star caught in the shield, and then Sidarth let the star slide beyond the shield and beyond Mellik's control. Mellik started to grab hold of the air around him with his mind, but Sidarth was quicker, and his magic buffeted around him, striking like a hundred hands. Sidarth mixed illusion, fire, and healing magics into the attacks. Mellik had to use all his concentration just fending off the furious assault.

Mellik was being driven back. He stumbled against Querin as he took a step back.

"What's happening?" asked the elf.

Mellik had no time to answer. He had to get a good look at Sidarth's shield to go on the offensive. He tried to split his concentration, but a volley of fire singed his pants, doing nothing more than making his leg warm thanks to the belt. The shield was as complex as Sidarth's attacks, seeming to change and weave back and forth through magics as Mellik watched. Mellik tried to cave in the stone above the apprentice, but the magic hit the shield and became as inert as his throwing star. A strong fist of air swatted Mellik's ear for his trouble.

Mellik lashed out with fire, air, water, and earth. Each burst was absorbed by the shield, barely causing a ripple in its spin. He was rewarded by a patch of frozen shirt on his stomach, and then his shoulder went tingly numb. Mellik couldn't spare the time to think about his shoulder as Sidarth's attacks became even more rapid, a staccato burst of healing magic. Mellik managed to counter most, but many got through. His legs, one whole arm, and his other shoulder became numb. One ear filled with a ringing. He could barely make out Querin asking what was happening. He was having trouble keeping his balance, and his movements were sluggish and jerky. A fist of air slammed into his stomach, and then another part of his pants was burnt away. His other ear began to ring, and now one eye couldn't focus.

"Run," he tried to yell, but his tongue didn't seem to work.

Another fist of air drove him to his knees. In his blurred vision, Mellik saw a shadow glide up behind Sidarth. It grabbed Sidarth's head and twisted. There was a crackling sound, and Sidarth slumped to the ground. Mellik collapsed as well. A hand twitched in front of his one good eye. It was Mellik's hand, but he couldn't feel or control it.

A scaly finger pressed lightly against his temple, and suddenly he could hear again.

"What elsse iz wrong?" asked Fesskah.

"Tonn na wagng."

Fesskah pressed a finger against Mellik's cheek, and his mouth came back under his control.

"My legs, right shoulder, and left arm are numb, plus my ears are ringing, and my left eye is blurry."

"Your body wantss to fix itsself. Uze your training. Make yoursself right."

Mellik closed his eyes and imagined the way his eyes had felt during those days of self study. His right eye was working correctly. That gave him a good starting point. He could feel the dissonance between the two: there was a buzz to the mana in the area that shouldn't be there. Mellik didn't want to try and remove that buzzing mana. He felt like the mana was correct, it just wasn't behaving correctly; but if he just tuned it down... Mellik opened his eyes while keeping hold of the feeling he'd discovered there. He slowly decreased the buzz, and his left eye came into focus as the buzz decreased to the steady throb of his heartbeat. After fixing his eye, Mellik found that righting the rest of his body was easy. Sidarth had set up the same buzzing effect everywhere he had struck, and it was the same process to revert it to normal. Fesskah had been right about his body wanting to fix itself. By the time Mellik got around to his ears, he was already starting to hear over the high pitched whine.

"I'm ssorry my friend," Fesskah was saying to Querin.

"It's alright. I knew it wasn't something anyone could heal. So did they," replied Querin.

"Then all that'ss left iz revenge."

"Shouldn't we try to get back to the college and warn them?" asked Mellik as he pushed himself back to his feet.

"There isn't time," replied Querin. "Sidarth was coming to get us. I could tell it was him by the tone of his shield magic. That means they're ready to begin the summoning."

"But without us, there's no one to sacrifice to the demon."

"I told you, there are other ways. That was just the quickest and easiest."

"Querin iz correct. We musst try to sstop them."

"But what are we going to do?" asked Mellik. "There are four of them, and one is a master."

Fesskah shrugged, "There iz no one elsse. And there are five. Carcarosse iz with them."

"That makes sense," commented Querin. "The summoning circle was altered to prevent something like this from being attempted. They would need a skilled stoneshaper to fix it. Fesskah is right. We three are all there is. The elves still remember the last time a major demon was summoned. The Emperor is right to fear demons. It's how he took control after all."

"What happened that time?" asked Mellik.

278

"The Emperor overthrew the academy of magic and began his conquest of the world. The demon killed more people than there are stars in the sky. If these fools succeed, they will start a war that could rival the Emperor's initial war of conquest, maybe even surpass it, and our friends above will be the first casualties. If Marran and his cronies fail, it could be worse. They could lose a demon on the world completely uncontrolled, or even allow multiple demons to cross over at once."

Mellik thought they'd have a better chance of running or hiding, but his pride wouldn't let him admit it.

"Then I guess we should get going," Mellik tried to keep his voice from quavering.

"Mellik," Querin groped over to where he sat and found his hand. He gave it a squeeze. "You killed two of them, and Fesskah has taken care of another two."

"Three," interjected Fesskah.

"There. You see, even captured or on the run, we have been able to succeed. Now we are together, and are on the offensive. We can do this."

Looking at Querin's blind face covered in bloody rags did not help the pep talk. Mellik wanted to comment that, for his own part, he felt luck had as much to do with his victories as any skill.

"Okay," was all he said.

"Good man," and Querin gave his hand another squeeze before straightening slowly. "Fesskah, you know the way, I assume?"

"Of coursse. My friend, we sshould make hasste. Would it hurt your dignity to be carried?"

"Yes, but it's a toss-up between my dignity and the lives of thousands of people, so maybe you should just risk it and carry me."

"Of coursse." Fesskah picked him up easily and turned back the way he had come from. Mellik scrambled after him.

On his way by, Fesskah shoved Sidarth's body out of the way with a negligent kick.

Chapter 35

Mellik played with his ring as he ate. Fesskah said they would need the food to help replenish their energy. Fesskah himself had gone to scout the summoning room.

"From your description, what Sidarth was using was a wizard's shield," Querin commented as he nibbled at some cheese and bread Fesskah had purloined from their camp for them. "They are relatively easy to bypass. Whatever mana they are using must be kept swirling, so you just hit it with a stream of your own mana, any kind will do. This puts a hole or gap in the defending Mage's shield and you can channel through that gap to defeat them."

"That would have been good to know half an hour ago."

Querin shrugged and felt around for his next wedge of cheese. "It likely won't come up that often."

"Why not?" asked Mellik. He leaned over to place the cheese in Querin's questing hand. Querin grimaced.

"Because it's a purely defensive magic that is so easily bypassed. The only reason Sidarth didn't do any serious damage to you was because he couldn't see you through that thick shield of mana. He was shooting spells randomly down that tunnel knowing you were there somewhere. He didn't even realize his fire magic was having no effect."

"It worked well enough," commented Mellik, holding the ring up for examination. The ring had felt comfortable on his finger, but Mellik wasn't used to having it there. The play of earth magic through the golden loop was beautiful. Mellik held the ring up to the rough stone wall to compare it to a more normal earth mana. He gasped.

"What!" exclaimed Querin, scrambling to his feet.

"It's okay. I think I may have just found something."

"Hasn't anyone ever told you not to gasp around blind people?" grumbled Querin, settling himself back down. "What did you find?"

"One second."

Mellik looked at the stone through the loop of the ring. Was it just the earth mana of the ring obscuring the normal patterns of the rock's mana? Mellik brought the ring away from the stone and slowly brought it up to his right eye. The gold ring fit comfortably there, as easily as it had fit on his finger. Looking at the stone's mana now was different. There was contrast and definition where none had existed before. He could look deeper into the stone as well. It was like he had lived by a river all his life only seeing it's surface, and now he could see the stones and sand beneath, the weeds and fish and even the silt floating along in it.

Mellik tried to explain what he was seeing to Querin.

"It's almost like your describing it to a blind man," commented Querin.

"Oh, Querin - I'm sorry."

"No, that was supposed to be a joke. Some fae have this exceptional acuity for a mana type. The kelpies can see water mana this way. They call it a "deeper" vision. It doesn't make them more powerful with that type of magic, but they can accomplish subtle things, like allowing someone to breathe underwater, that someone without the deep vision could not. Unfortunately, I don't know what you can do with a deeper vision for earth. A dwarf might. I can't believe I'm saying I wish we had a dwarf with us right now."

Mellik grinned.

"It'ss me," whispered Fesskah right near Mellik's ear.

Mellik nearly jumped out of his skin, stifling a scream. Fesskah grinned at his reaction.

"Good news?" asked Querin.

"I'm afraid not." Fesskah settled himself between Querin and Mellik. "They've pozitioned Car on watch in the tunnel to the ssummoning chamber. I don't think he ssaw me, but he'z erected a barrier of sstone with nothing but a narrow sslit to ssee through. He could throw up a Mage sshield and the sslit'ss ssize would block the uzual way to defeat it. In the time it would take to get passt the sstone bulwark, he'd be insside and they'd be ready for uss. He'z likely looking for the glow of magic too, sso that would give uss away."

"How wide is the slit?" asked Mellik.

"Az narrow az your finger, but he would ssee your throwing sstarz coming and block the sslit with his shield."

"I thought you said it wouldn't come up that often?" Mellik commented to Querin.

Querin shrugged, "As often as me being wrong apparently."

"What about something non-magical, something that would be hard to tell from all the other stone around it with the second sight?" asked Mellik.

"What did you have in mind?" Fesskah asked. "And why do you have a gold ring on your eye?"

Mellik laughed, "Hopefully I can answer both questions. How good are you at throwing a spear?"

"How good are you at getting beaten up?"

"Braggart lizard," commented Querin. "No one is that good."

Mellik grinned.

*   *   *

The result was almost anticlimactic. The hardest part was shaping a stone spear that was weighted and balanced to Fesskah's standards. Mellik was surprised at how easily shaping and reshaping the stone was while looking through the ring. He could see and move the mana that kept the rock connected, and even strengthen that connection so that the stone was hard but still light enough to use effectively.

Fesskah had improved the plan mightily by shrinking and making his outline more human so that in the dark his profile looked very similar to Jopin. Fesskah was carrying Mellik as if he was still unconscious, and Querin shuffled behind holding a glow globe. It was hoped that the light from behind Fesskah would hide the reptilian features he couldn't change.

The three rounded the last corner before the tunnel straightened in front of the summoning chamber. Mellik tried to relax and lay limp, but he was abuzz with nerves.

"Who is that? Jopin?" Carcarose called out from inside his stone shell.

Fesskah grunted noncommittally.

"Jopin, where are Sidarth and Guy? Hold on . . ."

Fesskah's body shifted under Mellik and he felt the muscles bunch and flex as he dropped Mellik. Mellik tried to roll and catch his fall while staying out of Fesskah's way. There was a meaty thunk and the sound of Fesskah's soft footfalls running up to the shell.

By the time Mellik righted himself and looked up, Fesskah was standing right at the stone shell, looking through the eye slit. There was a lack of tension or movement in his pose that told of success. Mellik grabbed Querin's hand and almost dragged him up to join the goblin.

"Is he . . . ?" asked Mellik.

Fesskah looked up, "Dead? Yess. Can you remove thiss?" He gestured at the stone shell Carcarose has constructed against the door.

Mellik put his ring up to his eye and studied the small stone fortification. It was nothing more than a rearranged form of the natural stone.

"I can detach it in several places, almost like cutting it into pieces. How big a piece can you move without making too much noise?" Mellik didn't want to use too much of his energy cutting up the stone. He knew he'd need it all on the other side of the door.

Fesskah felt the thickness of the stone with his hand. "Four piessez eazily."

Mellik nodded and began to quarter the shell. It was much like cutting a piece of cheese with a knife extending from his fingertip. Unbinding the stone from itself was easy now that he could see the mana that held it together.

Fesskah removed the first piece as Mellik continued to work. Mellik didn't want to notice the lifeless form of Carcarose laying inside, but he saw that Carcarose was wearing his cape. He tried not to look at the body. He couldn't help but see the blood pooling up from the black stone spear jutting up out of Carcarose's head, staining the golden cape and hood a bloody copper. Mellik breathed through his mouth to avoid the sickly sweet smell of blood mixed with the biting stench of feces and urine. Mellik was just finishing when he notices that the spear had gone right through one of Car's eyes. He quickly looked away and stepped back.

"All done," Fesskah announced a moment later. "Mellik, is the door fuzed as well?"

Mellik looked back and saw that Fesskah had moved the body as far to one side as possible and partially covered it with the last piece of stone shell. Mellik studiously avoided looking at the stone spear the goblin was carrying, but then Fesskah held the cloak out to him.

"I, I don't think I can wear that," Mellik muttered.

Fesskah frowned at him. "We are going to battle, thiss iz all the armor you have. Do you not think blood will be involved? Better ssomeone elssez than yourz."

Fesskah shook the cloak at him and Mellik tentatively reached out to take it. Fesskah continued to stare at him, so Mellik carefully draped it about his shoulders. Mellik tried not to think about the stickiness at his neck.

"Hood," ordered Fesskah and gestured at it.

Mellik grimaced, but pulled the furred hood up over his head. Blood didn't seem to stick to the sandsnake mane.

"Good," commented Fesskah and turned to the door.

Approaching next to Fesskah, Mellik could see that Car had, in fact, fused the door in a couple of spots. The large stone door swung inward, so it would have been simple for Car to disconnect it and then dart inside. The shell would have hampered anyone from following long enough to seal the doors and mount a defense. Mellik disconnected the door from the wall.

"Are we ready?" asked Fesskah.

"Wait," said Querin. "I can help."

"You are blind, my friend."

"Yes, but so was Sidarth when he attacked Mellik, and he almost won. If I stand in the doorway, I'll know the battle is somewhere in front of me. At least I can be a distraction if nothing else."

"How will you defend yourself?"

"If you lose, I die as well. There's no point in my staying out here waiting to die."

"But how will you keep from hitting us?" asked Mellik.

"I could use fire. You are protected from that with the belt."

"I can harden my sscalez and form a brille, a clear eyelid, to protect my eyez," added Fesskah. "A large blasst of fire could sstill harm or kill me."

"I will make them small bursts. I think I will be more of a distraction than a threat anyway."

"Mellik, you go left, I will go right," Fesskah instructed. "We need to divide their attention. We will be outnumbered, sso try to disspoze of them quickly. Don't hold anything back. Are you ready?"

Mellik and Querin signaled their ascent. Mellik adjusted the ring on his eye and flooded himself with mana. Fesskah placed Querin's hand on the door and had Mellik stand to his left.

"I'll go in on the count of three," Fesskah whispered. "One . . . Two . . ."

Chapter 36

"Three!"

Fesskah slammed the door open and sprinted into the room. He boosted his leg muscles for maximum speed as he followed the wall to his right. He spread his eyes out for better peripheral vision. There was an apprentice ahead of him, Zanic, a fire mage. Master Marran was opposite the door, and Brin and another apprentice were now behind him. He would have to trust Mellik to at least keep them busy for now. Balls of fire sizzled past at random from Querin in the doorway.

A cone of flame shot from Zanic toward him, but Fesskah had already prepared his body for fire. Fesskah launched himself into the air toward Zanic, flipping backwards so his harder back scales were toward the flame as he tucked himself into a ball. He felt the flames engulf him, and then the spines along his back ripped into flesh as he crashed into Zanic.

Fesskah uncurled as he rolled off the human and spun. His index claw grew into a razor sharp poignard and he slashed it across Zanic's neck. Bright blood sprouted from the wound and spread across the dark floor.

Fesskah looked up just in time to see Master Marran levelling a crossbow at him. He leaped aside a moment too late, and the bolt ripped across his forearm, gouging through the thick scales there. Fesskah closed the wound and regrew the scales even as he dodged another bolt. Fesskah was glad that Master Marran had apparently run out of the stream of knives he'd used to chase him off after killing Tanay.

Marran continued to fire bolts, a crossbow appearing loaded in his hand as soon as he'd fired the last one. Fesskah dodged each one, steadily closing the gap between them even as the Master backed slowly away. A dart of fire buzzed passed his face. Fesskah dove into a shoulder roll and came up hurling his spear. Marran wove a pair of magic circles in front of himself, and the spear disappeared into one only to come shooting back out of the other. Fesskah was already diving off to the side, and the spear sailed wide of him. A crate etched with arcane symbols came crashing to the floor a hand- span away. He couldn't grow a third eye. He would just have to trust that his random leaps would be enough.

Fesskah began to throw small amounts of fire and healing magics in the middle of each leap. The small numbing spell Sidarth had used gave him the idea. The spells wouldn't kill if they landed, but they'd keep Marran busy and maybe do a little damage. He would show this Mage what a Battle Prince of the goblins could do. Marran disappeared.

*   *   *

Mellik raced in on Fesskah's heals. He veered left and found Hespir in front of him, with Brin a few paces behind him. Hespir was also an air Mage.

Mellik spun three of his throwing stars at Hespir, one at head height, one at his stomach, and one at his knees. Hespir caught the three blades with air and trapped them against the wall next to him with shackles of air. Mellik had already released his control of the stars and channeled a thin, quick beam of earth magic under Hespir's feet. Hespir countered with a fist of air. Mellik sidestepped and turned just enough to let the air glance off a shield of his own air formed about his body. He let another of his stars fly. This one Mellik kept control of, darting it right to circle around Hespir before it was close enough for him to grab with air. Hespir tried to turn and track it's path as he threw another, larger blast of air at Mellik, but Hespir's boots stayed put from the stone Mellik had laced over them, and he began to fall, unbalanced from the unexpected trap. Mellik allowed the strong blast of wind to throw him up against the wall as he concentrated on turning his throwing star, forcing it around the falling apprentice to bury itself in his Hespir's back with a muffled splat. Hespir collapsed with a grunt.

Brin came bounding over Hespir's body, his rapier crackling and sparking in his hand. Mellik tried to raise his hand, but realized it was held fast by air. Mellik could feel the magnet's magic at his hip and sent it spinning at the onrushing Brin. Brin caught it in a fist of air, a psychotic grin on his face. Mellik reached back with his mind to release the stone where Brin's shackles of air were attached, but realized he didn't have time to worry the stone free. Instead, he wove a furious blast of air at Brin, hoping to disrupt his aim. A bolt of flame gouged into Brin's arm, and he cried out, spinning slightly as Mellik's air buffeted him.

Mellik wove a circle of fissures into the stone above Brin. It separated with a loud crack. Brin looked up as the piece of stone began to fall and shoved himself out of the way with a blast of air against the wall. The large piece of stone fell where he'd stood a moment before.

Brin tumbled to his feet and glanced at the door. A shove of air sent Querin reeling back into the tunnel. Another wave of air slammed the door shut.

Mellik had time to free himself from the bonds of air and magnetically pull his three throwing stars to himself from near Hespir's body. A shield of solidified air appeared on Brin's left arm as Mellik started his stars spinning. Lightning crackled along Brin's rapier, flashing from his hand down its length to dissipate into the stone floor. Through the loop of gold around his right eye Mellik saw it: the lightning wanted to go to the floor, was attracted to part of the stone. Could he use that? Brin feinted forward.

Mellik shuffled back. He'd practiced Kigana enough to know Brin wasn't close enough to land a hit even with a hard lunge, but he wanted to keep his distance nonetheless. He started two stars spinning, but kept them close. They were excellent weapons, but he'd already seen that he couldn't maintain control of them once they were closer to another Mage than himself.

Mellik shot a stream of earth mana at Brin. Brin's shield of air swirled with mana, and he brought it up and blocked Mellik's spell. Brin let the shield become transparent to the second sight again. It was a neat bit of spell casting Mellik had to admit, but Brin would be blind if he had to bring the shield up in front of his face.

Mellik channeled earth magic again, aiming it at Brin's face. The shield came up, and Mellik sent another bolt of earth magic just over Brin's head and shield. A small piece of the wall, shiny and black, fell out to clatter against the floor.

Brin glanced back and smiled at Mellik. "You missed, rockhead."

Mellik stayed silent and channeled again. Brin blocked the first one again, and another chunk of wall fell next to the last. This time, as Brin peeked around the edge of his air shield, Mellik channeled again. The earth mana narrowly missed him. Brin countered with a stream of air mana, but Mellik easily blocked it. Mellik brought his two stars together so he could control them with a single stream of mana and began channelling double strikes of earth mana. Brin began to dodge and block the mana strikes. Mellik made sure the strikes were just far enough apart that Brin couldn't block both strikes with his shield. This meant half the strikes went to strike the wall behind Brin. A significant number of stones from the wall were piling up there.

"Keep it up, rockhead, I can do this all day," Brin yelled from behind his shield.

Brin was right, of course. Mellik was rapidly depleting his mana reserves, while Brin was using barely any. Mellik kept up his barrage. None of it would matter if he lost. He just hoped his stars would create enough of a distraction when he needed them.

*　　*　　*

Querin was afraid. He stood at the door listening to Fesskah's instructions, and all he could hear was the sound of his own heart telling him to cower and hide. He, who had stood on the highest branch of the mother tree as the autumn winds howled. He, who had volunteered to come alone to the college of magic and be poked and prodded by human wizards. He, who was now blind. The darkness threatened to engulf him.

"Three!" called out Fesskah, and Querin felt the door move away from his fingertips.

Querin formed a Mage's shield in front of himself. It was as ineffective a defence as he had told Mellik, but it was all he had. He thought he was making it smaller than normal, but without his sight it was impossible to tell. At least he could feel it in front of his hand, swirling with life energy. He groped to his right until he found the wall and then the door. With his luck he had probably gotten turned around. The bards would forever sing of brave Querin, facing the wrong way hurling barbs of fire into an empty tunnel. If the Emperor hadn't managed to kill off all the bards of course.

Querin dropped his shield and began to shoot fire magic at random into what he hoped was the summoning room. He couldn't maintain the shield and shoot through it while blind. If someone killed him, he hoped the next darkness would be more comforting.

Querin shot more and more fire into the room. Few elves were as skilled with fire magic as he, even among the elders. He shot two and three bolts at a time into the room, trying to spread them at random, hoping he was helping at all. Each sound around the room made him flinch in fear. He'd never felt so helpless. He stood and kept firing flame into the room.

A body of air slammed into him and hurled him backwards. He landed hard, cracking his head against the rough stone floor. He heard the stone door slam shut behind him. He had been swatted away like a fly. He lay there on his back for a moment, stunned, just like a fly would.

"But I'm not a fly," he said out loud. His voice rang hollow and alone; afraid to be heard.

"I'm not a fly!" He raged at the darkness.

He turned over and felt the coarse stone floor beneath his hands. He remembered that the floor just in front of the door was smooth like the summoning room. Querin reached out and felt the floor around him. There: it was smooth just to his left. Querin scuttled along the floor, feeling his way forward. His questing hand touched the vertical plane of the wall and the door in it. Querin gave the door a push. It held fast, moving just a hair, but it moved. That probably meant it was being held by air.

Querin felt for the mana with his hands. He could feel the stone door's mana: like a dry, steady heat. The air at the crack had a more wispy, flickering quality. Querin couldn't feel far enough to find the magicked air holding the door closed. It had to be a temporary enchantment. If Mellik and Fesskah were still alive, Querin couldn't imagine someone maintaining an air binding while battling them. That meant it had to be small and focused. Querin would just have to find it by chance. Most wizards cast spells at chest level by instinct and habit. Brin was the most likely candidate for an air spell, and he was almost as tall as Querin.

Querin placed his hands at the door's seam, right at chest level, and then brought them down half a hand's width. He channeled a focused burst of air mana through the crack. There was a slight puff of air above and below his casting, but the air mana seemed to travel through the crack unimpeded. Querin brought his hands down another half a hand width and tried again with the same results. He went lower and tried again, and this time he felt the air push back against his hands and rush out above and below them. He'd found it. Going down a little further, the air once again was unimpeded. The spell was even more focused than he had hoped for.

Querin switched to fire magic. Most apprentices thought you had to fight air with air. That was fine if you could see it and exert more control than your opponent, but for a binding you couldn't see, fire was much more reliable. Air expanded as you heated it.

Heat it enough, and the binding magic would draw far enough apart that it couldn't hold any longer. Querin poured fire mana into the gap. He leaned against the door as he poured more and more fire mana between the door and jam. Some would go into the door, but it took far too much fire mana to heat a piece of stone this size for him to worry about it.

The door gave way and swung open. Querin was ready for it and caught his momentum by shoving the door wide. He immediately poured out a wide fan of fire in front of himself. He hoped his friends were still alright.

*   *   *

The door swung open, and Mellik saw Querin stumble through behind Brin. A sheet of fire shot across the room from the elf, and Mellik braced himself to ignore it.

He shot his stars at Brin as the fire swept into Brin's back. Brin burst with air magic as he cried out in pain. The air pushed the fire and stars away from him, but Mellik had already released control of the magnetic blades. Brin was engulfed in the globe of defensive air magic. The wave of fire swept over Mellik. His buckle grew warm, but Mellik felt only a warm breeze. Mellik concentrated on the lightning magic he'd seen Brin produce so many times, but his was not the controlled little bursts Brin made down his blade. Mellik's magic was a wave of uncontrolled electrical energies pouring from both hands into the air.

A bolt of lightning shot from the air in front of Mellik. It leapt right through Brin's globe of air to find the pile of black, metallic rocks Mellik had made behind him. There was a thunderclap like the world was breaking and when Mellik's vision cleared, Brin's bubble of air magic was gone. Brin lay twitching and smoking on the ground. Mellik magnetically picked up his two throwing stars and sent one whipping into Brin's face, just to be sure. Now, to help Fesskah.

*   *   *

Fesskah leapt and spun as Marran disappeared. Mid-leap he saw the Mage appear from behind where Fesskah had begun. He fired a bolt of fire at the Mage, but it was met midway by a torrent of water that came streaming from the Mage in a geyser.

The water hit him just as he was landing and sent him staggering backwards. Fesskah slid farther back as the stream of water continued to buffet him, and the smooth floor became slick. He sprouted setae from his feet and hands, stopping his slide. He couldn't see the Mage through the gout of water, but he unleashed a stream of fire mana into its path. He widened the fire mana into a small shield in front of himself, vaporizing the water and creating a huge cloud of steam. A crate slammed into him from above, sending him sprawling. He'd stayed in one place too long.

*   *   *

Mellik set his last two stars spinning. He turned to see Master Marran send a huge spout of water at Fesskah. Fesskah was knocked back, but he stopped, and a cloud of steam erupted from in front of him. Mellik threw both stars at Marran as hard as he could. A large black crate appeared above Fesskah just as Mellik's stars struck Marran. The teleportation Master cried out, and then his cry was cut off as he disappeared.

Mellik ran to where Fesskah lay. A bolt of fire cut across his path.

"Querin, stop!" Mellik called out.

"Did we win?" the elf asked, his voice shaking.

"I think so, but Fesskah's hurt."

"Bah, I'll be fine," Fesskah grunted as he shoved pieces of the crate off of himself. One arm dangled awkwardly as he sat up.

"Mellik!" Fesskah's eyes dilated, and he jabbed his good arm to point back where Mellik had come from.

Chapter 37

Mellik spun, and the world seemed to slow and grow quiet as he saw Marran kneeling at Brin's side.

"Oh my beautiful boy, what have they done to you?" sobbed Marran. Mellik could see blood soaking the front of Marran's robes.

"Master, my love," gasped Brin. Mellik sucked in breath at hearing him still alive.

Marran turned at the sound, and a knife came hurtling from in front of his hand. Fesskah shoved Mellik out of its path and rolled the other direction. More knives flashed out. Marran was not concentrating on his aim, but it was still enough to keep Mellik and Fesskah dodging and weaving out of their path.

"My boy, my love," Marran crooned to Brin. "It's not too late. Give me your power. Combined, we can finish them, and I will have your beauty restored."

"Yes, Master . . . love," sighed Brin.

Watching with his second sight even as he dove beneath another knife, Mellik saw Master Marran begin to draw in power from Brin. Brin seemed to relax, and a smile creased his bloody, burnt face. Then, as Marran pulled more and more, faster and faster, Brin's eyes popped open, and his mouth gaped in silent protest. Marran pulled the last bit of life from Brin's body, and a sound finally escaped - a soft, keening cry of despair. Brin's body relaxed in finality, collapsing in on itself.

Marran's body pulsed with the energy of two Mages.

"What's happening?" Querin shouted, edging in from the doorway.

"Marran just . . ." Mellik was interrupted as a roar of wind, heat, and sound erupted from the center of the room.

Mellik was sent sprawling. His body slid before the torrent of air, and his shoulder crashed painfully into the wall. He levered himself around to look back into the room, lifting a hand against the waves of air and heat to see. In the center of the room, a portal had formed: not the vertical slashes and brief openings that Master Marran had used before, but a horizontal ring that was part of the floor, but not. The light, heat, and wind came flowing from it like a waterfall turned on its side. Smells came with it too - scents of blooming flowers and rotting leaves, burnt flesh and a clean spring rain.

Something worse rose more slowly from the gaping gateway: a figure that shifted and blurred like shadow, but with the hint of familiar things - a hoof here, an eyeball there - misshapen and distorted, but still recognizable. The form rose up and seemed to hover over the portal for the blink of an eye, and then the gateway snapped shut. The sudden calm was like a slap. The figure stood shifting and oozing in the center of the room. Eyes and other appendages rotated and flicked, taking in its surroundings. The eye stalks locked onto Querin for a brief moment, and then its form shifted and flowed. A head, much like Querin's, appeared, seeming to grow from the eyes, which were still too large and lacking any iris or color. The body was fat and bulged in odd places. The arms bent and twisted like snakes, and the hands were odd parodies, with no thumbs, and fingers splayed straight out in a half circle. Another pair of oversized hands were where feet should have been. A third leg ending in an arm shot out from the creature, catching itself as it began to topple over in its new bipedal form.

"Where?" a deep, resonant voice asked in Mellik's head. It wasn't the word itself as Mellik knew it, but the thought, the question, was somehow clear.

"Ah," it replied to an answer Mellik hadn't heard. Mellik somehow knew it was speaking to Marran now. "We thought so, but it has been a while. We thought the worlds might have moved apart. Of course: the bargain. It is ever thus."

An eye swivelled to focus on Mellik.

"Kill it!" roared Fesskah, and Mellik saw him charge toward the monstrosity.

Mellik set his last star spinning when something slammed into his head and knocked him flat onto the floor again. Mellik's vision swam from the impact, but his cape had protected him from the crossbow bolt lying shattered next to him. Mellik looked up to see Master Marran standing with his hands out. A loaded crossbow appeared in Marran's hands, and Mellik shot a ray of air out to knock it away. Marran threw up a mage shield to block the air, but he couldn't shoot the crossbow, and Mellik scrambled to his feet.

Mellik began shooting small bolts of air and fire at the Mage, who maintained his shield to block them, but Marran was smiling.

"I can keep this up all day, Mellik," he commented drily. "You're using more of your limited energy than I, and that demon will make short work of the lizard without your help."

Mellik tried to ignore him. He could see Fesskah fighting against the demon out of the corner of his eye, but couldn't worry about how he was doing. He walked carefully forward and kept pelting Marran with his small magics. Marran kept smiling and paced backwards, the crossbow held up at the ready waiting for a break or weakening in Mellik's attack.

Mellik knew why Master Marran felt so confident. Mellik could feel his own weakness as each bolt of magic sapped his dwindling power, and he knew Marran could see his weakness.

Mellik finally came next to Brin's body. He reached down . . .

"It's just a shell. Do what you want," taunted Marran.

Mellik felt the small iron balls next to Brin's body, and channeled. He shot the balls in Master Marran's general direction, not bothering to aim, and not changing their direction once they shot out from his hands. First one, then another, and then a stream of balls shot from Mellik's hand, singing through the air. Marran shifted his shield to air to deflect the balls, but as the final burst of iron left Mellik's hands, Mellik added a stream of transformation magic, like he'd once used on himself. Mellik heard a few of his iron missiles strike home when Marran's spinning shield of air failed to deflect all of them, and at the same time he saw his stream of magic hit Marran in the neck. Master Marran's neck colored gray and stiffened. The Mage disappeared.

*   *   *

Querin knew the minute it happened. He had never seen a summoning, (*still haven't*, his mind teased), but he had been drilled on what a demon felt like even more than what it looked like. He could feel its presence come into the room, and its voice ripped through his mind like fire in a fierce wind. He knew where it was by the sheer magic it radiated. He knew what to do, and hoped that Mellik and Fesskah could protect him long enough.

He strode forward, hands stretched out before him. He didn't channel a shield of any kind. His only hope was that the creature would not notice him or think him a threat.

*   *   *

Fesskah saw Querin stride forward but had no time to wonder what the elf was doing. It took every ounce of skill and concentration just to keep himself alive. The demon did not understand its new environment or the working of magic in this place, but it knew very well how to use magic to transform and manipulate its own body, and it had power to spare. Fesskah only had time to block its many incoming attacks, with nothing left over for offense. Fesskah was one of the best warriors his people had ever produced. He had been told this and knew his own abilities far surpassed any other goblin alive, but this demon could do things he'd never thought of and would never have the skills or power to accomplish.

Spears of bone shot out at him from its torso, and clubs swept out like fourth and fifth legs, while living whips would lash out at him, and tentacles would try to wrap and entangle him. Fesskah hardened his scales and concentrated on not being grappled by the tentacles and whips. He knew instinctually that being entangled by this creature would be death. He was cut and bruised in a dozen places within moments, but at least he was still alive.

Then Querin was beside him. The elf was older by decades, from a race that knew its history from millennia before his own kin, and he was Fesskah's friend. Fesskah gave no though to blocking the spear-like appendage that shot out toward the elf. He blocked again and again, and suddenly realized that the demon was all but ignoring him in order to get to the elf. The elf had no tough skin to protect him, and Fesskah was forced to give up all his transformations except the long, blade-like claws in order to concentrate on more and more speed to counter each and every attack. He paid the price with cuts and lashes scoring his arms and hands. He could feel his life blood leaking out of them, but could not afford the power to close the wounds.

"Quickly, my friend," Fesskah wheezed out.

*   *   *

Querin knew Fesskah was holding the demon off. He wished he could go faster. On its own plane, or with even a few hours to adjust itself to this new world, the demon wouldn't have been vulnerable to Querin's attack, but here, on this world, the demon didn't know how to fight off the basic intrusion of a Mage trying to suck its life force away from it. The rules were different here, and it was Querin's one chance to defeat it.

Querin was older by far than his friends suspected. Querin was indeed young for an elf, but elves measure their lives like the coming and going of forests. He could absorb and hold more mana than any but the greatest Mages in human history, yet the demon held reserves beyond what Querin had ever imagined.

The demon attacked Querin in a new way. It reached out with its mind and bombarded Querin with images, sounds, and scents from its own world. Some images were impossible for Querin to process, with multiple perspectives or from dozens of eyes, sensations that Querin couldn't comprehend. Querin walled off his thoughts. The demon could still force its senses through, but now they came slower, and Querin hoped it would be enough. He hoped it helped Fesskah. He hoped he could take in enough mana to kill or at least weaken the creature.

*   *   *

Mellik looked up to where Fesskah battled the demon. Querin was there now as well. The elf was . . . he was sucking energy from the monster like it was a river. Querin shone almost as brightly as the demon in Mellik's second sight.

Mellik was weak. He wasn't even sure he could make it over to where the battle was taking place. He looked down to see a few of the little iron pellets still lying next to him. He looked back at the figure of Fesskah furiously blocking appendages in a blur of martial action. What good would a few pebbles do? Mellik needed to do something.

He took the dead magic pouch from around his neck; his only thought that it had worked once. It was empty, and Mellik began to gather up the iron pieces and place them inside. His hands were shaking, and he was forced to go slowly and carefully as he missed and dropped the first couple of lumps. When he had the bag almost full, he held it up carefully toward the demon, the open end of the bag towards himself. The fight was blurry, and his hand and head seemed to sway back and forth. Mellik tried to time his burst of magnetic energy to when the demon's blurry brightness crossed into the path of his swaying hand. Mellik felt the bag shoot from his, burning his palm with its speed. Mellik collapsed.

*   *   *

Something changed. Querin sensed it, could feel it through the link the demon had tried to forge between their minds. A moment of confusion seeped through Querin's wall - not a memory, but a thought. Querin knew he could handle little more of the creature's energy.

"Fesskah, get down," Querin shouted. He waited half a heartbeat for Fesskah to comply and then unleashed a torrent of fire energy from his entire body. He could feel the blistering heat even as he pushed at its edges with air magic to direct it and keep it contained. He felt like he was transforming his entire being to flame, that he was pouring out his soul into this inferno, a flame that would consume everything in its path, would even consume and devour its source.

*   *   *

Mellik heard a howl of rage and pain reverberate through his mind. He looked up to see Querin limned in orange-red fire mana, fire magic pouring from his body like Master Kaleed's forge gone berserk with unchecked power. Mellik could still make out the form of the demon writhing in the bath of flame like some quasi-bipedal serpent. Then it dropped, and the screaming in Mellik's mind was snuffed out. Mellik closed his eyes.

Chapter 38

"You're dragging him crooked," commented Fesskah.

"Then slow down," replied Mellik. "Or you can do this yourself."

"I would, but I only have one hand," and Fesskah held up the stump. "And my right leg iz broken in sseveral plassez and will not hold hiz weight yet."

"I'm sorry, Fesskah. You're just so much stronger than I am. I have all my unbroken limbs and I still can't keep up with you."

"It'ss okay. We will take a break. Resst and we will drag the elf further when you are ready."

"You're not supposed to drag an elf," Querin muttered, his head coming up and wobbly rotating to stare sightlessly in their direction. "I must insist that you stop immediately. It's disrespectful."

Querin's speech was slurred, lacking the clipped diction Mellik was used to.

"Your timing iz impeccable," commented Fesskah, "since we just stopped."

Mellik helped Querin to sit up.

"Oh," Querin commented. "Then I guess you are forgiven. Why were you dragging me?"

"I am unable to carry you right now," replied Fesskah.

"Yes, yes," and Querin waved the answer away and almost fell over, Mellik just managing to catch him. "But why did I need to be carried or dragged anywhere."

"You were unconsciouss."

"I . . ." Querin turned to Mellik. "Do you understand my question?"

"We weren't sure how long you would be out, so we were going back to the group camp where the supplies were. Plus, it smelled horrible in the summoning chamber."

"You see how easy that was," Querin shot at Fesskah.

"You didn't assk where we were going," and Fesskah held out

his arms, in helplessness.

"How's the hand?" asked Mellik.

"It's fine," Fesskah replied.

"What happened to your hand," and Querin waved vaguely at Fesskah.

"The demon kept hitting it until it fell off."

Querin nodded as if that was perfectly clear and acceptable. "And what happened to the demon?"

"You killed it," Mellik supplied.

"Well, of course I did," replied Querin. "I was the only elf there, so I had to, but what made it pause, gave me the opening?"

"Thiss," and Fesskah pulled Mellik's pouch from his belt.

"My pouch!" exclaimed Mellik.

"Yess, I am ssorry. I pulled it from the demon'z remainz. I had forgotten to give it back until now."

"How did a pouch help me?" asked Querin.

"It iz a dead magic pouch," explained Fesskah.

"I shot it at the demon," Mellik replied at the same time.

"It went right in," explained Fesskah. "The demon'z sskin and tisssue iz normally very ssoft, it only hardened itsself to attack. I think it could ignore mosst phyzical attackss that way. The pouch flew right in, but then the demon didn't know what to do with it."

"Dead magic," repeated Querin. "Brilliant. An idea worthy of an elf."

"Don't give me so much credit. I was barely thinking at all. I don't even know why I used the pouch other than it worked the first time, when we were breaking out of the crystal prison."

Querin shrugged, "Luck and intuition are as valuable to a Mage as knowledge and skill at times. You do well to have all four." Querin was sounding more like his usual self.

Querin raised his head to sniff at the air in the stone corridor they had stopped in.

"You left the smell behind a long time ago," he commented. "I couldn't have been out that long. Why the rush to get back to the camp?"

"Marran iz sstill alive," replied Fesskah.

Querin's expression turned quizzical.

"He teleported away," explained Mellik with a shrug, forgetting for a moment that Querin couldn't see him. "I hit him, but he was still alive enough to teleport away, so he could teleport back. Fesskah had me mess with the circle, change and mar the inlaid gold."

"That should do the trick," replied Querin, nodding, "but you are wise to be cautious. Marran could know the chamber so well he doesn't need the circle itself. Although we did some damage to that room beyond the circle, so we're as safe here as we can be from Marran. It's hard to catch a teleportation master."

Fesskah grunted in reply.

"The Emperor will hunt him down for what he's done. We've done our part," said Mellik.

"We'll see . . . " commented Querin, settling down cross legged across from Fesskah. "Or I guess you two will see, I'll hear about it."

"What do you mean?" asked Mellik.

"We're the three most disliked apprentices in the college, three freaks mothers scare their children with. Our entire party is dead, many by our hands, and the only other witness is a respected Master who will be at the college for days establishing his side of the story before we get there."

Mellik sank to the floor, his legs growing wobbly. "But . . . we won."

"It takess many battlez to win a war," said Fesskah, laying a hand on Mellik's shoulder. "Be glad that we won thiss one."

FINI

ABOUT THE AUTHOR

Chandler York Shelton lives in the Seattle area with his wife, two kids, two cats and a dog. He is an avid gamer who loves cards, Catan, DnD, and too many others to list. He's also an ardent camper including car camping, backpacking, canoeing, snowshoeing and anything else that gets him outdoors. Someday he'd like the first line of his bio to read, "...bestselling author of," but for now, he'd just like to thank you for reading his first novel.

Made in USA - North Chelmsford, MA
1064156_9781980835776
03.27.2020 1104